RECRUIT OF TALIONIS

TALIONIS SERIES
BOOK ONE

C.J. MILACCI

To my mom, who believed in this story from its inception until now.

Mom, you taught me what it means to have hope that breaks through the darkest of times, and where that hope comes from. I love you!

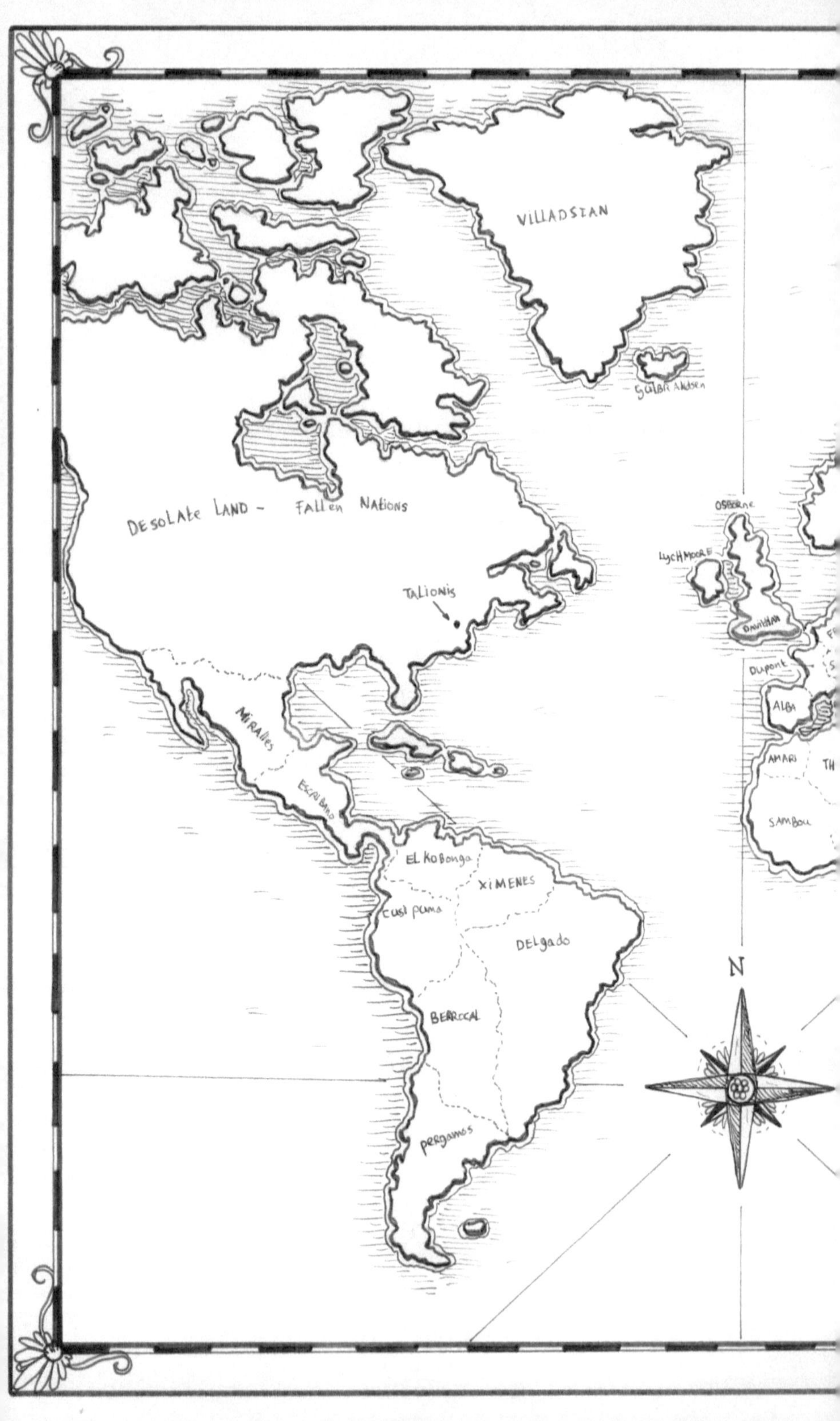

VILLADSTAN
Gulbrandsen
DESOLATE LAND - FALLEN NATIONS
TALIONIS
OSBORNE
LYCHMOORE
DAVIDIAN
DUPONT
ALBA
AMARI
SAMBOU
MIRALLES
ESCALBANO
EL KOBONGA
XIMENES
CUSI PUMA
DELGADO
BERROCAL
PERGAMOS
N

ROSH
POPOV
SERDA
WOJTEK
NISHAN
KAWASHIMA
mysthia
Junyu
DIVIDED
JING-TING
Myung
ZEKI
PERSIA
Bodhi
Tsai
posadas
LABBISA
ABN-EL-kader
JORA
Linkang
nigena
SuTRiya
NGO
RONalia
hopeRa
Chaim 2022

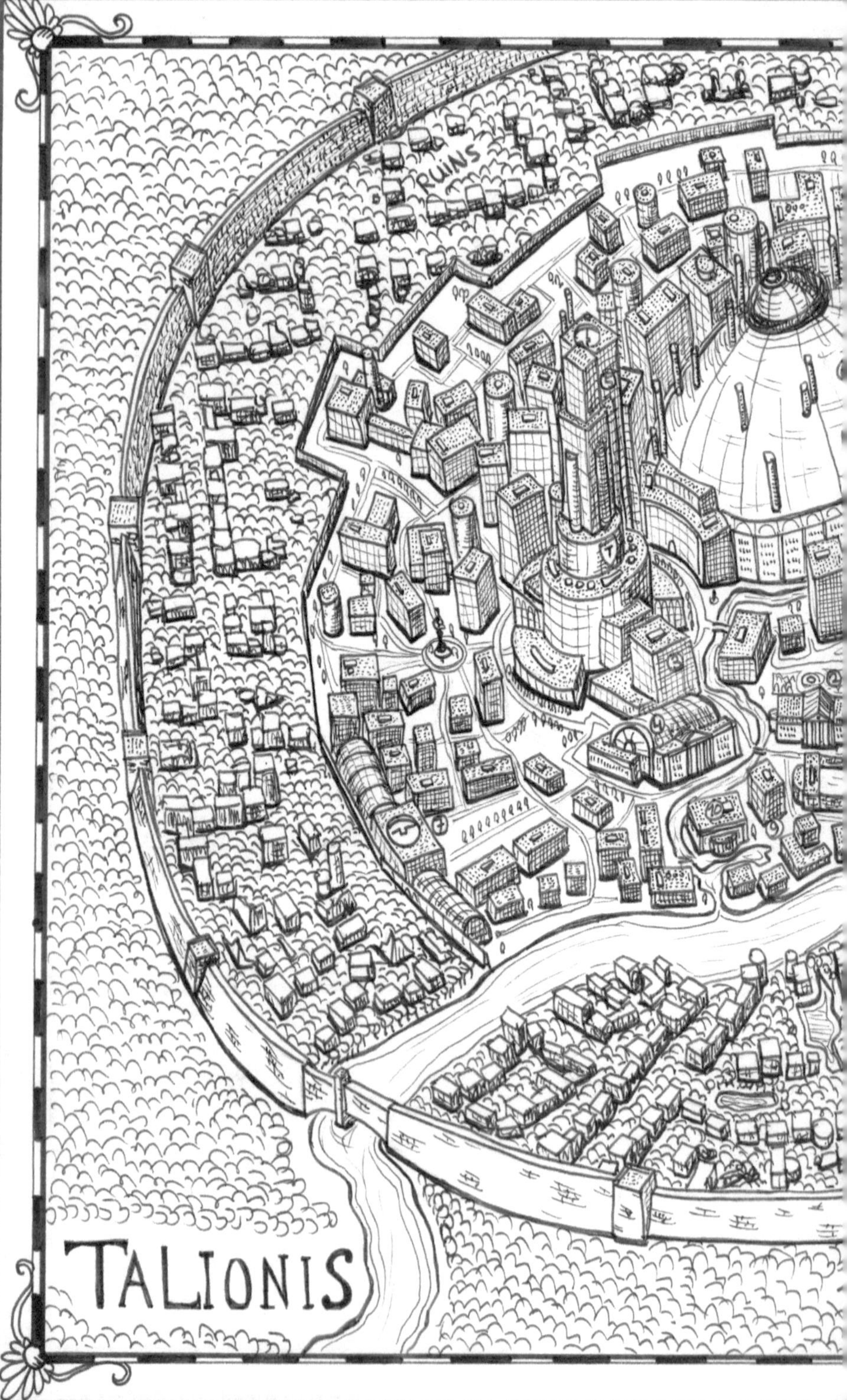

RUINS
TALIONIS

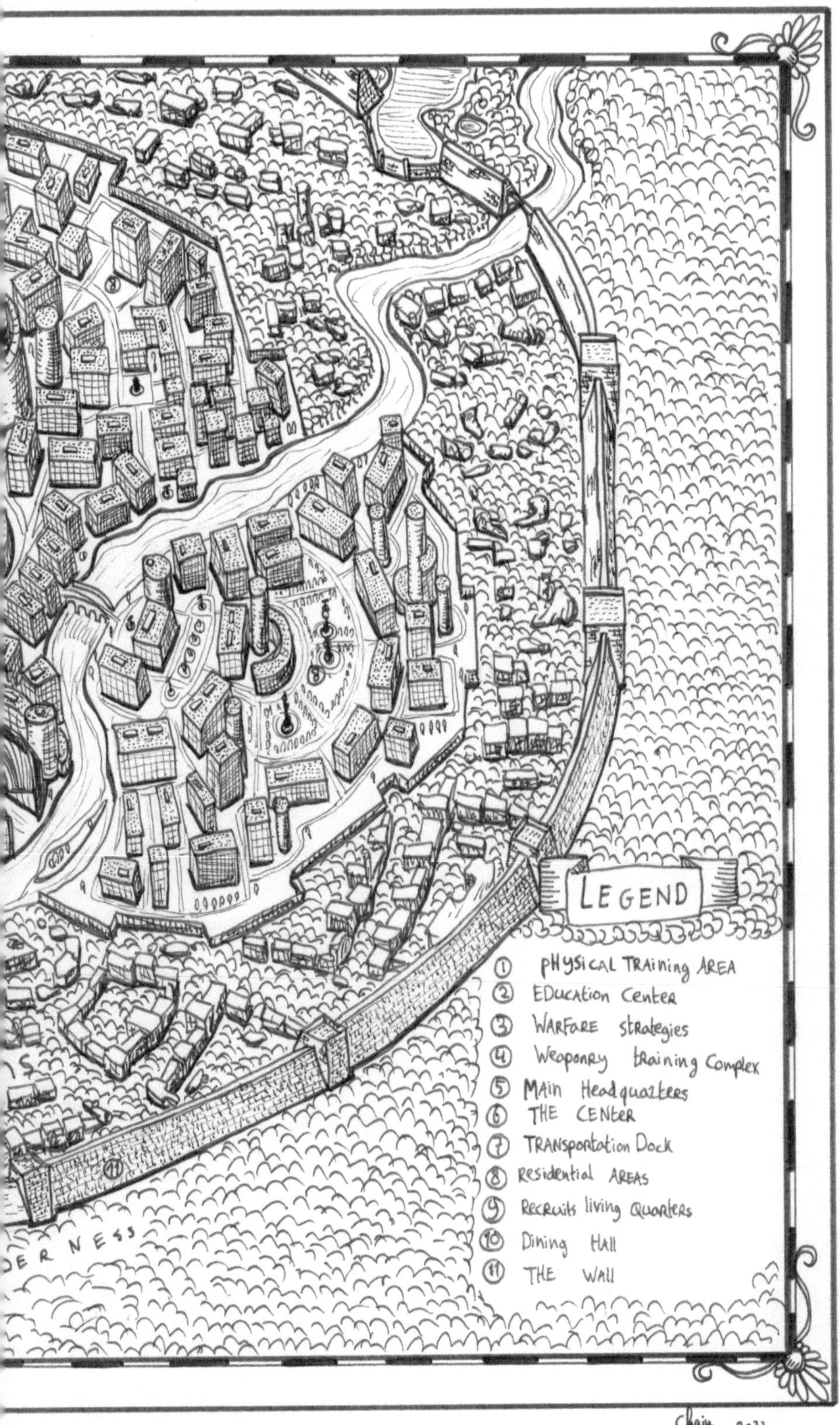

LEGEND
1 pHYSiCAL TRAINING AREA
2 EDucation Center
3 WARFaRE strategies
4 Weaponry training Complex
5 MAiN Headquarters
6 THE CENTER
7 TRANSportation Dock
8 Residential AREAS
9 Recruits living Quarters
10 Dining Hall
11 THE WALL
ERNESS
Chain 2022

PROLOGUE

Talionis was ready.

Finally.

A thriving city built in a desolate land, forgotten by the rest of the world. Perfection concealed from the eyes of the nations and the eyes of Demetrius Ark's father. The best part was, the old man thought Talionis was his idea.

Demetrius surveyed his creation from his office at the highest point in the city. His most trusted officers waited behind him, their eagerness pulsing through the room.

He turned to face them. "It's time."

Some of them smiled. Others kept their faces a mask, but Demetrius knew they were all ready for this moment. It was the one they'd been preparing for for years.

The next piece in the plan that would lead to his father's destruction and to Demetrius claiming all he was destined for.

"We'll prepare the squadrons, Commander," Lieutenant Colonel Keenan Valarius said. "What day should we set the extractions for?"

Demetrius walked to his desk and slid out his chair. Screens came to life around him, images and videos showing the city he'd spent fifteen years building.

"Tell the Watchers to set everything in order for September 25th." He allowed himself a small smile. "You're dismissed."

They saluted and marched from the room.

Demetrius leaned back in his chair and released a satisfied sigh. The North American region wouldn't know what hit it. And now that everything was in place, no one would be able to stop him.

CHAPTER
ONE

hree Weeks Later

September 25th has tormented me every moment for six years. Darkness clings to the morning, unwilling to relinquish its hold and allow light to enter the world. But that's fitting for today.

The anniversary of my brother's death.

My gaze probes the murky depths of the bay as waves lap at the shore, spitting up pieces of plastic, cloth, and whatever else the ocean has churned up today. Wind blows sand over the rusty frame of a pre-Demise car several feet to my right, creating a haunting tune. Chills inch up my spine. I hate this place, and yet can't seem to keep myself away.

Bria... Bria... Bria...

The waves whisper my name with every splash on the shore, mocking me and beckoning me at the same time. My nemesis. The monster I must face—must defeat because of what it took from me.

My throat thickens, the memories stirring.

I take a step forward, then stop again.

Light edges its way over the horizon, brightening the surrounding landscape. I know it by heart. Every bit of forest and rock around the tiny beach. The cliffs to the east, stretching into the water. The old car wedged between boulders, half-buried in the sand. My stomach roils like the waves. It's the same as it was during my last moments with Ezri.

His laughter echoes in my mind, his exuberance and life. His trust in *me.* Then it's drowned out by the memory of my scream. His cold body.

The sand at my feet becomes like needles. I take a step toward the water. A flutter of anticipation ripples through my stomach, and an eagerness, a *need,* to dive into the waves collides with the anxiety I feel each time I face the bay. My hands twist the damp towel I brought with me.

Bria! Bria! Bria!

The waves shout my name now. I take a shuddering breath. Then I throw my towel to the ground and charge into the water. It grabs at my ankles and then strikes my thighs and splashes up my body as I press forward.

The bay consumes me to my chest. I dive under. The chill of the water engulfs me in its smothering embrace. It's time.

I surface, and my eyes find the cliff wall, pick out a small crevice as my goal, and then I swim. The current pushes against me as I cut through the water, and memories scream through my mind, refusing to drown. I kick harder.

Swim faster, Bria!

My arms reach and grab and pull me forward, my legs moving at a rapid pace. I can do it. I can out-swim the memories. I can be strong enough today.

But do I want to be?

My movements slow, weighed down with the question. The cliff wall comes closer, and I push the final distance to my goal. I wasn't fast enough. I failed. Again.

Same as six years ago. Same as every time since then.

I scream at the waves, some of the salt water sloshing into my mouth. I spew it out and find a point across the bay—an old buoy.

Faster this time.

I plant my feet on the smooth stone of the cliff and push off toward the buoy, knifing through the water. My muscles burn. The memories attack again, like a monster in the waves. I have to swim harder, faster. I have to be *better*. I can't fail again.

But I do.

It takes me too long to reach the buoy. I hit its rubbery surface and grind my teeth together. *Again.* I pick a point on the cliff and dive under.

I swim lap after lap. The memories start to fade, but I pull them back. I need them. If I can't have Ezri, I *must* cling to his memory when I'm here. No matter how painful.

Later. It'll fade later.

I lose track of how often I fail, how many times I don't reach my target in time. No matter how fast I am, it's never enough.

Taking a deep breath, I plunge beneath the surface and dive to the bottom. It doesn't take long before my fingers sink into the sandy floor. The gentle ebb and flow of the current mocks me, like the monster cradling me just to whisper in my ear, *"His death wasn't my fault, but yours."*

The need for air burns my lungs. Pushing off the ground, I shoot to the surface, bursting through in a spray of water. A sob lodges in my throat, but I swallow it and turn to stare up into the clear blue sky.

I want to do another lap, but my body is done for now.

"Ria!" The water distorts my name, just like it does everything else.

I turn to the shore. The familiar form standing on the beach beckons impatiently. I groan. The wind picks up her red hair, billowing it out like a warning.

What is Shay doing here?

I debate diving under the water and pretending I didn't see her, but that will only delay the inevitable, so I swim until I'm in shallow water and slosh the rest of the way to the beach. My hair clings to my face like leaches, and streams of water run from the rolled up legs of my pants. Shay's nose turns up so high she could get a nosebleed from the altitude. That would be nice.

I tuck my necklace into my shirt, the sea-glass pendant resting near my heart.

"Out for a morning stroll?" I scoop up the towel I dropped.

Shay sniffs derisively. "Your aunt told me to come find you."

And I'm sure she didn't get to witness your crappy attitude.

"So nice of you to bend to her every whim," I say. "Why is she looking for me?"

Sand stuck to the towel rubs against my skin, as grating as Shay.

"You're really that stupid? Today is The Festival." Her eyes squint, and her lips curl like she's ready to spew something out of her mouth. Probably more insults.

My hands bunch around the fabric of the towel, but I force myself to stay calm. "Well, thank you, Shay. What would I do without you?" I scrub the towel around the dripping ends of my hair.

"Hurry up."

"Get off my back. It's still early."

"Bria, it's after nine."

"*What?*" How long did I swim for?

A glint of triumph sparks in her eyes. "Aw, lost track of time again?"

"Shut up." I tug on my shoes, then march toward the forest, ineffectively rubbing the towel against my sopping clothes.

Shay saunters after me, but I ignore her and half-run, half-stagger as I desperately try to sponge my clothes dry before I get home. Aunt Elena will be furious, but I'm more upset at the idea of my mom being disappointed. Maybe I can distract them by mentioning how Aunt Elena left her lantern lit all night.

The Lassen River murmurs as though in pessimistic disagreement. I know it's right. My aunt loves nothing more than an opportunity to lecture me. Especially when it comes to my regular swims in the bay.

We skirt around the pile of twisted metal and debris that was cleared to make Derbe, and it glints in the morning light. Out of habit, I tap the dilapidated green sign that reads *Portland, Maine* as I pass it. Every pre-Demise city was destroyed, but my parents have taught me to respect the history of the region. Even though I don't understand why it matters.

Scattered trees force their way through the mess, and I almost envy them. Usually, I don't want to think about the Demise at all, but at the moment, I'd rather sort through the rubble of destroyed cities than face my aunt and the lecture I'm sure is coming.

Hopefully, my mom reins her in before my aunt and I end up in a shouting match. Again.

Smoke rises from the chimneys of the houses clustered on the eastern rim of Derbe, and the smell of cooking meat fills the air. The Festival is this afternoon, and everyone is going. It's expected, even though it's not required. But it's the last thing I want to do. Maybe, if I can get out of this lecture without losing control of my anger, I'll convince my mom and dad to let me stay home.

They'd understand my need for quiet. My aunt, on the other hand, won't like the idea one bit. Still worth a shot.

As I approach my house with Shay trailing behind me, the door bursts open, and my aunt comes sailing out.

Perfect. She was watching for me. No chance I'll be able to sneak inside to change my clothes before seeing her.

Shay rushes to my side. "I found Bria for you, Ms. Elena." Her tone is sweet enough to set my teeth on edge. "I hope you don't mind if I run home. My mother probably needs my help getting things ready."

I glare at Shay, but she doesn't so much as spare me a glance.

My mom comes out as my aunt responds. "Thank you, Shay."

Aunt Elena smiles at her and waits for her to leave before turning on me. "Bria, where have you been? Your mother and I have been preparing food since seven this morning."

"Elena." My mom's voice has a cautionary tone to it, but my aunt ignores her.

The two are over ten years apart in age, and, though they have some physical similarities, I still find it difficult to believe my mom is the younger sister.

Aunt Elena's sharp gaze examines my still-dripping clothes.

"Why are you so wet?" She pinches the bridge of her nose. "Please don't tell me you were swimming." The words force themselves past her gritted teeth.

"Would you believe there was a downpour this morning?" The sarcasm wafts out of me, and I can't find any way to stop it. I lock eyes with her.

She purses her lips, foot tapping. Waiting for another answer, more details, a reason to lash out at me.

I stare off into the forest. "I needed to get some exercise."

"You traipse through the forest alone with no protection, and then you dive into the water while it's still dark out. You don't know what's out there!" Her sharp words slap at me like a wet rag. My shoulders tense. "Six years ago, Ezri *died* in the ocean. Why would you—?"

"Stop!" My head whips back toward her, and I clench my hands. "You've been living with us for years. Why does this shock you?" I spread my arms out. "Have any of your lectures convinced me you're right before? Just leave it alone." My voice rises in volume, and my face burns. If she had physically smacked me, it would have hurt less than hearing her say my brother's name.

Aunt Elena's lips purse even more, making her look like she drank sour milk.

My mom steps forward and rests her hand on my aunt's arm. "Let it go, El."

Aunt Elena opens her mouth to say more, but my mom's stern expression stops her. "There's no way we can keep Bria out of the water."

"But—"

Mom cuts her off with a shake of her head.

She turns to me, eyes gentle, yet rebuking. "And Bria, whether or not you agree with your aunt, I expect a more respectful attitude."

"Sorry, Mom."

She quirks an eyebrow at me.

I sigh. "Sorry, Aunt Elena."

Aunt Elena tilts her head in acknowledgment of the apology but doesn't utter a word of one to me. No surprise there.

"Good," Mom says.

Aunt Elena turns and marches back into the house. Mom comes closer to me. She tucks one of my damp curls behind my ear, her eyes watchful. "I'd ask how you're holding up today, but I think it's pretty clear."

Every one of my raging emotions settles, and a lump thickens my throat. I swallow hard and shrug.

"My sweet girl." She traces her finger down my cheek, her face compressing in pain briefly. "I miss him too. Why don't you tell me what's going on in that head of yours?"

The lump in my throat pulses, and my eyes burn. I look up into a sky that's too blue, too clear. The motion breaks the contact with my mom.

"I don't want to talk about it," I say, but with no edge to the words.

We've had this conversation before, but I can never do what she asks of me. I deserve all the pain I feel. I can't allow myself the comfort of sharing it with her.

"Okay," she whispers.

My gaze falls from the sky back into focus with her.

She smiles, but it's tinged with sadness. I feel bad for not being able to talk with her, even just to let her share her own pain and grief. But it hurts too much, and I can't bear it.

I search for another topic and suddenly note the unusual quiet. "Where are the boys?"

My twin eight-year-old brothers, Eli and Zeke, are always up by now and always loud.

"Dad took them to the shop," she says.

I blink in surprise. "Really? Today? Why?"

Her smile widens. "They were terrorizing Aunt Elena by sneaking cream cakes."

I shake my head. "I can imagine." My grin fades. "But why did Dad take them to his shop? No one works on the day of the Festival."

Mom releases a low sigh. "You're not the only one who's struggling today, my girl." She links her arm through mine before I can come up with a response and leads us toward the house. "Now. We have a lot of work to do before the Festival."

A rush of gratitude fills me. This is so like her. Always there for me but also willing to give me the space I need and not push me, even when I change the subject when I shouldn't.

I lean over and kiss her cheek. "Thanks."

She pats my arm. "I'll always be here for you, Bria."

"I know."

Before we enter the house, she pauses. "Today will be hard, but activity will help. Fighting with your aunt won't."

I roll my eyes. "But she's just…"

"Protective?" Mom offers.

"That's definitely not how I would put it. Can I just stay home? Please?"

She tilts her head to the side. "How about this, you go to the Festival with the rest of us—"

"But, Mom…"

"And I'll take you with me tomorrow," she continues, as though I didn't interrupt.

The rest of my argument freezes, and some of the pain from the day ebbs away as curiosity probes me. "Take me where?"

"A village about fifty miles away called Sontone. I've been commissioned to make another map, and I'd like you to come."

"Really?" Excitement ripples along my veins. "Yes, of course. Yes."

She laughs. "I had a feeling that would be your answer."

This will be my thirteenth cartography trip with my mom, and I've loved every single one of them. I fling my arms around her. "Thank you!"

She returns the hug. "You've become my best assistant." She leans back to look at me. "Bring the tools your dad and I got for you. I'm going to teach you how to create my multi-dimensional maps. You've got the basics down, and it's time you learned the finer aspects of cartography. After all, the greatest mistakes and the most profound discoveries are—"

"In the details," I finish with her.

"Oh, have I said that before?" She smirks and then nods at the doorway. "Let's get inside before your aunt comes to find us." She gives a small shudder and then winks.

I smile and follow her inside, more of the strain releasing. Maybe I'll be able to get through today after all. As long as I can keep my focus on tomorrow and not on my brother.

Two hours later, with my dad and the twins back from the docks, the six of us head to the village square. The last thing I want to do is go to the Festival. There are too many people. Too many memories. But the promise of the upcoming trip with my mom propels my feet along. *I can do this. I hope.*

I focus on the familiar landscape I pass, trying to keep myself from falling into the trap of my memories. We pass dozens of small cottages, much like ours, made from logs cut down in the Delamere Wood with thatched roofs and chimney stacks. The closer we get to the square, the more crammed together they are.

A few specialty shops are sprinkled among them, but mostly homes populate the two miles between our house and the square. Narrow walkways separate each home, and wider roads for horses and carts run between the housing sections. Occasional patches of old concrete dot the lanes.

People crowd the square, and the smells of roasted meat mixed with freshly baked pastries waft through the air. My stomach grumbles. Brightly colored blue and green fabrics are draped throughout the square for the Festival, and a temporary stage is set up in the midst, filled with musicians playing an upbeat tune.

We drop off the creamed cakes and pies my mom and aunt made

at the dessert table—one of many tables situated around the square. Most of our trading bonds this week went to purchasing supplies for the treats, which is like just about everyone else in Derbe. The town goes all out for the Festival, celebrating surviving another year after the Demise.

As soon as they can, Eli and Zeke race over to join the kids in the public meeting house, where they'll spend most of the day playing games and winning prizes. I smile as I watch them go. That was my favorite part of the Festival when I was their age. Ezri loved it, too. My smile fades. Why does everything remind me of him?

I shove the memories down into the place I keep them locked away.

"Bria!"

I peer through the crowd, searching for the face that accompanies that familiar voice. Lencie beams at me from several feet away, Jaxon next to her. I make my way toward my two closest friends, thankful for the diversion. If I have to be here, at least I can spend the day with them.

Jaxon's muscular frame and serious expression almost make Lencie look like a child with her petite build and pigtails. Her face isn't as pale as usual, and the dark smudges under her eyes seem less noticeable. She gives me a hug, her squeeze a little tighter.

As she pulls away, an impish grin lights her face. "I signed you up for the tug-of-war contest."

"What?" I groan and take a step back. "Come on, Lence."

"You'll have fun. Jax is doing it too."

Jaxon's eyebrows rise. "Don't bet on it," he says in his low voice. "I'm gonna split from here as soon as I can and go fishing."

"Shocking." I roll my eyes.

Lencie and I share a knowing look. Jaxon hates crowds. I'm surprised he showed up at all. The most likely explanation is that Lencie nagged him about it.

She turns her light blue eyes on me, her mouth pulled to the side, the way she does whenever she's about to say something, and she doesn't know how I'll receive it. I brace myself.

"How are you handling things today?" she asks.

"Fine." The word is sharper than intended, but Lencie doesn't seem fazed by it.

She opens her mouth.

"Uh, guess what?" I say. "My mom is taking me with her on another commission. We leave tomorrow."

Lencie lets out a long-suffering sigh but allows the change of topic. "That's great." A sparkle lights her eyes. "You'll become an Eryndale Scout one day. I just know it."

"You really think so?" I tuck my lip between my teeth.

Lencie nods. "Definitely."

Jaxon shrugs. "I still don't understand why you want to be a scout for Eryndale. You'll have to leave Derbe, train in the mountain refuge, and probably never live by the sea again."

I smirk. "Not all of us love fishing as much as you do."

"I'm just saying." Jax lifts a hand up, the hint of a smile teasing his mouth as he looks out of the corner of his eye at Lencie.

"Jaxon." Lencie whacks him on the arm, the reaction I'm sure Jaxon expected. "Don't be ridiculous. Scouts get to travel, see new places. They do a lot of good. Derbe wouldn't even be here if it wasn't for Eryndale and their scouts." Her hands fly into the air. "Bria will be a part of that."

I duck my head, brushing at a stray piece of lint. Even though Lencie's illness keeps her from certain dreams, she always encourages mine.

I've wanted to be a scout for as long as I can remember. Two and a half years, and then I'll be twenty and old enough. Though on days like today, when the memory of Ezri is so close to the surface, the dream seems foolish.

The tenor in the square changes as the contests begin, and I do my best to focus on what's happening and on the conversation with my friends. But my mind is having too hard of a time suppressing memories of my brother and telling me I'll never be worthy of being a scout.

"Go on. You're up!" Lencie prods at Jaxon and me.

My forehead furrows. "Huh?"

"Told you she wasn't listening," Lencie says to Jaxon. "It's time for the tug-of-war competition. Can't wait to watch." She gives us a cheery smile.

"No," I say, flatly.

"Oh, come on. Don't be so boring," Lencie says.

"I'm not doing it." I lift an eyebrow at Lencie, preparing for her argument.

She opens her mouth, then closes it again. "Fine," she huffs. "When you get all stubborn, no one can make you do anything."

I grin. "Thanks."

"It's *not* a compliment." Lencie whips her head around to face Jaxon. "You'd better hurry and get over there before it starts."

He shakes his head. "I don't want to do it eith—"

"Jaxon Riston, go do the tug-of-war—" A fit of coughing cuts her off.

I tense. Jaxon's hand goes to support Lencie as the cough racks her body. After a few minutes, her coughing dissipates, but her shoulders stoop.

She removes her arm from Jaxon's hold and gives him a weak shove. "Go. Do the competition."

Jaxon glances at me, and I nod for him to go.

"At least *he* listens to me," Lencie murmurs as he walks away. There's an airy quality to her voice.

"Let's sit over here and watch," I suggest.

She agrees without argument, which is almost as concerning as her cough.

Some of Lencie's strength comes back as we cheer on Jax's team. Despite his half-a-dozen concerned glances in our direction, his team wins.

After a while, the competitions wrap up, and as evening approaches, everyone finds a place with their family at the tables for dinner. Lencie joins her family, though based on her weary face, I doubt they'll be staying long. There's no sign of Jax, which means he probably left to go fishing.

I find my family and settle between my mom and Zeke. Eli is on the other side of Zeke, and the twins talk over each other as they tell me everything they did. Their antics and enthusiasm actually make me smile.

My stomach grumbles, and I gaze longingly at the food, ready to fill my plate. But, just like every other year, we have to wait for the mayor to give his speech and toast, which will be longer and more boring than necessary. Like it always is.

Mayor Jasper Tessan shuffles to the center of the stage holding a glass of apple cider, prepared by the Grendens for today. He clears his throat, and conversations die as everyone gives him their attention.

Eli puffs out a sigh, and Zeke flops back in his chair.

"Why does he always gotta talk?" Zeke folds his arms across his chest. "He's boring."

I almost burst out laughing but manage to keep it together. "Just be quiet for a bit, and then you can eat."

"Fine," he mumbles with a frown.

I ruffle his hair.

"What a wonderful day we're having today, thanks to an excellent harvest," Mayor Tessan begins. "But we would be remiss to celebrate without remembering *why* we're celebrating. We would not be where we are today if we hadn't banded together after the Demise." When he says *Demise*, he deepens his voice and tilts his head down, his face taking on what, I'm sure, he thinks is a grave, serious expression. But to me, he resembles a distressed cow, which makes me want to laugh.

He clears his throat, and I settle in for what I'm sure will be some variation of what he's said every year since he became mayor seven years ago. Why he feels the need to tell us about the Demise, even though we all know about it, I haven't yet figured out. Everyone knows it's the reason we have the Festival each year on the last Saturday of September.

I zone out. It hardly seems like reliving the destruction of North America is relevant. After all, I don't remember the "great nation" it once was. It seems to me our time would be better spent discussing how to continue moving *forward*, not looking back. Looking back is dangerous. Painful. At least in my travels with my mom, it doesn't seem like every village harps on the Demise like we do. My parents think it's important to remember, and I respect them. But all I want is to move on and leave the past where it is: in the past.

Mayor Tessan's arms shoot up above his head to emphasize whatever it is he's talking about, his large belly jiggling with the effort. The quick movement causes some of the cider to slosh out of his cup, but he doesn't seem to notice.

A laugh bursts from me, and I quickly disguise it as a cough. My mom glances over and smirks, which almost starts me giggling.

He drones on in his irritating, squeaky voice for several minutes as the food cools and the rest of us shift in our seats. The mayor is oblivious.

I bounce my leg up and down. I wish my mom had just let me stay home. Eli pokes Zeke with his fork, who in return shoves him in the arm. I grab pull Zeke toward me and reach around him to flick Eli in the ear.

"Stop," I hiss.

Both sets of eyes grow large as they settle back into their seats. For now. Maybe I should switch seats with Zeke, since they can't stay this still for long. Before I can move, the mayor brings his speech to a close.

"And so today, as we celebrate that we've survived another year," Mayor Tessan says, "let us remember how far we have come, and celebrate how far we will go!"

We all lift our glasses of cider and say the toast: "To Derbe, a town born to survive!"

Together, we all take a drink of the cider.

THREE

Crying chips its way through my dreamless sleep. Foggy clouds muddle my brain, and I don't want to let them drift away. But the crying persists. Zeke? Strange. He hasn't woken up crying in years. Keeping my eyes closed, I roll over to reach across the small gap to his bed and mumble something comforting. Hopefully it works, so I can go back to sleep.

I stretch my arm out and drop my hand to the soft blanket covering him. But there isn't a blanket. Something cool and wet pricks my hand. Grass. My eyes spring open, all of my senses alert. The last vestiges of sleep evaporate from my body.

I'm outside.

Chills inch up my spine as the icy fingers of anxiety tighten their hold on my thoughts. Where am I, and why am I here? My heart races as my mind frantically searches for the one piece of information that will force this to make sense.

The whimpering, soft cries that woke me up cut through the night again. It's a child crying, but not Zeke—I know my brother's cries. I take a deep breath, trying to calm the panic rising with each moment, and sit up.

I'm in a clearing in the middle of a forest, dark lumps surrounding me as far as I can see. The night is dark and eerily quiet.

The only light comes from the flickering red and orange embers of a dying fire. Trees rise in black silhouettes against the midnight sky. The familiar scent of pine needles mixes with the lingering smoke from the fire. But why can't I hear the ocean waves crashing on the cliffs? Or the Lassen River rushing through the trees? There's only one answer to those questions. This isn't Delamere Wood.

I don't know where I am.

My eyes adjust to the darkness. The dark lumps are sleeping people. I pull my knees to my chest and clasp my arms around them, squeezing my eyes shut as I try to recall how I came to be here. It's a blank.

I rub my hands up and down my arms and rock back and forth. "Breathe, Bria," I whisper. "This is a dream. It has to be a dream."

"Hate to break it to you, but this isn't a dream." The menacing voice startles me.

My eyes fly open, and I spin toward the voice. I squint through the dark, struggling to glimpse him, but the night itself seems determined to hide his identity from me. I tremble.

He speaks again. "You weren't supposed to wake up for a few more hours." He clicks his tongue twice. "We can't have that now, can we?"

I sense more than see his body close the distance between us. Before I can move away, his hand snakes out and covers my face with a cloth. A sickening smell slithers into my nose, my mouth. I push against him, turning my head, trying to get away from the stench, away from him. With his other hand, he grasps my upper arm in a bruising grip.

I kick him in the shin. He grunts and, with the hand he has on my face, pushes me to the ground, pinning me in place. His grip is tight, painful. I need to fight, but my limbs seem weighted. My head spins, and everything fades.

What is happening?

CHAPTER

FOUR

"Ugh." I grunt. Pain shoots through my side as a foot slams into my rib cage.

"Wake up, dirtbags. Time to move," a woman's voice yells from somewhere to my left as I'm yanked up by whoever kicked me.

"Ow!" The cry escapes my mouth before I can stop it.

My head is throbbing, my side hurts, and my wrists are tied together behind me so tightly that my fingers are almost numb. The man hauls on my bound wrists, dragging me to my feet. The pain makes one thing clear—this is not a dream.

The man who pulled me to my feet tugs on my bindings. The motion and pain force my head down, and I stagger forward.

"Stay here." He moves on to another person lying on the ground.

I squint against the early morning sun as they startle others awake and bring them to stand in straight lines all around me. The frightened expressions on their faces confirm that they're as confused as I am.

They're all close to my age, give or take a year or two. I scan the crowd for Jaxon or Lencie but don't see them anywhere. There's no one I recognize. What is going on? Loose, dark curls are blowing about my face, but my bound hands keep me from pulling them into a braid like I normally would.

All of the adults are dressed the same: black cargo pants, boots, gloves, and a dark green shirt. Some have a gun slung across their backs as they move around, while more men and women surround the clearing with weapons in hand.

We are in a manmade clearing large enough to contain the few hundred people who now fill it.

A noise to my left grabs my attention. A dark-haired guy slams his head back into the face of the man trying to drag him to his feet. The man lets go, and a uniformed woman runs over, a weapon extended. A loud *zap* cuts through the air, and white lights shoot out and shock the guy. His body shakes, and then he drops to the ground, wheezing. When the man pulls at his bound wrists this time, he doesn't resist.

My stomach knots. Who *are* these people?

And what is happening?

My fingers pulse and ache behind me, and I long to reach for the smooth, well-worn leather cord of my necklace, grasp the one thing from home I can hold on to. The weight of it rests against my neck. At least they haven't taken it. Yet.

I squeeze my eyes shut. What happened before I woke up in the forest? I search my memory.

The Festival.

We lifted our glasses for the toast, and then...

What happened next? I clench my hands, and the bindings bite harder into my wrists. Frustration tightens my shoulders. Why can't I remember!

I pry my eyes open and blink. Shay is standing in the line in front of me. They must have just brought her over. This might be one of the few times I can remember that I've been happy to see her.

"Shay!" I hiss her name, my eyes darting around.

"Bria?" she whispers and begins to turn her head.

"Don't look back." For once, she listens. "Do you have any idea what's going on?"

"I, uh..." She clears her throat. At least she's keeping her voice low. "I heard some of them talking earlier before they started waking everyone up. They said something about a transport that's arriving soon and making sure all the recruits are ready in time." Her hands are shaking, and there are red marks on her wrists where the plastic bond cuts into them.

None of what she's saying makes any sense. "Transport. Recruits." I stop talking as they shove another person into line several rows up from us. "Did they say anything else? Anything that could explain what's going on?"

"I don't know!" she snaps, a frantic undertone to her words. The prim, poised, and know-it-all Shay is nowhere to be found.

"Shay." I almost wish I could put my hand on her shoulder to comfort her. Then again, she *is* still Shay—even if I can relate to the fear in her voice. "Calm down. Just think for a second. Can you remember anything else?"

I hope I seem calmer than I feel and that she doesn't hear my desperation for answers.

She takes a deep breath that shudders when she releases it. "Um." She swallows. "They mentioned something about a commander or something." She shrugs. "I don't remember."

She sounds like she's about to cry.

Please don't cry.

"I'm just—" She takes another breath, hopefully trying to pull herself back under control.

"No talking in formation!" The voice makes my stomach churn. It's the same voice that startled me last night. The voice of the man who drugged me.

He's not very tall, but he's lean, and I know from personal experience, he's strong. There are scars scattered across his face, but his nose is straight and unmarred. Golden eyes stand out against his tanned skin in a startling and eerie way. They shift back and forth between Shay and me.

"Is that understood?" he shouts, inches from me.

"Get out of my face." My voice trembles as I speak, and my eyes narrow as I stare at him. I don't know what's going on, but I already hate this man.

He grins. His hand flies up and smacks me across the face so quickly, I don't have time to flinch. My head rocks to the side from the force. A burning, tingling pain flares across my cheek, and tears rush to fill my eyes. I blink them away and clamp my teeth together, refusing to acknowledge the pain.

"Never talk to me like that again." He barks out the words and leans his face in closer.

He's waiting for me to pull back, turn away, mutter an apology of some sort, but I can't. I won't. He will not see weakness in me. No matter how terrified I may feel. Each second that ticks by feels like an hour. Neither of us breaks eye contact. My cheek stings. His breath assaults my nostrils, coating me with its putrid smell.

"Knock it off! Finish securing them for transport," a man calls over. "Make sure they're all lined up correctly."

He stares at me for another moment, and then pulls back. "You've got a lot to learn, kid. You don't want to mess with me." He shoves Shay into the line next to me and then struts away.

Our confrontation hasn't gone unnoticed. With the way he shouted at me, there's no way it could have. I feel the stares of those around me, teens and adults alike, but keep my gaze fixed on the ground. A few moments pass. Then there's shuffling and murmuring as people go back to whatever they were doing before.

A sharp intake of breath from someone in front of me draws my attention. The soldiers are securing the teens' legs to one another, making a chain. A tendril of fear scurries up my spine and back down.

Whatever's happening, wherever we're being taken, I can't let it go down without a fight. And there will be no way to fight once they attach me to others.

One man approaches me and Shay, pulls a cord from the package bound at his side, and bends down to our feet.

No no no. I can't let him do this.

Terror claws at me, and one word flashes through my mind.

Run!

I fling my knee up into the man's stomach, knocking him off balance, and then turn and shoulder my way past the few people who stand behind me and sprint to the edge of the clearing, slipping through a gap between the guards. There's a shout, gasps, the sound of others moving, but I ignore it all and run as fast as my bound hands allow me to.

I have no idea where I am. No clue which direction home is. I only know that I have to escape. I run as hard as I can away from the clearing. Away from the dozens of teens and young adults being led away to a horrifyingly new life. Away from the man I have learned to hate, even though I don't know his name. Tree branches scratch at my face, my arms. I stumble over a root and barely keep myself from falling to the ground. A warm, sticky substance trickles down my wrists. Blood.

Tears spring to the surface. I blink hard, force them away. Now is not the time to cry. I need to put as much space between myself and my captors as possible. I race as fast as my legs will carry me over the uneven forest floor, ducking under branches, sidestepping trees. My breath comes in short bursts now, my lungs burning. I stumble again. Fall to my knees. Strain to get up without the use of my hands.

Then I run again. A branch hits the bruise on my side where I was kicked earlier.

Noises sound behind me. They're coming for me.

I try to run faster.

"Get the others!" A familiar voice bellows. "The girl is mine."

Panic spurs me on, expelling any weariness. My eyes dart around the forest, searching for a direction to go, hoping at least for a place to hide, hindered by my bound hands.

A bullet whizzes by my head, blasting into a rock mere feet to my right.

I dare a glance back and see a man with his gun trained on me. They're closing in. I race around a thick tree, leaping over a rock in my way, then come to an abrupt halt.

Standing in the path before me is the golden eyed man.

Ragged breaths tear through my body as I stare at him in horror. Others form a circle around us, their weapons drawn.

One woman places a hand on her ear. "Copy," she says. "We've secured the other runners. Transport is fifteen mics out, sir."

The golden-eyed man doesn't take his gaze off of me as he nods. "Good. I'll deal with her." The others drift away. The man's eyes narrow, and he breaks eye-contact. "Not you, soldier."

A soldier stops, a look of terror on his face. It's the man who was about to secure my leg to Shay and the other teens.

"Yes, sir." His voice trembles, and sweat breaks out on his forehead as he casts a glance at the golden-eyed man.

I want to step backward, move away, but fear washes over me in a sudden wave, anchoring me in place.

Golden Eyes flicks his gaze at me and then back to the soldier. "What. Happened?"

"She kneed me, sir," the soldier says. "Knocked me down."

In a move so swift, I barely see it happen, Golden Eyes is next to me, hand gripping my hair. I try to pull away, but pain seizes my scalp. He gives it a hard jerk, turning my head to face the soldier. I wince.

"She's untrained, bound, and she *knocked you down?*" The words are ominously calm.

"I-I'm sorry, sir."

A blast sounds near my ear, and the soldier cries out in pain, falling to the ground. Golden eyes holds a gun in his other hand. I gasp, try to pull away, but his grip tightens.

"You serve the Commander, soldier. Be worthy of that, or face the consequences."

He holsters his gun and then drags me by the hair toward the injured man. Blood runs from the bullet wound in the man's leg, and I look away as my stomach lurches.

"Get back to the extraction point." He kicks him in the side. "And don't give me another reason to notice you."

The man struggles to his feet, the pain apparently overshadowed by his fear of Golden Eyes. "Yes, sir." He salutes and then limps away.

Leaving me alone with a man I realize I need to fear.

Panic grips me, and I struggle under his grip.

"No, no," he says in a voice that's calm, measured. Terrifying. "We're not done here."

My heart pounds in my throat, and my eyes connect with his.

"You have a lot to learn, recruit."

I blink. Recruit? What is he talking about?

"My reach goes farther than you will *ever* be able to escape from. Try to remember that." He tilts his head to the side. "And if you forget, I will remind you." He releases my hair and grabs my upper arm in a grip so tight, I can feel the bruise forming. Then he pulls me back toward the extraction site. "Hopefully, you didn't set our timeline back too far."

My head pounds as I try to sort through what he's saying, but the words don't make sense. I stumble on a root, but his grip on my arm keeps me from falling to the ground, and he doesn't stop walking. Instead, he picks up his pace, half dragging me until I can get my feet back under me enough to keep up.

Anger boils within me, burning my stomach. I will not be broken. Not like this. Not by him.

My mind flashes back to the guy from earlier. Without giving myself time to think, I pull my head back and smash it into his face. My forehead connects with his nose. There's a crack. He screams in pain and releases my arm as his hands go of their own accord to his broken nose.

I seize the opportunity and turn to get away.

"I don't think so." Golden Eyes grabs my arm and whirls me around to face him, the warm blood on his hands sticky against my skin.

I flinch as his grip tightens. His eyes water from the pain, and blood slowly pours out of his nose, enhancing the rage twisting his face into a snarl. My heart pounds in my chest as fear takes over rational thought. I tug my arm, try to pull back, to get away from him. His grip becomes viselike. The reality that I can't escape him flits through my mind, but still I fight. He pulls me closer, grabs my other arm, and lifts me off the ground. I kick my feet, but it does nothing. He's too strong.

"You will pay for this," he growls.

He hurls me into the air.

My body twists. There's no way to catch myself, to break my fall. For an instant, everything slows down. I'm floating in midair. The sky stretches above me, my body turns, and I face the ground. It rises to meet me. A rock jutting out of the earth fills my vision, and I brace myself for the impact.

Bam! My head slams into the rock. Pain bursts through me as everything goes black.

CHAPTER

FIVE

A shock zips through me, and I bolt upright, gasping for breath.

"She's alert, sir," a woman kneeling on the floor next to me says.

The empty syringe in her hand causes me to try to move away from her, but my bound hands and feet make it almost impossible. With a rush, everything comes back to me.

Waking up in the forest.

The soldiers.

The other teens.

Golden Eyes.

The man comes into view as though he could read my thoughts. "Good. We're two mics out. Prepare for landing."

"Yes, sir." The woman puts the needle in a box, seals it, and then stands.

My muddled brain struggles to process everything. I look down and immediately wish I hadn't. My stomach roils. I'm suspended in the air, the tops of trees passing by in a blur beneath me.

"Where am I? What's going on?" The questions burst from my mouth, coated with fear.

The soldiers ignore me, and I open my mouth to ask again, desperation pushing aside any sane thought.

"Girl, I would stay quiet if I were you." The words are a whisper, but they catch my attention.

The girl who spoke is bound inches away from me on my right, and as I crane my neck to look behind me, my mouth drops open. Somehow, all the teens from the clearing are in this vehicle, but the ground beneath us and the sky above us are as clear as if we were floating in midair. It's like being in an enormous bubble.

The glass darkens, and there's a shift as the vehicle goes downward. Gasps sound from among the teens.

"Silence!" Golden Eyes shouts.

There's a whimper from one girl, but it cuts off quickly.

I look at the girl next to me, the one who risked speaking to warn me. Dark black curls frame her face, and her creamy brown skin is smooth except for her forehead, which is wrinkled in concentration. Piercing eyes study me, and I want to squirm under the weight of her inspection. Then she looks away, staring straight ahead. Almost as though she's dismissed me.

Before I can decide if the action annoys me or not, the vehicle descends rapidly, and then settles with a light thump. My heartbeat quickens. A door on the side of the vehicle slides up, and a massive man's shadow is outlined against the brightness of the outdoors.

He enters, each footfall shaking the floor as he approaches Golden Eyes. His hair is a little longer and more unkempt than the other men in uniform, and a scar runs over his left cheek.

Golden Eyes salutes him.

"You're late," the big man says, saluting him back.

Golden Eyes slides a glance at me, and my skin prickles under the hatred in his eyes. His nose has an ugly red mark across it. "Not too late."

Before the big man can respond, Golden Eyes turns toward the other soldiers.

"Get these scumbags up, out of the transport, and to the hall for their first briefing."

"Sir, yes, sir!" the soldiers respond in unison, and then they are among us, yanking people to their feet.

One of them approaches me, grabs my arm, and pulls me up. My head spins, and aches I didn't even know I had suddenly make themselves known. I blink and take a staggering step, hindered by the bindings on my legs tying me to teens on either side of me.

The girl who spoke to me earlier nudges me gently with her shoulder. "Breathe through the pain," she mutters under her breath. "And for the love of anything that is good, *don't* do anything else to make them notice you. Especially since I'm standing right next to you."

Before I can respond, they propel us out of the transport. The brightness outside slams me in the face, and my head throbs as they lead us toward a building close by. I try to look around, get an idea of where I am, but there's no time as soldiers push and shove us into the building.

It's as though I'm walking in a pain-filled fog, and there's no opportunity to process anything. I'm living in a nightmare. How did this happen?

The room they lead us into is cavernous, and the lighting is far different from anything I've experienced before. The soldiers shove us and yell at us until we are in straight lines and fill the space. Once we are in the positions they want us in, they remove the bindings on our legs and wrists. When they remove the bindings from the blonde girl on my left, she thanks them.

"Silence!" the soldier shouts in response.

The girl's eyes widen, but she nods once.

As soon as mine are removed, I rub my hands over my chafed wrists. Each throb, every pulse of pain, all of it a reminder that this is real. The pounding in my head intensifies.

"Attention!" The voice thunders from the huge man who entered the transport upon our arrival. He strides into the room, followed closely by Golden Eyes.

The lines of young people around me seem to stand straighter, and tension pulsates through us, pulling us together tighter than the plastic bindings that were just removed. Only one row of teens stands between me and the two soldiers as they come to a stop at the front, turn on their heels, and face us, hands linked behind their backs. Golden Eyes scans the room, and then his attention lands on me. His eyes narrow, and, though I don't break eye contact, I can't help but wish I was farther back and hidden among the other teens. Or able to inflict more damage on the man than I already have.

"I am Staff Sergeant Andor Valarius, and I am your senior Drill Instructor," the big man says. "I am assisted by Drill Instructor Sergeant Laban Meritas." He gestures to Golden Eyes, who takes a step forward and then steps back.

At least now I have a name. But the man doesn't seem worthy of a name.

"You will call us Sergeant Valarius and Sergeant Meritas." The words are precise, measured, and very loud.

One thing I know already. I won't be calling Golden Eyes *Sergeant,* or giving him any title that would show respect. Even if it's only in my head, I'm calling him Laban.

"You are in a city called Talionis, and you are our first wave of recruits," Sergeant Valarius continues.

"What?" the curly-haired girl on my right mutters so quietly, I almost don't hear her.

"I'm sure you have questions," Drill Instructor Valarius continues, "but I'm not interested in hearing them. Follow the orders given to you by the soldiers of Squadron Seven and by your instructors. Is that understood?"

We all stare at him, silent.

"He asked if that was understood!" Laban shouts. "We need to hear a, 'Yes, sir!' Now!"

"Yes, sir!" Everyone shouts in response.

A sadistic smile spreads across his face.

My heart skips a beat. Before he says another word, I know I don't want to hear it.

"Forget where you came from," Laban says. "Forget the life you knew. You are now recruits of Talionis!" His voice rises as he speaks, his fist pounding the air.

Terror claws at me. I shake. *No. No. No.*

Slow clapping from the back of the room interrupts my frantic thoughts. I turn with the other teens to find the source, and my jaw drops open. My head injury must be worse than I thought, because I'm sure I'm seeing double. The man who just entered the room looks strikingly like Drill Instructor Sergeant Valarius, except for his well-groomed hair, and the look of gratification on his face that's the opposite of Sergeant Valarius's impassive, closed expression. I'd bet a week of trading bonds they're brothers.

"Well said, Sergeant Meritas, well said." The man strides to the front of the room with a confidence bordering on arrogance.

Both sergeants are at attention, and the newest soldier salutes them. "At ease."

He spreads his legs shoulder width apart and tucks a hand into his pocket. He has a red band around his left sleeve with black streaks running through it, which is something I haven't seen on anyone else's uniform.

"Good morning. My name is Lieutenant Colonel Keenan Valarius, and it's a pleasure," he places his free hand over his heart, "to welcome you to Talionis. I'm sure you're all wondering about what's going on. Your questions are completely understandable, and I'm here to personally welcome you and give you an explanation of what your lives will look like in the days to come."

I lean forward.

"We have recruited you into a special military force. This is not something to fear. You're about to enter a new life, and this will give you opportunities that, I guarantee you, are unlike anything you have ever even dreamed of." He smiles, looking as pleased as if he had just given us all a wonderful gift.

"We recognize that this life will be a complete departure from what you're used to, but we're certain that with time and routine, you'll come to see the many benefits of being recruits of Talionis."

My eyes narrow as he speaks. It's like they expect us to be happy we're here.

"Your days will be filled with lessons and trainings," Colonel Valarius continues. "In the beginning, they will include physical conditioning, training in technology, and education in the history and ways of Talionis. After a while, you'll be introduced to weaponry training and warfare strategies. You are here to become vital parts of this city and ambassadors for Talionis in the North American region. Do well, and we will reward you."

This doesn't make sense. The wound on my head throbs. Weapons. Warfare. Physical conditioning. What exactly are they planning to do? And what purpose could I possibly have in their plans? My heart pounds out a staccato beat with each question.

"The first month and a half will be the same for all of you as you become familiar with the city and go through basic training and preparations. You"—he fans his arms out at us—"were each chosen for a variety of reasons, and you'll be placed into groups and assigned training to reflect those reasons."

Chosen. I never thought that word would sound like a curse, but right now, it does.

"During these beginning weeks, we will observe you to confirm if your original assignment is the best fit for you. After that, you'll enter more intensive training geared toward specific areas."

"Whoa, wait a second!" A dark-haired guy in front of me steps forward. "Stop acting like this is some kinda honor or something. We don't want to be here."

A spark of admiration for his bravery ignites in me, but it's immediately squelched when I glimpse Colonel Valarius's face, pinched in frustration. Laban stalks toward the young man, his golden eyes raging. His arm flashes out and collides with the dark-haired boy's face, knocking him backward. Before he can raise his hands to defend himself, Laban hits him again. He crashes into me, and I stumble back. He pushes away from me, and Laban throws an uppercut into his jaw.

I look at Colonel Valarius, half-expecting him to stop Laban, but he's ignoring the situation, brushing at a stray piece of lint on his sleeve.

"Never talk to a soldier of Talionis that way again. Show some respect." Laban steps back, and the ragged, pain-filled breathing of the boy who voiced his opinion haunts the air with a clear warning.

Blood pounds through my veins and thunders in my ears as I

stare at the boy, who seems almost unable to stay on his feet. A part of me wants to step forward, help the guy. I don't want this to be as bad as it seems. It can't be. Then I look up and find Laban studying me, as though he's daring me to do something, *anything*, to give him an excuse to beat me too.

The whispered words from the girl on my right about not doing anything to make them notice me come to mind. I stifle a groan. I haven't done anything since we arrived, but Laban Meritas knows who I am. Maybe I'm not as brave as the guy in front of me, but I can at least be brave enough to not cower in front of this tyrant. I thrust out my jaw and stare back at him, earning a scowl in return.

"Drill Instructor Sergeants Valarius and Meritas will be primarily responsible for your basic training." Colonel Valarius continues as though nothing happened, a small, insidious smile curling the corners of his mouth. "Because of your delay, Professor Mandeville could not be here to meet you, but he will be your technology instructor. Ms. Elva Trill will teach you about Talionis. In the coming weeks, you will be introduced to your instructors in Warfare Strategies and Weaponry Training. There will be others who will assist your primary instructors, and you'll meet them as you go about your training."

My hands twist together. I don't want to hear anything else. What I want is for none of this to be happening. I shift, and a flare of pain burns from a bruise on my side. The shoulders of a girl in front of me are shaking, like maybe she's crying. I swallow hard. I refuse to break down like that. Whether or not I want it to be happening, it *is* happening. I clench my jaw and drag my attention to Colonel Valarius.

"This is a lot to take in, but you will find serving Talionis and the Commander well worth everything." He spreads his arms wide. "Welcome to your new home. I'll leave you in the capable hands of your Drill Instructors."

With those words, he turns, says something to Laban that causes him to nod curtly, and exits the room through a side door.

Sergeant Valarius steps forward. "You will now be led to the tailors to receive your standard recruit uniform. Change immediately and give your old clothes to the tailors. Males will then be given haircuts, and females will be taken to their living quarters to drop off their second uniform. You'll then be led to the dining hall for chow and further instructions."

"Obey every command immediately," Laban shouts. "Delays will be punished. Understood?"

"Yes, sir!" echoes around the room.

"What did you say?" Laban barks.

"Yes, sir!" The shout is deafening, and as much as I don't want to join in, I say it along with the other recruits. Laban's watching me, and I need more information about what's going on here before I do something that gets me beaten.

Or worse.

"Squadron Seven," Sergeant Valarius says, "take the recruits where they need to go."

"Yes, sir!" The soldiers in the squadron pull sticks from their belts and direct us through a set of doors on the opposite side of where Colonel Valarius exited.

I scan the room as I follow the crowd of teens toward the door, searching for a sign of Jaxon or Lencie, both wishing for the comfort of having them here and also desperately hoping they're still back in Derbe and not facing this nightmare. Relief and disappointment add their discordant ripples to my muddled brain when I don't see any sign of either of them.

"My name's Ari," the blonde girl on my left says, interrupting my thoughts. "What're your names?"

I glance over, unsure if she's serious. Somehow, she's smiling right now.

The girl on my right snorts out a laugh. "Girl, after all that, you're really introducing yourself?" She shakes her head. "I'm Nika."

They look at me.

"Bria."

"Nice to meet you both." Ari squints over at a nearby soldier. "What do you think those sticks do? They seem crafted for a purpose, but I can't figure it out."

Nika and I exchange a quick look, and I have the strangest urge to smile.

With everything going on, all we just heard, we're exchanging pleasantries, and Ari is interested in a stick. The mix of normalcy and strangeness feels odd.

A zap from behind us cuts through the air. I spin around to find a recruit on his knees, clutching his side.

A soldier stands over him, stick poised, an electric current buzzing on the tip. "Get up, recruit, and get moving! We don't have all day."

When the guy doesn't immediately rise to his feet, the soldier zaps him again with the stick. He cries out in pain.

The soldier leans down into his face. "Get. Up."

"Why are you all standing around?" A female soldier near the door shouts. "Did we tell you to stop? I don't think so. Move, or be shocked." She smacks her stick against her palm, and everyone half-walks, half-jogs through the door.

I fall into step with Nika and Ari, strangely comforted by the two girls I just met, and pass through the door. My body aches. My mind can't process everything I've seen and heard in the past hour, and one thought throbs above everything else.

My life, as I knew it, is over.

CHAPTER

SIX

The trek down the passageway to the tailor is filled with zaps as recruits who are slow, stop, or question what's happening are shocked by the sticks in the hands of the soldiers. Every command they give, every word they speak, comes out as a shout.

My heart races as I try to stay in the middle of the hoard of teens, some with eyes wide, others with tears openly streaming down their face, and a few with scowls. A guy bumps into me in his effort to move further away from a soldier with her shock stick, hitting a bruise. I suck in a quick breath as pain ripples through me. Somehow, I doubt I'll get to rest and recover before I'm forced to do whatever conditioning they have planned for us.

"Halt!" The soldier at the front shouts loud enough to cause an echo in the hallway, but I can't see him through the crowd of recruits in front of me. "The tailors are through the door on my left. Fifteen recruits will go through at a time, retrieve their uniforms, remove their personal clothing in the changing area, and leave all personal items with the tailors. Males will then receive their haircuts, and females will go to their barracks. You will all be given HaloAct bands which you will wear at all times. These bands, along with sensors throughout the city, will allow us to electronically monitor you and your progress. Understood?"

"Yes, sir!" We all shout the words, though they feel like sandpaper scraping my mouth on the way out.

Although I'm not sure what the soldier meant by electronically monitoring us, I do know it will make it harder, if not impossible, for me to disobey without facing major consequences. I don't want to give in or conform to whatever this is. But right now, I need to do what they say and give my body time to heal. I'm not strong enough to handle being shocked. Or a beating.

"I really want to see one of those sticks." Ari chews on her lower lip as she stares at one of the nearby soldiers.

"What?" I say. Who is this girl?

"I don't think asking to hold one of their weapons is going to go over real well," Nika says.

Ari sighs. "Maybe not."

The line moves forward several feet and then stops again.

"Does that hurt?" Nika nods at my head.

I gingerly probe the lump and grimace. It starts on the right side of my forehead and extends past my hairline. It aches and stings, and the rough edges of scraped skin cut across the bump.

I drop my hand. "It's fine."

Nika quirks an eyebrow. "Sure it is."

"Bria." Shay's voice behind me causes me to turn around and gives me a reason to ignore Nika's sarcasm.

She's slowly weaving her way through the handful of recruits separating us, shooting wary glances at the soldiers stationed around us. When she reaches me, she sighs.

"Are you okay?" she asks. "You don't look so good."

"Told you," Nika mutters, with a self-satisfied smirk.

Shay glances at her briefly, then focuses on me, chin tilted up.

I brace myself. Here comes a lecture.

"Whatever is happening right now, I don't think it's a good idea to make an enemy. You shouldn't have provoked Drill Instructor Sergeant Meritas in the woods."

I set my jaw and force myself to inhale and exhale before replying. These people have taken us from our homes, and she thinks it's a good time to lecture me on what I should and shouldn't do? Typical.

"Look, I don't think it's a good idea to stand out right now," Nika says, "but give the girl a break. At least she tried to get away."

Shay takes a step back and crosses her arms over her chest. "Excuse me. This is a private conversation."

Nika sniffs. "We were having our *own* private conversation before you butted in."

Shay's eyes widen, and her mouth drops open. Then she pulls herself together. "Bria causes problems wherever she goes. I was only trying to help."

"Thanks for that, Shay," I snap.

Shay taps her foot. "They brought you, while you were *unconscious,* onto the transport before everyone else. Clearly, they wanted to make an example of you. Do you think that's a good thing?" She pauses, nose tilting up. "It's not."

"They separated me from my brother when they brought us onto the transport," Ari says. "I haven't seen him since." Her voice breaks, and she turns away.

Some of my anger toward Shay dissolves as I recognize the pain in Ari's words. I'm not the only one struggling.

Before the conversation can go further, the mass of recruits moves, and we're next in line to enter the tailors.

The soldiers position fifteen of us three-by-three, and thankfully, I'm next to Nika and Ari. Shay is in the set behind us, giving me a momentary reprieve from her condescension. I want to thank Nika for sticking up for me, but I also don't want to risk being noticed by the soldiers right in front of us.

"Next," the closest soldier shouts and opens the doors.

They herd the fifteen of us into the room. A long counter runs through the middle, and two women stand behind it, both dressed in black skirts and white blouses buttoned up to the neck. Uniforms hang in rows behind them.

"My name is Sampta, and this is Presidia," the one woman says.

Sampta's eyebrows arch unnaturally high, and her hair is tied back into a tight bun. Her lips are pursed like she recently sucked on a lemon, and wire-rimmed glasses perch on the tip of her nose. Presidia's hair and eyebrows look almost identical to Sampta's, but she's a few inches shorter and doesn't have glasses.

"We will issue you your uniforms." Sampta spits the word out as though it tastes bad. "And I suppose we will be made available to you in the event that you need alterations or mending."

"Come now, let's go." Presidia waves a hand at us impatiently. "We don't have all day."

"Why we are *forced* to do this is utterly beyond me." Sampta fingers a uniform with a sniff of disdain.

Nika, Ari, and I step up to the counter and stare at the women.

They blink in unison. Then Presidia turns to Sampta. "Truly, why must we stoop to this level and deal with such incompetence?"

Sampta tilts her head in agreement, and then they face us again. "Names, please."

"You can't call us incompetent if you don't tell us what you need from us," I say, both annoyed and somewhat amused by the eccentric women.

Nika elbows me in the side, hitting a bruise. I let out a shallow huff and glare at her.

"I'm Nika Bromeliad," she says before Sampta and Presidia respond to me, which is probably for the best.

Presidia and Sampta scowl at me. Then Sampta picks up a small, thin, clear board. She pokes at it with her finger for a moment. It looks like she's tapping on glass.

Ari leans forward on the counter. "What is that?"

Sampta and Presidia both take a step back.

"If you must know, it's an AVID-screen," Presidia says.

"What does it do?" Ari asks.

I bite my lip to contain a grin. This girl is something else. Either she's completely oblivious, or she really doesn't care if she's irritating people with her questions and comments.

"Do we look like your technology instructors? Really." Sampta flicks her hand at Ari. "Off the counter. Now."

Ari obeys, and Sampta steps away and retrieves two uniforms from one of the racks. She holds them with two fingers from each hand, like merely touching the fabric is more than she wants to do. With a shudder, she passes them to Nika along with a pair of boots.

"Your name?" Presidia says to me.

"Bria Averton."

"And you?" Sampta asks.

"Ari Willowpen. Can you show me what you're doing?"

Sampta uses one finger to push her glasses further up her nose. "No."

Moments later, they give Ari and me our own uniforms and pairs of heavy black boots, and then Sampta and Presidia smear disinfectant gel on their hands.

"Next," Presidia says.

As the three of us walk away, Sampta mutters, "Once we're done with this arduous task, let's design something for the Commander. I need to put my hands to better use than this."

Presidia agrees promptly, and I shake my head, unsure of what to make of the women.

A female soldier ushers us to the changing area. "Change into your uniforms quickly, and remove every personal item. If we find you with any personal items from this moment forward, you will be brought to the sandpit and forced to do extra PT. Now change!"

She doesn't give us time or opportunity to ask what her words mean.

The three of us enter a room filled with other girls who are already in their uniforms or in the process of changing. I make my way to a corner to give myself some sense of privacy and swallow the lump that's forming in my throat.

Now is not the time to get emotional.

I set the boots and spare uniform on the floor, and I focus on the uniform in my hands. It's a green camo shirt and pants and a dark green t-shirt, and they stamped my name on the front and again on the left sleeve. Under my name reads Unit 6. I don't know what the words mean, and I'm afraid to find out.

As I strip off my clothes from home, my throat thickens. The crushing pain in my heart overshadows the pain I feel with the movements. I'm stripping away the final fragments of my identity. I carefully fold up the shirt I made with my mom, as memories of her sketching out the pattern and design rush over me. Later that same day, she let me sit with her as she worked on a map. It was the beginning of hours spent together as she gently taught me. Only yesterday, I believed we still had hours more of those lessons, of traveling together, working together.

Swallowing the memories, I carefully set the shirt on the ground with the rest of my clothing and put on the uniform. The starched fabric is stiff and unfamiliar against my skin. I reach for my necklace, the silky sea glass coming to rest naturally in my fingers. Familiar and comforting but also a painful reminder of Ezri.

The last thing he gave me before he died.

I squeeze the pendant before tucking it beneath my uniform. No matter what the consequences may be, I won't remove it.

I finish buttoning up the uniform, put on my boots, and gather my clothes before heading toward the changing room exit. At the door, two soldiers take everyone's personal items and throw them into bins. The girl in front of me resists for a moment and is shocked. She releases a cry and then relinquishes her clothing.

I hug my clothes to my chest, inhale the scent of home, and then force myself to give them to the female soldier when she reaches out her hand.

It's like a piece of me is torn away as she carelessly tosses them into the bin. I want to retrieve them, fight against what's happening. But I can't. Not now.

Not yet.

The soldier hands me a bright yellow sash.

"You will wear this until you have completed your first week of training. Put it on now."

I obey.

Next, she retrieves a bracelet from a box at her feet along with what looks like the same type of screen thing Sampta and Presidia used. She eyes my name on my uniform, taps on the screen, and then lays the bracelet on top of it.

"*Activated,*" an unnatural voice chirps.

The woman hands me the bracelet. "Wear this HaloAct band at

all times. It contains your training assessment information, your schedule, and a map of Talionis. It will also monitor you and track your progress throughout Physical Conditioning. Your Tech Instructor will give you a more in-depth explanation of how it works."

I fit the HaloAct band to my wrist as she speaks, feeling more bound than when my hands were tied together.

"For now, all you need to know is that you press this button," she gestures to a button on the band, "to view your schedule, and this one to view the map of Talionis." She points to the button next to the first one.

She pushes me forward. "Next!"

I exit the changing area, and I'm greeted by another soldier who instructs me to join the group of other female recruits waiting to be led to our barracks. Every step I take feels weighted with uncertainty and trepidation. I squeeze my eyes shut, and images of my family dance in my mind. Are they even okay?

At least there aren't any other kids around Eli and Zeke's age. I would hate to see what this place would do to my exuberant, full-of-life little brothers. As much as I want to hug them right now, what I want more is for them to be safe. I push the thoughts of them aside. If I let myself linger there, I'll end up breaking down. And I can't afford that right now.

I fidget with the band to get it to rest comfortably on my wrist. The other girls around me are unfamiliar. A few talk in hushed tones, and almost all of them focus on the HaloAct bands on their wrists.

The thing that most intrigued me about the band is its map feature. Since we're waiting for the rest of the girls to finish changing, I push the upper right button to see what it looks like. A three-dimensional map shoots out of the band. The buildings in Talionis, buildings I haven't yet seen more than a glimpse of, spring out from my wrist in detailed, miniature form. A small gasp escapes.

It's incredible. But is it accurate? I tilt my head and study it, searching for inconsistencies.

A blinking dot catches my eye.

"These are amazing, right?" Ari pops up next to me.

I jump back a bit, dropping my hand to my side. The map disappears back into the band. "Uh, I guess so."

Ari pushes buttons so rapidly, I almost can't keep up. She opens her map, and I see the same blinking red dot on hers.

"What do you think that is?" I ask.

Before she can answer, a soldier steps into our conversation.

"That's you." He stares into my eyes, letting his words sink in. Then he walks away.

Panic spirals from the top of my head down to the bottoms of my feet and then back up again. That was what they meant when they said we'd be electronically monitored. As long as I'm wearing this band, they will always know where I am.

Ari doesn't seem as disturbed by the news as I feel. She remains focused on her band, bringing up different features that I'm not sure she's even supposed to know about yet. For the moment, she's quiet as she focuses.

The rest of the girls exit the changing area, and then we are marched to our barracks. As we move, my thoughts come down from their panicked state. The band is disturbing, but it might be useful. They want to frighten me with the fact that they know where I am, but I'll find a way to make this band a tool I can use to escape. The details on the map were remarkable. I'll study it once I've seen more of the city.

And I'll do whatever it takes to get out of here and back to my family.

CHAPTER
SEVEN

They lead us out of the building and instruct us to speed walk down a short path to another building one soldier refers to as the Recruit Living Quarters. Once inside, the female soldiers guiding us bring us to the right wing of the building where there's a long hallway with open doors on either side, leading to cramped rooms with three or four beds. Nameplates on the doors indicate which recruits are assigned to which room, and, though I know it's going to happen, my stomach still drops when I approach a room halfway down the hall with my name on it.

Everything about this shows they were *preparing* for us. And the knowledge doesn't comfort me.

I pause at the doorway.

"Enter your room, recruit," a nearby soldier says. She doesn't shout at the same volume as the other soldiers, but her words are firm and leave no room for argument.

I walk into the room and find Ari and Nika already inside. I approach the third bed in the space and drop my spare uniform onto it.

"Guess we're roommates." Nika makes a sound in the back of her throat. "If we're going to be associated with each other, please try not to get into too much trouble."

I roll my eyes but without any annoyance. A part of me is relieved to be with Nika and Ari. I don't know them well at all, but somehow I've connected with them through the trauma of our arrival in this place.

"They're tracking us...do you think they're listening to us too?" I ask.

"Not in here," Ari says. "I scrambled the frequencies using a feature I found on the band so we can speak freely."

I stare at her, not comprehending anything she just said, but she doesn't notice. Her back is to me and Nika as she straightens the already perfectly straight sheets on her bunk. Her bed's not far from the one I'm sitting on. Nothing in the room is far away. It's only big enough for the three beds and dressers in it. The walls and ceilings are white. The dressers and beds are black. There aren't any windows in here, making the space feel even more confined.

"I've never seen anything like this place," I say.

"Tell me about it," Nika agrees. "Even the lights are weird. Nothing like the lanterns I'm used to."

I sigh. I miss the soft glow of lantern light.

"You use lanterns?" Ari turns to face us.

Nika and I both nod.

"I knew different parts of the country had different tech, but I had no idea there were areas without electricity," Ari says the words almost to herself.

"What did *you* use?" I ask.

"Lights. Like these." Ari waves her hands at the lighting in the ceiling.

Dozens of questions leap to mind.

But then Ari tucks her lip between her teeth and drops onto her bed. "What are they planning to do with us?"

The urge to spring up from my bed and sprint from the room fills me, but I stay seated. Ari's question makes sense, but I don't want to think about it, reason it out.

Because that will make it even more real.

"Seems like they're going to try to make us into something," Nika says.

My hands grip my blanket. I don't *want* to be made into some-thing. Based on Laban's little performance and Colonel Valarius's failure to even attempt to restrain him, their plans aren't for our benefit.

Ari's forehead wrinkles. "I keep hoping this is all some kind of mistake, and they're gonna send us home. But it's not, is it?"

"Play with your band thing." Nika ignores the question and its obvious answer. "Us speculating about all of this isn't going to help until we know more."

"But you said I couldn't analyze my HaloAct Band in the room anymore," Ari says.

My eyebrows rise, and I can't help but wonder why Nika made the rule.

"If you can manage to look at it without exclaiming over every little thing you find, you can play with it."

"Analyze it," Ari corrects absently as she pushes a button on the band and brings it to life.

"Whatever." Nika shrugs at me.

I smirk. Ari is unique. That's for sure.

Pounding on the wall outside of our room causes me to spring to my feet. I sway as my vision darkens and then clears, a headache pounding behind my eyes.

"Chow time!" one of the soldiers' shouts from the hallway. "Out of your rooms and in the hall *now!*"

Nika and I head for the door, but Ari smooths her sheets where she sat. In another time and place, I would find her quirks amusing, maybe even tease her about it if I knew her better. But right now, I'm almost afraid for her and what the soldiers will do to her if she delays too long.

"Come on, Ari," I say.

Nika is halfway out the door and glances back, eyes wide.

When Ari moves to straighten the final wrinkle, I grab her arm and pull her out of the room.

"I wasn't finished," she protests with a scowl that reminds me of Eli when he doesn't get his way.

A pang ricochets through my chest at the thought of my brother, but I push it back.

"Girl, your bed is fine," Nika says out of the corner of her mouth.

"It's better when everything is tidy," Ari says.

A soldier down the hall bangs against a door several times. "What is the delay? Move! Move! Move!"

She enters, and a moment later drags a girl from the room and slams her against the wall.

"When we give you an order, you obey!" She leans into the girl's face, screaming the words.

The girl is trembling but gives a quick nod.

"Don't give us a reason to notice you again, understood?"

Another nod from the girl, whose face is almost as pale as the white wall behind her.

"I need to hear a response, recruit!"

"Yes, ma'am," the girl says, her voice small and quavering in the hallway's silence.

The soldier stares at her for another second and then steps away. "What are you all staring at? To the Dining Hall, now!" She points past us and down the hall, and she, along with several other soldiers, herd us in that direction.

I pass a door marked *Stairs*, and there are signs directing the way to various rooms and meeting areas, but the soldiers keep us moving too fast for my mind to process any of it. I want to slow down, collect each detail, find the mistakes they don't know about.

This can't be the end. This can't be my life.

When we arrive at the Dining Hall, which is in the same building as our living quarters, I hesitate. I don't want to go in. I don't want to hear any more of what these people have to say. And I don't want to be given orders to follow. But I need to know what's going on to find some answers. And I'll follow the orders they give me if it means being better prepared for when I can escape.

I inhale. Exhale. And step into the room with the rest of the recruits. Nika and Ari are ahead of me now, but I find I don't mind the solitude.

The Dining Hall is as big as the first room they brought us to.

Tables and chairs fill the space, with one long stretch of tables running through the center. Several doors line the back wall, and the faint aroma of food wafts through the air.

The soldiers instruct us to find our seats and await further instructions. Then they drift to the edges of the room. I pass tables crowded with recruits, some talking, others silent, but I don't see Shay, Nika, or Ari. And right now, I don't have the energy to engage with new people.

I find an empty table at the back and settle into a seat. The cool metal of the table beneath my hands draws my attention. It's solid. Real. As much as I want to leave, pretend none of this is happening, I know it's not possible. If I left today, at this moment, everything I've already experienced would mark me.

That's what trauma does.

I stare at my hands. They're shaking. I squeeze them together, trying to still them. It doesn't work, so I drop them into my lap to keep anyone else from noticing. Even if I denied it all day, there's the proof I'm afraid. I hate it.

Several men and women enter through the back doors carrying trays of food. They set them on the center table and leave as others take their place. My stomach churns as the smell of the food takes over the room. I rest my hand on my abdomen, hoping it will help. It doesn't. At home, when my stomach is sick, my mom always fixes me some tea with mint leaves from the garden.

My stomach protests again, but images of my family parade through my mind. I swallow the lump in my throat. My eyes burn, so I squeeze them shut. No. I can't let this happen. My emotions, the pain of thinking about my family—I can't let it overwhelm me. I take a deep breath and force the thoughts away. The same thing I've always done whenever it hurts too much to think about Ezri.

Thinking about my family here will only distract me, and I can't afford any distractions. I need to be focused, to find a way to escape.

Three slow breaths later, I open my eyes.

"Listen up!" a woman who brought food in says.

Conversations stop as everyone turns their attention to her.

"The food has been served. Line up on either side of the tables and fill your plates. Someone will be in shortly to instruct you on what you'll be doing next." She leaves through the back doors.

Recruits stand and line up to get food, and I rise from my chair and fall into line with the rest of them. Platters of eggs, bacon, shredded potatoes, bowls of fruit, and sweet rolls fill the table. I haven't eaten since the Festival, which has to have been over twenty-four hours ago now. I should be starving. The food should look great. But it doesn't. Nothing is how it should be.

I add a few things to my plate, not even filling it halfway, and head back to my table.

"Bria! Over here!" Ari calls.

I pivot at the sound of her voice and find her a few tables away, half out of her seat, waving at me. Nika is there as well as two guys, both with freshly shaved heads. I head toward her, almost relieved to not have to go sit by myself.

"I looked over to say something to you when we walked in here, but you were gone," Ari says as soon as I sit down.

I offer a half-smile but say nothing.

"Oh! This is my brother, Bryson." Ari points to the boy sitting next to her.

I tilt my head at Bryson in acknowledgment of the introduction. The blond fuzz left on his head and his blue eyes are a striking match to his sister's, and he has the slight, athletic build of a runner.

"He found me when I walked in here." Ari rests a hand on her brother's arm as she speaks.

He gives Ari a small smile, the strain in his eyes not lessening the affection he has for his sister. "And this is Shane Malton." She gestures to the boy sitting two seats away from me. "We just met." The hint of a blush tinges Ari's cheeks.

"Hey," Shane says, before taking a bite of his slightly burnt toast. Chiseled features, light brown hair, and deep brown eyes set off Shane's good looks. He sits tall and has a confident air about him.

"Nice to meet you both," I say, the manners automatic.

"Wish it was under better circumstances though, huh?" Bryson replies with a choked chuckle.

"I hear that." Nika lifts her fork in the air.

I stab a forkful of cooling eggs and force myself to eat. They taste like sawdust in my mouth, and I reach for my water. Maybe the sweet roll will taste better. I pick it up and pull off a chunk.

Shay approaches with her plate of food and sits next to me, and I'm shocked at the comfort I feel at seeing her. This is *Shay*. We're not friends.

But I know her. She's from home, and right now, that alone is enough.

Ari goes through another round of introductions. Then she focuses on Bryson, discussing the features she's discovered on her band as he eats his food.

"You doing okay?" I ask Shay.

She stiffens. "I'm fine."

"Okay then," I say, unsure why I thought it was a good idea to care.

Then she sighs. "Sorry. It's a lot to process. I don't understand what's going on or even how they took us from Derbe in the first place."

"Yeah, I can't figure that out either. Have you seen anyone else from home?"

She shakes her head.

The door to the Dining Hall is thrust open, and I drop the piece of roll I was about to eat. The room goes quiet. Sergeant Andor Valarius and Laban walk in, their footsteps thundering in the sudden silence. They stop several feet into the room, Laban in front, Sergeant Valarius slightly behind and to the left.

"Listen up," Laban bellows. "Meal time is over."

I glance at my plate. Most of the food remains, but we've only been in here for about fifteen minutes.

"If you didn't finish, you'll learn to eat faster next time. You should all be observant enough to be aware of your unit number. If not, you won't last long," he scoffs. "We'll divide you into groups and give you a tour of the city. Units One, Two, and Three, you're with me. Units Four, Five, and Six, you're with Sergeant Valarius." He points at him with his thumb. "My group," he turns and begins walking away, "let's go!"

There's scrambling all throughout the room as the recruits in units one, two, and three get up and shuffle past the rest in order to catch up to Laban. Everyone at my table remains seated. A quick glance at their uniforms shows Shay, Nika, Ari, and Shane are in my unit. Bryson's in unit four.

The last of the first group of recruits leaves, but Sergeant Valarius says nothing. He studies the room, frowning. I can't pull my eyes away from the scar marring his face. It's hideous, frightening, and it begs to tell a story. One that, I'm sure, is unpleasant. Andor allows the silence to continue. A recruit nearby shifts nervously in his seat.

"Make two lines. Males on the left. Females on the right," Sergeant Valarius finally says, his voice deep, commanding attention.

Chairs screech, some even toppling as the couple hundred recruits move to do as instructed. I stand slowly, trying to maintain some sense of control, and get in line behind Ari, who's standing behind Shay.

"We'll use a transport vehicle to conduct your tour of Talionis. It's like the one you arrived on. These are the rules you will follow during this tour. Do not speak unless spoken to. I don't want to hear any talking. If you have a question, stow it. It'll get answered eventually if it needs to, and I don't want to waste my breath as you try to figure out what's going on. Life changed. Deal with it. And finally, follow all instructions immediately." He clenches his jaw, and his scar bunches, pulling his skin taut across his cheek. He surveys the two lines. "Let's move out."

CHAPTER

EIGHT

Sergeant Valarius is different from his brother. Colonel Valarius spoke with passion and excitement. He acted like we should thank them for letting us be a part of Talionis. Sergeant Valarius, on the other hand, speaks in a detached, routine manner. No enthusiasm, no passion, no elaborate words. Just firm commands.

I emerge from the building and squint as the harsh sunlight mocks me with its brightness. A sneeze rises, but I choke it back, focusing on the ground and allowing my eyes to adjust. A slight breeze blows, pulling one of my dark brown curls the rest of the way out of the braid before dropping it on my neck. I reach up and tuck it back in.

The transport waits on a landing pad not far from the entrance. I still have a hard time processing seeing the enormous machine. It's like a giant tear-drop that's been placed on its side and has grown wings. The mirrored glass covering it reflects the images of the surrounding area. A long walkway extends from the back of the transport to the ground, and the line of recruits winds its way toward it. Sergeant Valarius stands at the bottom, arms crossed over his chest, watching the recruits enter.

A wave of nausea sweeps over me as I move closer, but I push it back. I've been in one of these already, though I only remember the last moments of the flight. I will not show fear. No matter what I feel, I will not let these people see me as one more person they can control.

As I step up to the walkway, the hair on my neck stands up. I shift to the left and find Sergeant Valarius's eyes boring into me, as though he's evaluating me. I lift my chin. We stare at each other for a moment, and his lips twitch as though he wants to smile. My eyes narrow, daring him to underestimate or laugh at me. He gives a subtle nod and breaks eye contact. I release a breath I hadn't dared allowed to escape. Ari is several feet in front of me now, and I hurry past the soldiers stationed throughout the transport to catch up. I slide into the nearest seat, and Nika plops down next to me.

"Guess we finally get to see our new prison," she whispers.

Sergeant Valarius's steps vibrate through the floor as he comes up the walkway, and there's a dull thud as the door is closed. The transport lifts off the ground, my stomach lifting into my throat with it.

Sergeant Valarius presses his way into the center of the transport, spreads his legs shoulder width apart and allows his body to sway in a practiced rhythm with the movement of the vehicle—not unlike the fishermen at home when they're out on their boats in a rolling sea.

"This is Talionis, a place vastly different from anything any of you have known." He talks as though he's memorized a script, each word practiced and rehearsed. "You have the privilege of becoming a part of this glorious city. Today, from the sky, you will see your new home. Tomorrow, you will begin your new life. I'll be pointing out the main areas you will need to know. You'll discover the rest of Talionis in the days to come."

I grip my armrests until my knuckles turn white. The ground has now dropped far beneath us. The large, square building they housed us in rises several stories high, but we soar over it. Below us, paths crisscross their way to various buildings, and the transport moves over them slowly.

Sergeant Valarius continues droning on, his tone flat. "We are now above the Physical Training Arena."

"Woah," Nika whispers.

And I have to agree. The Physical Training Arena is huge, shaped in an oval with half of it covered by a roof, the other half surrounded by a wall but open to the sky. The outdoor area is sectioned off, and a variety of large objects are placed throughout it. From up here, I can't figure out what they are. The transport moves on. The wall cuts off at the far end, where a river provides the final barrier.

Next, we pass over a building which isn't nearly as imposing as the Arena. It's much smaller and more ornate. Sergeant Valarius identifies it as the Educational Center. We continue over the Warfare Strategies and Operations building and the nearby Weaponry Training Complex.

"These buildings will become more important to you later as you develop in your training," he says.

Their names alone tell me I don't want anything to do with them.

The transport continues, making its way into the center of the city, where a huge building towers over everything else, glistening in the late morning sunlight.

"That building is the Main Headquarters. All the high-ranking officials of Talionis have their offices there." Smaller buildings surround it, and people crowd the streets, moving in different directions.

Talionis is nothing like Derbe. The buildings rise higher than any I've ever seen. The housing districts we pass over are elaborate and expansive. And the colors are cold and harsh—black, white, and gleaming silver.

"What in the world?" Nika says under her breath.

I look out the window to see what she's gaping at and can't stop my mouth from dropping open.

"And this," Sergeant Valarius says, "is the Center. Evaluations and any major gathering will take place here."

The mammoth structure is stark and imposing. I think it could swallow up the entire town center of Derbe and still have room to spare. It's a giant oval with a domed roof that arches into the sky, the silver spikes on top shooting even higher. I crane my neck to keep looking at it even as we travel past.

"Talionis offers many wonderful things, but one of our greatest attributes is our security," Sergeant Valarius says. "Soldiers patrol the streets, day and night. They're also stationed at every building, and our electronic monitoring sensors, cameras, and communications system allow us to quickly and efficiently deal with any security breach, no matter where it happens in the city. You are safe here."

My mind spins. How is all of this even possible? It sounds like pre-Demise stuff. But even though I'm struggling to process it all, the implication of what he's saying is clear. We're trapped.

"We're now exiting the city limits and flying over the Ruins. The Ruins surround Talionis, providing an added barrier against the dangers outside."

We approach a fence overgrown with vines and vegetation. The buildings nearest it are not nearly as opulent as the others we have passed. They're much smaller, some even a bit rundown. We cross over the fence, and my skin crawls as I view the area below.

Rubble from collapsed, and long-ago abandoned, buildings clutters the area. Trees and bushes have forsaken their originally intended limitations and burst through the debris, twisted metal and parts of old vehicles gripping the branches and lifting toward the sky. What must have once been roads are now jagged concrete teeth, gnawing through the undergrowth. There's a loud crack, and a building standing on feeble supports shudders and then crashes to the ground. Clouds of dust billow up around where it once stood and soon hide the crumbled structure from view.

This place is unlivable. Hostile.

A few of the soldiers nearby mutter to one another, casting furtive glances down at the Ruins. Like they fear it.

"Let's go, let's go," one of them says under his breath, hand tapping against his leg.

Their unease sets me more on edge. Isn't this all just a way for them to demonstrate their control? Then why are they afraid?

We continue forward. The dilapidated structures disappear, and dense vegetation takes their place, hiding the ground from view.

Trees rise, their limbs outstretched claws, ready to grasp anything that might come close enough. Shadows cling to everything, hiding the dangers lurking inside. As we pass a small clearing, a burst of flames shoots up into the sky, then quickly diminishes. One soldier jumps, and another lets out a startled cry. I press back into my seat.

"This place gives me the creeps," Nika whispers.

A tree sways and then falls to the ground. A jolt ripples through me. "Yeah."

Sergeant Valarius clears his throat, and Nika and I both startle at the sound. "We're coming to the edge of the Ruins now, where we find the last layer of security."

A wall stretches up from the earth, standing high in front of us. I crane my neck, trying to see over it, to glimpse freedom. The wall fills my vision. Which I'm sure is intentional.

They claim they're protecting us and keeping us safe. But, in all I've experienced in my life, it's difficult to imagine anything more dangerous than the place I'm in now.

"The Wall is electrically charged. If a person touches it, the result is unconsciousness, possibly death. It's almost as though lightning has struck them." Sergeant Valarius's voice is matter-of-fact. "When a charge is emitted to an external source, an alarm goes off at the nearest wall tower, and guards are deployed to investigate. There are false alarms such as when branches or animals hit it, but each time the alarm is activated, it is checked."

The transport flies parallel to the wall, passing one tower where several soldiers stand at attention.

"Another important function the walls serves is supporting the Net. Those who advance in technology training will learn more about that." Sergeant Valarius turns toward the pilot. "Make good speed heading back. No need to delay out here."

Several of the soldiers release audible sighs, and then the transport turns, and we head back toward Talionis at a much faster speed. As the trees rush by in blurs, and we're whisked away from every danger they claim to be protecting us from, a feeling I loathe wraps itself around me, clinging to my skin, sinking into my pores.

Helplessness.

And it disgusts me, because I know it's not an accident that I feel this way. It's by design.

I'm trapped. That's really what they wanted to show us with this excursion. There's no way to escape. They call it security. But it's really imprisonment.

CHAPTER

NINE

I'm alone in the room, sitting on the bed assigned to me. Both Nika and Ari are still in the bathroom getting ready for bed. I pull my braid to the side and begin unwinding it, the unbound curls scattering in any direction they choose.

After the tour, the rest of the day passed in a blur. More introductions were made that I couldn't keep track of, and brief explanations were given about what tomorrow will hold, during which my brain struggled to process half of what they said and what they meant when they talked about technology. We ate again, another meal I could barely choke down, though I ate fast since it's clear we won't know how long we have to eat at each meal.

Then we were ushered back to our rooms by soldiers, and an overly cheery woman told us over an intercom in the hallway to "get a good night's rest because you have a full and exciting day coming."

My lips twist into a frown at the memory. Why does everyone act like we should be thrilled to be here?

Nika enters, walks over to her bed, and drops her boots and uniform in a pile against the wall before facing me. "What a day." She plops onto her bed. "How's that head wound treating you?"

I drop my hands from my hair. "It's fine."

She squints her eyes and studies me. "I got a bump like that once.

The day after it happened, my head hurt so bad, all I wanted to do was lay down and close my eyes. I know you're not tougher than me."

I quirk an eyebrow. "You don't know me well enough to know that."

A serious expression washes over her face. "Do you have good parents?"

"Uh, yeah," I say, confused by the change in topic.

"Then I know I'm right."

"I'm sorry," I say, understanding that Nika just allowed me an insight into her life that probably wasn't easy.

She waves a hand as though batting away my words, then leans forward, elbows braced against her knees. "One thing I've learned in my life—don't fight against a bully that's bigger than you until you know exactly what moves you can make to stop him."

"Okay," I say, drawing out the word.

Her gaze shifts to the door before coming to rest on me again. "You're a fighter, and I respect that. But we can't do anything crazy. Not yet. Not until we know what we're up against."

The door opens, and Ari steps in, but Nika doesn't acknowledge her. She waits for my response.

I nod. "I'm not planning to."

She sighs, as though relieved, and settles back into her bed.

A twinge of guilt pricks me. I just met Nika today, but already she's becoming a friend. And I may have just lied to her. Because, when it comes down to it, I'll do anything I can to escape, no matter how crazy.

THREE HOURS. I'VE BEEN LYING ON MY BED FOR THREE HOURS, AND I CAN'T sleep. The glowing clock on the wall ticks off another minute. My achy limbs are weighted down with fatigue. I should have fallen asleep as soon as I put my head on the pillow. But my mind won't stop racing as question after question marches through.

What exactly is going on in Talionis?

What are they preparing us for?

Why me?

Why the other recruits?

Why not Lencie and Jax?

How did they choose us?

How did they get us away from our families without anyone stopping them?

Or did someone try to stop them and fail?

Does Derbe still exist?

Is my family still alive?

These questions pummel me, driving sleep further and further away. No answers come. I can't bear to even consider the possibility of my family being gone. They have to be there when I get back home. But with what I've seen of Talionis...

Tears press behind my eyes, clamoring for release. I take a deep breath. Then another. I'm going to get out of here. I'm going to get home. I'm going to see them again.

But what if I get home, and they're not there?

I sit up abruptly. These questions aren't getting me anywhere. I rise from my bed as quietly as possible and slip out into the dark hallway.

The Recruits' Living Quarters is big, with a wing for the males and a wing for the females, divided down the middle by a meeting hall and dining area. Turning left down the hallway means heading toward those common areas and most likely soldiers. I go right.

The hallway is dark, but my eyes don't need time to adjust as a result of staring at the ceiling above my bed. I pass the closed doors of other female recruits, the sound of muffled sobs coming from more than one room. Guess I'm not the only one not able to sleep.

I pick up my pace and soon come to the end of the hallway and a door marked Stairs, the faint glow in the letters yet another reminder of how removed I am from everything I understand. I pull the door open and move past it, turning once I'm inside to ease it shut with an almost silent click as it latches behind me. My room and the common areas are all on the first level. The stairs stretch above me, and I climb.

At first, I take the steps at a normal pace, but the questions continue to hound me. I go faster. My sock clad feet are whisper soft. I pass the door to the second level, and then the door to the third. As I approach the fourth floor, my breath comes in puffs, my heart beating faster from the exertion. I'm outrunning my thoughts. It feels good. For the moment.

The stairs end on the fifth floor. I pause in front of the door, not ready to go back to my room.

I crack the door open and peek down the hallway before emerging from the stairwell. If, for any reason, soldiers patrol this level, I don't want to have a personal encounter. No one is in sight. Good.

The corridor is identical to the one outside my room. Nothing new to see here. I walk down it anyway. It's better than lying in bed, alone with my questions.

A noise assaults my ears, and I freeze.

CHAPTER
TEN

I press my back against the wall and wait. The noise comes again. The hiccuping breaths of someone crying. I push away from the wall and start toward the sound. It grows louder. It's a child, and something about it is familiar, like I've heard this cry before. I slow down, trying to determine where the crying comes from. A door a few feet ahead of me is open.

The child sniffles. Those sobs. The memory assaults me. This is the crying that woke me up in the forest. This is the child I assumed was Zeke before I realized my world had come crashing down on me. Unable to stop myself, I enter the room. The faint light on the wall illuminates a small girl, only nine or ten, alone, with tears running down her cheeks.

A child.

Fear grips my heart, echoed in the mask of terror that falls over the girl's face when she realizes I'm in her room. She scoots back into the corner of her bed, drawing her knees up as a shield.

"It's okay. I'm not gonna hurt you," I say, hoping she believes me. Why is there a *kid* here?

The girl quivers, tears still streaming down her round cheeks. Blonde hair, in shocking contrast to her light brown skin, springs out in tight curls, forming a halo around her face.

"I'm Bria. What's your name?"

She stares at me for a moment, then relaxes her hold on her legs. She draws in an unsteady breath. "Storm. I wa-want my mom," she stutters past tears, the soft cries starting again.

I slowly close the distance to Storm and sit near her on the bed. A moment later, she's in my arms, crying against my chest, clinging to me. My shirt grows wet with her tears, and I awkwardly pat her back. This isn't what I imagined finding when I went looking for a distraction, but I put aside my own frantic thoughts—and the new ones for my brothers threatening to drown me—as I try to comfort her.

Her small body shudders against me as she continues clinging to me. But that's okay. I don't want to leave her like this, terrified and alone. Why would the soldiers kidnap a child? I was sure my brothers were safe, but seeing Storm...

I clench my jaw until my teeth hurt and hold her a little tighter. No. I can't let my mind go there, or I'll be as inconsolable as the little girl.

Her breathing evens out, and her tears come to a stop. Maybe she cried herself to sleep. I move slightly, preparing to pull myself away from her and leave.

Storm turns to me. Teardrops clump her eyelashes together, her face red and blotchy. But her eyes are clear and bright. She reminds me so much of my brothers. Without thinking, I pull a strand of damp hair from her cheek and tuck it behind her ear. A deep ache for the boys weaves itself around my fears and settles in my chest, along with a sense of protectiveness for Storm.

"How did you end up here?" I murmur the question and immediately wonder why I said that out loud. I don't want her to start crying again.

She wipes a small hand over her wet cheek. "I saw them."

"What do you mean?"

She scoots out of my arms so she's facing me. "It was dark, and I shoulda been asleep." She shifts her eyes down to the left. "My mama thought I was, but I wasn't." Her gaze connects with mine again. "I love the stars, and I went out on the roof to look at them."

She stops.

"What did you see?" My voice is low as I try to keep my desperation for answers from leaking into the words.

"Shadows came out of the trees. I thought it was just deer at first, but when they got closer, I could tell it was people. One of them snuck into a house and came back out carrying someone."

The small gap between us vanishes as Storm huddles closer. I feel a twinge of guilt for making her relive it, but before I can tell her she doesn't have to, she rushes on.

"I didn't know what was happening. Then I saw two of them go into the house next to mine where Cade lives. He's always really nice to me. When I leaned over to get a better look, I saw them coming out carrying him." Her shoulders scrunch up toward her ears. "I guess I said something. One of them looked up and pointed at me. I got scared, so I went back inside and got into bed."

A tear leaks out of the corner of her eye, and I catch it with my thumb.

"A lady came into my room and took me. I tried to scream, like my daddy told me to if something scared me real bad, but I couldn't. She had her hand on my mouth. It smelled funny." She wrinkles her nose. "She carried me downstairs and outside, but I don't remember anything else. I woke up in the forest."

She starts crying again and buries her face into my shoulder. I run my hand over her hair.

"Shh, it's okay. It'll be okay." Without thinking, I say the words I've spoken to my brothers when they were scared or hurt.

Storm wipes a hand across her face, smearing her tears more than drying them. "Really?" Her voice is small.

I swallow hard. I'm *not* sure if it'll be okay. It probably *won't* be okay. Instead of answering her, I offer a small smile.

She throws her arms around my neck and holds on tightly. Slowly, I bring my arms up to hug her back. Several moments pass. Storm's story doesn't answer my pressing questions, but the fact that they took her instead of killing her when she saw what was happening offers me a thin strand of hope that those I love are still alive.

I shift and glance toward the door. I should probably go back to my room, but the idea doesn't sound at all appealing. Storm's arms lessen their grip, and I feel her small body rise with a yawn. She pulls away enough to look at me with a sleepy gaze.

"Will you stay with me 'til I fall asleep?" Her eyes are big and imploring, just like my brothers'.

"Sure." I grab ahold of the chance to put off my return to my own worries and questions, to focus on her instead of myself.

I move off the bed, and Storm crawls beneath the covers. She settles the blankets up to her chin and blinks a slow blink.

"Bria?" My name comes out on a yawn.

"Hmm?"

"I'm glad you found me."

"Me too."

"Can you sing me a song?"

Her eyes close, and she settles deeper into the bed, as though I said yes.

I shift on my knees awkwardly. No matter how bad my brothers' dreams were, I never gave into their pleadings for a song.

"Please." Her voice is even softer with exhaustion.

An old lullaby my mom used to sing to me falls over my lips, and soon, the peaceful countenance of sleep cloaks her face.

Tears clog my throat. I wish I had done this for Eli and Zeke every time they asked rather than brushing them off, frustrated that it was me that had to be the one to comfort them. They would drive me crazy, but they were the best little brothers. Right now, I'd give anything to have the assurance that I'll be able to do something like this again. I stand and silently leave the room.

ELEVEN

Day 1 of Training

The alarm echoes through the room, jarring me awake. I shoot out of bed, disoriented and confused. A bright light turns on, and I squint.

Nika throws her covers off her body and sits straight up in her bed. A muffled sound comes from Ari as she falls to the floor.

"Ow," she mumbles in a sleepy voice as she holds her elbow, her blonde hair sticking out in every direction.

"What is going on?" Nika says. "And what time is it?" A yawn punctuates her question. She drops her legs to the floor and stands.

I rub a hand over gritty eyes. "I don't know."

"Attention all Recruits," the speaker in the hallway chirps out an annoyingly chipper female voice, "this is your 0400 wake-up call. You have fifteen minutes to exit your barracks and be led to the Physical Training Arena. Any late arrivals will miss breakfast."

"Well, that answers that," I say. The lack of sleep will catch up with me at some point, but for now, adrenaline has pushed the fuzzy exhaustion aside.

Nika murmurs something under her breath as she pulls on her uniform.

Ari stands and works at gathering her hair into order. I don't want to even think about what my hair must look like. I run my hand through it, and it catches on a knot. With a grimace, I pull it all back into a ponytail. I'll deal with it later.

Once the three of us are ready, we enter the hallway and join the rest of the female recruits exiting the building. There's little conversation, and the fear in the eyes of the few girls who look my way speaks volumes.

"Let's go, recruits!" A soldier hollers as we near the exit. "Move, move, move!" He claps his hands in time with each word, and the soldiers with him herd us toward the male recruits who are outside.

The bright lights blazing from poles around the area shatter the darkness of the early morning. A fog lays close to the earth, and a breeze sends the damp air through me. Bumps rise on my skin, and I wish it was only because of the cool morning.

Four soldiers enter the building and half-drag the recruits who are straggling outside. None of us say a word as we stand clumped together, and I'm not sure if it's because we're exhausted or because we all know talking will get us in trouble, even though they haven't told us that.

I keep my eye on the soldier who's pacing in front of the group. Occasionally, he barks an order at one of the other soldiers, and they immediately obey.

The lead soldier stops and faces us. "I am Corporal Mitts. Before we go to the Physical Training Arena, you need to know three things. First, obey every order given to you immediately. Second, when we arrive at the Arena, you will go to your unit's holding area. And third, from now on, you will stand at attention until you are told, 'at ease.' And before any of you weaklings ask how to stand at attention: *Attention!*"

As soon as the word is out of his mouth, the soldiers all around us move in quick, precise movements, fisting their right hands and placing them over their hearts and bending their left arms so they are behind their backs. Feet snap together, their chests out, all of them standing tall.

"At ease!" Corporal Mitts commands.

The soldiers link their hands behind their backs, and spread their legs shoulder width apart.

"Understood?" Corporal Mitts barks.

"Yes, sir!" I say, along with all the other recruits. The words leave a sour taste in my mouth. They came out too easily.

"Good! Let's go. Double time!" Corporal Mitts turns and marches down a path.

The soldiers pull shock sticks from their belts, and none of us wait around to see whether or not they will use them on us. We jog down the path after Corporal Mitts.

After a few minutes, we arrive at the Physical Training Arena. There's a platform just inside, but before I have time to take in the view of the Arena, Corporal Mitts is yelling at us to get to our unit's' designated areas.

There are signs on the wall behind us with each unit number. Everyone shuffles around to get to their space. I elbow my way through the crowd to the Unit Six holding area, Nika and Ari not far behind me.

"It's way too early for all this yelling," Nika mutters.

"Somehow, I think we have more to come," I say.

She grunts something between a laugh and a groan.

The soldiers move among all of us, situating each recruit until we are in perfect lines. I'm positioned near the front of my unit.

"Why aren't you at attention?" Corporal Mitts screams as the last several recruits scramble to their holding areas.

Everyone mimics the movements demonstrated earlier, and soon we're all at attention. I clench the hand fisted over my heart, my nails digging into my palm. I don't want to do this, but Nika's words from last night ring through my mind. Before I do anything rash, I need to better understand the enemy I'm up against.

Last night. I inhale sharply. *Storm.*

As subtly as possible, I try to look among the recruits for the little girl, but I'm limited in movement by the need to be at attention. I turn my head a bit.

"Eyes forward!" Corporal Mitts shouts, snapping my focus to him.

He's staring right at me.

I force my face to remain neutral, even as desperation claws at me to frantically search for the little girl. Right now isn't the time. If she's here, I'll find her later.

But they wouldn't put a kid through training with us... would they?

I stare out at the Arena, attempting to distract myself with the view. The space is divided into two sections with a track running along the outer perimeter. One section holds equipment: weights, pull-up bars, ropes, sacks, and additional training gear that is more advanced than anything I've seen before. The other has several raised and padded squares with steps leading up to them.

Along one wall, from floor to ceiling, there are varying sizes of rock-like bumps protruding from the wall. This place is even more immense than it seemed from the air. The gates at the back of the room leading to the outdoor portion are closed, cutting off the area from view.

The door opens, and Sergeant Valarius and Laban enter. Corporal Mitts steps back and snaps to attention, and Sergeant Valarius takes his place in front of us.

"At ease!" he says.

Unlike the soldiers, we don't drop into the at ease position with simultaneous fluidity. There's an awkward moment as everyone finds the position, and Sergeant Valarius crosses his arms over his chest.

"That was ugly. You are recruits, and you will move with precision and as a unit. Understood?"

"Yes, sir!" we shout.

"I didn't hear you." Laban strides up next to Sergeant Valarius. "Your commanding officer just asked if you understood. Say it louder!"

"Yes, sir!" we scream the words, and my throat feels scraped raw.

"Let's try this again," Sergeant Valarius says. "Attention!"

I snap to attention, along with every recruit and soldier around me.

"Better. At ease!" Sergeant Valarius gives the order, and this time we drop to the at ease position together.

He nods once. "This morning, you will receive basic instruction in physical conditioning. These soldiers and I will be your primary instructors in this area. They will indicate with a nod of their head who they are when I say their name: Corporal Mitts, Corporal Cromer, Specialist Saylano, Specialist Quinsy." He lists them from left to right, each nodding at their name. "And you already know Sergeant Meritas."

I clench my jaw and manage not to look at Laban.

"The rest of the soldiers will assist us in training you. Units One, Two, and Three, you will go outside with Corporal Mitts and Specialists Cromer and Saylano and begin your training there. You may leave."

They turn away from us and head down the opposite stairwell. Though I watch intently, there's no sign of Storm. Not in any of those units.

"Units Four, Five, and Six will remain inside with Sergeant Meritas, Specialist Quinsy, and myself." My stomach clenches. I can't be in Laban's group. "Meritas will lead Unit Four, Quinsy Unit Five. And Unit Six will be with me."

The barest hint of relief whispers through me as I watch Laban approach his unit and march them past us as they head toward the stairs. Being in Sergeant Valarius's unit doesn't thrill me, but at least he isn't as predisposed to hate me as Laban is.

Quinsy takes his group down after Laban's, and then Sergeant Valarius leads us downstairs. I breathe a little easier after I crane my head around to look behind me for Storm. She's not here.

A young guy, dressed differently from the rest of us, is on one of the raised mats fighting against a soldier. Sweat gleams from his deeply tanned face, and brown hair lies haphazardly against his forehead. His movements are fluid, graceful almost, as he dodges the soldier's attacks and blocks punches and kicks. A smile dances across his face, as though he's toying with the man. And then, with movements so fast they're almost a blur, he attacks the soldier, landing him on his back.

Impressive.

The young man looks up, and his gaze connects with mine. He smiles and then winks at me. My face burns, and I turn away.

"I can see why you've been looking all around to catch a glimpse of him. That boy is *fine*," Nika says out of the corner of her mouth.

Sergeant Valarius comes to a halt, saving me from having to find a response to Nika.

"Your assessment begins now," he says. "Stretch out. You're about to run."

Running is never something I feel like doing. Occasionally I run through Delamere Wood, or along the shoreline, but that's usually only because I know if I don't get home quickly, I'll be in trouble. But if there's an alternative to running, I take it.

Today, I don't have much choice.

I bend over and stretch my stiff limbs. I groan when I press on a bruise on my shin, but otherwise it feels good. We stretch for several minutes.

"Line up on the track," Sergeant Valarius commands.

Everyone obeys.

"This track is a half-mile long. I want three laps as fast as possible. Go."

We take off. Halfway through the first lap, my body is screaming at me, each bruise throbbing to its own excruciating beat. Shay races past me, face set in determination. She's always been a runner—one more thing that makes us different. But she's here, and she's familiar. That's something. Maybe we can be friends.

I push through my pain and find a rhythm, thankful for my regular swims in the bay. I stay in the middle of the group and maintain my pace for the rest of the run.

When I finish, my breath comes in short bursts, and sweat drips off my face, down my back. My tongue is dry, and my mouth feels coated with dust. I collapse to the ground with the others who have finished.

"Those of you who were first to finish the run and received a green band, see Private Mendes. You've earned yourself a water break."

Shay stands along with several others, and the rest of us watch with longing as they're handed cups of water. A girl who doesn't have a green band stands and takes a step toward the water station.

Sergeant Valarius leaps into her path. "Do you have a green band, recruit?"

The girl takes a step back. "No, sir. But I need a drink."

"Then make sure you run faster next time," Sergeant Valarius says in an even tone. His gaze scans the rest of us. "That goes for the rest of you as well. You want to be rewarded? Then work harder."

I swallow, and pull my attention away from the water, almost wishing I could go back in time and push myself to run faster. Too late now.

The last group of recruits is staggering more than running as they make their way down the track. Ari is at the front of the group, and even from a distance, I can see her gasping for breath. Her arms fly out from her sides like broken windmills, and under any other circumstance, the sight would make me laugh.

But right now, I'm more concerned about one of the soldiers hurting her and the other stragglers.

"Move faster!" Sergeant Valarius shouts. "Go! Go! Go!" He makes a quick gesture, and two of the soldiers run toward the group.

I get to my feet, ready to chase after them before they can hurt any of the recruits. Nika comes up beside me, and we both take a step forward. The soldiers don't remove their shock sticks. Instead, they get in the faces of the runners, yelling at them to run faster, pick up their pace, stop holding everyone up.

A breath releases from my lungs. They're not going to hurt them. Not yet anyway.

Ari leans forward, arms drooping more at her sides.

"Come on, girl, you can do it," Nika says under her breath.

A soldier sprints toward Ari. "Stand up straight, recruit! Move faster!"

"Yes, ma'am!" Ari gasps out the words, pulling herself up straighter.

"You keep falling behind like this, and we'll send you to the Ruins."

Another soldier barks out a laugh. "Entire squads of soldiers have disappeared in there, never to be seen again. The lot of you can't even run a couple miles! The Ruins will devour you before you've been in there five minutes."

One recruit looks to be on the verge of tears, and a soldier crowds close to her. "If you're afraid—and you should be afraid—then run *faster!*" He screams in her face.

"Stop staring," Sergeant Valarius says. "Their delay will not hinder the rest of your training. Time for strengthening. Let's go!"

I hesitate, taking one more look at Ari. She's closer now, almost in.

"Now, recruit!" Sergeant Valarius is right next to me, yelling in my ear.

My heart jumps. "Yes, sir!"

He presses his hand to my back and thrusts me forward.

Don't stand out, don't stand out, I chant to myself, hurrying to join the others from my unit. When I move toward the line facing Sergeant Valarius, he puts his hand on my shoulder, stopping me.

"You'll demonstrate this next task," he says.

I don't dare argue.

"Everyone pair up." Sergeant Valarius issues the command, and the three soldiers assisting him ensure everyone does as instructed.

Ari stumbles over before they pair everyone up, clutching her side, panting. "That...was exhausting." She runs a sleeve over her face and then flops to the ground.

Sergeant Valarius is next to her in three quick strides. "You do not stop or rest until I tell you to, recruit."

"Sorry, sir." Ari blows out a breath and then gets to her feet. "I just haven't done anything like that ever. In my whole life."

I bite my lip, wishing the action could stop the words spilling out of Ari's mouth. The look on Sergeant Andor Valarius's face is anything but amused, and Ari is clueless.

"Your work is not done," Sergeant Valarius says, his voice low. "Drop and give me twenty!"

Ari's face falls, and I'm almost afraid she's going to cry at the prospect of twenty pushups.

"Maybe she just needs a break." The words rush out of my mouth.

Sergeant Valarius pivots toward me, eyes narrow.

"Sir," I add on. Ugh. What did I just get myself into?

His jaw clenches. "You think she needs a break, Recruit Averton? Fine. Then *you* drop and give me twenty!"

I lower myself to the ground. It could be worse. He's not beating me. I get into position and get through ten pushups, but my arms are burning.

"Sir, what's that?" A soldier asks.

Eleven. I lower my body and somehow push myself up again. *Twelve.*

"What?" Sergeant Valarius snaps.

"On her neck, sir," the soldier says.

My arms shake, but no longer from the exertion. They can't be talking about me. It couldn't have slipped out. I fall to the ground, unable to summon the strength to finish the set.

"On your feet, recruit," Sergeant Valarius commands.

I get to my feet, horror mingling with the sweat dripping down my body. My necklace, *Ezri's* necklace, is exposed.

CHAPTER

TWELVE

I stare into Sergeant Valarius's eyes, my pulse throbbing in my throat.

"Remove the necklace, Recruit Averton. Now." Each word Sergeant Valarius says is measured, firm.

I clench my hands at my sides, unable and unwilling to do as he commands.

A stick slams into my back, knocking the wind out of me. "Do as your instructor says."

"Please, no," I say, ashamed of myself for pleading with these monsters. But I have no other choice.

Sergeant Valarius turns to the other recruits, all of whom are watching us. "Did you all receive the order to remove *every* personal item and article of clothing upon arrival?"

"Yes, sir!" the recruits say, some shouting the words.

"Do you think it's fair for Recruit Averton to be an exception to this rule?"

"No, sir!" This time, not all the recruits respond.

Every part of me quivers. This won't be good.

"Then one of you remove her necklace, and you'll be rewarded with water."

At first, no one moves. Then three recruits who came in last in the run come toward me. I step back and into the soldier who hit me. He grabs my arms, pinning them to my side.

A male recruit reaches me first. "Sorry," he mouths.

He drops his gaze, and then takes my necklace and pulls it from my neck. The clasp breaks.

The cry I want to release catches in my throat, suffocating me. Drowning me. No. Not this. Not my last tie to Ezri. The boy walks away, a wheezing cough ripping through him, and hands the necklace to Sergeant Valarius, who takes it and puts it in his pocket.

I want to hate the recruit for what he just stole from me, but more coughs spasm out of him. He's thirsty, and my necklace was the only way for him to get a drink.

Tears burn my eyes, and it takes everything in me to hold them back. I can't give in to them.

Sergeant Valarius waves a hand, and the soldier holding my arms releases me and steps away. "Recruit Averton, you will complete the next portion of physical conditioning twice as punishment." He takes hold of my arm, his grip firm, but not as tight as the other soldier. "Follow me," he shouts.

Then he pulls me along with him as he leads the rest of the recruits to the next portion of training. I tug on my arm, despising the feel of his hand on me. Hating him for doing this to me. And disgusted with myself for not doing more to keep my one remnant of Ezri from falling into their hands. I pull against his grip again, but he doesn't release my arm.

"Hate me all you want," Sergeant Valarius says. "But know this: you're lucky I'm the one who discovered your insubordination."

He stops and shoves me forward.

I want to give up right now, but I can't. Again, I'm standing out in a bad way. And I can't afford to continue to do so. I have to obey them for now. But as soon as I find a way, I'm going to escape.

"There are ten low walls," Sergeant Valarius says, addressing everyone. "You are to pick up a sack weighing between twenty and fifty pounds, throw it over the wall, jump over the wall yourself, retrieve the sack, and throw it over the next wall, until you have gone over every wall. Then turn around and come back, doing the same thing. Understood?"

"Yes, sir!" Everyone says, and somehow I say it alongside them.

"Recruit Averton, you'll go first."

I grit my teeth and step forward. I pick up a sack and throw it over the first wall, then scramble after it. All of my anger, frustration, pain, I channel into each movement. It feels good. Distracting. I hurtle the sack over the next wall, my arms burning, and then hoist myself over after it. The sound of other recruits following echoes around me, but I don't look back. Just press forward.

The walls get progressively higher, though none is taller than me. By the time I'm at the seventh wall on my third time through, I can barely lift the sack over. Somehow, I manage to, and I half-leap, half-fall off the wall to the other side.

Other recruits pass me. I lift the corner of the sack off the ground and drag it to the eighth wall.

"Faster, recruit!" One of the soldier's screams at me.

I force my legs to comply, picking up my speed. He moves on to scream in someone else's face. Letting out a slow breath, I bend and pick up the sack. This wall is up to my chest. I push the sack up, but my arms give out, and it falls back onto me. How am I going to do this *again*?

I bend down to pick up the sack but don't stand up right away.

"Don't stop now," Nika says from my left. She throws her sack over. "Don't give them another reason to see you. Come on." She grabs one side of the sack. "Take the other side. We'll get it over together."

I want to protest that I can do it on my own, that I don't need her help. But the sad truth is I do. My body hasn't completely recovered from my injuries in the forest, and at least Nika's not scolding me. Or screaming in my face. I pick up the other side, and we throw it over.

We work together to get both our sacks over the next wall, and, somehow, none of the soldiers try to stop us.

"Thank you," I say when we get to the other side of the tenth wall.

"Don't thank me yet." Nika points with her thumb back in the direction we just came from. "We still have to go back through."

"Right." I reach for a sack.

"I'm sorry about your necklace," Nika says.

My throat thickens, and I clear it. "Me too."

"Now let's get this done."

Together we lift first one, then the other sack over the wall. At least I'm not alone in this awful place.

Once every recruit has finished at the wall station, Sergeant Valarius has the soldiers with him give each of us a heavy rod. Then he instructs us to squat low to the ground with the rod on our shoulders until he tells us we can stand. My body can't hold the position for more than a few seconds before I collapse to the ground. But I'm not alone. Others are dropping all around me.

Sergeant Valarius is in my face. "On your feet, recruit! Hold the position!"

I comply, staying up a little longer . . . but not long enough. Another soldier drags me to my feet, hands me the rod, and forces me into a squatting position.

I fall twenty-three times before a shrill whistle cuts through the air.

"Unit six, that's all for now," Sergeant Valarius says. "You're dismissed to the dining hall for breakfast."

I let the rod clank to the ground.

CHAPTER

THIRTEEN

As I round the bend in the path leading to the dining hall, I realize the soldiers have backed off. There are far less around now, and they aren't yelling at us to do anything, which is disconcerting.

The group of recruits ahead of me turns the corner to the dining hall, and a shot rings out. A recruit falls to the ground, screaming in agony.

More shots sound. More recruits drop.

They're shooting. At *us*.

Shay comes up next to me. "What's going on?"

I grab her and pull her flat against the closest building with me.

Other recruits are clumping around us, and my stomach sinks. The more of us in one place, the more likely we are to be noticed.

"Why are they shooting at us?" Shay asks, her voice shrill.

A shot sounds from behind us, and I whirl toward it as a recruit near me grabs her leg. Laban is standing there, gun pointed at our little horde.

"Never drop your guard for one second," he says, taking aim at another recruit. He fires, and the guy lets out a grunt.

But there's no blood.

"You want your breakfast, recruits?" Laban shouts. "Then earn it!

Get through the Kill Zone without being shot, or push through the pain even if you are. These are training bullets. They won't kill, but they hurt like fire."

He pulls his gun back up, but this time everyone scatters, including Shay. His eyes lock with mine, and anger burns my cheeks. He's evil. They're *all* evil.

Before he pulls the trigger, I sprint around the building.

I'm about a hundred yards from the dining hall. A couple dozen recruits are on the ground crying. Others are running forward, not even attempting to dodge the bullets as they focus on getting to the entrance. If I wasn't still recovering from my injuries, I would follow suit. But right now, I'm not interested in more bruises.

I scan the buildings that surround the path to the Dining Hall like ominous guards. Laban was right to call it a kill zone. They stationed soldiers on the roofs, and it seems almost impossible to find a route clear enough to avoid getting shot. Maybe it *is* impossible. That would fit well into everything I've seen of these people so far.

A soft whisper echoes through my mind. *The greatest mistakes and the most profound discoveries are in the details.* Tuning out the sound of the gunfire and the ensuing screams, I search the area again.

That's it.

An alley across from where I'm standing now seems like it will provide a way around the back of the buildings, circumventing the Kill Zone. I'll be exposed for twenty seconds. Fifteen if I sprint fast enough.

Without giving myself time to think, I race toward the small gap between the buildings. A training bullet slams into the ground at my feet, but I keep going. Almost there.

A whistling sound rushes by my head, and then I'm in the alley.

I don't stop running, though my body is shaking. I follow the winding alley between the buildings and then around the back and toward the dining hall. The sounds of gunfire dim. I was right. They aren't back here. I reach a side entrance, rip the door open, and rush inside.

I made it.

Recruits throughout the dining hall are crying, most having been shot at least once. No one else found the alley. At least, not that I can tell. Too bad the group around me scattered before I realized there was a way around.

I move through the line and fill my plate with food, keeping an eye out for Storm. So far there hasn't been any sign of her, and I'm not sure if I'm relieved or *more* anxious. This is not the place for a child. They wouldn't have shot at *her* if she was out there...would they?

I squeeze my tray and force the thought aside. She wasn't out there, so maybe she's okay.

My stomach rumbles, and I add an apple to my tray. Eggs, potatoes and onions, some kind of hot porridge, toast. It's probably more food than I need, but the exercise left me famished.

I break from the line, eyes scanning the room. Recruits are shoveling food in, some attempting to hold ice packs to bruised areas with one hand and eat with the other. I should join them. We may have just gotten shot at, but who knows when they'll interrupt us and drag us onto some other training. I move toward the table Nika's sitting at, but then a puff of blond hair at the back of the room catches my attention.

Storm.

I stride toward her, haphazardly balancing my tray as I weave around tables, and almost release an audible sigh of relief. She's at a table in the back corner of the room with only one other occupant: a tall Black guy with an athletic build. He has the shaved head and uniform of a male recruit.

Their backs are toward me as I approach. The guy has his head angled down toward Storm as he listens to something she's saying. A red welt is rising on his forearm, but Storm looks uninjured. I circle the table and set my tray down on her other side.

I'm halfway seated when the guy speaks.

"Find another table." There's a steel edge to his words.

His dark eyes stab at me. It's making perfect sense why this table is empty except for these two. He's intimidating, sure, but right now, I don't care. I've been told what to do by enough people lately, and

I'm not interested in adding him to the list. Plus, I need to make sure Storm is okay.

I ignore him and settle myself next to the little girl. "How are you?"

She grins at me and is about to speak when there's a scraping sound.

The guy has both hands on the table, and he's rising out of his seat. "I said, find another table." He sets his square jaw in determination, and something else. Desperation?

Before I can respond, Storm pipes up. "It's okay, Cade."

The name is familiar, and I remember her talking about her neighbor who was taken. This must be him.

"This is Bria. The one I told you about."

Cade's gaze flicks to Storm, and he settles back into his seat.

"Alright. Stay then," he says, a bit begrudgingly.

Cade's gaze catches on the bruise on my forehead, and a flicker of recognition lights his eyes. I hold my breath, half expecting him to tell me off like Nika did and force me to leave the table. If he claims it's not good for me to be around Storm, he would probably be right. Another second passes, and then he goes back to his meal.

I release a breath, and focus on Storm. "How are you?" I repeat my question and then shovel some food into my mouth. I've wasted several minutes, but it was worth it.

"Okay," she says.

Then she launches into a story, chattering away between bites of food. The brightness of the new day seems to have put to rest some of her fears. For now, anyway. She talks about anything and everything that comes to her mind. Her village. The games she played with her friends. Her family. The girl talks more than Ari. I respond when it's expected, but mostly I listen. There's something familiar and strangely comforting about having breakfast with a kid.

Cade and I make quick work of the food on our plates, but Storm takes her time, and I find the fact reassuring. Maybe they aren't rushing her from one thing to the next, like the rest of us.

A question gnaws at me, and I wait for her to take a bite of her food and pause in her storytelling.

"What did you do before breakfast?" I ask her.

She swallows and shrugs. "Nothing. Someone came upstairs to get me to eat. She was nice."

I'm impressed that she slept through the alarm, but the difference in her routine is a good sign, right? "What are you going to do after breakfast? Did anyone tell you?"

A shadow of the fear that cloaked her last night falls across her face, and I wish I could retract the words.

"No." She looks unsure for the first time this morning.

"Where's the lady who brought you down here?" Cade pushes aside his empty tray.

Storm rises off the bench a little and stretches her neck, searching the room. Before she can find the woman, the door to the dining hall opens, and Sergeant Valarius comes in.

Storm shrinks down in her seat and presses her little body as close to Cade as she can. He drapes a protective arm around her, and his jaw tightens as he glares across the room at the source of Storm's distress.

"That's enough sitting around, recruits." Sergeant Valarius's voice thunders around the room. "You have interacted with the Kill Zone. Everything you experience in Talionis will train you, hone your senses, and sharpen your skills. The Kill Zone will not be active before every meal, but it *will* be active again. Be alert. Keep an eye out. And learn how to get through without getting shot. Understood?"

"Sir, yes, sir!"

Colonel Valarius enters with two other soldiers.

"Good," Sergeant Valarius says. "All of you are to report to the Educational Building in ten minutes. Head out!"

The room erupts into a whirlwind of activity. Seven or eight soldiers disperse through the room, yelling at recruits to move faster, pointing out every piece of trash and demanding they pick it up. Cade, Storm, and I are far enough in the back that none of them are near us.

Yet.

Cade and I stand, and Storm joins us. Together, we drop our

plates in a nearby bin, dispose of our trash, and then we make our way to the door.

Storm slips her small hand into mine, and I almost jump. She smiles up at me, and I squeeze her hand gently. It's such a familiar feeling, holding a child's hand, but my stomach churns, and I regret eating.

Don't go there, Bria.

Halfway through the room, a soldier stops us.

"The girl isn't going to Educational Training," he says in a high voice that pierces my eardrums and doesn't fit with his bulky build.

"Then where is she going?" I ask, tucking Storm behind me.

The soldier studies me. "That's none of your business, recruit. Now, move out of the way and report to your assigned training."

He reaches around me to grab Storm, but I push his arm aside. He scowls.

"Not until I know what you plan to do with her."

The soldier spits out a foul word and reaches toward me, ready to lift me out of his way. Cade steps up next to me, crossing his arms over his chest. The soldier's face flushes red.

"What's the holdup?" Colonel Valarius strolls over. The soldier snaps to attention. The Colonel's eyes land on me. "Ah, the runner. Causing more trouble, are we?"

He knows about me. Goosebumps rise on my arms.

He turns to the soldier. "What's going on?"

"Sir, my orders were to bring the young girl to Observation with Sanchez. These two have impeded the process."

"I just want to know what he's going to do with her." The words rush out of my mouth before I can stop them.

"I told you, Recruit," the soldier began, "that's none of—"

Colonel Valarius lifts his hand.

He looks at me. "She's going to receive her own individualized training." There's a cold hardness in his eyes that doesn't fit with his smooth words. "We were not expecting a recruit as young as she is, and we don't expect her to perform at the same level as those several years older than her."

He focuses on Storm and turns his lips up into a smile that could almost be engaging, except that his dark eyes are not at all penetrated by it. They remain calculating, their focus sharp. I hear Storm's quick intake of breath as she moves further behind me. The fabric of my uniform bunches as she clenches my shirt.

At the sight of Storm's anxiety, a flicker of enjoyment cracks Colonel Valarius's gaze, but it evaporates as quickly as it appeared, and I almost wonder if I saw it at all. "Does that satisfy you, Recruit Averton?"

"Yes, sir." It doesn't. Not really. But I've already done more today to gain attention than I should have. At least they're not putting her through the same training as the rest of us.

There's nothing I can do to keep the soldier from taking Storm, especially with Colonel Valarius right here. And the last thing I want is for my actions to cause her, or myself for that matter, any more trouble.

I move to step aside and allow the soldier access to Storm, but she moves with me, the hold she has on my shirt tightening. I turn as best as I can, trying to get out of the soldier's way. She lets go of my shirt and wraps her arms around me, burying her face in my stomach.

A fresh wave of protectiveness washes over me, and I press my lips together. I can't tell her to let go, even though I know I need to.

"Hey." Cade drops to one knee and rests a hand on her head. "You need to go with this man, okay? We'll see you later."

Storm nods. A single tear rolls down one smooth cheek, and Cade wipes it away. She lets go and follows the soldier from the room.

"Get these recruits to their training!" Colonel Valarius says, but he isn't looking at Cade and me.

Several other recruits and soldiers have paused in their exit to watch the drama unfold. I wish I could melt into the floor.

The soldiers spring into action at Colonel Valarius's command, and they're soon yelling at the recruits and herding them out the door.

"Enjoy your training," Colonel Valarius gives me a calculating smile and strides away.

"Enough delay! Let's go!" A soldier prods me in the back, and Cade and I join the last recruits exiting.

We trot toward the Educational Building.

"Thanks," Cade says, once the soldier behind us moves on to yell at another recruit to move faster.

I glance over. "For what?"

"For standing up for Storm. She shouldn't be here."

I nod, unsure of what to say. But at least he and I seem to have moved from adversaries to allies. He rubs his hand over his jaw and then opens his mouth, but Nika joins us before he can say anything.

"I was looking for you," she says to me, "and then I saw a crowd gathered." Her tone is light, but her eyes are serious.

"Wasn't planning on that," I say. "This is Cade."

Nika waves a hand through the air. "We've met. Girl, just be careful. People who love power, who want others to obey them no matter what—it's not good to stand out in front of them. Trust me."

The words are heavy with meaning and experience, and they settle on me like one of the weighted bars from Physical Conditioning.

"That wasn't about her," Cade says, drawing my attention. "She did it for Storm. Beat me to it, actually." He gives a wry grin, and the weight lifts slightly.

"Get inside, recruits!" A soldier yells down to us from his position at the door of the Educational Building.

The three of us jog up the steps along with several others, and we're ushered inside and down the hallway to a classroom.

"Still," Nika whispers as we file into seats near the back of the room, "please be careful. Being someone they know, someone they recognize, is dangerous."

Her words bring the weight back onto my shoulders with a thud.

CHAPTER

FOURTEEN

Our instructor hasn't arrived yet.

The soldiers remain around the perimeter of the octagonal room, keeping conversation among the recruits at a minimum. No one wants to be hit or shocked or made to do pushups. My arms ache at the thought. Chairs are lined up in rows all around the room, on wide stairs descending to the center floor, where a podium stands. Narrow aisles break the rows of chairs into pie-shaped sections, and glass-like panels line the walls and the desks in front of us.

I catch sight of Shay in the front row, posture rigid. The strange desire to reassure her fills me, but I shake it off. If I go down there, I'll, once again, draw attention to myself—and to her. I know Shay well enough to know she'd be furious about that.

A door opens across the room, and a woman enters. She's not in uniform like the soldiers. Instead, she's wearing a black skirt, red blouse, and heels that click against the floor as she bustles to the podium.

"What are all of you doing here?" She waves her hand at the soldiers. "Out. Now. You know you're not welcome in my classroom."

I watch with wide-eyes as the soldiers salute her and then leave the room.

Once the doors close behind them, the woman offers a warm smile. "I am so sorry about that. From now on, I'll ensure the soldiers don't follow you in here for your Educational Training. This is a safe place for you."

I blink. What is going on?

"Now, let's begin." She taps at a screen on her podium, and then her head flies up. "Dear me! I forgot to introduce myself. I'm instructor Elva Trill, but you can call me Ms. Elva."

She moves out from behind the podium and stands to the right of it, one hand still resting on the top. "In this room, you will learn what it means to be a part of the marvelous city of Talionis. If you aren't yet sure *why* you should become an integral part of our Commander's plan, then I do hope you will find every reason to right here in Educational Training."

Trill repositions herself behind the podium. Her fingers tap away at something I can't see, and suddenly the room is plunged into darkness. A moment later, the panels around the room light up with a picture of a map.

"Today we will begin with a brief history of the rest of the world, one you are unfamiliar with, because it is the synopsis of what happened after the Demise of North America."

I lean forward in my chair, studying the map.

"On the screens around the room, you are seeing a map of the world as it once was and how the nations and lands were divided. There was tension among these nations, but a sort of understanding was in place that kept the tension from escalating. Until that fateful day when everything changed."

The image changes to another map of the same regions but with specific countries highlighted in red. A picture of an intimidating group of mostly men and a few women appears next to the map.

"The nations in red, led by the countries called Russia, China, and Iran at the time"—those places on the map seem to rise higher than the rest, popping out from the wall—"but including all the other nations highlighted, created an Act that they planned to bring to the International Meeting for the Maintenance of Peace. It was called the Redistribution of Power Act, informally known as

R.O.P.A., and the nations who formed the Act called themselves the Alliance."

The photograph next to the map increases in size, and the words *The Alliance* are now displayed below it.

"The Act dictated that all world powers at the time were to remove their troops and embassies from wherever they were stationed around the world. When R.O.P.A. was presented, it was immediately ridiculed and voted down, the loudest opposer of the Act being the president of what was once the United States of America, President Lena Oberville."

The map and picture fade to the background and a picture of a woman appears over them, blondish-brown hair cascading about her face, and green eyes flashing.

I stare at the image, almost wishing I could feel a sense of camaraderie or attachment to the woman who once led the land that I've grown up in. But I don't feel anything. Maybe that's because the country she led was nothing like the region I know and call home, even though it's only been two generations.

"The Alliance grew silent in the face of the opposition, and the rest of the world believed the Act was no longer an issue. They were wrong." Trill's voice drops to a grave tone, and all the images on the wall fade to black, immersing the room in darkness.

A beat of silence follows, and then she speaks again. "The United States of America was unexpectedly and brutally attacked."

The screens on the walls burst to life, and moving images of people and attacks and terror project from them, filling the room. My heart skips a beat.

The image of a child near Storm's age pops up in front of me. She's crying, frightened. And then there's an explosion, and she's gone. I press back into my seat, gasping. But as much as I want to, I can't look away from the surrounding images.

They draw me into a story and a time that, before this moment, I never really cared to think about—a time that I didn't think mattered. But it did. These were real people, and my parents were right to insist we respect their memory.

It's silent around me as we all take in the unimaginable destruction and death of a nation. The images change, showing different places, different people, one instant living their lives, bustling about a city or a town, appearing as though they are walking among us, and the next gone. I can almost smell the smoke rising from the ruined buildings, taste the desperation of those writhing in pain on the ground. Each image is more disturbing than the last, and I find myself unable to watch any more. I close my eyes.

But I still see the images.

"The devastation was so great," Trill interrupts the silence, and my eyes crack open—the pictures are back on the walls, no longer people moving around us, "the attacks so rapid and fierce, that the entire landscape was drastically altered."

Out of the corner of my eye, I can tell more images are flashing across the screens, but I keep my gaze focused on Trill.

"Before any nation could come to the aid of the small fraction of survivors in North America, the Alliance moved to attack countries around the world. The World War for Power had begun."

I sit and listen as Trill describes a war I knew nothing about. A war that impacted the world. She details the nations involved, countries and names that mean nothing to me, and, apparently, they now have no meaning anywhere else in the world. Everything has changed from what it was before the Demise of America. Before the World War for Power.

A pain pulses in my right hand, and I realize I'm gripping the arm of my chair with such force that my hand is turning white. I pry my fingers up, wiggling them until the feeling returns.

"It appeared the Alliance would win until a special task force, formed to find a weakness in the regime, found a way to defeat them. The Alliance's weaknesses were exploited and, in a final death blow, they were brought down."

I dare a glance at the screens and see overhead images looking down at armies surrendering, destroyed buildings and cities, and the weary but relieved faces of those who had stopped the Alliance from gaining complete power.

"After the destruction and havoc that was wreaked across the globe, old borders and nations were done away with. New countries were formed, and, by international vote, the leaders of these new nations were to be the members of the special unit that was responsible for bringing down the Alliance."

Trill pauses and pushes a button. The picture of a stern-looking woman with black hair and a deep olive complexion, her face lined from hours of worry and strain, fills each screen.

"One of the people in the unit was a woman named Donatella Sitreea. The country of Sitreea was named after her, and she became the Chancellor of Sitreea. The territory includes pieces of nations that were once a part of the European region."

Another map appears, focusing in on the country of Sitreea.

"North America was, in a great sense, forgotten as the rest of the world rebuilt after the war. Many believed there could be few, if any, survivors after the attacks and the fallout from them, and because of the work ahead in rebuilding the rest of the world, everyone was content with that assumption."

A flicker of anger sparks in me at those who would ignore our needs, but the weight of what I've learned and seen quickly extinguishes it. At least we had Eryndale. I wonder why she didn't mention the mountain refuge. Maybe they don't know about it or the role it played in helping survivors not only immediately after the Demise but in the years since.

"Years passed, and rumors of survivors lingered." Trill's voice takes on an animated tone. "One man from Sitreea decided to take matters into his own hands to see if those rumors could be true. Fifteen years ago, after receiving the permission of the Chancellor of the Sitreean Region, Commander Demetrius Ark, set out with men, women, and children to create a city where those desolate and broken survivors could live. Indeed, not just live, but thrive!"

Trill's hands paint the words in the air, the excitement in her voice increasing and carrying with it a note of awe.

Some of the weight of the past dissipates as I watch Trill fling her arms into the air, her actions reminiscent of an awkward bird.

"This undertaking was difficult. Our Commander was met with challenge after challenge. From clearing away debris," a new picture flashes on the screen of men and women clearing land, "to building the beautiful structures you see surrounding you," another picture of the buildings being built, "to creating a safe environment where young and old alike could flourish," a picture of families gathered on a grassy knoll, smiling and eating a meal together, "to dealing with the heartbreaking betrayal of those whom he thought he could trust. But he has greeted each challenge as an opportunity to better himself, for the sake of his people." Trill's voice crackles with emotion.

"You, the survivors of the Demise, were not brought in before now because our Commander wanted everything to be functioning and ready, not one thing out of place. But the time has finally come for us to open the gates of Talionis and bring in the survivors, to show you a life unlike any you have ever before experienced."

She seriously expects us to believe this? Her words about the history of the world held the substance and pressure of truth, but this stuff about Talionis and whoever this Commander is...there's more going on than what she would have us believe.

"In his wisdom, our Commander has decided to begin by bringing in the youth—the young, talented, strong, and the brightest of every village of survivors. And you," she spreads her arms wide to encompass all of us, "are the ones he has chosen to be recruits of Talionis. You have received a great honor and privilege in being selected. The training will not be easy, but once completed, he will place you in a position that suits you best, where you will thrive and be able to serve the purposes of Talionis in unfathomable ways. You will be those who will go forth to create and lead new cities and villages across North America. You will bring a new hope and life to this region under the leadership of the Commander."

She continues droning on about the greatness of "our Commander" and the wonders of Talionis, but I stop listening. For years, I've wanted to be someone who brings new hope and life to this region by being a scout for Eryndale. I've wanted to be part of rebuilding what was destroyed, to help remove the sting of the past. My chest tightens. That can't possibly be what they're doing here. You don't make someone's life better by wrenching them away from everyone and everything they love. There's no way they could desire to help this region when their first act here is to kidnap all the young people.

I shift in my seat. That's the other thing that doesn't make sense. Trill is the second person to say we were chosen. How could they have possibly known which ones to choose? I'm not sure exactly what this "Commander's" agenda is, but it's not what Trill is saying. It can't be. How could the very things I've wanted to do to make my life mean something be the things Talionis is trying to accomplish? The mere possibility makes me sick.

The room brightens again, the screens going black.

Trill finishes her monologue. "My greatest advice to you is to be excited about the journey you are about to embark on. I, for one, am excited to be one of your guides as you begin."

Does she actually have *tears* in her eyes? This woman is crazy.

"Now, before you go on to your next training, I have a little something for you." She pushes a button, and the doors around the room open.

Men and women dressed as kitchen staff enter with trays full of cookies and set them on the tables.

"What is going on?" Nika asks.

I shrug. This is not what I expected.

The servers leave. Everyone stays frozen in their seats. Maybe this is a test.

"Eat your cookies. Take some time to relax. You've gone through a lot of change, but I promise it will be worth it." She smiles. "I'll come back to get you when it's time to head to your next training."

With that, she goes to the table in the front row, picks up a cookie, pats Shay on the shoulder, and leaves the room.

Shay reaches for a cookie, and other recruits follow suit.

They've left us alone. Or at least they want us to *think* they left us alone. I don't understand how things work here, but I know these people can't be trusted.

Recruits stand, form groups, chat with one another, and enjoy the cookies. But I stay seated.

Nika elbows me. "Want a cookie?"

"Nah, thanks."

She eyes them but doesn't reach for one. "Probably a good idea."

Shay saunters up the aisle, nibbling at her chocolate chip cookie. Her eyes brighten when she sees me, and she comes over. "That was something, wasn't it?"

"Yeah. I didn't realize how bad things were," I say.

"Wish I could unsee all those images," Nika adds.

Shay nods and then leans forward. "They were disturbing. But the Commander's plan... maybe this place isn't as bad as it seemed at first."

I gape at her. "What?"

"Didn't you hear Ms. Elva?" When she says the woman's name, Shay's voice softens like she's referring to her favorite aunt. "Talionis is going to help the survivors of North America."

"Is she serious? She can't be serious," Nika says.

I don't respond. I *can't* respond. How could Shay believe anything these people say?

She reddens. "Well, I just think maybe we should hear them out more. See if this training and everything could be worthwhile."

I shake my head. "Don't believe what they're saying, Shay. This place isn't safe."

CHAPTER

FIFTEEN

"This will be amazing," Ari says as we enter the Technical Operations Building.

"If you say so." I almost have to jog to keep up with her.

We've been in Talionis for five days, but this is our first Technical Training Session. So far, our days have been consumed with physical training and educational indoctrination. Elva Trill comes off like she's there for us, wants to help us, but there's something about her I don't like...don't trust. But I'm in the minority on that feeling. Most of the other recruits look forward to her class, and some of them seem to buy into what she's saying.

The soldiers leading us to our training direct us to the left wing of the building.

Ari pauses. "What else is in here?"

The female soldier she asks looks surprised to be addressed, and I stifle a smile.

"The rest of the building is restricted access. Special Clearance only. Now move on."

"Yes, ma'am." I grab Ari's arm to pull her along with me before she can ask any more questions.

"I wonder what else they do in here," Ari says, more to herself than to me.

She pushes some buttons on her HaloAct Band and then scrolls through a long sequence of text. Her pace slows as she reads, and most of the recruits we passed earlier now pass us.

"Interesting," she says.

I don't ask. "If we don't hurry, we'll be late for class."

"Oh!" Ari's head springs up. She closes out of whatever she was reading, and we join the other recruits filing into the tech lab.

The room is square, with tables with large screens set up in perfect rows with four chairs behind each. Nika waves at us from her seat in a middle row, and Ari and I make our way to her.

"With the way she took off, I thought you two would be here before everyone else," Nika says.

I plop down next to her. "Band distraction."

"Again?" Nika rolls her eyes. "What'd she find this time?"

"I didn't ask," I say.

"Smart." Nika looks past me at Ari, but she's powered up the screen in front of her, and she's engrossed.

Shay slips into the seat on the other side of Ari with a small wave. I wave back but find I'm not upset that Ari is between us. The past few times I've talked with Shay haven't been ideal.

"Oh, this is incredible," Ari says. "The HaloAct Bands connect to the screens. I synched them, and now I can download all the information I type onto the screen." She pulls her attention away from the screen for an instant to glance at me. "Want me to sync yours up for you?"

The clock on the wall chimes, and a small, strange looking man enters the front of the room. His uniform hangs loosely from thin shoulders, the pants bagging at the ankles. A few days' worth of stubble clings to his jaw and neck, and wild salt and pepper hair sticks out at every angle from his scalp.

"Class has begun," he states. "My name is Professor Mandeville, and they have given me the arduous task of attempting to teach you about Talionis Technology."

He paces back and forth as he speaks. "The first thing you need to know is that this class will start on time, *every* time. I do not tolerate tardiness."

He shoves a hand through his hair as though the very thought aggravates him.

"I need order. Order in my classroom, order in Talionis, order in life. It is the only way things run as they ought to. And part of order requires those functioning in a society to arrive where they need to, *on time*. My time is far too valuable for it to be wasted."

He comes to a stop. "If you are late, you will receive one warning. If subsequent tardies occur," his body twitches, "you will be punished. Is that understood?"

"Yes, sir!" The response echoes through the room.

"Good. Then let's begin."

Mandeville explains how to sync our bands to the screens in front of us, and Ari gives an audible sigh before typing away and moving on to things that don't look like they have anything to do with what Mandeville is talking about.

Once Mandeville confirms on his screen that everyone's bands have synced, he rattles off different features of the HaloAct Band, displaying the information from his screen onto the individual screens in front of each recruit.

"This is boring," Ari mumbles. With a few quick strokes, she bypasses the reflected screen and busies herself with something else.

The sideshow of Ari is amusing, but I focus on what Mandeville is saying. He gives us instructions on how to access the progress report indicator for each level of our training and explains how the bands are used to monitor the physical health of each recruit, from heart rate, to blood pressure, to brain function. If we remove the band, they will know. Then he reminds us that the bands can track us and electronically monitor us. A fact I want to forget.

The part I find most interesting is when he reviews the map function and gives details on how to use it more fully. I've used the map feature more than once, looking for any potential flaws, but everything about it seems perfect. Mandeville demonstrates how we can zoom in and out, see street-views, and find directions to different places in the city, and each new feature enhances my fear that I'll be unable to find an inconsistency I can use to my advantage.

He gives a few more details about the bands, but my mind is spinning as I try to take it all in.

"As you progress in your trainings, we will give you higher levels of access, including access to more in-depth features on your bands," Mandeville says. "Features you will find—"

The clock chimes out the hour.

"Ah, end of class," Mandeville says, apparently more interested in things running on time than finishing his sentence. "That's all for today." He pushes a button, and the screens around the room go black.

Except for Ari's.

Mandeville's eyes zero in on her. I shrink down in my seat.

"Recruit Willowpenn's table will remain back," Mandeville says.

At the sound of her name, Ari looks up, closing out her screen without focusing on it. Shay sits up so straight, it looks painful.

"The rest of you are dismissed."

"Here I thought the only roommate I had to worry about getting me in trouble was *you*," Nika complains to me.

I smirk. "Maybe you're the one who's a bad influence on me and Ari."

The comment earns me an elbow in the ribs.

The other recruits file out, and Mandeville waits to address us until they're all gone.

He approaches us. "Recruit Willowpenn, you seemed a bit distracted today." His face reddens. "Let's see if you paid enough attention to answer questions from class correctly, shall we? If you fail to answer satisfactorily, you and your friends here will spend time in the sandpit for some incentive training."

All the humor I felt moments before evaporates. I haven't yet been sent to the pit for disciplinary PT, but I've seen others who have. Laban oversees that area, and he pushes recruits until they're physically sick or bleeding in order to "teach" them "loyalty" to Talionis and the Commander.

"I understand everything you taught today, sir," Ari says, sounding more serious than I've ever heard her.

"Very well," Mandeville snaps, splaying his fingers and thrusting them through his hair. He rattles off five questions in a row and then stares at Ari.

With no hesitation, Ari answers each question. Even the last two, which, I'm pretty sure, were not covered in the lesson.

Mandeville tilts his head to the side and studies Ari. "You are impressive, recruit. As was promised."

The words send a chill down my spine. How much do they know about us?

He taps at the screen Ari was using. "I've increased your level of access on your band, Miss Willowpenn. Now leave. All of you. I have other matters to attend to."

The four of us almost run from the room.

"You got lucky in there," Shay says once we're in the hall.

"Correction," Nika says. "*We* got lucky in there. Girl." She takes Ari by the shoulders. "You are *so* fortunate that you could answer those questions because if I had to do pit time... mmm. No."

"Sorry?" Ari says the word like it's a question.

Nika releases Ari's shoulders, and we start walking. For the first time in five days, we're alone in a hallway. The soldiers who have been taking us from training to training must have all gone with the rest of the recruits.

Shay picks up her pace until she's soon outdistanced us. I'm sure she *hated* being associated with anyone who was breaking a rule. She struggled being here until Trill's class, but now she seems to believe everything they're saying—at least everything Elva Trill says.

I shake away the unpleasant thoughts and turn to Ari.

"How did you know the answers to all his questions?" I ask.

Ari shrugs. "He didn't ask anything complicated."

"Speak for yourself," Nika says.

Ari wanders to a door leading to another wing of the building. She fidgets with the electronic keypad lock for a moment, and the door swings open.

"How did you...?" I don't finish the question.

"It's dinnertime," Ari says, eyes sparkling. "Want to explore a bit?"

"Is she crazy?" Nika asks. "I think she's crazy. We almost all had to go to the *pit*, and now you want to explore a secure section of a building?"

"Why not?" Ari says.

"You're getting to be worse than Bria," Nika says.

I roll my eyes. "I'm right here."

"It's a terrible idea," Nika says, ignoring me. "If they catch us in here, they'll probably send us to the Ruins like they're always threatening. And if *half* the things they say about that place are true, I never wanna step foot in there."

Ari bites her lip. "I know...but...I saw something when I was going through code during class. It made me curious. Please. We'll be fast."

"Okay." I step toward her.

"Ya'll are insane. We're gonna get in so much trouble," Nika says. But she follows me and Ari into the restricted hallway.

Ari leads the way as though she's been here dozens of times, passing several doors and hallways until she stops. No one is around, but my heart is pounding in my ears. This was a bad idea.

They're tracking us. They probably know exactly where we are right now. But somehow I can't make myself turn around.

Ari bypasses another locked door, and we enter a lab. A low wall with large windows separates us from machines pouring liquid into vials on one half of a room and rats and other small animals in glass cages on the other half. Each cage has a screen displaying information I can't quite read from here. Different machines pour the liquid into tubes in the rats' cages. A faint chemical smell lingers in the air.

A screen overhead catches my attention: *Drug manufacturing and experimentation zone. Proceed with caution.*

"What is this place?" My question comes out like a choked whisper.

"This is freaking me out," Nika says. "Let's get out of here."

"One second," Ari says. She's typing on a screen that's attached to the glass window and then poking at her band. "Let me finish downloading the information I need."

A door on the side with the machines opens, and all three of us drop behind the low wall. My heart beats out a frantic rhythm.

Voices filter through to us. "We need the next dose ready to send to the Watchers within six months." Mandeville.

"It'll be ready, sir," a woman says.

"Make sure it's right this time. No more mistakes."

Ari nudges me and Nika and gives us a thumbs up. She gestures to the open door, and we crawl out.

Once we're in the hallway, we run back the way we came and burst outside.

"That was too close," Nika says.

"But I got what I needed." Ari holds up the wrist with her band.

"What are you recruits still doing here?" Sergeant Valarius's voice freezes us in place.

All three of us turn and salute.

"I said, what are you doing here?" He repeats, eyes narrowing.

"Professor Mandeville held us after class, sir," I say.

He stares at me for a long moment, as though weighing the truth in my words. "At ease."

We drop to the at ease position.

"Very well," he says. "But now you need to head to the Dining Hall. Join the rest of the recruits and wait for further instructions."

"Sir, yes, sir!"

CHAPTER
SIXTEEN

Nika, Ari, and I jog away from Sergeant Valarius and toward the Dining Hall.

"I hope we're not about to get shot at again," Nika says.

"Did getting hit hurt really bad?" I ask. Nika's tough, and I'm surprised at the wariness I hear in her voice.

The Kill Zone has been active three times over the past five days, but there's no indicator of when they'll be firing at us. Just gunshots. So far, the alley has been clear each time, so I've taken that route, but I'm always nervous that they'll realize they left a hole or that it's some kind of trap.

She slows almost to a stop. "You haven't gotten hit?"

"No." I draw out the word.

"*Everyone* gets hit," Nika says. "Most of us more than once every time they're set up."

I glance behind my friends before responding. "I found the way through."

"There's a way through?" Ari asks.

"Yeah. I'll show you guys if we need it when we arrive. But keep it quiet. If it was an accident, I don't want them closing off that option."

"Deal," Nika says.

We move again.

"Okay, now that Bria has taken out the possibility of getting shot on our way to dinner," Nika says, "how about you tell us why we just risked our necks to sneak into a lab?"

Ari's eyes light up. "That place was amazing, right?"

"Try to stay focused for me, girl. Please."

"Oh, right. Well, I wanted to get more information about the Watchers and, according to the code I was scanning during class, I needed a direct connection to the screens in that lab in order to download the information to my band."

We're nearing the dining hall, but all of us are walking slower. Dread coils in my stomach, dissolving any appetite I may have had, and questions for Ari rise in my throat, choking me.

"What are the Watchers?" I manage to ask.

We're a hundred feet or so away from the Kill Zone, and Nika holds up her hand. "I want that answer too. But first"—she focuses on me—"am I about to get shot at?"

I scan the area, forcing myself to focus on the buildings surrounding us. There's no sign of anyone on the roofs, no glimmer of a gun's muzzle. The Kill Zone isn't active. Not now, at least. "I don't think so."

"Maybe you should show us the safe way just in case," Nika says.

"Fine." I lead them down the route I discovered. "Ari. What is a Watcher?"

Her face grows more serious than I've ever seen it.

"It's not a *what*. They're people. Talionis spies in villages, towns, cities all over the North American region."

"But how? My town is small," Nika says. "Anyone different would stand out right away."

Ari bites her lip. "I think they used people who already lived in the villages to get them the information they wanted. About us."

I want to protest, yell that she's wrong, but I'm drowning in the logic of her words. It makes too much sense. That's how they would know enough to *choose* us.

A pounding begins in my temples.

Ari holds up the wrist with her band like she did earlier. "That's why I needed to get in. To get the list of Watchers. See if I'm right."

"When will you know for sure?" Nika asks.

"The files are encrypted. It may take me a few days to break through but shouldn't be longer than a week."

I lead them down the alley to the side entrance of the Dining Hall, and Nika and Ari keep talking, but it's like I'm hearing their words while I'm underwater. Nothing penetrates clearly. Right before we open the door, Nika stops me and makes sure I agree with them that we should keep this information to ourselves until we know more. I must nod in agreement, because next thing I know, we're in the Dining Hall, and someone is handing me a tray.

One ugly truth is forming in my mind. I was betrayed. By someone I know. Someone I probably *trusted*. Someone who knew all I went through, all my family went through when we lost Ezri, but they did this to me anyway.

And if Ari's right, she has the information to show me exactly who that person is.

The question is: will I be able to handle knowing?

I automatically fill my plate with food and trail Ari and Nika to the table we've made our own. Shay, Bryson, Shane, Cade, and Storm are all there already, almost done with their meals.

I slip into the seat next to Storm and somehow find it in me to smile at her, but the questioning look in her eyes tells me she can sense something's off. I take a bite of food, searching my mind for something to say to her, a topic to bring up, a question to ask— anything to shield her from my own fears and worries at this moment.

The door to the dining hall slams shut before I can swallow.

Laban struts in. "Clean up and get to the Arena, recruits! You're gonna get a little exercise before you tackle your chores for the night. You have five minutes to report."

He leaves, and the dining hall erupts in activity. Recruits jump up from their tables, disposing of their trash as fast as possible. I shove a piece of chicken into my mouth and then toss the rest of my barely touched plate into the trash. I'm not hungry anyway, but I know I'll wish I'd eaten more later tonight.

Storm is right next to me, eyebrows drawn together.

I put my hand on her shoulder. "I've gotta go. Sorry, I couldn't spend more time with you."

"I don't like when they come in and yell like that." Her little voice quivers.

"Bria," Shay says. "We have to go. Now."

I grit my teeth against a sharp retort. Shay's right, but I don't need to be bossed around right now. I focus on Storm.

"Sorry he scared you." I give her a quick hug, not knowing what else to say.

Her little arms tighten around me, and when I let go, it feels like some part of me shreds. I hate that I have to listen to what the soldiers tell me to do, that I have to leave her alone when she's scared. But I do. I offer her one more smile and then jog from the room.

If Ari is right, if there are people in Derbe who betrayed me and Shay, who spied on us for Talionis, then are my little brothers safe? Or are they in as much danger as Storm?

I ARRIVE AT THE ARENA WITH THE LAST OF THE RECRUITS AND LINE UP IN THE Unit 6 holding area with seconds to spare. The two bites of chicken I had roil in my stomach, but I stand at attention.

Everything Ari said, all the implications if she's right, slam into my mind with bruising force. The pieces fit together in a sickening way. They make sense.

Sergeant Valarius and Laban march onto the platform.

"At ease, recruits!" Sergeant Valarius says.

Everyone obeys.

I obey. Am I going to continue to do everything they want? Fall in line with their plan, whatever it is?

Laban steps forward. "I'm going to ask you a question, and I want a response, understood?"

"Sir, yes, sir!"

He paces in front of each unit, his golden eyes flashing in the light like an animal. "Do you want to be a part of saving lives?"

"Yes, sir!" I say the words along with everyone else. I *do* want to be a part of saving lives, but I doubt Laban and I have the same idea of what that means.

"Then you will give yourself completely to the Commander's plan." Laban shouts every word. "He knows what this region needs. Every bit of training you go through has a purpose. Push yourselves, give everything you have. Do it for your families. Do it for yourselves. Do it for the future of the region."

"I'm not doing it his way." The dark-haired guy who has spoken up more than once steps away from his unit to say the words. His face is bruised, but resolved.

Laban strides over until he's inches from the guy. "Mason Procleon, do not test me again."

Mason doesn't back down or say a word in response.

"No comeback this time?" Laban sneers. "Let's take a walk."

He signals to two soldiers, and they each take one of Mason's arms. He doesn't struggle. As he's led away, something in me churns. There have been two recruits who have gone missing that I've known about since we arrived. Gone without any trace of them being here to begin with. Will Mason be next?

If I defy them the same way as Mason, or fail as badly as the other two recruits were failing, what will they do to me? If it wasn't for Storm, maybe I would risk it, but even though she has Cade, I can't leave her here. She's lost enough already.

Maybe I can't completely defy them, but I refuse to be everything they're trying to make me into.

Sergeant Valarius claps his hands, and everyone focuses on him. "Today, you will attempt to go through an obstacle course. From now on, your meals and your chores will reflect how well you're doing in your trainings. The better you do, the better you'll eat, and the better chores you'll be given."

I'll do enough to get by, making sure I'm around for Storm, but nothing more. I can deal with not eating as well and with having the worst chores.

Sergeant Valarius marches all six units outside to a course. There are walls to climb, ropes and bridges, pits to jump over, and weighted sacks to deal with. I barely focus as he explains the course to us, and then he's sending us through it in groups of five.

I sprint with the group to the first obstacle, my body obeying the commands of the soldiers to move faster, push harder. But then I slow down, taking the last position as the five of us cross the first rope bridge. By the time they're over the first part of the walls we have to scale, I'm just arriving.

Corporal Mitts gets in my face. "Faster, recruit! Do *not* let them leave you behind! Move! Move! Move!"

I grind my teeth against the urge to give in and only increase my speed a little.

"Be better than this, recruit!" Corporal Mitts doesn't let up as I hurtle the first wall. "Do you want to go to the Ruins? Think you can survive against the wild dogs and spontaneous explosions?"

I grab a sack and toss it over the next wall.

"Soldiers better than you have died in that place. Do you hear me, Averton?"

"Sir, yes, sir!" I yell. But we both know I'm not pushing myself the way I can.

"Then, *move!*" He screams the word in my face, his spittle coating my cheek.

I pick up my speed enough to get him to move on to another recruit, but when I complete the course, my time is one of the slowest.

CHAPTER

SEVENTEEN

A Week Later

The soldiers try to be discreet, but, over the past week, I've learned to tell when the Kill Zone will be active. They move differently, give us more space, don't yell at us to get to the dining hall faster. Most of the other recruits don't seem to notice the subtle changes, other than Cade.

Today, there will be an active Kill Zone.

As I make my way toward the dining hall with Ari and Nika, I hear the shots. My friends hardly tense anymore. They know I'll get them through to safety. I mentally go through the four routes I've discovered and sort out how I'll divide everyone who's found their way to me.

More and more of the recruits have learned that I can get them through the Kill Zone without getting shot, which is why I've had to figure out alternative routes to the alley I originally found. It complicates things, but a part of me is happy to help protect other teens from the cruelty the soldiers of Talionis seem to enjoy doling out.

The group began to grow when Ari told her brother, Bryson, and Shane, because she has a crush on him. Then she mentioned it to her friend from Tech Training, Nalani. I felt bad when I saw Shay grimacing over a large welt after being shot, so I told her I'd get her through. And then I lost track of how others found out.

We round the bend to the meeting point I've established, and I almost stop. Instead of the fifteen recruits I expected to find waiting for me, there's about thirty. I roll my shoulders and step toward the group.

This will be a challenge, but I welcome it. My brain and body need to be pushed a little since I'm barely trying in any of the other trainings.

"Okay, you ten." I point to a group of recruits. "Go with Ari and Shay." I focus on them. "Take them through the alley."

Shay nods. "Let's go!"

They jog away.

"Cade, take these six through the garden entrance."

He inclines his head and leads them back the way we came so they can double back through the garden.

I send seven with Bryson to take a more obscure route leading up an outdoor staircase, into one building, through the hallway, and then out onto a raised breezeway between two buildings, downstairs of the next building and out the side door.

The five left with me and Nika are some of the best recruits in Physical Conditioning, which is necessary since the one route left takes us directly through the Kill Zone.

"The rest of you are going to have to stay tight with me," I say. "This route is risky, and unless you do exactly what I do, you could end up shot. Okay?"

"Yes, ma'am," one guy I don't recognize says.

I flinch and focus on him. "I'm not a soldier."

"Sorry, ma'a—" he cuts himself off before finishing, but the words he was planning to say grate on me.

I know it's become a habit for everyone, but I don't want to be associated with the Talionis soldiers in any way. I swallow back my emotions and race toward the Kill Zone, crouched low, sensing the others right behind me.

About four days ago, the area in front of the dining hall was set up to look like a marketplace, with stalls, tables full of goods, and even a few mock buildings. At first, it didn't make sense why they would do it, but then I realized they'd created a way through the Kill Zone. If you knew the right places to hide and crawl through.

I lead the little group to the entry point on the outskirts of the Kill Zone and dive under a table and into a stall. I pause inside, the shots and cries of recruits being hit thundering close by.

"Why do I always end up taking this route with you?" Nika grumbles as she comes up next to me.

I smirk at her. "You could have gone a different way."

She rolls her eyes. "Then who's gonna watch your back? You've been making yourself enough of a target as it is."

I ignore the comment and crawl to the next point on the route by one of the mock buildings. A training bullet hits the dirt a few yards away, heightening my focus. One wrong move along this route, and someone could get shot. The bullets aren't real, but these people trust me to get them through safely, and I can't let them down.

We weave through the fake marketplace, crawling, running in a crouched position, and shimmying through windows in the mock buildings, until we end up on the other side of the Kill Zone.

One of the new guys laughs and smacks me on the shoulder. "That was great! Thanks."

I can't help but smile at his relief. "No problem."

We enter the dining hall, and I part ways from the group and head toward the line of the lowest ranking recruits. Sergeant Valarius wasn't kidding when he said our meals would reflect how well we're doing in our trainings. My nose wrinkles as I'm handed a plate of some kind of leftover gruel. The stuff tastes like mushy, slimy, nothing.

But it's the price I have to pay for doing things my way—at least a little my way.

I go toward the table I always sit at and try not to look with too much envy at the chicken, broccoli, and roasted potatoes most of those at my table are eating. My stomach rumbles when I sit next to Nika and catch a whiff of garlic coming off her plate.

Conversation flows around me, and I let myself breathe. After an active Kill Zone, they give us a longer meal time. No need to rush.

I plunge my spoon into the gruel in front of me and take a bite, swallowing without chewing. Not that chewing this mush is necessary. I can't blame my friends for trying to do well in their trainings. The food and better chores they receive as a result almost make me second guess my decision to slack off. Earlier today, I had bathroom duty—which was disgusting—and tonight, after dinner, I have to scrub dishes.

Nika and several others who performed well in Physical Conditioning today have a free period tonight. I take another bite.

Ari had some trouble breaking through the encryption to find out the list of names of the Watchers, but she told Nika and me she should be able to get to the list tonight. Maybe, if it's not someone I know well from Derbe, I'll reconsider my decision, try harder in trainings. After all, I don't have to agree with everything they're saying, but I would really love something that tastes better than this.

Storm plops down next to me, her enormous shadow not far behind.

"Hi, Bria!" Blonde curls shoot out in every direction and bounce in their own greeting as she settles into her seat.

I smile at her and nod at Cade when he sits. His eyes wander the room, even as he eats, as though he's constantly gauging and assessing what's going on.

"We both know you're not as bad at trainings as you're pretending to be." His low voice draws my attention, but he's still observing the rest of the room.

I shrug. "So?"

"You just got over thirty recruits through the Kill Zone unscathed." His eyes find mine. "Be careful. They're gonna notice."

The caution in his tone makes me grip my spoon tighter. "I'll be fine."

He goes back to his food, and, after a moment, I do too, but his words gnaw at me. Before I can dwell on it for too long, Storm dives into her meal-time chatter, and I allow myself to focus on her instead.

This has become Storm's habit. She finds me whenever there's a meal and plants herself next to me. Then she talks. And talks. And talks. All I have to do is listen, which doesn't require too much effort.

Nika asks Storm a question, and the two talk around me.

My eyes scan the room, following Cade's example, as I mindlessly eat the bland food on my plate. Some recruits look haunted. A few seem almost defiant. But most of us have learned how to put on the show we need to for the soldiers. What's most disturbing to me is that, for some, I don't think it's a show. I've heard recruits *repeating* Elva Trill and buying into the propaganda of this place. And it makes me sick.

I stir my half-eaten bowl of nastiness. I should finish it, but I don't think I can stomach it tonight.

"Why are you always eating that stuff?" Storm asks, face scrunching in distaste.

"Good question."

I drop my spoon at the sound of Shay's voice. The conversations around us stop. She's standing on the other side of the table, arms crossed. She's distanced herself from me since I've fallen behind in training, and the most I see or talk to her is when there's a Kill Zone. Otherwise, I only have to endure her disapproving looks when I answer questions incorrectly in Educational Training or come in last in Physical Conditioning.

But, knowing Shay, we're about to progress beyond disapproving glares. Her lips are pursed, and her brow lowered. Here comes a lecture.

"Bria, what's your problem?"

My jaw cramps as I bite back my frustration. When I feel as though I can respond in an almost normal tone, I risk opening my mouth. "What do you mean?"

"Don't give me that." She tilts her chin, her nose hefting itself higher into the air. "Why don't you ever do what you're supposed to do?"

I force myself to pick up my water and take a drink as calmly as possible. Shay's just trying to adapt. She's upset because of how everything has changed. She misses home. I feel guilt clamp its hot fingers on my neck. Even though we've never gotten along, maybe I can cut her some slack.

I set my glass down. "It's been a difficult adjustment—"

"Adjustment? You're not trying to *adjust* to being here." She shakes her head emphatically. "You're such a hypocrite."

She jabs a finger at me. "In Derbe, everyone knew you wanted to be a scout, to make a difference. But here you have the opportunity to do that. The Commander has chosen us to be trained to do great things, to save lives. And you refuse to do what you have to to be a part of that."

She presses her hands on the table and leans forward. "But what's new? You always had to do things your way, even if people had to die so you could."

Her reference to Ezri snaps the thin cord of control I had tethered around my frustration. I shove back from the table and stand so fast my chair topples over.

I glare at her, jaw trembling in fury. "Do you want to say that again?"

She doesn't respond.

I spin around and walk out of the room, out of the building, and into the night.

The temperature dropped with the setting of the sun, and I tilt my chin up, letting the icy air cool my flushed face. I pace in front of the building, and pressure builds behind my eyes. I squeeze them shut.

I've suppressed my feelings over these past couple of weeks, but Shay knew which buttons to push to unleash them. I focus on my breathing. I won't let myself break down.

How could she believe the things they're saying? And how could she drag Ezri's death into this?

A headache pulses from the center of my forehead. I massage it, but it just seems to get worse. I sit down on a bench near the fake marketplace of the Kill Zone. At this moment, I would almost welcome the pain of being hit with a dozen training bullets, but there aren't any soldiers nearby. Not that they need to be. They can monitor everything I do through my HaloAct Band.

Fallen leaves rustle along the ground. I pull my legs up onto the bench with me, rest my arms on top of them, and drop my head onto my arms.

Maybe if I told her what I know, then what I'm doing would make more sense to her. But I can't do it. Just the thought of telling her that someone we both know betrayed us makes my stomach churn. I may not like Shay, but I can't crush her like that. And I promised Nika and Ari I wouldn't tell anyone else. Not yet.

The crunch of gravel causes me to shift a bit to see who's approaching.

Storm grins at me. I lift my head from my arms and feel my lips tilt up in a genuine smile. Funny how she can do that—break through the fog that always rests on me and make me smile. Nothing, no one, can anymore, except for her. At home, I used to smile and laugh. I think.

My smile falters, and I shake the thought away. She skips over, plops herself down on the bench, and starts chatting away as though we've been talking and are continuing the conversation.

"Guess what? Today I got to climb as high as I could! It was so fun!"

"Did you really? You're a little squirrel." I chuckle at the face Storm makes at me.

She crosses her arms. "I'm not a squirrel!"

"Are you sure?"

"Yesss!"

"Okay, if you say so."

Her little mouth twists to the side, and her eyes search mine. When she's satisfied that I agree with her, she smiles and leans into me.

I play with a springy strand of her hair, loving the texture.

"Bria?"

"Yeah?"

"Are you okay?"

I shift so I can look her in the eye. Worry creases her brow.

"Of course I'm okay."

"You looked really upset when you left the dining hall."

My eyebrows inch up. "I was a little upset. But I'm fine now."

"Do you ever miss your mom and dad?" She sighs. "I miss mine."

I blink at the sudden shift in conversation. "Yeah, sure I do." A lump forms in my throat at the admission. I swallow to clear it. "But it's okay, because at least I have you, my little squirrel."

She smiles a little, but her face turns serious again. "You know why my name is Storm?"

I hesitate. Does she ever stay on one topic? "No."

"It's because when I was born, there was a bad storm outside, and everybody was scared. Trees fell down, and the wind blew really hard." Storm leans against me as she speaks, playing with the fabric of my uniform. "But my dad, he read in the Bible about how God is always in control, even in the storm. They told me they named me Storm so I would remember that even when life is really scary, God is still with me."

She turns, her piercing brown eyes boring into me. "Do you believe in God, Bria?"

An alarm blares, and my HaloAct Band vibrates on my wrist.

CHAPTER

EIGHTEEN

I leap to my feet, and Storm does the same, hand clutching mine.

"What's happening?" she asks.

I give her hand a light squeeze. "I don't know."

My heart is racing, but I keep my voice calm. I thought I was used to everything in Talionis, but this is new. And I don't like it.

My band continues to vibrate, and then the map feature opens on its own, and a voice comes over the speakers sounding the alarm.

"Recruits proceed to bunkers. This is a drill. Recruits proceed to bunkers."

The alarm and the words continue to echo as people—recruits, soldiers, and Talionis workers—spill out of buildings.

The map on my band shifts to a street view of where I am, and a road lights up with a red arrow.

"Follow the path to bunkers immediately."

Soldiers run out of the dining hall, some marching to various buildings, others herding recruits.

"Let's go, let's go! To the bunkers!"

A soldier is emphatically pointing down the path my band is telling me to take, so I guide Storm over to the swarm of recruits heading that way. We half-run as a small group of soldiers guides us, yelling at us to go faster, and maps on all the recruits' bands echo directions. We pass the training Arena, then the Educational Building, and then they take us to the back of a building I've never been in before.

It's small, and the entrance is almost invisible until we're walking through it. Low red lighting is the only thing to break the darkness inside. Storm's hand shakes in mine, and I pull her closer. A part of me is ready to turn and run from this place, no matter what the consequence, but there's no opportunity as the press of recruits entering behind me pushes me forward.

Anytime someone asks a question or says anything, a soldier yells at them to be quiet. If he or she is close enough, they're zapped by a shock stick. I keep Storm in the center of the horde, as claustrophobic as it feels. She's safer with a barrier between her and the soldiers, who seem desperate for us to head through this dark, dank tunnel.

There's a shift in the ground, and I realize we're heading down. Lower and lower. My pulse thrums in my throat. Why are we doing this, and where are they leading us?

Then the hall opens into a spacious area. I squint against the brighter lighting but breathe a little easier as we all disperse throughout the space.

The only sounds are those of recruits entering. When the last recruit files in, Sergeant Valarius steps through the doorway.

Everyone snaps to attention. Even Storm, which twists my stomach. What have they been doing with her during our trainings?

"At ease. This is your first Bunker Drill," he says. "You may speak quietly with one another, but you are not to leave the bunker until you are told to, understood?"

"Sir, yes, sir!"

"If you attempt to leave the Bunker, the soldiers are ordered to stop you, using lethal force if necessary. Get comfortable. You'll be here for a while."

With that, he turns and exits the way we came. A gate-like door slides into place over the entrance, and for a moment, no one moves. Then recruits break into groups and spread out through the area.

Storm takes my hand again. "I'm scared."

I drop to a knee and place my free hand on her shoulder. "It's okay, little squirrel. How 'bout we find Cade?"

Any activity is better than standing here wondering what's happening. Storm's bottom lip quivers, but she gives a small nod. We weave our way through the space. We're underground on a concrete platform. There are benches scattered throughout the area, and groups of recruits cluster around them.

I accidentally brush the back of a girl I don't know, and she jumps, a yelp escaping.

"Sorry," I mumble as I pass. Guess I'm not the only one feeling nervous down here.

A group in the far corner of the room catches my eye. They're the same age as the rest of us, but they're not recruits. Their uniforms are blue, not gray, and they're somewhat separated from the rest of us. Cadets. According to what Corporal Mitts told us when we first arrived, they're children of soldiers and residents of Talionis.

They're laughing and joking and far more at ease than the rest of us. Like they've done this before and know exactly what's happening. The gaze of one guy connects with mine, and he grins, his white teeth glistening against his bronze skin. My face heats as recognition spills over me. He's the guy who was at our first Physical Conditioning lesson. The one who caught me watching him.

He waves. Unfortunately, it seems he recognizes me too. He takes a step toward me, and I spin away.

"Bria, over here." Ari's voice catches my ear, and I hustle over to her and the group with her, grateful for a reason to move *away* from whoever that guy is.

Cade is there, and Storm breathes an audible sigh of relief when she sees him—relief echoed in his eyes—but she doesn't let go of my hand.

"What's going on?" I ask.

"No idea," Nika says.

Cade leans against the wall, arms crossed. "My guess is something is happening up there they don't want us to be a part of."

His words crash against me like a tempestuous wave. We've already seen so much. What could they possibly be hiding from us? Yet it makes sense.

"Seriously?" Ari groans. "My band shut off completely." She frowns, and I realize my band isn't on either. "There must be some sort of signal block down here."

"I'm sure you'll survive," Bryson says, settling onto the ground.

I follow suit, leaning against the wall so I can look out at the sea of recruits around me. Storm sits so close to me she's almost on my lap. I put an arm around her, and she rests her head against me. My friends chat, and as my adrenaline drains away, Storm's question floats back to mind. Do I believe in God?

The question bombards me, forcing away the questions I would rather dwell on, like why am I in a bunker right now? And how can I escape Talionis?

But no matter how hard I try to focus on something else, Storm's question is the one that echos in my mind, consuming my thoughts.

My parents never cared much for what they called "religious things." They always said they were good people, kind to others, and that's what mattered. But all of that changed. Ezri's death changed their mind. They clung to God that day, but I couldn't. Not after what happened. God became a big deal for them, so I perfected tuning them out whenever they brought Him up.

It was so easy to ignore them. Why can't I ignore Storm's question?

WE REMAIN IN THE BUNKER FOR OVER AN HOUR, AND, WHEN WE'RE FINALLY cleared to leave, Sergeant Valarius dismisses us to return to our barracks and waives all duties for the evening. Which is a relief.

Storm has relaxed back to her normal self, and, though she gives me a longer hug than usual, she seems okay going to her room with the woman who comes to get her.

I bypass my room and go to the bathroom to wash up for bed, exhaustion hitting me in waves. I'm physically and mentally wiped out and grateful I don't have to scrub dishes in the kitchen like I was supposed to. Whenever I think I'm getting used to the routine here, they disrupt it. Like Bunker Drills, whatever that was for.

Maybe that's the point.

Nika is already here, and I join her at the row of sinks.

"Sorry about what happened earlier." She turns off her sink.

I pause.

"With Shay," she says. "I don't know what she was talking about, but it seemed like she crossed a line."

I turn on the faucet and splash water on my face before answering. "There's no line Shay *isn't* willing to cross. Not if it can benefit her in some way." The words are harsh and maybe not entirely true. But I'm too tired to offer disclaimers.

I rub the soap onto my face.

"Wanna talk about it? Death is hard..." her voice trails off.

"Come on, you know I don't talk about it, Lencie—" My head snaps up, and I stare at Nika as water drips down my face.

Her eyebrow quirks. "Lencie? Friend from home?"

My throat thickens, and I nod, unable to find words. I'm tired. Way too tired.

Nika nods as though understanding words I can't speak, pats my shoulder, and then leaves the bathroom.

I brace my hands against the sink and stare down at them, eyes burning. I haven't thought about Lencie in weeks, but Nika's comment sounded so much like something Lence would have said. Homesickness hits me, taking my breath away.

I swallow.

No. I can't lose it. Not now. With more effort than I wish it required, I shove thoughts of my friend, of home, back down and wash away the feelings that found their way past my defenses.

When I enter my room, Nika and Ari are on Ari's bed, huddled over the screen she smuggled in. They look up when I close the door, and the expressions on their faces freeze me in my tracks.

"What?" I ask, but don't want the answer. Not really. I want to ignore them and crawl into my bed and fall asleep. Pretend, for a few hours, that life isn't a confusing, painful mess. But I'm not a kid, and make-believe games don't change reality.

"Ari did it," Nika says. "She broke through the encryption."

I don't move from where I'm frozen by the door.

"We have the list. We know who the Watchers are."

CHAPTER

NINETEEN

My feet move of their own accord to Ari's bed, and next thing I know, I'm perched on the edge. I need to know. Right?

"We waited for you," Ari says.

I think I nod, but I'm uncertain.

"Who's first?" Ari asks.

"Let's look at a town none of us are from, see if we can figure out exactly what the Watchers do before we discover who the ones from our home towns are," Nika suggests.

"Yes." I say the word too quickly, but my friends don't seem to notice.

I scoot further onto the bed, next to Ari, so I can see over her shoulder.

She picks a town at random, opens the file, and a list of Watchers populates the screen. Four Watchers from this town. Four names, four faces. And underneath them, a list of the teens in the town, with stats next to each name. Like they were grading them. Determining their skill levels.

A few of the names are bold, with the word RECRUIT next to them. Ari clicks one of the names. *Lex Penatov*. His face appears in the top right corner on a new screen. A face I vaguely recognize from trainings. He's not in our unit, but I've seen him around. Under his name and picture are more stats, including a psychological profile.

The three of us are silent as our eyes scan the words, confirming what Ari thought. The Watchers *are* spies for Talionis. They're the reason we're here.

Ari goes out of Lex's profile and returns to the list of towns. She scrolls a moment, finds the city she's from, and then opens the file. I barely register as she says names aloud, names that mean nothing to me…but everything to her. She shrinks back when she's finished, face pinched in hurt and confusion. Now she knows the names of the people who betrayed her, the ones who sent her here.

"Who's next?" Her voice is higher than normal.

"Nika," I say.

I'm not ready. Not yet.

Nika's lips press into a grim line, but she takes the screen when Ari offers it to her. That Ari is parting with the tech rather than insisting on doing it for Nika tells me more than words ever could.

There's no hesitation as Nika scrolls and then taps on the name of her hometown. Her face hardens as she reads silently.

She looks up after a moment. "I know all of them, *babysat* for one lady after her husband died in an accident. And yet, here I am." She passes me the screen.

List after list of towns fills the screen. My eyes scan the names listed in alphabetical order. I scroll quickly past the A's, B's and C's, and come to the D's. Dabin, Danein, Deerin, Delonto. Derbe. My town. My home.

Dread climbs up each vertebra of my spine, twists down my arm, and pulsates from my finger. When I push this button, I'll find out the name of the people whose actions destroyed my life. The ones who betrayed me. I need to know. I want to know. Don't I? Suddenly I'm not sure. My finger drops, and I open the file.

Three names are listed. Mayor Tessan and Mrs. Grenden, but it's the third one that seems to rise off the screen, consuming my vision. Shock and horror slap against me in waves that alternate between hot and cold as I stare at the name.

Elena Blyweiss.

My aunt.

I force myself to look at her picture, into her eyes. Her stern gaze stares back at me. Blood drains from my face. No. No, this can't be right. Aunt Elena and I may have had our differences, but betraying me to these people? She would never have done that.

But the protests in my mind sink before I can cling to them, like trying to use seaweed as a floatation device. Foolish.

I'm gripping the screen so hard, my fingers are turning white.

"You knew them." Nika says.

I nod once. "Yes. One of them was my aunt." I sound detached, disconnected.

Ari inhales deeply, but neither says a word. What is there to say?

I was betrayed, just like they were, but the one who sent me here was family.

I hand the screen back to Ari and get off the bed. I take two steps and then face Nika and Ari.

"What now?"

"I don't know," Nika says.

I nod again, then exit the room. As soon as I'm alone in the hallway, a rushing sounds in my ears until I can't hear anything else. *You were betrayed. You were betrayed. You were betrayed.*

The words are branded on my eyes, echoing in my ears, capturing each breath until I can only manage sucking in oxygen in quick and shallow bursts. My entire body shakes. I lean against the wall as my aunt's betrayal tears through me.

I slam my fist into the wall. Why did she do it? She claimed to love me, and yet she let them kidnap me. No. She *told* them to kidnap me.

She looked me in the face day after day. Pretended to care about me. Played with me as a girl. Taught me how to do things as I grew up. And it was all an act! Empty words of love. Empty promises of wanting the best for me. All just preparing for the day when she would sell me away to strangers.

Everything was ripped away from me forever, because of her!

I reach for where my necklace should be, my hand finding the bare place on my neck. Everything I ever cared about has been torn from me. Or destroyed by me.

Time passes, but I'm not sure how long I stand here. Lights dim. Noises from the other rooms cease. Recruits are going to bed, and I can't move away from the wall. What now? The question I asked Nika earlier pulses in my mind.

How do I move forward knowing everything I know?

"Sir, yes, sir!" a girl screams out the words from a room a couple of doors down the hall.

I flinch.

They're breaking us, haunting us in our sleep. And we were all sent here by people we *knew*.

I push away from the wall and ease open the door to my room. It doesn't matter how much gruel I have to eat, or how disgusting the chores are they make me do. I'm *not* giving them the satisfaction of seeing me work hard and becoming the recruit they want me to be. My skills are all I have left, and they're not for sale to make my life easier.

My band buzzes and beeps out a steady alarm on the nightstand next to my bed, growing louder with each second. I pry my eyes open and rub my hand over them, but it doesn't wipe away the grittiness. I fumble through the dark and grab my band. The alarm stops, but the buzzing continues. That won't stop until I enter the kitchen for my pre-training chores.

It feels like I *just* fell asleep. And I probably did. Nika and Ari were still awake when I entered the room last night, and the three of us were up way too late talking. Well, Ari and Nika talked. I mostly sat there. They concluded that there must be more to the Watchers than what we know. But my conclusion is that what we know is enough. Even after we stopped talking, I couldn't fall asleep. Just stared at the ceiling.

And now I have kitchen duty.

Somehow, I get myself up and dressed and out the door before my band starts up another alarm. I enter the kitchen to find the cook, Tilly, already bustling about the room. For a plump little woman, she moves around the kitchen with impressive speed. She looks over when she hears me enter.

"Oh good, you're here!" The words rush out of her mouth. "Prep the eggs."

The other recruits assigned kitchen duty make their way in, and the kitchen swarms with activity. I move toward my designated station, my eyes drooping. I just want to go back to bed.

Someone enters the kitchen, his arms overladen with sacks of produce. He sets the bags down, and I recognize him immediately as the guy I've seen in Physical Conditioning and in the bunker last night. I turn back to the multitude of eggs I'm supposed to be cracking, glad that this time he didn't notice me.

A shell drops in. I try to fish it out, but it gets lost in the egg goop. Someone's in for an unpleasant surprise, though it won't be me. Day old oatmeal is my typical breakfast. I yawn, and my jaw pops.

"Hey."

The low voice by my shoulder makes me jump and causes me to drop an entire egg into the bowl. I spin toward the voice.

Mystery guy stands next to me grinning, white teeth blazing against his dark skin, his blue eyes sparkling. "Sorry to startle you."

I glare at him and then turn and attempt to remove the slimy egg from the bowl.

"Since I've been seeing you so much, I figured I'd introduce myself." He pauses, but I keep my focus on the egg retrieval as it slips from my fingers. "I'm Matthias."

I give a curt nod but say nothing. I've made enough of a fool of myself in front of this guy already, and I'm not interested in him knowing anything about me. Even my name.

He stands there, watching me as I finally remove the egg.

"Well, hopefully I keep seeing you around," he says.

I make the mistake of looking at him. He flashes a smile and a wink, then saunters off whistling. I frown. He's in way too good of a mood this early in the morning. And what is a cadet doing delivering produce to the recruit's kitchen, anyway?

I go back to prepping the eggs, but, to my irritation, I can't get Matthias's face out of my mind. Must be more exhausted than I thought.

CHAPTER
TWENTY

The days pass by in a blur. I'm going to all of my trainings but doing even worse than I was before. And I'm hardly sleeping. At night when I close my eyes, I keep picturing my aunt. I know she wasn't happy with me most of the time, but this? How could she do *this* to me?

The worst part is, I'm afraid that maybe I deserve it. All of it.

I almost wish I believed in God the way Storm seems to. Even Nika has talked about praying to Him. If I thought I could do that, that He actually wanted to hear from me, maybe I'd ask Him why all of this is happening. But I'm afraid of the answer I'd receive.

I enter the Arena and line up in my place in the second to last row of my unit. I'm not sure how there are recruits doing *worse* than me, but I'll probably be in last place soon enough. I stand at attention.

Sergeant Andor Valarius strides into the room a minute later. "At ease! Units one through five, you will follow the conditioning schedule laid out on your bands as usual. Dismissed."

The five units double-time it down the stairs and into the Arena, leaving only my unit, Sergeant Valarius, and Laban.

Sergeant Valarius paces down the line, then back to the front of the platform. "Unit 6, your training today will be different."

Something about how he says *different* sends a chill through me.

"Sergeant Meritas and I will evaluate your swimming capabilities in the river, with a two and a half mile swim."

Every particle of saliva decides to evaporate from my mouth. Laban stands slightly behind Sergeant Valarius, and he's staring at me. This is about *me*. I'm not sure why or how I know, but I *know* they're doing this because of me.

Numbness takes over me as Sergeant Valarius and Laban march us through the Arena and outside, past the obstacle courses, and to the bank of the river. It churns past, the water hazy but not as murky as the Lassen river.

Bria... Bria... Bria...

This is my first opportunity to swim in weeks, and the water calls to me. The monster followed me here, and it waits for me, lurking in the depths of this river.

Sergeant Valarius instructs us to swim down the river until we reach a net, which is where we will come back onto shore.

Ezri's face swarms into my mind, and a need to dive into the water, to fight the monster haunting me, takes hold of me.

"The results of this evaluation," Laban shouts over the noise of the water, "are of interest to the Commander. Show him your loyalty. Honor him by doing well!"

I recoil, taking a small step back from the river's edge. I'm fighting two monsters now: the one from my past who stole my brother from me, and the one in this city who's trying to control me. And I can't defy them both today. If I swim fast, maybe I can out swim the memories waiting for me in the water. But doing so means playing right into what Laban and his commander want.

"Prepare to enter the water," Sergeant Valarius says.

I step toward it with the other recruits. Despite myself, a flutter of anticipation dances along my nerves. I want to do this. To swim. Need to do it.

"Enter now!" Sergeant Valarius's words spur everyone into action.

I dive in. The cool water sweeps over me, familiar, painful. Exhilarating. I surface and swim against the current, my body knifing through the water. For a moment, I forget everything. Talionis. My past. Aunt Elena's betrayal. It fades as I swim, the current pushing against my body, the water rushing past, the rhythm and movements I know so well propelling me forward.

Water whacks me in the face, going up my nose. I slow, sputter. And it all comes rushing back. A few recruits pass me, and I realize I've taken the lead. I'm doing exactly what they want. But not anymore.

I find a slower pace, forcing my body to do the opposite of what it wants. The monster laughs in my ears, like it knows it's winning. Again. And I have to let it.

A net stretches across the water ahead of me, marking the end. I cut toward the bank of the river, diving under one last time before coming to the edge. A hand stretches out to me. I take hold of it and clamber up the muddy bank. Most of my unit is already on the shore.

Shay stands near Laban, both of them observing me with expressionless faces. I turn my back to them and watch the last few recruits swim in.

Nika hands me a towel. "That was some impressive swimming at the beginning there."

I towel off my hair. "Thanks."

Two more recruits scramble onto the shore, panting. One girl is left in the water, still a distance away.

Nika's voice drops. "It might be good to at least try, Bria. I know this place is awful, but..." her voice trails off.

I tighten my grip on the towel. Nika's a good friend, and I don't fault her for doing what she's doing, for trying. But I can't.

The last girl, Ava, makes her way in, shaking and pale as she struggles to get up the river bank.

Laban approaches. Something in my gut seizes. This will not be good. He shoves Ava so she falls back into the water. Everyone goes silent. He grabs her by her hair, and my scalp twitches at the memory of him doing the same thing to me. Then he dunks her under the water and holds her there.

My throat closes as I watch in horror.

Gasps echo around me, but someone chuckles, like he thinks this is *funny*.

Laban yanks Ava back up, and she spews out water, choking coughs racking her body. He leans his face into hers. "Is this how you thank the Commander for everything he's done? By failing so miserably? Maybe this will help you remember to try a little harder in your training."

Ava's crying now, which only seems to make Laban angrier. My heart pounds. I can't let this happen. But what can I do to stop it? Tortured, I watch as Laban moves to push her down again.

"Enough, Sergeant," Sergeant Valarius says. "We have other work to do."

Laban half-drags Ava over to the rest of us and then releases her with a shove. She collapses on the ground, shuddering.

My hands shake as I finish drying off, and I want to pretend it's because I'm cold. But I know better. Maybe Nika is right. Maybe I shouldn't be failing this badly.

A FEMALE SOLDIER APPROACHES THE TABLE, AND CONVERSATIONS CEASE. Even Storm stops talking.

"Recruit Averton. Come with me," she says.

I set my spoon back into my untouched bowl of mush. I just sat down. Why am I being summoned away now? I don't ask the question. Instead, I stand up and follow the soldier from the room, feeling the eyes of my friends and other recruits staring after me.

She ushers me out of the building and into the rainy day. We go at a fast pace, water kicking up as we march through puddles. The rain makes tracks down my face and begins soaking through my uniform, along with a sense of anxiety. The soldier is bringing me into the center of Talionis.

We approach a building I haven't been in before and march up the steps. She shoulders through the door, and we enter an ornate, open area in a spray of rainwater. Hallways shoot off from the lobby to various areas of the building.

She leads me down a hallway, up a flight of stairs, and then stops at a closed door and knocks with two quick raps.

"Enter." The voice is familiar, though I've only heard him speak a few times. Colonel Keenan Valarius.

Why am I being taken to him?

The woman opens the door and waits for me to proceed her inside. When I don't move, she gives me a shove. I stumble into the room.

Next to Colonel Valarius is Laban. And Shay.

My mouth parts, and I stare. What is going on?

"Thank you, Private. That's all." Colonel Valarius dismisses the soldier who brought me, and she closes the door behind her.

As much as I want to stare at Shay and Laban, I force my focus on Colonel Valarius. Control and confidence clothe him as perfectly as his tailored uniform, and there's something about him that demands obedience. Or promises a consequence.

"Recruit Averton. Your name is more familiar to me than it should be. And not for a good reason." He cocks his head, and a lock of black hair dares to fall out of place and land on his forehead. "Do you think we're fools, Bria?"

The way he says my name sends a chill down my spine. I swallow and shake my head no.

He leans back in his chair and folds his arms across his chest. "Then why do you insist on this charade?"

"What charade, sir?" I immediately wish I could force the words back in.

Colonel Valarius's eyes narrow. "Perhaps you're the fool. Though based on what I know of you, that's most likely not the case." He snaps his fingers, and Laban and Shay step forward like they rehearsed it. "Recruit Bellingdon."

"Yes, sir," Shay says.

Why is she here right now? I clench and unclench my hands. I don't think I want to know, but I'm about to find out.

Colonel Valarius doesn't take his gaze off of me. "Please relay the information you told Sergeant Meritas and myself earlier."

I focus on Shay, dread coiling in my stomach. No. She wouldn't.

"Bria, I mean Recruit Averton, is a skillful swimmer, sir. One of the best I've ever seen." There's no hesitation in her speech.

Blood pounds in my ears.

"Additionally, she has successfully helped dozens of recruits navigate the Kill Zone and brought them to safety without being shot." She doesn't spare a single look in my direction as she relays the information.

Every word is spoken with no sign of remorse. She doesn't care what her words will cost *me*. All she cares about is how she looks in front of these people. And it makes me physically ill.

"Don't look so stricken, Recruit Averton," Colonel Valarius says. "Your friend has only confirmed what we already knew to be true."

Friend?

He stands up from his desk. "There is a greater purpose here than you or any one individual." His eyes bore into mine. "Shay has found trusting the Commander and his plan to be well worth her effort. Perhaps Sergeant Meritas can incentivize you to a similar loyalty."

My mind screams, but my mouth is frozen shut as Laban shoves me toward the door.

"Time for you to experience the pit." Laban's raspy voice grates against my ears.

"Oh, and Recruit Averton."

At the sound of Colonel Valarius's voice, Laban jerks me to a stop.

"Since you are so keen on doing things to ensure others are kept safe..." Colonel Valarius pauses.

My heart races so fast, I'm sure they can see my pulse pounding in my throat.

"If you don't do everything Sergeant Meritas demands, we'll ensure your roommates experience the ramifications. Do I make myself clear?"

"Yes, sir," I say, unsure how the words force themselves past my lips.

Laban chuckles as he takes me from the room and leads me outside. It's no longer raining.

I'm shocked—no. I *want* to be shocked that Shay could betray me like this, turn me in just to benefit herself. But with each step to the sandpit, the surprise and haze of what just happened slips away. Shay believes every word they tell her, does everything they want. She eats well, has the chores that aren't even chore-like, and is praised regularly by soldiers and instructors for her performance.

The real question is, how could I have *ever* believed she would guard my secrets from these people?

Maybe I should tell her why we're here, that people from home betrayed us. Bile rises in my throat. She won't care. In fact, Shay would probably think those traitors, my *aunt,* did us a favor.

We arrive at the sandpit, a large area in front of the Arena, open for everyone to see what happens when you're disciplined in Talionis. I've passed many recruits doing their time in the pit, but somehow I've never been dragged here before.

Laban shoves me, and I fall to my knees in the wet sand. A jolt rings through my body at the impact, and, along with it, a steely defiance. I take my time getting to my feet, brushing off the sand clinging to my uniform. The last thing to rise is my head. My eyes connect with Laban's.

His lips curl into a snarl, his golden eyes glimmering. "I'm going to enjoy this."

I want to spit in his face, curse him out. Do something—*anything* —to defy him. But Nika and Ari's faces come to mind. I have to obey.

"Sanchez, with me!" Laban shouts to a female soldier nearby.

She jogs over and snaps to attention. "Sir, yes, sir!"

Sweat glistens on her forehead, and there's a tremor in her voice as though she's nervous. From the smile on his face, my guess is that Laban notices it too.

"At ease," he says. "Let's show Recruit Averton what it means to get slayed."

"Sir, yes, sir!" Sanchez rounds on me. "You heard your sergeant! It's time to think of what you've done wrong and beat it out of your system." She screams the words in my face. Any bit of fear I thought I saw earlier is gone.

"Drop and do pushups until I say stop!" Laban shouts.

I do as he says. Both Laban and Sanchez scream at me to keep going and I obey. Because I have no other choice. My arms burn. Sweat drips down my back. Laban shouts for me to do sit-ups, then he's telling me to get on my feet and do high knees. Everything is harder in the sand than in the Arena, as though the sand itself is fighting against me.

Whenever my pace slows even a little, Sanchez and Laban are in my face.

Laban grabs the fabric of my uniform and slams me into the ground. "Get into a plank position and hold it!"

Pain ripples through me, but I obey. I'm not sure how long they have me in the pit, but they push me to a point beyond anything I've experienced before. Pushups, high-knees, planks, sit-ups, burpees, and anything else they think of, over and over again.

My body rebels, and I vomit, which brings Laban over, screaming at me to keep going because he didn't say stop.

Moments later, I'm in a plank position again, arms quaking beneath me. A part of my brain registers that another soldier has approached and pulled Laban away, but Sanchez is crouched next to me.

"Get your butt down, recruit! Hold a perfect plank position! Does it hurt? Then don't get sent here again!"

"Yes, ma'am!" I say through gasping breaths.

I can't keep going like this, and I know it. Laban probably does too. But if my body gives out, if he decides I didn't do everything he commanded, what will Colonel Valarius do to my friends? Maybe making friends here was a bad idea.

God, I'm not even sure I think You're there, and I know if You are, You have no reason to listen to me. But please don't let my friends get hurt because of what I've done.

I push away the thoughts. Storm's question about God got to me more than I want to admit. My shoulders burn in agony, and I almost drop into the sand.

Don't think about the pain, Bria. Come on. My personal pep-talk doesn't do much to help. Sanchez keeps screaming at me, but I focus on the murmur of conversation between Laban and whoever is with him, not attempting to process a word of what they're saying, but hoping the distraction works.

Sanchez pauses to take a breath, and two words Laban says ring through the air and whip me across the face.

"Get Storm."

CHAPTER

TWENTY-ONE

I collapse to the ground, ignore Sanchez's screams to get back into position, and scramble to my feet. I lunge toward where Laban stands several feet away. Two soldiers are jogging to the Recruits' Living Quarters.

Sanchez tries to grab me, but I sidestep her, and then I'm in front of Laban.

"What are you going to do with her?" I ask, my strangled voice echoing fear I can't hold back.

Laban's nostrils flare, but he whirls to face Sanchez, who stands beside me. "Corporal Sanchez, didn't I leave this recruit in your hands while I saw to some business?" He speaks through clenched teeth.

"Y-yes, sir," Sanchez says.

His golden eyes crackle with anger. "I'll deal with you later. Dismissed."

She salutes and then leaves. If I wasn't so concerned about Storm, I might be afraid for the soldier. But she's a soldier which means she must have chosen to be here. Storm did not.

"What are you going to do with Storm?" I repeat the question, despising myself for how desperately I need answers from Laban, of all people.

And like a shark smelling blood in the water, he senses it too. His lips curl into a grin. "The littlest recruit can play a role in the Commander's plan, just as well as the most difficult recruit." He tilts his head. "Perhaps even more."

Goosebumps rise on my skin. "Leave her out of this. She's just a child."

"Oh, she's more valuable than that." His gaze focuses on something behind me, and he smiles. "She may just lead us to a whole new source of recruits."

My heart stops beating for a moment, then races as the impact of his words settles on my chest. They're going to *train* Storm, treat her like a recruit. If she does well, they'll bring in more kids…Eli and Zeke. And my aunt will be there to sell them off. Terror slams into me, more painful than a thousand hours in the sandpit.

"Bria!" Storm's choked cry causes me to spin around.

The two soldiers are pulling Storm toward Laban. Her cries intensify, and she reaches her small arms for me.

Desperation spurs me into action. I run to her.

"Don't interfere, recruit," Laban says.

A soldier steps into my path, blocking me from Storm.

I punch the man in the face, all the force of my rage and fear behind my fist, and then kick him in the shin. He drops to the ground. and I move past him. Two other soldiers grab my arms. I resist, trying to pull away, but their grip only tightens.

A crowd has gathered, but they part to let the soldiers and Storm pass through. Storm turns her little body around as much as she can, reaching for me, sobbing uncontrollably. No, this can't be happening. This is my fault. I failed her. I should have protected her, told her not to do anything to make them notice her. My rage turns into a weight of failure that settles onto my chest.

"It's okay Storm! You'll be okay!" I yell out the words of comfort, unable to believe them for myself.

My mind is numb as I'm led, hands bound behind my back, into the Tribunal. I'm being brought before the Council on charges of assault since I attacked the soldier. It doesn't matter what my punishment will be. They took Storm away, and I have no way of knowing where she is or if she's even okay.

Since Laban is involved, I fear the worst. I could have prevented this. I should have recognized they were evaluating her by the things she was telling me she was doing, but I missed all the signs. And now she's been taken away from everything and everyone she trusts here.

How could I have let this happen?

The room I'm brought into has a domed ceiling and an elevated table that follows the curve along three sides of the room, dominating the space. I'm positioned in the center, the door to my back and the table engulfing my view. A soldier places metal straps around my ankles, securing me to the floor, and leaves me to stand alone in the cavernous space, waiting.

An ornate clock on the left wall ticks away the seconds. Over and over, the image of Storm sobbing and reaching for me as they took her away repeats in my mind. And now I wait for a punishment that will only keep her further from my reach. I hang my head. She trusted me, believed I would keep her safe. And I failed her. But why does that surprise me? I fail everyone.

The door opens. I lift my head, but don't turn. Muffled voices filter in from the hallway as several men and women enter the room and take their places at the Tribunal Table. The Council. The ones who will decide my punishment for an assault that I'm not at all ashamed of. If they're expecting an apology, they won't be getting one.

There are fifteen members of the Council. Many of them are unfamiliar to me, but I recognize Elva Trill, Colonel Keenan Valarius, Mandeville, and Sergeant Andor Valarius. The center chair is elevated higher than the other chairs. I didn't focus much during Instructor Trill's educational lectures, but I remember the one on disciplinary proceedings in Talionis. The Council are the ones who dole out punishment for crimes committed against the laws of Talionis. The High Council is the one no one wants to appear before.

They're the only disciplinary proceedings in which the Commander himself is present. They deal with high crimes against the state and against the Commander. Every case brought before the High Council has resulted in execution.

Laban enters and stands near me. I clench my jaw, wishing my hands were loose so I could wrap them around his neck. I'll never forgive him for terrifying Storm. At the same time, I hope terrifying her is *all* he's done.

Colonel Valarius sits down in the center chair and brings the proceedings to order.

"We gathered the Council today to discuss disciplinary measures to be taken in the matter of Recruit Bria Averton of Unit Six and her assault against a soldier of Talionis. This action, witnessed by Sergeant Laban Meritas, will receive the punishment that is due." Colonel Valarius pauses, and his cold and calculating eyes pierce me, pronouncing me guilty. "I move for the punishment to be twenty-four hours in the Ruins, without food or water."

The word *Ruins* does a better job than anything else of pulling me from my numb stupor. He can't possibly be serious about sending me there.

There's a slight gasp from one of the female members of the Council.

"We need all the recruits we can get," Sergeant Valarius says.

His brother glares at him, but the sergeant doesn't seem to care.

"She's skilled and could be useful to the Commander. We just lost another squad of soldiers to the Ruins last week. If you send her there, she'll die."

"Or she'll prove she's the kind of recruit we need." Colonel Valarius shifts his attention to me. "Averton, you have rejected every opportunity we have placed in front of you, hidden your skills, and now assaulted a soldier. Since it's clear you don't want to be here, let's see how you fare in the Ruins."

My mind tortures me with replays of every threat the soldiers made to send us to the Ruins, all the things they've said about the place. I don't want any of it to be true, but I've seen the genuine fear in their eyes when they've discussed it among themselves. Still remember their jumpiness when we flew over them our first day here.

Soldiers far better trained and more skilled than me have gone missing or died out there. This can't be happening. What have I done?

Colonel Valarius stands, and his gaze sweeps over the other members of the Council. "All in favor of Recruit Averton's punishment being twenty-four hours in the Ruins?"

A massive Black man with a shaved head stands first, and Mandeville and two others I don't know quickly follow suit, showing their consent. The rest move slower, but eventually all are standing. Even Sergeant Valarius.

"Recruit Averton, your punishment is unanimously sealed by the laws of Talionis. It will be executed at 1800 hours. We will retrieve you from the Ruins tomorrow at 1800 hours."

He slams a gavel down onto the table. The sound echoes in my ears long after I'm led from the room.

———

At eighteen hundred hours, I'm led out of the Detainment Center and into the evening by a small entourage. Outside, recruits are lined up in formation, all eyes fixed on me. Soldiers stand at attention, lining the pathway from the door we just exited to the small transport that will take me to the Ruins.

I don't know what I expected, but it wasn't this—to be publicly humiliated as I'm marched past hundreds of recruits. Probably for the last time.

Then again, why not show them what it looks like when you don't fall into line with Talionis and its commander?

I lift my chin up a notch and keep my focus on the transport. No matter how terrified I am, I won't show it. Not to the soldiers and not to the recruits. It feels like it takes forever, but we finally arrive at the transport. Out of the corner of my eye, I catch sight of Ari. She's at attention in the front row of unit six. Too bad all her tech abilities can't help me in the Ruins.

A pang zips through my chest.

Again, I'm being forced away from friends, people I care about, with no chance to say goodbye. This time I get to see them, but it doesn't make it any better. Still, I focus on Ari, give her a small nod. I catch sight of Nika and Cade. All three of them are grim. If only half the things the soldiers have claimed about the Ruins are true, I'm in trouble, and they know it as well as I do.

"Alright, let's get this over with," Laban says, from the door of the transport. He addresses the crowd. "Recruit Bria Averton has been sentenced to a stint in the Ruins for assaulting a soldier of Talionis. Let this be a warning to all of you. Understood?"

"Sir, yes, sir!" The shout echoes through the air, pulsating through me.

Laban orders four soldiers to board the transport with me, and none of them look pleased, but the two on either side of me remain in position, staring straight ahead.

Sergeant Andor Valarius strides over and shoves a jacket into my arms. He stares down at me, his shaggy hair messier than usual. "As an acknowledgement of your potential, you have been issued a jacket to protect you against the elements." His voice is a low murmur. "I'll bring her on board," he says to the soldiers.

They step away, and Sergeant Valarius leads me up the ramp onto the transport.

"I've got it from here," Laban says.

The two men eye each other.

"Leave her in the clearing on the south side," Sergeant Valarius says.

Laban opens his mouth to protest.

"That's an order, Meritas," Sergeant Valarius says.

"Yes, sir," Laban growls.

With that, Sergeant Valarius leaves, and they shut the transport door.

"Doesn't matter if you have a jacket or where I drop you in the Ruins," Laban sneers. "There's no way you'll survive this."

With that, he barks orders to the soldiers—all of whom appear jumpy and agitated. I guess I'm not the only one who's anxious about entering the Ruins. At least they don't have to stay there.

I put the jacket on as the transport takes off. The front folds across my body and zips up my left side. I want to pretend it's an added layer of protection, that it will deter whatever I'm about to face, but it's a foolish thought.

We travel for about ten minutes before crossing over the fence that separates the Ruins from Talionis. As soon as we pass the border, the pilot begins weaving an erratic path, turning left, then right, bringing the transport higher, then dropping us low. I fall into a seat.

"Pilot Jones," Laban shouts, reaching for an overhead support to steady himself. "Why are you taking evasive action?"

"Protocol sir," the pilot says. "Something took out a small transport a couple of weeks ago. We're still unsure of what it was, but to be safe, they instruct every transport below certain specifications to take evasive action when entering the Ruins."

The soldier near me inhales sharply, her face pale.

My stomach lurches when the pilot makes a sudden drop, and I grip my armrests. At the moment, I'm not sure if I'm more afraid of the Ruins or dropping from the sky with the way the pilot is flying this thing.

A few minutes later, the transport descends and hovers a few feet above the ground of a small clearing.

"Get her up." Laban paces the transport, looking out all the windows.

There's something about his actions that's surprising, and then I realize what it is. He's nervous.

I'm yanked to my feet by two soldiers, and Laban opens the door. He grabs my arm, presses a button on my wristband, clips a lock over the clasp, and then scans it with his device.

"Now we'll know where to find your body when we come to pick you up," he says.

Without letting go of my arm, he leads me to the door. "Enjoy your stay."

With that, he pushes me out of the transport.

It's only a few feet to the ground, but I land with a hard *thud!* Before I have the chance to get to my feet, I hear the whirring of the transport lifting. It leaps into the air and resumes its erratic flight pattern until it's out of sight.

I stand in the silence that follows in a small clearing surrounded by trees that rise ominously to the sky, thorny vines wrapping themselves around their trunks. The limbs of the trees jut at odd angles, threatening arms waiting to grab anyone who would dare intrude. An odor, like rotten eggs and moldy cabbage, infuses the air. I pull the collar of my jacket up and bury my nose in it, but the smell seeps through. I gag.

Night is falling, the increasing darkness making the shadows of the forest grow in length until they begin to slowly capture the clearing. The temperature has dropped since I boarded the transport. I shiver, sink down to the ground, and wrap my arms around my knees. There is no way I'm going into those woods.

My mind races with the things I've heard about this place, the things I witnessed during the tour we had on our first day here. The collapsing buildings. The spontaneous fires. I clench my hands into fists and draw my knees in closer to my body. Plus, there're all the stories the soldiers tell the recruits. Based on Laban's nervousness alone moments ago, somehow I know each story is true.

A dog howls in the distance, and I shiver again. Maybe if I can sleep, I'll be able to keep myself from playing out every possible scenario that ends in my death.

I curl into a ball on the ground, skeptical. This will never work. There's no way I'll be able to sleep out here. I close my eyes anyway.

TWENTY-TWO

I jerk upright, startled awake by something. I can't believe I fell asleep. The night has grown black, clouds hide the moon, and nothing is visible. What woke me up? I blink, trying to see. Chills of apprehension tickle the base of my neck. I stand, turning in a circle.

The first low growl sounds to my left. I pivot to face it. A cloud slips from its cover over the moon, and a shred of light pierces the darkness, reflecting off a pair of yellow eyes. Eyes fixed on me. The animal stands at the edge of the forest. I step back. There's the low, guttural sound of a growl behind me, another to my side. I stop moving and scan the ground for a weapon, something, anything, that will help me defend myself. There's nothing.

The animal in front of me lifts its massive head and howls. I scream and wave my arms, trying to scare them. They growl louder.

Time slows. I envision them tearing into my flesh and the agonizing pain I'll face before I die. One of them howls again, breaking me from my imaginings. I refuse to go down without a fight.

I turn and sprint to the right, flailing my arms, screaming, and making as much noise as I can. There is barking and snarling as the dogs take off after me. Fear urges me on. I smell them behind me, the musty scent of wet, matted fur and foul breath. They're closing in. Thorns grab at me as I enter the forest, unwilling to grant me entrance, but somehow my feet find their way over the rough terrain. A branch scrapes my arm.

Paws strike my back, knocking me to the ground. The animal's weight presses down on top of me. Instinctively, I cover my head with my arms and wait for the dog's teeth to rip into my body, to feel what I imagined feeling moments before.

A shrill whistle pierces the air.

The dog on top of me steps off. I keep my head buried under my arms, ragged breaths tearing through me.

Something prods at my side, and I flinch, curling into myself. This is it. I'm going to be eaten.

"Good. You're alive." The voice is low and husky, like someone who just woke up.

I uncover my head to peer up at him, but the face of my protector is hidden beneath a hood. Maybe I'm not about to die.

I sit up and gasp. The dogs haven't left. They're all sitting in a circle around me and this strange man.

"They won't hurt you."

"I'm not so sure about that," I say.

Without a word, the man gives two short whistles. The dogs get up and trot into the woods.

I scramble to my feet. "Who are you?"

He doesn't respond right away, and, though I can't see his face, I feel him scrutinizing me. I shift, caught between wanting to be with someone, *anyone*, and fearing this man that wild dogs obey.

A light shines in my eyes, and I squint against the brightness.

"What is a recruit of Talionis doing in the Ruins?"

I step back, heart racing. "How do you know I'm a recruit?"

A sound bursts out of him—almost a laugh but not quite. "The uniform speaks for itself." In a blink, he closes the distance between us. "Did they send you to search this area?"

"What are you talking about? No. It was my punishment." I step back, stumble over a root, and land hard on my backside, but the pain barely registers. Whoever this guy is, I'm a little freaked out.

He looms over me for another moment, shrouded in darkness on the other side of the light he's shining in my face. The sounds of the forest echo in his silence. "Who'd you make mad enough to get you sent here?"

It's a simple enough question, but somehow it feels like a test. Like the answer will determine what happens next. The ground is damp, and it seeps into my pants like my growing unease. People don't survive the Ruins, but this man is comfortable here, unnervingly so.

"Well?"

"I, uh, it doesn't matter," I say.

Then his staff is pressing into my chest. Not painfully, but with enough pressure that I know he could pin me to the ground faster than I could scurry away.

"Yes. It *does* matter." The pressure increases slightly. "Start talking, kid."

I squint into the light, trying to see past it to the man, but I can't. There's something about him, something I can't put my finger on. But he's different from the soldiers. It's almost like he's wary of me, even though he has the upper hand.

I answer his question. "Colonel Valarius and Sergeant Meritas. They sent me here because I refuse to do everything they want me to do."

"I'm sure there's more to it than that." The pressure on my chest lifts. "How long were you sentenced for?"

"Twenty-four hours."

He grunts. "What'd they charge you with?"

"Assault of a soldier."

He removes the staff from my chest. "Really?"

"Yes."

The light shifts, and I can almost make out part of his face. The shadow of a dark beard with flecks of gray clings to his jaw, but his eyes are still hidden beneath his hood. Then he reaches down toward me and offers his hand. Black words tattoo his arm: Honor God. With a small cross underneath. Who is this guy? Other than Storm, no one in Talionis speaks of God.

I hesitate for a moment, then take his hand and allow him to help me up.

"Fighting against Talionis doesn't come without its price. Be careful." He turns to go away, then pauses. "You should never have had to face the things you're facing. It's not right."

His words wrap themselves around me, reach into my heart. Whoever this man is, whatever he's doing out here, those words capture me.

He walks away, and I step toward him.

"Wait."

He doesn't turn around.

I chase after him. "Where are you going?"

"I have work to do."

I walk faster and close the distance to him. I grab his sleeve. "But I don't know where to go."

He sighs.

"Please. Don't leave me here alone." Desperation has found its way into my voice, and I don't know how to remove it.

I'm terrified of this man but also drawn to him.

He approaches me again, looming over me. His hood falls off, and for the first time, I glimpse his face. It's bronzed and weathered, and his hair is charcoal black and sprinkled with gray. But it's his dark, searching gaze that freezes me in place.

I hardly breathe as he studies me.

Then he nods. "Fine. Let me see your wrist."

"Why?"

He grabs my wrist and examines the HaloAct Band. Leaning his staff against a tree, he retrieves something from his pocket. He fiddles with the lock on the clasp until it comes undone and removes the band from my wrist.

"I have work to do tonight. If you don't want to be alone, you can come with me." He grabs his staff. "But I can't say it'll be any safer than waiting in this clearing."

With that, he sets off at a pace just shy of a run.

I hesitate for less than a second before I take off after him.

He moves over the forest floor and through the maze of trees and fallen buildings with the ease of familiarity. I stumble over a rock, and the whisper of uncertainty threads its way through me. Is this the best idea?

I have no idea who this man is, and he's comfortable here. No one is comfortable in the Ruins. I regain my footing and hurry to catch up. Whether or not this is a good idea doesn't matter. It's definitely a better option than waiting around for a pack of wild animals to finish me off.

A few minutes later, the man approaches a dilapidated building, then disappears inside. I pause. Buildings collapse out here for no reason, so entering one seems like a bad idea.

The darkness of the night is thick now that the man has stepped inside with his light. Something rustles in the trees behind me. Okay. Inside it is.

I step over broken bits of concrete, enter. And stop.

This is *not* what the inside of an abandoned building should look like.

Debris and rubble have been cleared from the floor. The room is well-lit, and there's a table and entire communications center set up. At least that's what it appears to be. The man has multiple screens, and he has something up to his ear. His face is lined in concentration, and I almost think he forgot about me.

Which is probably a good thing.

I need to get out of here. He's probably working with Colonel Valarius, and this is all a trap. I step back, and something crunches under my foot. The man whirls toward me.

"You're one of them, aren't you?" My voice is unnaturally high. "You're a soldier of Talionis."

He sets down the device he was listening to and faces me, arms crossed. "No, I'm not."

I sweep my hands over his equipment. "You expect me to believe you?"

One shoulder lifts. "I don't expect you to believe anything, but it's true." He focuses on one screen, pokes at it.

And I stand there and watch. Because, as much as it terrifies me, I want to believe him. I want to believe there's a man who isn't like every other soldier I've encountered in the last weeks.

I move toward him, curiosity propelling me. "What are you doing?"

He doesn't look up. "Work."

"So, you do work for them?" Please let the answer be no.

He arches an eyebrow at me. "No."

A moment later, a nearby explosion rips through the night.

I collapse to the floor, hands covering my head, ears ringing.

"You can get up," the man says.

I lower one arm and peer over at him. He's at his desk, unfazed by the explosion. My heart is still pounding. "What was that?"

"What's your name?"

I guess we're just going to ignore the fact that something *exploded*.

I sit up. "Bria."

He taps away at a screen, then nods. "Your story checks out, Bria." He leans back in his chair. "I'm Cai. Welcome to one of my sites."

"One of your *what?* Who are you? What is going on? How did you end up here?"

The side of Cai's mouth quirks into a grin. "Your questions all lead to long stories. But I'll tell you this much. I escaped Talionis. Now I fight them from here."

I stare at him. None of that makes sense. There's no way he could be a recruit. He's at least thirty or forty years older than me, and Talionis hasn't been around for that long. "Were you a soldier?"

"No."

An alarm sounds on one of his screens. Cai leaps to his feet, taps on the screen, and then picks up a bag. "You're welcome to stay here. There's a cot in the corner, and you'll be safe enough. I'll be back in the morning."

"Where are you going?"

He's almost out the door before I can get the question out. "I have to handle something."

He disappears outside. I stare at the place he stood a moment ago, then run to the door. When I look out, there's no sign of him.

I move back inside and go over to his desk. There are seven screens set up, but they're all off now. If Ari was here, she'd be breaking into them and figuring out who Cai is and what he's doing out here. But I don't have her skills with tech.

I search the room, but there's nothing else of much interest. There's a cot in the corner, like Cai said, and it beckons me. Maybe I can rest. Just for a little.

Cai is an enigma, but, though a part of me knows I should fear him, I'm not as scared of him as I am of Colonel Valarius or any of the soldiers in Talionis. I sit on the cot. He said he'd be back tomorrow. I yawn, my eyes drooping.

My head hits the pillow, and exhaustion washes over me.

CHAPTER
TWENTY-THREE

The next morning, I wake to find a plate of food on a small table near the cot but no Cai. I sit up, mouth watering. There's dried meat and cheese and an apple. Food with *flavor*. Without giving myself time to question whether or not it's safe to eat, I dig in.

Cai enters the room a moment before I decide if I'll lick the plate clean. He looks from the plate to me.

"Guess you were hungry. What are they feeding you in there?"

I set the plate down and pull my legs up onto the cot. "I mostly eat gruel, but that's because I'm not really applying myself in my training. Other recruits eat better."

I'm not sure why I'm sharing this with him, but Cai's easier to talk to than I expected.

He settles into his chair and pulls another apple from his bag. "Still hungry?"

My stomach growls in answer, and he smiles slightly, then tosses me the apple. I take a bite, the sweet juiciness exploding in my mouth. So. Good.

"They reward you if you do what they want? Punish you if you don't?" Cai asks.

I freeze before taking another bite, lower the apple. "Yeah."

Uncertainty pricks at me. I'm getting too comfortable here. I don't know this man or why he's here.

He leans forward, arms resting on his knees. "Are there other rewards? Beyond just food?"

I spring up. "Why are you so interested in this?"

He stands as well, dark eyes observing me, seeing through me. "Because I need to better know my enemy in order to understand what they're planning."

I glance from Cai to the door.

"Leave if you want to. I won't stop you."

The urge to run lessens. "How did you end up in Talionis?"

"If I answer your question, will you answer mine?"

I nod.

"I was forced here."

I cock my head. "Where are you from?"

"Eryndale."

My eyes widen. "The mountain refuge?"

He nods slowly.

My heart clenches and twists as the dream that was shattered the moment I woke in the forest gets prodded. It's one more thing those in Talionis robbed me of. I'll probably never become an Eryndalian scout, never even *see* Eryndale.

I swallow back some of the bitterness and eye Cai with new interest, caught between wanting to know more about the sanctuary in the heart of the mountains that's the reason so many survived after the Demise, and also unsure if I'm ready to face the fact that the one thing I've wanted to do for years will never become a reality. A new thought pushes past my internal dilemma.

"But…" I shift, confused. "How could they find you? Let alone *take* you from there?"

The exact location of Eryndale is hidden, and getting into the refuge is supposed to be impossible without the aid of a scout.

Cai folds his arms over his chest. "I wasn't taken from there. I was on a mission." His eyes appraise me. "The details are unimportant."

A mission. He was a scout. I open my mouth to ask another question, but the look on his face stops me. He's not going to offer any more information about his capture. The desire to know more, not only about his capture, but about what it was like to be a scout, stirs inside me, but I clamp it down. He clearly doesn't want to relive any of it, and there's no point in me knowing more about something I'll never be able to become.

I change topics. "How did you end up in the Ruins?"

"I escaped. As I told you. Just didn't get as far as I had hoped I would."

"What do you mean, you escaped?"

He studies me, appearing to decide if he'll answer. He grunts. "When they first brought me to Talionis, I had no other choice but to do what they wanted."

I lean forward.

"I was helping them build their city, and it was grueling work. But one day, something happened." He stares at the floor. "And I had enough. It no longer mattered what they held over me. I couldn't be part of what they were doing. I wanted to leave and stop them. They *have* to be stopped." He rakes a hand through his hair and sighs.

"How'd you get out?" I whisper the question, hoping my voice doesn't stop his flow of words.

"I discovered a way to get into the Ruins undetected while I was working near them. One night, I used the passage and escaped. I thought I was free. Didn't realize they had erected the wall." Cai's head droops at the memory, and I find myself feeling defeated for him. "I tried to take the river and swim under, but they have it barred with lasers. I almost drowned."

I wince at the word. "How long ago was that?"

"Three years." He picks up his staff from where it's resting against the desk. "Now your turn. What rewards do they give to those who excel?"

Questions for Cai crowd in my throat, but I swallow them back. He gave me more of an answer than I expected. Time for me to return the favor.

"Beyond food, lighter duties and commendations. They say

they'll bring the best recruits into advanced training and give them higher security clearance."

Cai gives one nod. "Okay."

He heads toward the door.

"Where are you going?" I ask, not ready to be left alone again.

"Back to work."

"What do you mean? What work could you possibly have to do out here? It doesn't make sense."

He studies me for a long moment. "Come with me if you'd like. I'll show you some of it."

A thousand reasons *not* to follow a strange man into a dangerous place blast through my mind, but I go after him anyway.

For the next few hours, I follow Cai through the Ruins. We hike what he calls "trails" through the dense undergrowth and over the discarded remains of the old city, and he stops at different points to check things. I don't ask questions, though I have many. Instead, I watch, the picture of who Cai is becoming clearer.

He sets explosives under a couple of buildings.

There are four hideouts and platforms camouflaged high in the trees that he brings me to, each stocked with weapons and clear views of the sky and ground.

And the whole time he has had a com device in his ear just like what the soldiers wear.

He's not a soldier—I'm surprised at how certain I am of that fact. But he's also dangerous.

We come to the river, and, on its banks, is the burned shell of a small transport.

"You're the reason everyone's scared of the Ruins, aren't you?"

"Hard to say." Cai ducks into the transport and retrieves a weapon. "I'm not in Talionis to hear the rumors."

I gesture to the transport. "Did you take that down?"

He inclines his head in affirmation.

"The explosions, soldiers going missing, fires—all of that's you?"

Another nod.

"But who's out here with you? Who helps you?" I ask.

"No person. But I'm not alone."

"What?" That makes no sense.

"They'll be coming to pick you up in a couple of hours. I have one more thing I want to show you." Cai hikes away from the river, evidently expecting me to follow.

I'm tempted not to, just to see what he does, but I don't want to stay by the fallen transport alone, and I'm more and more intrigued by this man whose presence in the Ruins can terrorize an entire city of soldiers.

The air cools as the sun sets. My fingers grow numb, so I tuck my hands into my pockets and bury my chin in my jacket. It takes a while, but then we pass a huge bell with a thick crack in it and arrive at a fence covered in twisting vines and leaves, and Cai stops. The fence stretches as far as I can see in either direction until it's swallowed up in the forest.

Of all the things Cai's shown me today, this is the least impressive. "Why are we at a fence?"

"It's time for me to do more than hide in the Ruins and fight the ones who enter, but I need your help."

I stare at him, unable to comprehend what he's saying. "What are you talking about?"

"Escaping. Bringing down Talionis and Demetrius Ark."

"*What?*"

A bird screeches and flies out of a nearby tree.

I grip the back of my neck. "You can't be serious."

He doesn't say a word, but from the look in his eyes, he's definitely serious. Deadly serious. My heart leaps at the possibility he's suggesting, but I squelch the excitement. It's too much of a risk even *talking* about this. "There's no way we can do it."

"You're wrong about that." His face lights up. "We'll use their own system against them. I'll help you. Train you." His arms move rapidly as he speaks. This is the most animated I've seen him. "We'll gather others, and we *will* escape and defeat them."

Hope flares. What if he's right? What if we really could get out of here? Laban and Colonel Valarius's faces flash through my mind, and the hope gets buried by the reality of who my enemy is and what they're willing to do to stop anyone in their way.

What would happen to Storm or my friends if they ever found out I'm plotting to escape? Besides, how can I be sure I can trust Cai? I desperately want to believe he's offering me a real opportunity to get out of this nightmare, believe he's exactly who he says he is. But it's too good to be true. He's done enough to bring fear over any soldier who crosses into the Ruins, but he hasn't been able to actually get *out* of here.

"It won't work." I hear the hollow echo of defeat in my voice.

Cai reaches out a hand like he's going to put it on my shoulder but then pulls back. "Please, Bria. Work with me. Help me."

And I want to agree. To say I'll do it. But I can't. "No. I can't. I'm not going against them again. It's too risky."

He opens his mouth but then closes it and looks down at the ground. "Well, if you change your mind," he bends down and pushes aside a portion of the fence, "this is how you can return to the Ruins without being detected. You'll find this hole if you go through an abandoned building on the outskirts of the housing unit behind the Physical Training Arena. For the next two weeks, I'll come here every night at twenty hundred hours, and I'll wait. If you change your mind, I'll be here."

I'm about to tell him there's no way I'll change my mind, but something stops me. Instead, I simply nod in acknowledgment. Cai brings me back to where the transport will pick me up, finds the wrist band he removed and refastens it to my wrist.

I turn to enter the clearing, but Cai places his hand on my shoulder.

"God, thank You for bringing Bria here," he prays. "Protect her. Keep her from the darkness of this city, and show her the way you intended is one of healing, not the evil of Talionis. Bless her, Jesus. Amen."

With that, he disappears into the forest.

TWENTY-FOUR

I perch on a boulder in the clearing, barely noticing the cool and slightly damp surface. My time here has been nothing like I expected. The Ruins are everything the soldiers claim it to be, everything they fear. And I met the man responsible.

A man who takes down soldiers bent on harming people, and who prays for a girl he just met. The dichotomy plagues my mind. Yet it's because Cai has both those sides that makes him someone I want to trust—which is an uncomfortable feeling.

Could I take him up on his offer?

Is escape, stopping those in Talionis from accomplishing their plan, possible?

The muscles in my legs tense as I consider running after Cai and agreeing to work with him. I press my palms into the boulder until I feel the jagged surface imprinting itself on my hands and bringing me back to reality.

The risks involved in agreeing to help Cai are too great. What would happen to Storm or my friends if Colonel Valarius or Laban or whoever the Commander is found out I was plotting to escape? Or what if I *did* escape?

The rock vibrates, and I leap off it, afraid it's something else Cai rigged to blow.

Then I register the low, mechanical whirring of the transport descending to the clearing. I smooth my shaking hands down the front of my jacket, trying to calm my suddenly on-edge nerves and bring my mind back to the moment. I can't allow myself to be so distracted that I don't notice a transport approaching.

The hatch of the transport slides to the side, and Sergeant Andor Valarius steps into the opening. His hair is pulled out of his face into a stubby ponytail, and he scans the clearing before his eyes settle on me. Shock ripples over his features, but then his impassive scowl returns and he gestures for me to come to him.

I make my way toward the transport, each step weighted with the heaviness of discouragement. It's not only about the risks. I can't trust myself, let alone trust Cai. If I agree to his plan, he could end up betraying me, and I'd never see it coming. After all, that's what Aunt Elena did, and I never once suspected anything.

Sergeant Valarius unlocks my band and removes it, replacing it with a new one. "Your band malfunctioned while you were in the Ruins and stopped tracking you. You're lucky we got a read on your location again this evening, or you would have been presumed dead."

I take a seat in a chair facing the back of the vehicle. There are four passenger chairs in this transport, two looking out the back and two facing the front, along with the seats for the pilot and copilot. I mindlessly watch out the back window as we take off and head toward Talionis. The scenery passes by in a blur, and the pilot takes evasive action. Even with everything going on, the fact almost makes me smile.

These soldiers, with all their weaponry and technology, are afraid of one old man.

When we cross out of the Ruins, Sergeant Valarius moves from the copilot seat and sits in the chair across from me.

"Congratulations," he says. "You survived the Ruins. When we arrive back in Talionis, you'll be debriefed." He runs his thumb along the scar on his face, shooting a glance over my shoulder at the pilot. Then he leans forward, resting his forearms on his knees. "I must caution you, Bria," his voice has dropped to a low whisper. "There will be some who will not be happy you survived. If you continue to underperform or act out, the consequences will be more severe. Understand?"

His eyes lock on mine, awaiting my response.

I swallow, then nod. "Yes, sir."

I'm not sure if he's telling me this as a warning or a threat.

He leans back. "You'll miss dinner since you must debrief before returning to your unit." His voice is at a normal level now.

I pick at my fingernail, unnerved by the conversation.

The transport descends on top of the Main Headquarters, and Sergeant Valarius stands, grasps my arm, and pulls me to my feet. The door opens, and I'm escorted into the building. We walk down a flight of stairs and then a long corridor before we stop at the door to a private office.

Sergeant Valarius knocks three times, then clasps his hands behind his back as he waits to be admitted. I stand at an angle behind him and shift back and forth. Uneasiness inches its way through me. Before I can place my finger on why, the door opens, and Laban appears.

His eyes widen slightly when he sees me, but it's quickly replaced by loathing. I'm not happy to see him either, but I try to keep that from showing on my face, not eager to do anything to increase the trepidation I'm already fighting.

"Come in." He motions for us to enter the office.

Sergeant Valarius and Laban murmur to one another once the door closes behind us, but I ignore them, still on edge.

The room is boxy and might have been spacious if not for the enormous desk, cluttered with papers and file screens and a large monitor. An oversized chair rests behind it, with several smaller chairs cowering together on the other side. The heaters lining the wall emit a low hiss, like the warning of a snake before it strikes. Sunlight streams in through the windows, but the heavy drapes on either side seem eager to leap over them and plunge the room into darkness.

Several screens hang from one side wall, frozen on images of a city. The other wall is covered in shelves filled with books and a variety of trinkets. But it's the picture all the shelves have been built around that catches my eye. It's of a woman. Her deep brown eyes hold secrets that both intrigue and frighten me, and dark curls cascade around a beautiful, but almost haunted, light brown face. There's something about her that pulls me in and makes me want to know who she is. As I study the image, the shelves shift, and a gust of air blows against me as a hidden door opens, and Colonel Keenan Valarius enters the room. My jaw goes slack.

Laban walks over to Colonel Valarius and whispers something. Colonel Valarius's eyes lock on me before he turns and pushes a button, closing the door. I look past him at where the space once was. There's evidence of nothing more than shelves. If I hadn't just watched him emerge from the wall, I would never have even guessed the door was there. Where does it lead? What could—

"Recruit Averton." Colonel Valarius's sharp voice whips me around. He's sitting at his desk, and his dark eyes bore into me. "Come here."

I stand in front of the desk. Laban and Sergeant Valarius remain by the door at attention. Colonel Valarius's fingers drum against the desk in a slow rhythm as he studies me.

My palms grow sweaty, and my heartbeat thunders in my ears, drowning out the sound. I clench my hands into slimy fists at my sides and wait.

His eyes narrow as he studies me. The look on his face is murderous. In one swift movement, his fingers cease their drumming and grasp a gun I hadn't seen on his desk. He points it at me.

This time, he's not going to have Laban enforce the punishment. If only all I was facing were Laban's drills in the sandpit—or even his fists.

My hands tremble.

Colonel Valarius tilts his head.

I'm not ready to die.

He releases the safety.

Sweat drips down my back. *Ba boom. Ba boom. Ba boom.* My heart ticks off the milliseconds.

Colonel Valarius pulls the trigger.

Bam! The shot echoes through the room an instant before pain explodes in my right shoulder. My mouth opens in a cry I don't hear, and my left hand gropes for the wound. He shot me. Colonel Valarius actually shot me. The pain ebbs slightly. My body must be shutting down. I'm dying. My knees weaken, and I drop into a chair.

I stare at him in disbelief, and his lips curl into a satisfied smirk.

"Don't be so dramatic, Recruit. It's merely a training bullet."

I pull my hand away from my shoulder, sure I'll find blood seeping between my fingers. But there's nothing. The pain dissipates more, though there's still a sharp ache. I'm not dead. My body shakes as adrenaline releases.

No wonder so many recruits have been eager to escape the Kill Zone. Those bullets hurt.

Colonel Valarius drops the gun onto his desk with a clang, bringing my focus to him. The smirk is gone.

"Next time you stand before me because you've failed to abide by the rules of Talionis, I can assure you, I will use the real thing. I have given up much for the goals we're working to achieve. Do not for a second think getting rid of you would cause me to lose any sleep." His voice is deceptively calm, like the eye of a storm. "Now, I trust that I have your attention?"

I nod and grip my hands to stop the shaking.

He steeples his hands together on the desk. "Anyone who can survive a stay in the Ruins has the potential to do great things in Talionis. Just by doing so, you've proven that you're the kind of recruit we need. You're behind in your trainings, but now that you're thinking more clearly, I expect to see rapid improvements. Understood?"

"Yes, sir." My voice sounds choked.

"Very good." He pushes back from the desk and stands.

I remain seated until I notice the impatient expression on his face. I scramble to my feet.

"You're dismissed."

Laban takes my upper arm in a tight hold and escorts me from the room.

Fear grips my mind, but I can't keep myself from wondering how they could expect me to believe the creation of Talionis was all for the good of the survivors of the Demise. If that was true, I wouldn't be afraid for my life.

CHAPTER

TWENTY-FIVE

"Y^{ou'll} join your roommates in their nightly chores cleaning uniforms," Laban says as we exit the building.

I nod, but I'm confused. Nika and Ari *never* receive the same chore assignments as me. Nika is too skilled in PT, and Ari is a genius with tech. They do well enough in their respective areas to eat well and not have to join me in the worst chores.

So what did they do to get laundry duty? It's exhausting, dirty work.

We enter the tailor's room, and Laban hesitates.

Sampta and Presidia hunch over a recruit uniform at their workstation, holding up different pieces of fabric and murmuring to each other.

"What are you doing?" Laban asks.

The women look up simultaneously.

"Improving these atrocities." Presidia pokes at the uniform with disgust.

"Did the Commander give the orders for the change?" Laban seems to attempt more civility than I would expect from him, but his grip on my arm tightens.

"Well no," Sampta says. "But really, I'm sure he'll agree. He has fabulous taste."

"Doesn't he though?" Presidia clucks her tongue. "I mean, he did hire us to handle his wardrobe, after all."

"Oh yes, and that new jacket we designed for him last week is positively exquisite, if I do say so myself."

The two women giggle, which feels out of character for how I've seen them, but then again, they *are* strange.

"Ladies!" Impatience laces his tone. "You cannot change the recruits' uniforms."

They stand at the same time, as though they rehearsed it. "And why not?"

Laban's lips press into a thin line. He shoves me toward the laundry room. "Join the others. I have to deal with this," he says through clenched teeth.

A part of me would love to stay and witness what happens next. The two women are unafraid of Laban, which is a first. Every soldier cowers when they're addressed by him. But Laban doesn't seem himself with these ladies either. Maybe it has something to do with the fact that they apparently dress the Commander.

I slip through the door at the back of the room as Sampta starts explaining how adding color and style to the uniforms will be good for morale. Laban's voice is just shy of a strangled cry as he cuts her off.

"You're alive!" Ari leaps to her feet as soon as I enter the laundry room.

"Girl, it is so good to see you. But why are you smiling?" Nika says from her position, bent over a pile of soiled laundry.

I point with my thumb back through the door. "Sampta and Presidia are having a *discussion* with Laban."

Nika snorts. "I've never met anyone like those two. They came in here earlier, made a comment about how 'drab' Ari and I look, grabbed a clean uniform, and left talking about how they had to 'improve them.'"

I join my friends, and we add loads of dirty, smelly uniforms to the two massive washers.

Nika sobers. "We thought you were dead."

I add a few more uniforms to the washer. "How did you guys end up with laundry duty?" I ask, unsure of how to respond to Nika's statement.

"Because we're friends with you," Ari says with no hint of anger.

Nika studies me for a moment. "Guess they figured if by some chance you survived, we would be ticked with you for doing something that got us in trouble."

"Sorry," I say as we move to the dryers. "They took Storm, and—" I freeze. "Wait. Have either of you seen her?"

They share a glance and then shake their heads. As we add wet uniforms to the dryers, I quickly share what happened and how I ended up sent into the Ruins and my fears for Storm.

Nika shuts the door to a full dryer and turns it on. "They said you attacked a soldier for no reason. Not that I'm surprised they'd lie."

The dryer whirs to life, clothes thumping against the door.

"Right after they led you past all of us and flew you to the Ruins, they brought Shay up in front of everyone." Nika rolls her eyes.

She and Ari tell me how Colonel Valarius gave a speech, honoring Shay for her loyalty, commending her, and providing her with extra privileges for a week for reporting on me. Then he announced all recruits are encouraged to report any fellow recruit they find who is not adhering to the ways of Talionis or who isn't living up to their best potential for the Commander. Any recruit who reports on someone else will receive special commendations and rewards.

With each thing they share, my stomach drops. This will not be good. Not only is Colonel Valarius watching me with more intensity, Shay and every other recruit buying into this place will be looking for any moment I slip up.

One of the dryers beeps that the load is finished, and all three of us startle. We fold uniforms in silence for a few minutes.

"What were the Ruins like?" Ari asks. "How did you survive? I heard some soldiers talking earlier today about losing two more soldiers in there last night, but you made it back."

Cai. He's the answer to Ari's question, but I'm not sure if I can talk about him. Not yet. Not until I figure out how to process everything that happened...and the opportunity he offered me. Plus, if it's all somehow one elaborate trap, the less my friends know, the better. Once I figure it out more, and decide what to do, then I'll tell them.

"Hello? Bria?" Nika waves her hand in my face. "You there?"

I swat her hand away. "Yes, I'm here. The Ruins were everything the soldiers claim." Well, that's accurate enough. Cai has made the place terrifying for anyone who enters from Talionis. "But the most terrifying part was facing Colonel Valarius when I got back."

Ari folds a uniform and adds it to the stack. "What happened?"

"He shot me with a training bullet."

Ari gasps.

I force myself to continue. "And he told me, if I don't start improving, the next bullet will be real."

Nika lets out a low whistle. "I wish I was more surprised. I guess surviving the Ruins makes you valuable enough for them to keep around, rather than making you another recruit who disappears."

Like Mason Percleon. After his "walk" with Laban, he wasn't seen again.

The door opens, and Sampta and Presidia waltz in. They screech to a halt next to our pile of folded uniforms.

Presidia's eyes bulge. "You call *this* proper folding technique?"

"Abhorrent," Sampta says. "Absolutely abhorrent."

For the next hour, Sampta and Presidia watch us like vultures, making sure we fold every uniform exactly the way they want it.

I tune them out. The bruise on my shoulder pulses, and everything my friends and I just talked about, runs through my mind. I'm going to have to try harder in my trainings, do better. I don't have a choice. But, as much as the thought of giving in to them bothers me, another thought is more terrifying.

Where is Storm? And what are they doing with her?

I'm not sure what to do. I fold a uniform. Sampta gives my hand a whack when I go to set it down and tells me to fold it again. I suppress a retort. The hit didn't hurt, and at least this time they aren't making us hand wash every uniform, like they forced me to do another time I had this chore, but I'm tired, hungry, and have way too much on my mind to deal with these eccentric women.

By the time we finish, it's the middle of the night. We're all exhausted as we make our way back to our room. None of us says anything as we walk, but a thought forms in my mind.

"Ari," I say as we enter our room. "Do you think you can help me find where they're keeping Storm?"

She yawns. "I'll try. I can check the database and grids I have access to, see what I can dig up."

"Thanks."

She collapses onto her bed, not even removing her shoes.

"Careful," Nika says. "You don't want them to know you're in their system."

Ari pops back up. "Um, I'm way too good for them to know I'm there," she says indignantly.

Maybe Ari will be able to find Storm, and hopefully she'll be okay, but then what?

Go see Cai.

The whispered thought floats through my head. Cai's strength, kindness, resolve, understanding—his prayer—all flood my mind. As tired as I am, an urge to go find him right now fills me. Maybe he's right. Maybe we could escape, and I could bring Storm with me, save her from whatever they have planned for her.

But what if he's wrong? Or what if we fail?

My heart hammers as though I just finished a hard swim. The stormy waves of fear and anxiety slap at me, threatening to drown me.

I don't know what to do about Cai, but before anything else, I need to find Storm.

CHAPTER

TWENTY-SIX

I hurdle the last wall and race after my team to the next portion of the course. A shot rings out. I dive behind a fake bakery, those with me following suit.

"Aw, man," Belen groans. "Why are we always getting shot at?"

"I'm not sure we *want* to know the answer to that question." Cade scans the last portion of the race. "Bria, what do you think about doubling back and cutting through the alley over there and toward the church?"

I crouch next to him, eyeing the path he's suggesting. Cade sees paths through the bullets almost like I do, but whenever we're on the same team, he double checks with me before following the route he thinks will work. Where he really shines is in reading people. He always seems to know when someone's upset, or if something's about to change in our routine. It's uncanny but helpful.

"Looks good," I say. "We should try to stay close to the shed on the left side of the church once we hit that point."

Everyone agrees, and then we're taking the route Cade suggested.

The past few days since I've returned from the Ruins have been exhausting, mentally and physically. My instructors seem to push me harder than everyone else, and despite Ari's attempts, we haven't been able to locate Storm. Ari thinks they're keeping her out of the system or in a floating file—whatever that means. All I know is, she's somewhere in this city, and I can't go searching for her without risking both our lives.

Cade is worried about her too. I half expected him to hate me, or blame me. But he doesn't. All he's said about it is that he wishes he was more surprised.

I crouch low, leading my team down the alley. At the end, I pause, peer around the corner, and put my fist in the air, signaling for the others to stop. They follow me without question through any Kill Zone now—whether it's on our way to a meal or in an obstacle course. Their trust makes me more cautious.

Our route is clear.

I give the signal to move and then race out of the alley, toward the shed, and through the church. We come out on the other side and hit the finish line.

Before we can congratulate each other for getting through or find out what ranking our time came in at, Sergeant Valarius appears.

"Line up at attention with the rest of your unit for an announcement," he shouts.

We jog to where most of our unit is and join the perfect lines, snapping to attention. After a few minutes, the last team to be sent through the course finishes, and they line up with us. Nika comes to stand beside me, jaw clenched.

I can tell she wants to say something, but she stays quiet.

Soldiers march the other five units over, and once everyone is in position, Sergeant Valarius and Laban climb onto a raised mat to address us.

"Your first evaluation will be in four weeks' time," Sergeant Valarius says. "This evaluation will determine which squad you'll be placed in within your unit. Each unit will have five squads. The recruits with the highest ranking in the evaluation will be placed in Squad 1 of their respective units. The lowest ranking recruits will be in Squad 5. Everyone else will find their place somewhere in between. Understood?"

"Sir, yes, sir!"

"From today until your eval, we are going to push you harder and train you to be the best you can be," Sergeant Valarius continues. "Your schedules will also change. You'll begin training in hand-to-hand combat, Weaponry Skills, and Warfare Strategies. You will still have Educational Training once a week. Technical Training will also continue for the next four weeks. After the evaluation, things will change. Your bands have been updated with your new schedule."

Laban steps forward. "Are you gonna work hard, recruits?"

"Sir, yes, sir!"

"I can't hear you!"

"Sir, yes, sir!" The chant from the recruits is deafening, and it makes me nauseous that I have to say it with them, but I do.

"Good. Make us proud." Laban steps back.

The last thing I want to do is make that man happy, let alone *proud* of me, but when Sergeant Valarius tells us to gather closer for hand-to-hand combat demonstrations, I move with the rest of the recruits.

"I got shot three times in that Kill Zone," Nika hisses. "Three times. Please tell me you got hit at least once."

I shrug, and she rolls her eyes.

She lets out a disgusted sigh. "It's not fair that you and Cade were on the same team," she grumbles.

For the next twenty minutes, Sergeant Valarius and two other instructors demonstrate several defensive techniques and a few attack maneuvers. Sergeant Valarius moves faster than I imagined possible, defending himself and using the momentum of his attackers against them. There's no hold they try on him he isn't able to break, and both of the other soldiers end up on their backs on the mat over and over.

By the time the demonstration has finished, I almost feel sorry for the two guys.

They disperse our units throughout the arena, and Sergeant Valarius breaks up my unit into small groups to work on the fundamentals of hand-to-hand combat.

I end up in a group with Shane, Nika, Ari, and Belen. It doesn't take long before it's clear that Shane and Nika have the most potential in this area. They seem to understand what the instructor is telling them to do with very little instruction. The difference between the two of them is that Nika seems almost angry, and Shane looks like he's enjoying the praise from Corporal Mitts.

After Corporal Mitts works us through a few different combinations on our own, he has us divide into pairs to spar with each other. He puts Nika and Shane on a mat together, and Ari and Belen on another, leaving me to practice the series of strikes on the dummy available.

Left jab. Duck low. Right hook. Left jab. Step back. Front kick. The dummy shifts with each strike, then settles back in position.

"Want a partner?" Matthias is suddenly at my side, a grin smearing his face.

"What are you doing here?" Heat burns my cheeks. How long was he watching me before I noticed him?

"They asked some cadets who are skilled in hand-to-hand combat to come and help you guys train." He flexes, his bicep bulging, and winks. "You know I'm good at this, so here I am." He gives a slight bow. "At your service."

My cheeks heat more at the reminder of watching him spar, but I glare at him. "Can you *please* go bother someone else?"

"I'd rather work with you, Bria."

The way he says my name, the fact that he *knows* my name, makes me pause. "Why?"

"Because you clearly need the help, and I'm all about helping a pretty girl out." He wiggles his eyebrows.

Is he *flirting* with me? Seriously? "No."

"Averton, work with Matthias," Corporal Mitts shouts over. "Now!"

I want to smack the pleased expression off Matthias's face.

"Wow. The Corporal and I don't always agree, but I'm gonna have to thank him for helping me out on this one."

I roll my eyes.

In a blink, Matthias has dropped to the ground and done several one-handed pushups. "Just warming up." He springs to his feet.

"Okay, now I'm ready. And by the time we're done, we'll be friends." Another stupid wink.

What is with this guy?

"No, thank you. I'll work with you if I have to, but we will never be friends." I cross my arms. "You're just like everyone else here, with your agenda. I won't be a part of it."

Matthias steps close, his face dropping every trace of humor. "Don't assume you know who I am."

I shrug, but it's difficult. Something in his eyes catches me. "You're from here. I know enough." Even as I say the words, the conviction I want to feel about them is marred with uncertainty.

I turn back toward the dummy, hoping Corporal Mitts doesn't come back to confirm I'm obeying his order. I throw a jab, and Matthias catches it, his grip firm but gentle.

"No. You don't."

I try to tug away, but he waits a moment before releasing my hand. His words rattle through me, and I almost want to believe him. But I can't. Right?

"Now, let me help you." A small grin reappears. "Please."

I swallow. He is persistent, I'll give him that.

"Fine."

A full smile flashes. "Great. Now, let's work on getting out of your attackers' hold." Matthias turns his back to me. "Grab me from behind."

I stare a hole into the back of his head. I am *not* voluntarily touching him.

"Any day now, Bria."

"Can't you just explain what I'm supposed to do, and I'll work on the movements or something?"

He cranes his head around to look at me, eyebrow raised. "That won't really teach you anything. You have to practice." He looks forward again. "Now, grab me in a choke hold from behind, and I'll break away."

I let out a very audible sigh, but he doesn't appear to notice. I might as well get this over with. Stepping close behind him, I reach up, almost on my tiptoes, and wrap my arm around his neck.

A split second later, I find myself flipped over his shoulder and landing on my back, with a thud, onto the mat. Matthias reaches out a hand to help me up. I glare at him, shove his arm aside, and stand to my feet on my own. "I can see I'm going to learn a lot from you."

Matthias grins, unfazed. "I'll grab you this time and work you through how to get out of it."

I'm about to give an emphatic *no* when I realize Sergeant Valarius is watching us. "Fine."

Matthias grabs me from behind, his grip unyielding. He's too strong for me to get away from.

"Now," his voice is right by my ear, "start by elbowing me in the stomach."

I happily acquiesce, and I'm rewarded with a low grunt as he bends forward slightly.

"Not yet."

I smirk. "Oh, *sorry*."

"When I *say*," Matthias emphasizes, "elbow me in the stomach and stomp on my foot. Then, when I bend forward, shift, leverage my weight over your hip, and flip me to the ground. Got it?"

I nod.

"Okay, try it."

I do as he instructed and actually throw him to the ground. Maybe having his help isn't such a bad idea after all.

"Good. Now try again, but faster."

For the rest of Physical Conditioning, Matthias works with me through the maneuvers, correcting my positioning and movement almost every time I try to do something. I allow some irritation to show with each of his corrections, but by the time Physical Conditioning ends, I'm able to do much more than I could if I was practicing on my own. Not that I'll ever share that with him. He might be somewhat helpful, but his easygoing manner doesn't fool me. There's no way I'll ever trust anyone from here.

Sergeant Valarius dismisses us.

"Nice job," Matthias says. "I'll see you around." He flashes another smile that I'm sure gets plenty of girls' attention, then saunters away.

I watch him leave, unnerved. He's too *nice* to be from here. There has to be an angle.

"So did you have fun with the cute boy?" Nika asks, coming up next to me.

"He's annoying," I say. "You can have him next time."

This gets a laugh from Nika, and the two of us leave for our next training—Weaponry.

TWENTY-SEVEN

Nika and I enter the Weaponry Training Complex, and I force myself forward. I'm dangerous enough to people without placing a weapon in my hands.

The narrow hallway opens up into a rectangular room at the end. The ceiling stretches high overhead. Two long rows of tables, high enough so one can stand in front of them and not need a chair, run the width of the room, and cabinets filled with weapons clutter the perimeter, stopping where the second row of tables starts. Beyond them, the room stretches forward, empty space. The far back wall holds targets, and tracks mar the floor in intervals.

A man leans against the wall off to the side, observing us as we enter. There's an arrogance about him, even though he seems younger than the other soldiers in the room. Nika and I find a table near Cade, and Ari and Shane grab the other empty table nearby.

Once our entire unit has arrived, the guy pushes off from the wall. "My name is Lance Corporal Collin Sidon, and I'll be your instructor for Weaponry Training. Today, we will issue you your personal rifle. These rifles are to remain with you at all times. They will only be loaded on the firing range, and we will inspect each weapon to ensure it is not loaded before you leave the range." He paces the front of the room. "Your weapon will become a part of you.

Sleep with it. Keep track of it. Know its serial number. And go nowhere without it."

A soldier hands him a rifle.

"You have worked hard and earned the privilege of carrying your own weapon." He lifts the rifle. "This is a sign of respect. It shows you have achieved the status of a true recruit of Talionis." He lowers the gun. "But you must continue to prove that you have earned the right to carry your rifle. Understood?"

"Sir, yes, sir!"

"Obey orders, push yourselves, excel, and you will keep possession of this prize." His gaze almost caresses the weapon. "Disobey or fail, and have your weapon taken until you can earn it back. Understand?"

"Sir, yes, sir!" I shout the words, but the last thing I want is to carry around a gun, proving my loyalty to this place.

Lance Corporal Sidon signals to several soldiers, and they pick up crates full of rifles, and go about setting a gun in front of each recruit.

A soldier sets one in front of me. It settles on the table with a dull clang, the black metal glimmering in the room's light. It's menacing. I swallow the dread and wipe my sweating palms on my pants.

"The gun in front of you is your weapon. With it, you will have access to the lines for the best food at mealtime, and you will earn the respect of the soldiers around you." He nods toward us. "Pick it up. Get a feel for it."

Many recruits snatch their guns up, but I hesitate, along with a few others. Shay already has her weapon in her hands, and she's gazing at Lance Corporal Sidon with open admiration.

I look away, unable to watch. Closing my hands over the smooth surface, I take a deep breath and pick the gun up. The weight is unfamiliar, and the size and overall feel of the weapon, awkward. I want to drop it back on the table immediately, but I suppress the urge.

Ari hefts her rifle, eyes widening. "This is heavy."

My guess is she'd give anything to be settled anywhere else with a screen rather than holding a weapon, and for once I would happily join her. Anything would be better than this.

For the rest of class, we learn how to disassemble and

reassemble our weapons, clean and care for them, and the proper way to carry and hold them. By the end of class, as I'm leaving with my rifle slung over my shoulder, I'm sickened because I'm already more comfortable with the gun than I was a couple of hours before.

I jog to my room, the rifle on my back bouncing with each step, a constant reminder that they're happy with me. But now isn't the time to think about that. If I don't find Nika in our room, then there's no way the soldiers will stay happy with me . . . or her. Nika never misses a meal, but she missed breakfast, and now we're supposed to be going to our first Warfare Strategies training.

Though I want to find her and tell her class is about to start for *her* sake, I can't help but acknowledge that I don't really want to go to a training called "Warfare Strategies" by myself.

I reach our room and burst through the open door and stop short. Nika's here, and she's crying.

I stare, unable to stop myself. This isn't the Nika I know. My friend is strong, a fighter who keeps a clear head. She's not supposed to be the one who breaks down and *cries*. Ari, sure. I expect her to burst into tears at any moment, but not Nika.

I hesitate, unsure of what to do. I shift, and the floor creaks. Nika spots me. She takes a shuddering breath and swipes a hand over her face, brushing away the tears.

"You okay?" I ask, then wince. Dumb question.

Nika arches a perfectly formed eyebrow. "What do you think?"

"Sorry."

She shrugs and offers a half-smile. "We have Warfare Strategies soon, huh?"

I nod.

She sighs and rubs both hands over her face. "Kay. Let's go." She gets off her bed, knocking the comforter off, and grabs her rifle.

We exit the room at a quick pace, and I stay quiet. If she wants to share what's bothering her, she will, but I'm not going to push.

"I hate crying." She wipes a finger underneath her eye. "It's even worse when someone catches me."

I definitely understand that.

She sniffs. "Today's my birthday."

I glance at her but remain silent.

"I'm eighteen. I didn't think it would matter, you know? Didn't think it would be harder today than it's been every other day we've been here. But for some reason, I can't stop thinking about home." She adjusts her rifle, and we leave the living quarters building. "Usually, on my birthday, my sister and I spend the whole day together, just the two of us. I come from a big family, but my older sister always made sure to take care of me and make sure I felt...special."

Her shoulder lifts, then drops back down. "I miss her."

I sigh. "I get it."

We pass a group of recruits heading to Warfare Strategies.

"I hate it here," Nika says. "Some days I want to give up trying to find their weakness and just *fight*."

"Me too." The reality of where we are, of why Nika and I are even friends, suffocates me.

Maybe I should go see Cai, find out if his plan could actually work. I glance at Nika. Maybe she could be a part of it too. Something to think about. And maybe something I would actually *do* if I knew where Storm was, and that I could keep her safe.

We're about to enter the Warfare Strategies building, and I pause. "Nika."

She turns.

"Happy birthday."

She rolls her eyes, then smiles. "Thanks."

I open the door and stop halfway through the threshold to keep from pressing into the other recruits already crowded inside. It's quiet.

"What's going on?" Nika asks.

"No talking!" The grating voice screeches through the air, but I can't figure out where it's coming from.

Then the crowd parts, and I see the source. A short woman with black hair cut into a blunt bob and round black-rimmed glasses has her arms crossed tightly and her foot hammering out a staccato on the floor. She can't be much taller than Storm, and she has clearly learned to overcompensate with that voice.

"All of you can follow me. *Quietly.*"

She leads us down several hallways to a large open area. "Stow your rifles in your designated space on the wall racks, and then wait until your instructor arrives and tells you what to do." Without another word, she pivots and scurries from the room as fast as her little legs can carry her.

Nika and I find the digital tags with our names on them and add our rifles to the wall rack along with the other recruits. Then wait.

After a few minutes, the massive Black man from my hearing with the Council brushes by me and walks to the center of the room. His dark brown face is as hard as stone, and every hair has been shaved from his head so that it shines as the lights in the room reflect off it. He towers over everyone, and his muscles seem to have muscles.

"I am Major Tay Vasco." His deep voice rumbles through the room. "Warfare Strategies is going to play a huge role in determining how far you go in Talionis. The other trainings are important, but here we discover who will be great in this city. Those who excel will stand before the Commander himself."

I grimace, but quickly mask it. No need to advertise my revulsion to the mere idea of meeting the man in charge of all of this.

"The building is divided into eight sections. Each section has two zones. This is the Neutral Zone. We will meet here for each of your scheduled trainings with me." He crosses his arms over his broad chest, his muscles bulging even more.

"Today, I will assess you and determine what level of training you should be at. You'll be separated into groups, and each group will be taken to a different zone. Your group will be placed in a scenario, and in it you'll have to determine the strategy needed to defeat the enemy you come up against. Every scenario is vital, no matter how simple it may seem. You will face varying levels of difficulty. I'll put you in positions where you'll likely fail, but today, failure is expected." His eyes rove the room. "If you want to stand out, then don't perform as expected."

The only reason I want to stand out is because I'm fighting. Not because I'm performing better than expected. I don't even want to know what Warfare Strategies is all about, but the temptation to let myself just fail is pushed aside by the memory of Colonel Valarius, his gun, and his threat.

Major Vasco pulls a small screen from his pocket, taps a few buttons on it, and then puts it back. "We're ready to begin."

TWENTY-EIGHT

Vasco and a few others organize us into small groups, separating us according to our room assignments: one female room and one male room per group. Ari and Nika and I end up with Griffin, Asher, and Shane.

We're led down a series of hallways of black walls and white ceilings and stop before a room in section three, zone two.

"You're about to enter a scenario that will place you in a variety of environments." The woman who led us back rests her hand on a button near the door as she addresses us. "It's not real, but you'll feel like it is. It will condition all of your senses to believe what you're experiencing is, in fact, reality. You'll feel pain. You'll smell the environment. If you put something in your mouth, you will taste it."

I stiffen. How is any of this possible?

"Warfare Strategies contains some of the most advanced technology in all of Talionis."

Ari's face brightens, and I half-expect her to ask a question, but she stays quiet.

"While you're in the simulation, we will monitor your every move. What you do, how you interact with one another, and how you react to the scenario you're placed in will all be recorded. You'll be assessed based on these things. You'll be judged on how well you do as a team but, more importantly, how well you do individually. If your team does well in the beginning, your simulation will increase in difficulty. The higher you go, the better you'll look to the leaders." She appraises the six of us, and I fight the urge to run back down the hallway. "Good luck."

She presses the button. The door slides to the side as she steps away to reveal a black room yawning before us. Apprehension tightens my shoulders as we step through the door.

Once the six of us have crossed the threshold, the door clangs shut. Thick blackness engulfs us. I squint into the darkness, trying to make out the others. If I didn't know they entered with me, I would think I'm alone. I lift my hand in front of my face and accidentally hit myself in the nose. I've never been in a place this dark.

"You guys still here?" Ari's voice rises out of the blackness, cracking in fear.

"Yeah," Shane answers, sounding less assured than normal.

"Now what?" Nika says. If she's afraid at all, there's no way I can tell.

A light glimmers in the distance, but it's so faint, I wonder if my eyes are playing tricks on me.

"Do you see that?" I think it's Griffin who asks.

Okay, I'm not imagining it.

"Yeah," I say, the others echoing me.

The light grows steadily, and the room rumbles, the ground shaking beneath our feet. I blink, and in that instant, the room changes.

It's not a room anymore. We're outside, in the mountains some-where. The sun edges over the horizon, sending out its light into a new day. We're high on top of a mountain. I exhale, and my breath crystalizes. The smell of evergreen trees mixes with the scent of coming snow. Nika and I stare at each other.

"How is this happening right now?" she asks.

I shrug, beyond words.

There are a few trees scattered about, short and stumpy, cringing in the high altitude. We're standing on a flat, rocky ledge, barely big enough for the six of us, and there's an enormous pile of rocks on the right next to a medium size duffle bag that the guys go to. I lean over the side, and the sheer drop makes my stomach flip.

Ari tosses a rock over, and it bounds down the mountain.

"Wow," she breathes. "This is incredible. I wonder how they make it so lifelike." She pokes at her band, muttering to herself. "Maybe it's—"

Shouts from below cut her off and shatter the quiet of the early morning. Birds screech and rise out of the trees.

"Find them, and kill them!" The angry command is clear and close. Too close if they're coming for *us*.

All of us drop, and Shane and I ease ourselves to the edge. Fifteen soldiers, in uniforms I don't recognize, are marching up the side of the mountain, the barrels of their guns glinting in the early morning light. Shane signals to the rest of the group the direction they're coming from.

"Go that way." Shane mouths, pointing with two fingers to the left. We all nod, and Griffin takes the lead.

A small, precarious pathway is our only option. It's about a foot wide and slopes downward, with the cliff wall shooting up to the left and a straight drop to the right. I'm in the back of the group as we edge our way along the path. Griffin hesitates for a moment, stopping the rest of us in our tracks, and I crane my neck. The path curves, and it's impossible to see what's beyond. The sound of the soldiers moving up the mountain grows louder.

"Move faster," I hiss.

"Seriously? Do you *see* where we are right now?" Nika whispers back.

My feet shuffle forward, heart pounding in my ears. We round the bend, and the path opens up, continuing down into the trees. We race forward, into the forest. Our breath comes in short bursts as we try to take in as much of the thin mountain air as we can.

"What are we supposed to do?" Asher asks.

"Well, this is warfare training, so I don't think we're supposed to run," Nika responds.

Asher scowls at her.

"She's right," Shane says. "They want us to do something here. And I'm assuming that something is to take out the soldiers. We need a plan."

"I say we keep going down," Griffin pipes up. "Try to outrun them."

"Hello. That's still running," Nika says. "We need to *do* something." Her hands stress her words.

"They outnumber us and have weapons. Unlike us." Griffin snaps back.

"We've got weapons." Shane digs through the duffel bag. "Looks like a pistol for each of us, so not a lot."

"Bria, what do you think?" Nika asks.

"Um, excuse me?" I take a half step backward.

"You make it through every Kill Zone without getting shot, and you get others through," Nika says. "You see things no one else notices."

"She's right," Shane says.

Ari nods.

"That's different. I can find the way through a dangerous situation—not a way to *stop* armed soldiers." I pause. "Although..."

"There." Nika points at me. "That's the face I wanna see. You have an idea."

I stare through the trees, toward the soldiers. "Maybe."

Quickly, I outline a plan that divides us in half and has three of us returning to the ledge we just left to push the rocks over on the ascending soldiers while the others prepare to hit them from the side in case any get past the rockslide we hopefully create. It's risky, and a little foolish, but it's the best I can come up with.

Asher is hesitant, but when Shane agrees that it's our best option, he relents. Shane, Griffin, and I go to the ledge and Nika, Asher, and Ari take their positions.

"There they are!" A soldier yells as Griffin steps onto the ledge.

They're about seven hundred yards away.

Without talking, the three of us press our shoulders into the pile of rocks. It doesn't budge.

I grit my teeth and lean into them. The sharp edges scrape my hands and cut into my shoulder. Griffin and Shane grunt as they put all of their strength into pushing. Nothing seems to happen.

"Push together on three!" Urgency bruises my lungs with its weight and forces its way into my words. If this doesn't work, we've failed. Because of me. "One. Two. Three."

We push, and this time there's a shift. We clamber back as the rocks tumble over the edge on a collision course toward the soldiers. The ground beneath me rumbles as the rock slide picks up speed and debris. The soldiers cry out as boulders hurl toward them.

A few move into the path I predicted, still attempting to get to us. There's the sound of gunfire as the rest of our group fires.

The soldiers flee.

Before Nika, Ari, and Asher join us, everything goes black.

I slowly stand to my feet, my arms extended for balance. The room shifts, and I stumble, falling to my knees. Something creaks, and then wind rushes past my ears, and my hair flies around my face. I reach up to pull my hair together.

Then it's bright.

We're on the roof of a building overlooking a city. The building is tall but not as tall as the one across from us. That building soars into the sky, hundreds of feet above us. I crane my neck to stare up at it. The top extends over the rest of the building, almost like a hat, and it rotates slowly.

Buildings sprawl all around us, clustered together and glistening in the bright sunlight. The structure we're on top of has a flat roof, and it's empty of people except for the six of us. A short wall surrounds the perimeter. The air is thick and warm.

"Now what?" Asher asks.

Ari walks toward the wall. "What's that?" She reaches out and pulls a box out of the shadows.

"Open it," Shane urges.

Ari pulls off the lid, revealing a panel. There's a screen in the center with a strip of six squares underneath it, an unlit red light in the top left corner with a switch under it, and a large button on the bottom right.

"A Calintrone board," she mutters, more to herself than to us.

She flicks the switch. The screen springs to life with an image of the massive building across from us, and a mechanical voice relays instructions.

"Your target, the Intrentas Building, has been wired to explode. The device," an image of a bomb fills the screen, *"must be activated within the next three minutes. To activate, each of you must scan your right thumb on one of the finger strips below the screen. Once each of you has been identified, the light will flash. You then have thirty seconds to depress the button. If you do not complete this task, you will be executed by snipers positioned in nearby buildings."*

The screen blackens, and then a timer counts down from three minutes.

"Alright, let's do this," Griffin says. He stretches out his thumb.

"Wait!" I shove his hand away from the device. "Why are we supposed to blow up a building? There're probably *people* in there."

"Yeah. Based on the size of it, a lot of people." Nika's mouth tightens into a line.

"It's an order, and it's not real." Griffin gestures to a nearby building. "Plus, I don't feel like getting shot."

"It feels real enough," Nika says.

I nod. I can't bring myself to kill others just to save myself, even if this is all in my head.

"Two minutes remaining."

"We're running out of time," Asher says.

I step in front of the device. "No. We can't *do* this."

"Bria." Shane's eyebrows crowd together. "We don't have a choice. We have to follow the orders."

I look over at the building, our target, and watch as a young boy opens a door and steps out onto a balcony. I shake my head frantically. "No. No. I *won't* do it!"

"One minute remaining." The numbers turn from white to red.

Griffin shoves me out of the way and scans his thumb on a square.

"Recruit Griffin Dottle, scanned."

"Come on!" Griffin says.

Asher scans his thumb and then grabs Ari's hand and scans hers.

I back away from the device, away from the insanity of exploding a building and killing hundreds of people. I bump into someone.

Shane propels me back to the others. I push away, but his hands clamp harder on my arms.

"Sorry, Bria. We have to do it," Shane says.

I pull against his hold, but I can't find my voice to yell at him to let go. My traitorous feet won't resist enough to keep him from propelling me forward. I won't do this. I fight against his grip, wishing I had been working as hard as the rest of them, wishing I had enough physical strength right now to free myself from his grasp.

"*Thirty seconds.*"

Shane and I are only a few feet from the device, and Asher and Griffin are taking hits from Nika as they try to force her over.

"Get her over here!" Shane calls.

Asher grabs Nika from behind, but she throws him off and hits Griffin with a left hook.

Shane shoves me on the ground, pries open my fingers, and scans my thumb before I can get away. He jumps up and goes to help Asher and Griffin bring Nika over.

She puts up a fight, but the three of them are dragging her closer.

I race toward them, desperate to help Nika fight them off.

Griffin kicks me in the stomach, throwing me back.

"*Ten. Nine. Eight.*"

The three guys wrestle Nika to the box, and Shane scans her thumb.

Asher hits the button. The numbers stop flashing, and everything is silent for an instant.

Then the explosion rips through the air, piercing my ears until I hear nothing but ringing. The building we're on sways with the force. I can't look away as the tower buckles in on itself, smoke and flames devouring the structure. My ears clear, but I immediately wish they didn't as screams of horror take the place of the ringing.

"We did that." I'm gasping. "*We* did that." I turn on Shane and shove him. "*You* made me do that! They're dying. Because of *us*."

He winces at the accusation.

Blackness engulfs us once again.

TWENTY-NINE

The door slides open, and light from the hallway pours into the room. The silhouette of a man casts a shadow, his tall, broad frame filling the doorway. Major Vasco. He beckons to us, and we exit.

"Congratulations on completing your first challenge successfully," Major Vasco says as we emerge. "You'll continue to improve as we work with each of you in your unique skill sets. Your observation skills," his gaze connects with mine, "are good. We'll hone them until they're great. And in the first simulation, you worked well as a team." He shifts his focus to the guys. "In the second simulation, the three of you showed promise in obeying orders under pressurized conditions. However, you ladies have work to do in that area. You're dismissed," he says, and then exits the room.

I leave in a daze, angry about what they made me do. The screams of those about to die still fill my ears, and I press both hands to them to try to drown out the sound. But I can't. My stomach clenches and turns. I walk faster and then run into the closest bathroom, barely making it before everything in my stomach climbs up my throat and empties.

Numb, I retrieve my rifle from where I stowed it, and I head to the tech building. When I step inside the classroom, the familiarity of it wraps itself around me. This is probably the only time I've ever been happy to be here. Nika slips into her seat next to me a moment before class begins, and she looks livid.

"They had no right to do that to us," she says.

Her voice trembles with anger and something else. Something I can't identify.

"I'll tell you one thing," she continues, as Mandeville steps to the front of the class. "I'm gonna learn enough from Sergeant Valarius so that they can never force me into something like that again."

"Me too," I say, almost thankful for a reason to try beyond keeping myself from getting shot.

Then again, this reason feels almost as bad. I need to learn to fight so I can stop other recruits from forcing me to kill people in Warfare Scenarios.

None of this is okay.

The bell chimes, and Mandeville starts class. My screen displays the information and schematics of the tech he's talking about, and I let my mind grow numb as he waxes on about the item's uses. Ari is, as usual, working on something different from everyone else, but today there's an added intensity. Her fingers fly over the keys, and she's swiping at her screen with more force than needed. So much so that I'm almost afraid Mandeville will notice.

Class ends promptly, and I move with the surge of recruits to the door. I overhear Nika asking Ari what she could possibly see in Shane on the way out.

Several recruits laugh and joke with each other as they leave, but there are others who seem as shaken as I am.

I exit the building to find Matthias strolling by. He starts to smile and wave but then grows serious. I turn away from him and head to the dining hall for dinner. Not that I'm at all hungry.

Matthias falls into step with me but doesn't say a word. I glance at him, but he's focused straight ahead.

I stop, and he stops with me. "Matthias. Do you need something?"

"What's wrong?" His eyes squint as he studies me.

I pinch the bridge of my nose. "Nothing. I'm fine." Why didn't I wait to leave with Nika and Ari?

"No, you're not."

I blink. "Look. We're not friends, so even if something *was* wrong, you're the last person I would tell."

He nods. "It's Warfare Strategies, isn't it?"

I flinch at the reminder, giving myself away.

"The first one is always the worst." His face scrunches. "They get a little easier to handle the more you do."

My stomach clenches at the idea of doing another scenario, watching more people die, being responsible for their deaths. Yeah. Definitely not eating dinner tonight. I start down the street.

Matthias catches up to me, his hand resting on my arm to stop my progress. I arch an eyebrow at him, and he drops his hold.

"We could be friends, you know." His characteristic grin resurfaces, though not as fully as normal. "You might find I'm not as awful as you think I am."

"I doubt it." I again attempt to walk away.

He steps in front of me. "Wait. Just give me one chance. Come with me."

"No way." I try to step around him, but he moves with me.

"Come on. I want to show you something. It always cheers me up after a hard day."

A small part of me wants to go with him, to see if maybe there really is something that could get my mind off this day. I hesitate, trying to see his real motive, but he seems genuine.

He wiggles his eyebrows. "You don't have to come if you're too scared."

"Please. You don't scare me."

"Good. Let's go." He takes my hand and tugs me away from the recruits' living quarters.

I pull away, but curiosity keeps me following him through the streets of Talionis, even though the practical side of me says this is a bad idea. The sun is setting, and he picks up his pace. We pass areas I'm familiar with, and then we enter a housing district I haven't been in before. He walks us all the way through it until we come to an older, tall building with a large spire at the top. He opens the door, and I hesitate at the bottom of the stairs, adjusting the strap of my rifle. This is *such* a bad idea.

He turns back to me. "Quick." A grin splits his face. "If this is a trap, you've already gone too far to get out of it." He cocks his head toward the building. "One chance." He disappears inside.

I pull my lip between my teeth, then follow him in. He *has* helped me out, and he seems harmless enough. Though overly confident. Maybe he deserves this one chance.

It's dark inside, and I squint.

"Good," Matthias says from the dark shadows to my right. "You came."

I jump, which irks me. "What's so special about an old, dark building?"

"You'll see."

He disappears farther inside, and I try to follow but stumble over an empty box.

"Take my hand. I'll lead you through."

I shrink back. "No, I've got it."

"Let me help you, or we'll miss it."

"Miss what?"

His hand stretches out farther. "If you don't take my hand, you're never going to find out."

I tentatively take his hand, and his warm fingers curl around my cool ones in a solid grip. I immediately want to pull away, but he doesn't give me the chance as he urges me forward. After a few moments, we stop in front of a wall with a curtain draped over it. Matthias lets go of my hand, grasps the curtain, and pulls it aside.

My breath hitches in my throat as the exquisite colors in the image in the window reflect the light of the setting sun and cast the room into a mosaic of color. I turn in a slow circle, mesmerized by the dancing dust motes, the colorful blue and yellow and gold shapes marking the marred walls, the way the entire room is transformed. I face the window again, taking in the image for the first time. Some pieces of glass have been broken, but the entire picture is mostly whole.

It's of a cross, with doors flung open on either side. Beneath the picture are the words *Behold I have set before you an open door...*I draw in a shuddering breath. I wish someone would set an open door in front of me, but all I see are shut doors, locked tight.

"Pretty cool, right?"

I pull my gaze from the window and to Matthias. His head is tilted up as he studies the image, the colors lighting up his face.

"It is."

He sits down on an old, broken bench that has one side supported by a block. "This is where I come whenever a day ends up being more than I can handle."

He seems so peaceful, so...kind. Even though he can be a bit irritating, and can't seem to take a hint when I want to be left alone, it's hard to believe that he's actually from Talionis. But he is, and I can't let myself forget that.

"I'm surprised you ever have a day that isn't great," I hedge. "Aren't all of you cadets supposed to think everything about Talionis is wonderful?"

Matthias remains silent for a long moment, and I return my gaze to the window. The light is fading, the colors dying away with the setting sun. The beauty is evaporating, just like all illusions do.

There's a creak as Matthias leans forward, arms resting against his knees, head bowed. "You want me to be one way, Bria," his head comes up, and the last of the light spreads across his face as he stares at me, "but haven't I done enough to show you I'm different?"

I tuck a loose curl behind my ear, not sure how to respond. Moments that Matthias has helped me, stood up for me, tried to make me smile, pop into my mind. The room becomes more shadowy, just like my thoughts. Nothing is as clear as it was a moment ago.

"I don't understand you," I blurt out, realizing how true the words are once I've said them. I don't understand why he helps me, or sticks up for me, or even why he's trying to cheer me up.

Matthias stands and walks over. "You don't understand me, because you don't want to. You want everything and everyone here to be the evil monster you imagine they are."

He licks his lips and looks away. "And there *are* those people here —I'll give you that. But it's not how everyone is." He focuses on me again, the lines of his face accented by the shadows. "It's not how I am."

I swallow, disconcerted by his words, at a loss for a response.

"I know what it's like to have those you love ripped away from you. My family..." His voice cracks, and he clears his throat. "I lost my parents. When I was having a really hard time, when everything was falling apart in my life, someone was a friend to me, and it changed everything. Let me be that kind of friend for you."

My heart pounds in my chest, and my brain whirs like a piece of machinery as I try to figure out why Matthias would offer me his friendship, what his real motives are, why he acts like he cares that I'm struggling. And the thing that scares me the most is that all I see in his face, in his posture, all I hear in his words, is sincerity.

"I don't know if I can."

He nods, though his shoulders slouch forward. "We should go before someone comes looking for you."

He walks back the way we came, and my stomach lurches. I feel like I just wounded him, and, for a reason I can't identify, it bothers me.

"Matthias."

He stops and looks back at me.

"Thank you for showing me this, for everything you've done for me." I swallow. "Nothing is how it should be in my life, and I'm just..."

"Afraid," Matthias finishes the sentence.

Even though I don't like the word choice, I know he's right. I'm terrified of allowing him to be my friend.

He comes back toward me. "Don't let fear keep you locked up. Take a chance. I won't let you down..." The left side of his mouth quirks up. "Friend."

THIRTY

"Listen up, Unit Six," Sergeant Valarius says.

I drop my hands to my side and turn away from Matthias. My drive to become better in hand-to-hand combat has won out over my uncertainty about having Matthias around. He's good at this, whether I like it or not, and he's not the worst teacher. He's been giving Nika pointers as well, but I'm almost positive he has to try harder whenever the two of them spar. She's a natural.

"We're gonna do a pit drill," Sergeant Valarius continues. "Hand-to-hand combat in the sandpit. Three minutes for each match. Both recruits keep their rifles if it's a draw. If you pin the other recruit, you keep your rifle *and* theirs. If you lose, you lose your rifle for the duration of the day. Understood?"

"Sir, yes, sir!"

"Good. Then let's go."

Matthias touches my elbow, and I jump slightly. "You've got this." He winks. "I'll cheer you on."

We march outside to the sandpit, and memories of my last time here wash over me. Matthias is saying something to me, but I don't hear him. All I can hear is the sound of Storm crying for me, see her reaching for me. Panic throbs through my veins. Where *is* she?

Ari hasn't been able to find her, and I've had very little time to search for her. My worst fear is that Laban made her disappear, like he's done with other recruits who couldn't hack the training.

A whistle blows, forcing my attention back to the present.

She's somewhere in this city, and I'll find her. But first, I have to do what I can to survive myself. And that means staying focused.

Sergeant Valarius tells us there will be five sets of recruits in the sandpit at a time. Sparring will begin at the sound of the whistle and end when they hear two short bursts. Nika is one of the first ten he calls in.

I watch her for the full time she's in and can't help but be impressed. She moves with fluidity and strength, and when the time is up, she's landed far more blows than she's received, and she has her partner pinned to the ground—the only one of the ten to do so.

She exits and makes her way back to where I'm standing. Every soldier she passes congratulates her, tells her she was impressive, and a few pat her on the back.

"Check it out," she says when she arrives, pointing with her thumb at her back. "I've got two rifles."

I roll my eyes. She seriously can't be buying into this crap. "Nika. For real?"

Her smile slips, and she gives me a sheepish look. "Sorry. Got into the moment a little too much there."

I'm in the third group of ten to enter the pit, and the feel of the sand beneath my feet brings the memories back again. Laban screaming in my face. My muscles aching. Storm's cries.

The whistle blows, and I register the sound like I'm far away from it. I'm fighting Griffin, and he rushes at me. A moment later, I'm on my back, breath whooshing out of my lungs. Then he's on top of me, pinning my wrists into the sand.

"Come on, girl," Nika shouts.

"You got this, Bria," Matthias says. "You know how to get back up."

I grit my teeth, bridge my hips and throw my hands toward them, forcing him to release his grip as he falls forward. I turn my head to the side to keep him from falling onto my face, then grab him around the torso, climb up, pin his left arm, and roll him into the sand.

I get to my feet, into attack position, as Griffin springs back up.

"There you go!" Matthias shouts.

A small grin twitches my lips, and then Griffin attacks again. This time, I stay on my feet, turn away, and strike him in the side. The minutes seem to stretch on forever as we grapple with each other, throwing one another into the sand, getting out of holds, and delivering strikes. Griffin is good, but I find I'm able to hold my own better than I expected.

Matthias calls out pointers and takes credit every time I do something right, which makes me want to roll my eyes and smile at the same time.

By the time the whistle blows, neither Griffin nor I are pinned in the sand. We both get to keep our rifles. I go to the side of the pit and join Nika and Matthias, brushing sand off my clothes. Matthias is called away, along with the other cadets who were helping us train, and Nika and I watch on the outskirts of the crowd as the next wave of recruits goes into the pit.

Soldiers patrol the perimeter, observing the recruits.

Shane and Ari end up in the pit at the same time, though they aren't sparring with each other. Shane is good, and he fights his own opponent and helps Ari get out of the pins she's in. I want to hate Shane for how easy it is for him to fall into line here and follow every order given, but he's protective of Ari and seems to care about her.

The whistle blows, and she comes out without getting pinned.

"Next time, Willowpenn needs to go in without Malton," Sergeant Valarius says to Corporal Mitts, close to where Nika and I stand. "See how she can hold up on her own. Her numbers in PT are…" his voice trails off, and I risk a glance back at him.

He's staring at his screen, eyebrows drawn together. "How are her numbers this high? She's not that good!"

"What do you mean, sir?" Corporal Mitts asks.

Sergeant Valarius shows him the screen, and Corporal Mitts's eyes widen.

"Maybe she's better than we thought, sir. The bands are one hundred percent accurate in relaying the recruits' information."

Sergeant Valarius doesn't say a word as he puts his screen away, but curiosity pulls at me. Ari *isn't* very good in PT, but it sounds like her stats say otherwise. I'll have to ask her about it.

I ENTER MY ROOM TO FIND ARI ON HER BED, HUNCHED OVER HER SCREEN AS she types ferociously. I toss my dirty uniform in the laundry bin. The recruits who lost their rifles today in the sandpit are responsible for ensuring the rest of our uniforms are clean for tomorrow. Which is one thing I'm *not* upset about. Earning the respect of the soldiers as they see me around the city with my rifle is a grating experience, but the last thing I want to do after a long day is spend the night with Sampta and Presidia as they ridicule everything I do. I can only imagine how they're going to react when they see the amount of sand trapped in everyone's uniforms.

"I heard Sergeant Valarius say today that your numbers are looking good in PT. Almost too good," I say to Ari as I flop onto my bed.

"I heard that too." Nika enters and tosses her uniform toward the laundry bin. She leans her two rifles against her bed. "Girl. How is that possible?"

Ari pulls her attention away from the screen to grin at us. "Oh, I just go in after each training session and tweak the numbers a bit."

Nika and I share a look.

"How much do you 'tweak' it?" Nika asks.

Ari shrugs. "I try to keep myself near where you and Bria are."

My mouth drops open. Now that I've been trying, I'm moving up in my rank among the recruits in PT, and Nika was already near the top in our unit. Ari comes in with the last wave of recruits in every exercise unless she's with Shane in an obstacle course—then he gets her through faster. No wonder Sergeant Valarius was surprised when he looked at her ranking.

"What if they catch you?" I ask.

Ari laughs so hard, tears stream down her face. Nika and I stare at her. She gets herself back under control, shaking her head. "You're too funny, Bria."

A recruit knocks on our door and retrieves our laundry bin.

Once she's gone, Nika shuts the door. "Ari, seriously. What if they catch you?"

Ari's eyes widen. "I'm too good for them to catch me." There's no pride in her voice. Just an overwhelming amount of certainty. "Remember a couple weeks ago when the alarm went off at 0430 instead of 0400?"

"Sure," I say.

Nika nods.

"That was me." Ari smirks.

"The soldiers all acted like they gave us that break on purpose," Nika says. She retrieves the rifle that's not hers and begins cleaning it.

Ari waves the words away. "They thought it was some glitch. But really, I just needed a little more rest."

She looks so pleased with herself that I smile. I knew Ari was good at tech, but she's better than I realized.

A thought whispers into my mind. "But you couldn't do something like set a band to register a recruit as being in one place when they were in another, or something like that...could you?"

Ari snorts. "Simple. Give me your band."

I remove the HaloAct band from my wrist and toss it to her. She fiddles with it for a moment, does something on her screen, sets the band on the screen, and then brings it over to me.

"Now you can decide where they see you." Ari hands me the band. "Push this button and this button to set your location, and then you can go wherever you want. The band will think you're wherever you set it to begin with. If you push these two buttons at the same time, and then hit this one," she demonstrates, "you can adjust your workout and heart-rate levels." She grins. "I've used that one a couple times myself. When you want it to track you accurately again, just do this." She shows me a sequence of buttons to push.

I shake my head. "Impressive."

"Please don't use that newfound ability to get yourself in trouble." Nika clicks the piece of the gun she just cleaned back into its place.

Ari grins and goes back to her bed, picking up the screen.

"What else can you do on that thing?" Nika asks.

"I thought I wasn't allowed to talk about it in here?"

"You can have a pass tonight."

Ari scoots to the edge of her bed. "Actually, there's something I found earlier today. Something I wanted to tell you guys about."

She's serious now—almost *too* serious for Ari.

"What?"

"You know the Bunker Drills we've had?"

Nika and I both nod.

"Well, they've been bothering me. I don't understand why they have signal blockers down there. I mean, if we're going to be underground for a couple of hours, why can't we use screens or our bands?"

"I figured it was one more way for them to control us, keep us on edge," I say.

"It's not," Ari says.

Nika's movements slow down as she wipes the barrel of the gun.

"I don't think Sitreea knows we're here," Ari says.

"The country the Commander is from?" Nika asks, setting aside her cloth.

"Yeah. It's where all the soldiers are from. I broke into a different server than I usually spend time on. The military one."

She pauses, and Nika and I stare at her, waiting.

"Talionis is supposed to be a hidden intel gathering city for Sitreea. Not a training base." Ari taps on her screen and then shows us a file that corroborates what she's telling us.

There are communiques with intercepted intel on foreign military powers I don't know anything about, mission notes, and special forces operations—some with names of soldiers I recognize—but Ari's right. There's nothing about America or the survivors of the Demise. Or us.

"Are you sure this is everything?" Nika asks after a moment.

"As far as I can tell, this is everything being sent to and from Sitreea. And none of it says a word about recruits or a mission to help the survivors of the Demise. A few of the bunker drills we've had coincided with an inspection by Sitreean delegations. That's why they send us underground. They don't want the Sitreean's knowing we're here."

"If Sitreea's not involved, then why *are* we here?" Nika asks.

Ari closes out of the file on her screen. "I don't know."

THIRTY-ONE

No matter what Trill has said in her classes, I never once believed they took us for the good of the survivors of the Demise. Even so, Ari's revelation from a few days ago, that Sitreea knows nothing of what Talionis is doing with all of us, is unnerving.

Why are they pushing us so hard to train, and what purpose could all of this have?

I enter the Neutral Zone of the Warfare Strategies building and join Nika and Ari. The rest of our unit is scattered around the room, waiting for their assignments.

"Who do you think we'll be with today?" Ari asks, like she always does.

The three of us have entered every Warfare Scenario together, but we get paired with a different set of guys each time.

"We'll find out soon enough." I roll my shoulders, wishing I didn't feel like I was missing something. I've gotten so accustomed to carrying my rifle everywhere that when I check it for the Warfare Scenarios, it feels strange.

Ari nibbles on her lip. "I'm not looking forward to another one of these."

"I hear you," Nika says. "But I think we should get used to it."

The thought of getting used to these makes me want to be ill. For the past week, we've been in two a day. The scenarios are so *real*. Last night, every time I closed my eyes, I was once again reliving events I haven't actually *lived*. Seeing other recruits die, feeling the searing pain of a bullet, the ground rumbling as an explosion rips through a building—an explosion I helped create.

I'm doing, seeing, feeling, experiencing things I never wanted to, never even thought of. It's real. It has to be. Because something that scares me, that gives me nightmares like this, can't be all in my head.

I hate it. And what I hate most is that I'm good at it.

The one person who has actually proven to shake me from the fog of my nightmares is Matthias. He seems to know when I'm really having a hard day, and he does whatever he can to lighten my mood. As much as I might not want to admit it, I'm almost happy when I see him—which is good since he's decided to make an appearance as often as possible.

"They're putting us in more than everyone else," Ari's words are a whisper, but they grab my attention.

"What?" I say.

"The other recruits are doing one a day. And most of them do the same scenario at least a few times before they're given a new one."

"That doesn't make sense," Nika says. "Ours changes every time we're in there."

Ari rubs the back of her neck. "My brother told me what he's been doing, and so did Shane and Nalani. Plus, I went into the system and checked it out."

"But why?" I ask.

"Bromeliad, Willowpenn, Averton," Major Vasco interrupts before Ari can respond. "Come with me." He marches from the room, and we slowly follow after him.

I feel the eyes of the other recruits in our unit on us all the way to the exit. This is different. Every time we've been here before, everyone has received their assignment at the same time.

My mind races over the past few days, but I can't find any reason for them to be upset with my performance. I've done everything they've asked.

Major Vasco leads us down several hallways and into a small room empty of furnishings. Smoky glass lines the far wall, and there's a second door to the right. Nika, Ari, and I line up shoulder to shoulder.

Major Vasco faces us. "We have selected you to enter an experimental scenario." He takes a moment to look each of us in the eye. It's like staring into vacant space—cold and dark. "You're going to be placed with someone who the Commander has been personally observing. He's pleased with what he's seen." Vasco strides to the other door and opens it.

Laban enters the room, followed by Storm. I attempt to keep my face from registering my shock. She's here, and she's alive.

"Bria!" Storm starts to come toward me, but Laban grabs her arm.

Pain scrunches her face together for a moment, but then she straightens and gives me a small smile. Her smile is very different from her normal one. It doesn't stretch across her face, making it impossible for you to not smile back. It doesn't pull you from your sadness and remind you that there's still something good amid the chaos. It looks nothing like the Storm I knew.

She's changed. Something in me cracks, and I don't know if it's because her smile has changed or because she's actually still *trying* to smile.

I step away from Nika and Ari and anxiously look between Major Vasco and Laban. "What's going on?" I take another step toward Storm. "Why is she here?"

But I know the answer. They've been training her, just like they're training us. And the Commander has been watching, pleased with her progress.

Major Vasco gives me a glance that I imagine is the same as he would give to a pesky bug. "In your scenario, you'll be tasked with an item extraction." He pulls out a screen and taps at it, and the lights in the room dim. The smoky glass on the wall lights up like a screen, but the image of a small box pops out from it, like we could grab hold of it. The box rotates slowly, revealing every side.

Ari gazes at it, transfixed. "An albatrax box."

"Correct," Major Vasco says.

Well, at least one of us knows what we're looking at.

"Your scenario will take place in a factory. Find the albatrax box, retrieve it, and get out without getting caught."

But why is Storm here? They must have a reason, and it makes me sick to think of what they're about to put her through. I'm tempted to grab her and pull her from the room, away from the horror of what she's about to experience. But I can't.

"Sergeant Meritas will take you to your zone."

Laban shoves Storm toward us, and I put an arm around her. She hugs me back, and her body trembles.

"Are you okay?" I ask.

"Shut up, recruit," Laban says. "The kid's fine."

I glare at him as he exits the room, ready to attack, but Nika catches my eye and gives a subtle shake of her head before she follows Laban. Drawing in a steadying breath, I exit, keeping Storm close.

Laban brings us to a room down the hall, and doesn't say a word as he opens the door to the zone. He shoves me across the threshold, and then the door slams closed. Before anger can explode through me, Storm's grip on me tightens as the familiar, thick, pre-scenario blackness swirls around us.

"Bria, what's happening?" Storm's voice is clouded with fear.

I put my other arm around her, hugging her to myself. "It's okay. Everything will feel real and be a little scary, but it's all pretend."

"Don't worry, Storm," Ari says. "We're all right here. It'll be light soon."

The room shakes, and Storm whimpers. My gut clenches. I have to protect her. Maybe this won't be as bad as scenarios we've faced before. Soon the scenario has formed.

It's dusk, and we are just inside the walls surrounding a complex cluttered with buildings and smokestacks. Exterior security lights flicker on, but no one is in sight. The factory appears empty. Storm's hand slides into mine, her grip tight. I squeeze her hand.

"Well, Ari," Nika says, "What's an albatrax box?"

Her face lights up. "An albatrax box is used to create and control flight patterns for transports when entering a high traffic area. It encrypts codes that are then sent to the transport and read through a portenal. They're fascinating."

I stare at her for a moment. How she keeps all the tech details in her head is beyond me, but the sooner we can get the thing, the sooner I can get Storm out of this scenario. "Okay, well let's find it."

We wind our way through the complex, and with each step, the nerves in my stomach multiply. It's quiet. Too quiet. Storm doesn't let go of my hand, but then again, if she tried, I'm not sure I would release her.

We approach a building in the center of the complex, and the main doors slide open for us.

"This must be it." Ari steps toward the door.

"I don't know." I slowly shake my head back and forth. "It seems too easy. If it's so valuable and difficult to retrieve, then why aren't there any guards out here?"

Ari points at an electronic plaque next to the door. "See that symbol? This building has high value tech in it. This is where the albatrax box would be."

"With no security?" Nika says, incredulous. "I know you know your stuff, girl, but I'm tempted to side with Bria on this one."

Ari takes a step forward. "I really think this is where we need to go." She takes another step, bringing her to a foot in front of the threshold of the building.

"Something is off," I argue. "It's too quiet."

"Well, what will it hurt to look?" Ari steps through the open doors.

"*Intruder Alert! Intruder Alert!*" An alarm blares, and lights flash on, illuminating the complex as though it were high noon.

"It was a trap! They were expecting us!" I yell over the noise. "We have to get out of here."

"We need to find the albatrax first," Ari shouts back, stepping further into the building. "It has to be in here."

Nika moves toward Ari. "We don't have a choice now. The scenario won't end until we find the box or—"

She cuts herself off with a glance at Storm, but I know what she was going to say. We have to find the box or die before we can get out of here.

My heart hammers into my rib cage, and Storm crowds closer to me. I can't let her die— even in a scenario. The doors begin sliding shut.

"Bria, let's *go!*" Nika gestures toward me impatiently.

We jog toward her, getting through the doors a moment before they slam shut. Ari is ahead of us, and we hurry to catch up. Lights strobe throughout the building, blinding me. Ari glances at signs on doorways and through glass into workstations, but enters none of them. Storm's little legs pump to keep up the frantic pace, her blonde poof of hair bouncing with every step, her face set in determination.

Ari runs past another doorway and then skids to a stop. "In there! Go in there!"

Nika shoves open the door and, once we're all inside, presses it shut. No lights flash in the dimly lit space, and the noise of the alarm has been reduced to a low chirp. Stairs descend into darkness.

Boots pounding against the floor echoes in the hallway, and I dare a peek out the thin window on the door. Soldiers run past, some shouting orders over the alarms, others bursting into rooms.

"They're already here," I say. "There's no way we're going to accomplish this mission."

"We have to go down." Ari waves us forward. "Protocol in tech buildings would dictate checking the most valuable assets and high-profile rooms first. The basement will be the last part of their sweep."

We descend as quietly as possible. This is the most confident I've seen Ari in any scenario, but it makes sense. Tech is her world.

The basement is dark except for a couple of dim security lights. The dull sound of the soldiers' footfalls on the floors above us is a constant reminder that we are quickly running out of time. We go around piles of discarded metal, old and broken pieces of equipment, and stacks of boxes. On the back wall, there's a massive machine with tubes and ducts sprawling from it in every direction.

Ari gasps. "That's how we can get it." She clamps a hand over her mouth, glancing at Storm.

My shoulders tense. "No."

"That must be the reason they put her in here with us," Nika says.

"No. Way. Figure out something else."

"What's wrong, Bria?" Storm asks.

Ari clears her throat, and doesn't look Storm in the eye. "The only way to get the albatrax box is by going up through the electrotube." She gestures to the tube.

Storm looks between the three of us. "You're all too big. I need to get it."

A door bangs directly above us and echoes in the silence, following Storm's statement.

Storm looks at me. "Right, Bria?"

I swallow hard. "Maybe." I put my hand on her shoulder. "I'm going to see where it goes."

"Bria," Ari says. I don't look at her or acknowledge the warning in her tone, but she continues anyway. "There's no way any of us are fitting in there."

"She's right," Nika says.

I glare at them. "She's a *kid*. This whole thing was a setup so that she would be the one who would have to retrieve that stupid box. We are *not* sending her in."

"But I'll fit," Storm says.

I look down at her. The protests I was about to fling at Nika and Ari turn into a lump in my throat. She has her face set, just like Zeke does whenever he's determined to do something.

"It's okay. I'm a good climber." She tries to smile, but it falters on her lips. Then she turns, and my hand falls off her shoulder as she walks toward the small hatch.

Storm enters the electrotube, her little body easily sliding in. I'm frozen in place as I watch, memories of Eli and Zeke pelting me, driving the air from my lungs.

After a minute, I bend down to look in, but Storm is already out of sight. I want to call out to her and make sure she's okay, but it's too risky.

A few more minutes pass, and my anxiety increases. I pace in front of the opening.

Nika glares at me. "Stop. You're making me nervous."

I ignore her and continue pacing. "Why isn't she back yet?"

"I don't know." Ari twists her hands together and glances back toward the stairway. "They'll be coming to the basement soon."

I freeze. "What if they captured her?"

Neither of them answers. "We need to find her."

"We can't. We have no idea where—"

The sound of scraping and bumping comes from the hole, and then a box tumbles out, followed by Storm. She gets to her feet. "Is this it?"

Ari comes over to inspect it. "Yes!"

"We better get out of here," Nika says.

I crouch down and look Storm in the eye. "Are you okay?"

She nods, and some of my agitation eases.

We scramble back up the stairway. Nika peers through the small window into the hall. "They're only two rooms away. When they enter the next room, we leave." She doesn't look at us as she gives the instructions. "On my signal."

I grab Storm's hand. Ari clutches the box.

"Now!" Nika flings open the door, and we spill into the hallway.

We sprint past the door of the workstation the guards are searching.

"There they are!" someone shouts. "Stop!"

We run faster. I'm pulling Storm along now and hoping she doesn't trip. The strobing lights and blaring alarm wreak havoc on my senses. Every hair on my arms stands at attention, and an electric current zips through my veins.

The alarm cuts off abruptly. "Stop or we *will* shoot!" A man orders.

"Keep running!" I yell. "Don't stop!"

Everything seems to slow down, and the intensity of moments before fades. I feel my feet slamming against the floor, Storm's small fingers gripping my hand. And I hear nothing.

Then the pop of a gun cracks through the hall, the sound ricocheting off the walls, the ceiling, and the floor.

Storm screams, and her hand slips from my grasp as she crumbles to the floor.

"*Storm!*" The cry is barely out of my mouth when another bullet rips through my side and I'm falling, gasping. My vision blurs, but before it completely fades, I see Storm's lifeless body, surrounded by a pool of blood. I want to scream, I want to yell, I want to destroy whoever did this to her. But I can't fight the blackness that engulfs me.

THIRTY-TWO

Light filters into the room and I sit up, clutching my side, but as usual there's no blood, no sign of a bullet. I frantically search the room for Storm. She's an arm's length away, still lying on the ground, and she's shaking.

I reach out to her and lightly rest an arm on her shoulder. "Storm?"

She turns over, and her wet cheeks and red eyes hit me like another bullet. She flies into my arms, and her body shudders as shock rips through her.

"Let's go. Time for your debrief," Laban calls from the hallway.

Ari and Nika exit, but I don't move. I just hold Storm and let her cry. Laban walks in, but I don't look up. I despise him even more for making her go through this. He stops over us.

"Do you need *help,* recruit?" he sneers.

I stand and help Storm to her feet, not looking in his direction. If I look at him, I'll hurt him, and I can't risk him hurting Storm as a result. I walk out the door, still holding Storm's hand, and join Nika and Ari.

Laban leads us back to the room where they briefed us for our mission. Major Vasco sits in a chair, staring at a screen. He looks up when the door shuts. All of us, including Storm, stand at attention. Out of the corner of my eye, I see Storm take a deep breath and then she tucks her lip between her teeth, trying not to fall apart. Suppressed fury pounds against my head, causing it to ache. After what she just went through, she should be *allowed* to fall apart. No. She never should have experienced that in the first place.

Major Vasco stands. "You may not have successfully completed your mission, but you worked well as a team, even under pressurized circumstances." He approaches Storm. "Storm, you did well. You're brave."

Storm's hands twitch, but she remains at attention.

"We could use more recruits like you."

I step in between them. "What are you talking about?" I demand.

"Move back into position, recruit."

I set my jaw. "What do you mean, you could use more like her?"

He bends down and clamps his hand between my neck and shoulder. I gasp. He shoves me back into position.

"It doesn't. Concern. You." He enunciates each word, his hand tightening. Finally, he releases his grip, but my skin burns from his hold.

Elva Trill drones on about the ranking system in Talionis, but I can't focus on a word she's saying. They're training Storm, and, after our debrief with Major Vasco, they led her away, and I have no idea where they took her. No way to check on her and make sure she's okay.

The possibilities of what's coming for Storm...and for my brothers, weigh on my chest, wrapping their claws around my lungs. They can't make kids a part of whatever it is they're doing here. It's not right.

But they're already doing just that.

A message buzzes on my band, and I automatically open it. It's a personal note on an encrypted channel. Ari. She's sent Nika and me messages before, mainly because she *could*. But we never know how to send her a message back securely, plus her messages disappear after a minute. I scan the text.

I have to show you something. Meet me after class.

I nudge Nika and shift my wrist so she can read the message. Her eyebrows crowd together, confirming my suspicions. Something about it feels ominous. Not like Ari. Her messages typically have some new tech fact she learned or a note about how she hated PT or a correction to something a tech instructor says. This is different.

By the time Trill has finished class, I can't decide if I'm more anxious about Storm or about whatever Ari needs to tell me. I make my way over to where she's sitting with Bryson. This is one of the few classes where we're with the other units of recruits, and Ari always sits with her brother.

"What's up?"

"Not here." She shoulders her rifle.

We leave the room, and my heart trips over itself as my anxieties rise. Nika joins us, and the three of us pull away from the crowd of recruits as each unit goes to their different trainings. Our unit is supposed to be in Weaponry Training in fifteen minutes.

Once everyone is out of earshot, Ari speaks. "I know where they're keeping Storm."

"What? Where? How did you find her?" The questions rush out of my mouth.

"I used a decryption key I built into my band to access her band while we were in the scenario," Ari says.

We near a soldier and Ari pauses, waiting to continue until we've passed him.

"Now I can access the server with her training information and where they're keeping her...but that's not all."

I want to be excited about what she found, but somehow I know that whatever else she has to say isn't good.

"What?" Nika asks for me.

We're close to the Weaponry Training Facility now, so our steps slow.

Ari drops her voice. "I haven't dug too deep, but it looks like they're creating a whole new training system for a younger demographic of recruits. They're planning to kidnap kids with the next extraction."

It's like I've been plunged into icy water with her words. It makes sense. I suspected as much, but this confirmation still feels suffocating.

"What are you waiting for, recruits?" A soldier yells over at us. "Get into your training, or I'll take your rifles!"

Somehow, I enter the building, but my mind is frantic. I need to do something, to *act*. I could never forgive myself if I didn't at least try to save Storm and my brothers.

And, though it's dangerous, I only have one option.

I need to go see Cai.

THIRTY-THREE

I lay in bed, pretending to be asleep when Nika and Ari enter. If I talk to them, I'll end up telling them about Cai, and I can't do that. Not yet. I need to go to the Ruins tonight by myself. This whole thing is too risky, and I don't know how much I can trust Cai. He's taking out Talionis soldiers, so we have a common enemy. But is he safe?

Probably not.

Nika and Ari speak in low murmurs, and then they're in their beds, and the light is off. I stay still until I hear even breathing coming from both of them. Then I ease myself into a sitting position and slip out of bed. I push the buttons Ari showed me on my HaloAct Band and set my location as the bedroom and adjust my heart rate and fitness to what they typically are when I'm sleeping. Then I grab my boots and jacket and silently leave.

I slink down the corridor toward the kitchen, and there's no one in sight as I enter. There're always soldiers stationed at the doors around the building, so I'll need to leave through one of the large windows in the kitchen used for ventilation. Hopefully, they don't lock them.

I hold my breath as I test the window. It glides up with little effort, and I sigh with relief. I put my jacket on, zipping it up to my neck and then stuff my feet into my boots. Bracing both hands on the windowsill, I boost myself up and over the edge and land in a crouched position outside. The dark, moonless night greets me with a gust of frigid air. I shrink deeper into my coat and pull my sleeves over my hands.

I creep through the shadows until I reach the corner at the back of the building. I press against the wall and peer around the edge. The back alley is dark and empty. My heart trips over itself and my armpits prickle with sweat.

Something moves, and I jump back.

It's a leaf.

I press my hand against my chest, take a deep breath, and then pick my way through the alley, following it as far as it will go. I stop at the end, still hidden in the shadows, though only several steps away a light illuminates a street. It's the only main street I need to cross. After this, I'll be able to stick to the back alleys and sides of buildings and back yards until I reach the Ruins. But this part is tricky.

Guards and soldiers regularly patrol this section since it's near "buildings of interest." I inhale, the cold air cutting through my lungs, and hold my breath for a moment. I exhale, my breath rising above me in a white cloud. Adrenaline pumps through me, warming my body against the frigid night. It's time. I ease my head past the security of the building. Two guards stand down the road, talking to each other, their backs to me. Otherwise, no one else is in sight.

I race across the street, exposed for an instant by the streetlights, but in the blindspot of the cameras. *Don't look at me. Don't look at me.* A few more steps. Two. One.

Shadows swallow me up.

The rough texture of the building catches at my jacket as I lean against it and wait. Voices trickle through the darkness as the two soldiers walk down the street toward me. One of them laughs. They move past the alley I'm standing in without glancing in my direction. My heart slows. I made it.

Closing my eyes, I envision the map of Talionis that I've stared at time and time again, and trace my route. It shouldn't take me too long now. I jog down alleys and through backyards, staying in the darkness as much as possible. The Physical Training Arena towers overhead, casting sinister shadows. I skirt around the sandpit and pick up my pace. I don't want to be near it any longer than necessary.

Once I'm past, the buildings grow smaller, more dilapidated. An abandoned building the size of three houses crowds near the fence. This must be the building Cai was talking about.

I force myself to keep jogging toward the structure, knowing that if I stop, I won't have the nerve to continue. The steps are riddled with holes and missing boards, and I slow down as I climb them. Whatever door used to hang in the doorway has long since disappeared, and spiders have repurposed the frame. I cringe, reach my arm in front of me, and cut through the webs as much as possible. One still hits me in the face as I enter the building. I swipe my hands over my face as I walk, trying to rid myself of the sticky strands.

The darkness inside does nothing to ease my apprehension about entering the Ruins again. I shuffle my way forward, stepping over old boards, furniture, and the decayed remnants of a different era.

"Ow!" I yelp when my shin collides with an object. I clamp my hands over my mouth, let myself grimace in pain for a moment, and then continue forward.

When I reach the back of the building, I find a hole in the wall which offers a view of the fence leading into the Ruins. Dense vegetation has taken hold of it. I run my hands along it. The overgrowth of leaves and vines pulls at my jacket and scratches my hands, but I can feel the solid fence beneath the tangle of foliage.

Thoughts of the bugs, spiders, and small creatures possibly living in here creep through my mind, and I have to force them away. Not that more bugs will make much difference. I'm already strewn with webs and who knows what else. I bend a little lower, and suddenly my hand is no longer pressing against the fence. This is it. I explore the area with my arm first. It'll easily be wide enough for me to fit through.

Pulling the hood up on my jacket, I cinch it around my head and then drop to my hands and knees. I crawl forward. Back into the Ruins. Back into the place where I was supposed to die. Back to the only person who might be able to help me keep Storm and my brothers safe.

I break through on the other side and stand up, brushing the bramble off my shoulders and front.

"So, you decided to come back."

I jump and whirl toward the voice. Cai lounges on a low limb of a nearby tree, mostly hidden by the dark night. He climbs down from his perch and comes toward me, turning on a torchlight. I take a few deep breaths, attempting to calm myself before I answer.

"Hello, Cai," I say, pleased when I don't sound as frightened as I feel.

"Bria." He's in front of me now, one hand holding the light, the other resting on top of his staff as he studies me. "Can't say I thought you'd actually come."

I look away from his steady gaze. "Something happened."

"I'm not surprised." He nods at my wrist. "You should have removed that before coming out here." He takes a step back. "It's not safe for you to be here with them tracking you."

"Oh, it's fine! My friend showed me how to trick the tracking system." I open the map on my band and zoom into the Recruits Living Quarters. A sigh of relief almost escapes me when I see the red dot blinking right where it should be.

"Hmm. I might need to meet that friend of yours at some point." He turns and begins hiking back through the woods. "I have some work to do, and I want to get you set up with your training so you can do as much as possible before you have to leave."

"Don't you care about why I came back?" I hurry to keep up with him.

He comes to an abrupt halt, and I almost run into him. "Do you need me to know?"

I take a step back. "I...don't know."

"Okay then." He starts walking again.

"Wait!" I reach out and grab his shoulder.

He stops and faces me, eyebrows raised. I drop my hand.

"I want to leave, and I'll even help you with whatever your plan is so that can happen. But I can't leave alone."

His expression is shrouded in the darkness.

"There's a little girl that they captured. And I think they're planning on bringing in more kids like her." I break eye contact and stare off into the dark woods. "I can't—" My voice cracks, the thought of my brothers pressing desperation into the words. I clear my throat and try again.

"I can't let that happen. But I don't know how to stop it." I focus on Cai. "You're the only option I have. The only option she has."

We stare at each other for a moment.

He nods once. "Then we'd better get to work. "

I wait, expecting him to say more, but he resumes his trek through the woods.

"What do you mean?" I call out as I follow him. "Do you have a plan or something? Have you figured out how to get out of here? How to stop them? Because every possible option I've considered won't work."

He doesn't respond. Just continues forward, actually picking up speed. I grit my teeth and race after him.

"Cai! Come on! What are we going to do?"

He stops.

"First," he turns and faces me, a small smile turning up the corners of his lips, "you train."

He shifts to the side, and I realize we're standing in front of a structure covered in vines with a tree shooting up through the middle. Cai pulls back a curtain of vines woven together from where it rests against the wall and reveals a doorway. Light from inside spills out.

"Go in," he says.

I eye it warily. "What is this place?"

"One of my sites."

I sigh but walk forward and enter through the narrow opening and into a brightly lit, high-ceilinged building that's full of debris and old junk. I halt. I can't move farther into the room than a few feet. Nor do I want to. Torches line the entire perimeter, casting light on precarious piles cluttering a floor that's barely visible beneath it all. Dirt cakes the parts of it I can see. Webs hang from the ceiling and bridge the gaps between the various piles. The only semi-cleared area is around a crumbling fire pit in the center of the room.

This is nothing like the first site he brought me to. No screens or tech or lighting from Talionis. Just junk. Everywhere.

I spin back toward Cai. "I'm already training in Talionis. Can't we work on the actual planning of how we're going to get out of here?"

"Are you excelling as a recruit?"

"I'm doing better than I was," I hedge.

He stares at me.

"No, I'm not excelling, but—"

"For the plan to work, you have to excel."

He brushes past me. I follow him apprehensively, and when I round the corner, I find another section that's been cleared. There's a stack of items standing in the middle, about as high as a man, and there's a target on the far wall. Another staff rests on the floor.

It's a little better than what I first thought but still a mess.

"What if I train by helping you take out soldiers and the other work you do?" Anything would be better than staying *here*.

"Not yet," he says. "Once you know more, perhaps I'll take you with me."

I open my mouth to argue that I'm ready now, but he thumps his staff against the floor, cutting me off. "You came to me, Bria, and I refuse to place you in more dangerous situations before you've been properly trained. God knows you've already seen more than you should have had to in Talionis."

My protests die in my throat. This man doesn't know me, but he seems to care about my safety. "You brought me out with you before..." I let the sentence hang, almost like a question.

"I knew it was safe before. I took you with me to show you what I do. To give you a reason to trust I'm who I say I am."

I incline my head. Trusting Cai would be dangerous, but the tour he gave me of the Ruins last time I was here proved he is who he claims to be, at least. "Okay. What do you want to do?"

"You'll train first, and we'll review the plan after. I'll set you up with specific instructions on what exercises I want you to do and how I want you to do them." He uses his staff to point to a camera on the ceiling. "I'll be able to monitor you, and," he pulls a communications earpiece from his pocket, "instruct you."

"Where will you be?"

"Working, as I always do. Plus, I need to make sure no one followed you here and that no one's looking for you."

I don't love that I'm going to be left alone to train in this dirty site, but I also don't want to alienate the one man who may help me escape Talionis, save Storm, and protect my brothers.

"Fine. What do I have to do?"

THIRTY-FOUR

Cai twirls his staff in his hand. "First, I'll demonstrate what your training will allow you to accomplish. My methods are going to be different from what you expect, but you need to do exactly as I say. If you do, it will help you excel as a recruit and also prepare you for when we escape."

He faces the man-sized stack. "Watch."

In movements so fast, I almost become dizzy, Cai spins his staff in one hand, bends, spins it behind his back into the other hand, and then does a series of jabs, strikes, and what appear to be blocks. His arms and legs fly swiftly and deftly, each motion fluid and well-practiced.

He drops his staff and picks up two metal sticks that are around two or three feet long each. Both arms move in synchronization, beating the sticks against the dummy, rapidly delivering blow after blow, the sound a staccato piercing the air. Then he does a backflip, leaving the sticks on the ground, and retrieves three knives from a low table. He flings first one and then the other two simultaneously, embedding them into the target on the wall.

He stops, and the only sound is Cai's breathing. I realize my mouth is hanging open, and I quickly snap it shut as he comes back toward me.

"So, would you like to learn how to do this?" He swipes an arm against his forehead.

For a moment, I imagine Matthias's face if I could learn to move as quickly as Cai just did. I might actually get the better of him without him letting me. I can't help the small smile that lifts the corners of my mouth.

"Yes. But why not use guns?" I almost hate that I'm asking, but I can't stop myself. I've grown accustomed to carrying my rifle every-where, and, as much as I don't love weaponry training, bullets are faster than hand-to-hand combat.

Cai scoops up the two staffs on the ground and tosses one to me. "Guns are loud. Knives, staffs, arrows—they're quiet. The enemy doesn't have as much time to react." He pauses, mouth turned down. "I don't enjoy taking lives or harming people. But I've learned to do it well in order to stop evil men and women from hurting the innocent. I fight for those who cannot fight for themselves, and I'll train you to do the same."

Something in me rises. A sense of purpose and excitement. I grip the staff in my hands tighter. "Okay."

He shifts, and I notice a rectangular, leather pouch on his hip.

"What weapon is that?"

"My Bible." Before I can process what he said or ask anything else, he continues. "Since we agree, I expect you to do as I instruct with no complaints."

Something about the way he states the words makes me wonder what exactly he has in mind, but I agree anyway. I toss the smooth staff from one hand to the other, trying to get a feel for its weight, eager to get started.

"How do you spin it so fast?" I try to mimic his movements from a moment ago, but the staff clumsily turns and then clatters to the floor. I pick it back up.

"You'll learn, eventually. Before you can become accomplished in these movements, you need to train your body, master specific motions, and build the right muscles."

I nod, once again attempting to rotate the staff, but this time using both hands.

"So," Cai continues, "you'll do that by clearing the cobwebs."

I drop the staff. "Wait. What?"

"These webs need to be cleared, and I'm going to show you how to do so." Cai walks toward a pile of boxes with webs strewn above them. "Watch."

"Wait a second." I step toward him. "How is this going to help me learn anything?"

Cai rests his hands on top of his staff. "Did you or did you not agree to do as I instruct with no complaints?"

I shrug. "Well, yeah, but that was to train, not—"

"This *is* training," Cai interrupts. "This is how you are to clear the webs." He plants his feet, jabs the staff into the cobweb over one box, and then twirls the staff in a large, slow circle. "You try now."

I sigh, still unsure what this will do. I jab the staff into a cobweb and then do a quick little circle before bringing the staff back to my side.

"No, that's not right," Cai snaps. "Do it again. Make a larger circle, and do it slower."

I roll my eyes and then do as he says.

"Spread your legs more."

I follow his instruction, biting back a retort.

"Good. Clear another web."

I clear five more webs with Cai moving around me, telling me to do this or that differently. Once he's satisfied that I'm clearing them as he wishes, he gives me an earpiece and leaves to work, telling me he'll check on me through the camera he has installed.

For the next half hour, I clear dozens of webs from the site, and my shoulders become stiff with the repetitive motion. I set the staff down and rotate my shoulders. Another cobweb dangles nearby. Once I clear one away, three more seem to appear. An old dirty cloth is crumpled up on the ground, and I pick it up and swipe at the web. It detaches from the corner of the box it was clinging to and cascades to the ground. I fling the cloth at another web, easily clearing it.

"Bria." Cai's sharp voice in my ear freezes my movements as I'm about to fling the cloth at yet another web. "What are you doing?"

I cringe. "Cleaning," I mumble.

For some reason, I feel guilty for using the rag, yet at the same time I'm annoyed that I came all the way out here only to do his housework.

"Put the rag down, and pick up the staff."

"Seriously though, Cai," I face the camera and spread my arms out, "what is the point of this?"

"Each task I will give you has a purpose, Bria. I need you to trust me that you are learning and training, even when you don't think you are." He pauses. "Can you do that?"

I swallow and nod and then pick my staff up from the ground. My hands protest at the feel, my palms raw with the promise of blisters. I'll do it. Let him train me his way. I don't have any other options.

"Good. Keep clearing the webs, but make the movements faster."

I comply.

"No, that's not right." Cai then gives me detailed instructions on exactly the way he wants me to clear the cobwebs.

I have no idea how he's getting his *work* done with the way he's chirping in my ear, but eventually he seems satisfied and tells me to keep working and that he'll be back soon.

When I've cleared half of the room, Cai tells me he's returning and to take a break. I collapse to the floor. Sweat drips into my eyes, but I don't even bother wiping it away. I don't want to move or consider sitting up. Each muscle in my shoulders and back protests with a rhythm of its own, as if to yell at me for the abuse I just put it through.

The thumping noise of Cai's staff hitting the floor echoes around me as he reenters. Maybe if I don't move, he'll think I fell asleep or passed out and have some pity on me. I've been at this for at least two hours, and by now it's probably close to midnight. He stops near my head.

"Alright, Bria. Get up," he says, although not in the commanding voice he used while I was "training."

I roll myself into a sitting position and moan. "Please tell me we're done."

He hands me a cup of water, and the ghost of a smile flits across his face. "Almost."

My body clenches up at the idea of more work, but I'm too thirsty to protest immediately. I gulp down the cool liquid, emptying the cup.

"I want to see how you do throwing knives." He walks away before I can answer or agree. Not that he cares if I agree with what he wants to do or not.

"Sure, I'd love to do that," I mumble to myself as I get to my feet.

Cai is lining up a set of knives on a table several feet from the target when I approach him. He picks one up.

"Hold the bottom of the knife with your thumb and forefinger, and allow the knife to rest between them." He demonstrates. "Keep your wrist perfectly straight, with your thumb pointing forward. Bend your arm back, bring it forward, and release right before your wrist bends down." He throws the knife, and it sticks into the target. "You try."

I pick up a knife and do as Cai instructed, but the knife smacks against the target and falls to the floor.

"Okay," he says.

"Right." Clearly, knife throwing isn't my skill.

"Your form isn't bad. You may have some potential. Try again."

I press my left hand against my right shoulder and then rotate my shoulder. "I'm pretty beat, do we have to—?"

"Bria. Throw another knife."

I grunt, irked, but do as he says. He makes me throw ten more knives, and finally, the last one sticks with a satisfying thud. My head jerks back in surprise, and I feel inordinately pleased with myself.

"Fine. That's enough for tonight. Each time you come to train, you'll work on throwing the knives." He crosses the room and adds a couple of logs to the fire.

I lean against the wall and let my exhausted body collapse to the floor. Cai pokes the logs into position. When he finishes, he retrieves some papers and a screen and brings them to the table the knives were on.

I yawn, and he glances at me. "Well, do you want to hear the plan or not?"

I scramble to my feet, knocking over an old, empty box, and hurry over.

"Pay attention." He spreads the papers out. "I don't like to repeat myself."

I nod, even though he's not looking at me. As he turns on the screen, I catch sight of the tattoo on his left arm. Something pulls at me.

"Now." He pulls his arm back, but I still see the image of the tattoo.

It shouldn't distract me like this. I blink and refocus myself on what he's saying.

He points at the hologram map of Talionis coming out of the screen. "It's been a while since I've been in Talionis, and from the looks of this, the layout has changed."

I nod, confirming the map is accurate.

"Some of the changes will make what we have to do more complicated but not impossible." He picks up a stack of papers and begins spreading them out on the table around the map. Each one has a location listed at the top, a rough drawing, and a list of details about it.

"What are these?"

"Secrets of Talionis," Cai says. "I was here for the building process, so I know things I'm sure they would kill to keep secret. It's one reason you need to train and do well. If you receive higher clearance, you'll be able to access these areas and confirm things are still as I remember."

"Wait," I object, hating the very idea of actually excelling in Talionis. "Can't I just sneak into these places or something?"

"No. We can't risk arousing their suspicions before the time comes for us to act."

I'm about to protest, but the look he gives me out of the corner of his eye makes me clamp my mouth shut.

"Fine." For now, anyway. "What's the point of finding these places?"

"There's no easy way out of Talionis. They've thought of just about everything as far as I can tell. But I think I may have begun to figure out a way, and we'll use the secrets I know to help make it happen."

I raise my eyebrows. "How?"

"Sabotage."

THIRTY-FIVE

The word hangs in the air, settling around us. It makes sense. Cai's an expert in sabotage, at least in the Ruins. But how will it work in the city?

"If we can create significant problems in key areas, personnel would need to be moved to deal with them," he says.

"Right."

"So we create those problems. We map out our escape route and find the areas we need to target in order to draw the soldiers and guards away from our route. Areas that are vulnerable or of high value are what we look for. We'll need a mix of both. In the chaos, we'll steal a transport and leave. From here, we'll go to my home in Eryndale and find the help we'll need to stop Demetrius Ark for good. The Eryndalian scouts are well trained, and I'll convince the leaders that this is a necessary fight."

I tap my finger on the desk, lost in thought. Could it work?

"It's different in Talionis than out here," I say. "We won't have free rein to set things up like you do."

He inclines his head. "True. It will be difficult. But this is part of the reason you need higher clearance. We'll have to bring in additional people as well."

I stop tapping. More people *are* necessary, but how do I explain

Cai to my friends? And is he someone I trust enough to risk not just my life but theirs as well?

"When you come," he continues, "you'll train first, and then we'll plan."

The possibilities swirl through my mind, and hope stirs. Maybe I won't die in Talionis.

"One more thing," he says.

Something about the way he says that makes me pause. "What?"

"You'll need to get maps of the region."

"Aren't they in the system? Can't we just add them to a screen or something?"

"No." Cai hesitates. "There's only one copy. One map. Ark is paranoid, and he doesn't want anyone else having access to what he knows about North America." He picks up a piece of paper he had off to the side and drops it on top of the map. It's schematics for a safe. "The map is in the safe in his office."

I stare at him for a solid minute. The man is delusional. He's spent way too much time out in the Ruins alone. "Excuse me. Are you telling me you want me to break into the office—the *safe*—of the Commander of Talionis? I've never even seen the man! There's no way I'll be able to pull that off." A frightening thought grips my brain. "How do you even know there's a safe in Ark's office?" I take a step back. "Is this a trap?"

Cai leans back against the table. "Calm down, Bria. No, this isn't a trap." He looks down at the papers cluttering the table. "I know about the safe because I helped build the secret compartment he keeps it in." He focuses on me again.

I stare into his eyes, searching for any hint that he's lying, but he seems sincere. "Why would they trust you to do that?"

"I'm good at creating secret compartments and hidden spaces, and they found that out." He shrugs and then smiles slightly. "They just never figured on me using that against them."

I take a deep breath, willing myself to calm down. This is the man who has terrorized soldiers, taken out squads, brought down transports. This isn't a trap. But the plan is dangerous. "I don't know how I'll ever get in there."

"We'll figure it out. But first, you need to excel, be someone they notice and reward."

"I'll try," I say, unconvinced I'll be able to do what he wants. "But I'm pretty far behind. Our first evaluations are in two weeks. Then we'll be placed in ranked squads. I'm not sure I'll have what it takes to be among the top ranked recruits."

"Do what you can. Whenever you can get here, I'll help you prepare. Don't give up before you even start." Cai pushes away from the table and heads toward the door. "Let's go. You need to get back."

I follow him into the night.

We wind our way through the Ruins toward the fence. My limbs feel weighted with exhaustion, and my eyelids are drooping. I let my eyes close and then stumble. I catch myself before falling to the ground. Cai is silent as he leads the way. Apparently, he's used up all of his words. If I don't do something, I'm going to fall sound asleep while I'm walking.

"Cai?"

"Hmm?" He hefts himself over a log, and I follow suit.

"What's with your tattoo?"

He glances back at me. "It's a reminder. No matter what, I need to honor God. My life is His. He paid for it." He walks around a boulder.

"But." I run my hand along the rock as I pass it. "God let you end up here." I spit the word out. "Why would you still honor Him?"

Cai doesn't answer at first. Maybe he doesn't have an answer. A night owl hoots in a nearby tree, reminding me there are things around me I can't see right now. I think of the dogs and walk even closer to Cai, almost stepping on his heels. Perhaps another conversation will last longer.

Before I can come up with one, Cai responds. "I honor God because I know Him, know what He's done for me, how He loves me. And He's worth it. No matter where I am, no matter what happens, He's always worth honoring."

I duck under a low branch, my heart wrestling with his words. "I don't get it."

"God put each of us in this world to find Him, even though He's not far off." Cai stops, and I realize we're at the fence. "Until you seek

Him and find Him and start to understand all He's done for you, you're not gonna get it."

Annoyance flares in my gut. "I'm not stupid. You could at least try to explain it a little better."

Cai pushes his hood back, giving me a clear view of his face. Some of my irritation seeps away. He looks almost...sad. "Do you want to know God, Bria?"

"No." The response is instinctive and comes out before I even think about it. I haven't wanted to have anything to do with God since I was eleven, let alone know Him. Whatever that means. Besides, there's no way God would want anything to do with me.

"Okay." The word is more of a sigh. "Well, if your answer to that question ever changes, let me know."

I nod my agreement, surprised by the intensity in his eyes. A part of me wishes I could give him a different answer.

"I hope one day it does."

I shift uncomfortably and glance at the fence. "I guess I should, uh, go."

Cai nods. "Come back when you can. I have an alarm that triggers in my site to let me know when someone comes through this opening. If I'm not here when you arrive, I'll be here within a few minutes."

"Okay. See you soon." I pull my hood up, bend down, and crawl through the hole and into Talionis.

I force aside the thoughts of God and focus on the plan to escape instead. It will work. It has to work. I blow out a puff of air as I carefully make my way through the abandoned building. I have a lot to do.

The walk back to the living quarters is uneventful. I slip back in the way I came out, undetected, and soon I'm in my room. I shed my clothes and put on my pajamas before climbing into bed.

As I lie in bed, my mind plays over my time in the Ruins and Cai's plan. It might actually be possible to be freed from this nightmare. My thoughts shift from the plan to Cai's parting words, and no matter what I do, I can't force them aside. I squeeze my eyes shut, try to fall asleep. But I can't. Cai's words continue to haunt me.

Okay, God. If You're really there, if You're who Cai seems to think You are, show me.

My throat aches with unshed tears, and I roll onto my side. It's a nice thought, God wanting me to know Him. But after what I did to Ezri, why would God care about me?

CHAPTER
THIRTY-SIX

After my night in the Ruins, exhaustion has been my companion through each training session, but now that I have two hours of free time, anticipation is driving it away.

I'm going to see Storm.

Ari gave me the instructions on where to find her. They've placed her with a woman named Damara Lotz in the Modified Housing District. I asked Matthias if he knew anything about the area, and he said most of those who live there are assigned to specific duties in Talionis: janitors, cleaners, cooks. Going there, visiting Storm, is a risk. But I can't continue doing everything the soldiers, and now Cai, are demanding without at least knowing she's safe.

But there's one person I need to tell before I go: Cade. He cares about Storm and has been searching for her too.

I enter the Recruits Living Quarters building and slip into the room my friends and I hangout in when we have free time. Cade's in the room, and so is Nika, but they're alone, on their knees, *praying*.

I freeze and stare, emotions I don't know what to do with exploding inside me.

Cade's words filter over, as Nika nods her head in agreement.

"And, God, if there's a way for us to get out of this place, show us. But if not, whether in life or death, we'll still praise you."

The door slams shut behind me, and they both look up.

Nika breathes a sigh of relief. "Oh good, it's just you."

Anger rips through me. "You believe in God too? Both of you?"

Nika's eyes widen, and Cade stares.

I shake my head. "I can't believe this."

I rush out of the room, ignoring Nika calling out my name. Why does everyone I'm close to have something I don't have? Can't have. Fury burns in my veins, propelling me forward.

First Storm. Then Cai. Now Nika and Cade.

It's like I'm surrounded.

I press my hands to my face and release a muffled scream. Then I take a deep breath.

This isn't a big deal. So what if they believe in God? That's not what's important right now. There are other, far more pressing, matters—like checking on Storm.

I pause before leaving the building, set my band to register me as staying here, and then head toward the Modified Housing District. With each step, my anger cools, and I feel a little foolish. I must be more exhausted than I thought. And I probably owe Nika and Cade an apology of some sort.

But right now, I need to find Storm and make sure she's okay. Have they still been putting her through Warfare Strategies? Have they hurt her? Is this woman treating Storm well? The questions drive away my embarrassment and the strange ache I feel at the thought of God.

Before long, I've entered the Modified Housing District. Dilapidated houses that are crowded together flank the streets on either side. These buildings are old, maybe even from before the Demise. They've been fixed up enough to keep them standing, but it's eerie—like the buildings themselves have haunting stories to tell. The streets are empty, since it's the middle of the day, and most are working. Other than occasionally catching the whisper of movement behind a window, I don't encounter anyone.

After a few minutes, I find Lower Citizen Way, and stop at house number 6724. I stare up at the house. It's as crippled and old as every other house on the block, but warm light drifts out from the windows. I approach the door, but it opens before I get to it.

A Hispanic woman in her late-thirties peers out at me. Her brown hair is pulled into a bun on top of her head, and faint lines crease the area around her eyes and mouth. She's thin, almost too thin.

"Can I help you with something?" Her voice is stronger than I expected.

I try to look past her to see if Storm's inside, but the door is only open partway. "I'm looking for someone. A woman named Damara Lotz."

Her eyes narrow. "Why?"

"I was told she's watching over a girl named Storm."

The door behind the woman opens wider, and then I see Storm. "Bria?"

I walk the rest of the way up the path and drop my rifle to the ground as Storm pushes past Damara and runs to me, throwing herself into my arms. I hold her close, the familiar texture of her springy blonde curls against my cheek. She seems taller than before. Stronger. I lean back and take in her warm, light brown skin and deep chocolate eyes. "Are you okay?"

She smiles up at me with the same sad smile that broke my heart the day we were together in Warfare Strategies. My chest tightens, and I pull her back into my arms.

"We should probably continue this conversation inside," Damara says from the doorway.

I retrieve my rifle, and Storm and I follow Damara inside. The cramped home has a musty smell. Peeled wallpaper and chipped paint cover the walls, and the ceiling is laced with cracks, varying in size from splinter thin to almost two inches thick. I'm no expert on architecture, but even I can tell it's not the safest of buildings. The only thing I can say for the place is its clean.

Damara closes the door behind us. "Storm," her voice is soft as she speaks to her, "why don't you go upstairs and wash your hands? Lunch'll be ready soon."

Storm bites her lip and looks at me.

"I'm not going anywhere," I say, reassuringly. I glance at Damara. At least I hope I'm not.

She runs up the stairs.

"Lunch?" I ask when Storm's out of earshot. It's after 1400 hours.

"She just got back from training. Leave your gun by the back door. Storm doesn't need to see you with it the whole time you're here." With that, Damara walks toward the kitchen.

I do as she instructs, hating the fact that I have the gun and that it could frighten Storm, and then join Damara in the kitchen. She gives me some carrots, a cutting board, and a knife, and she stirs a pot on the stove.

"So you're Bria?" Her back is toward me.

My chopping slows down. "Yes." Why do I feel like I'm about to be interrogated?

She taps her spoon against the pot and then faces me. "Why are you here?"

"I needed to check on Storm and make sure she's okay." I chop a sliver off the carrot, and then set the knife down.

"She said they took her from you. She's cried for you, said you'd help her."

I wipe my palms on my pants. "I couldn't find her. I tried, but there were...complications." It sounds so lame. I should have tried harder, risked more.

She takes the cutting board of half-chopped carrots from me, deftly chops the rest, and then adds them to the pot on the stove. "The worst day she's had since living here with me was the day she saw you again." There's an accusing note in Damara's voice, but I also sense a fierce protectiveness toward Storm.

"Is she okay?" I blurt the question out, though I know the answer.

"Some days, no, she's not at all okay. But in this house, I promised her she'd be safe." Damara steps toward me. "My question to you is, if you're here, can I keep that promise?"

We stare at each other. I don't know how to answer her. It's not like before. I'm not defying them. I'm doing everything they want me to do. But is she safe? I'm planning to escape, which is for her, but it could also endanger her. Something I can't share with Damara.

The sound of Storm clunking down the steps reaches us. She reappears before I'm able to decide what the right answer for Damara is.

Storm presses close to me and takes my hand in hers. "Are you staying for lunch, Bria?"

I smile down at her weakly. "I don't know." I look at Damara. "Am I?"

Damara smiles at Storm. "Yes, she is."

I sit down next to Storm at a rickety table in the kitchen, and Damara sets out a simple meal. As we eat, I can't help but notice the clear affection between the two. Storm talks through the entire meal, but there's a shadow in her eyes that wasn't there before. Some of her sweet innocence has been lost, and I can't decide if that fact makes me want to cry or strangle the person responsible. Maybe both.

Damara excuses herself.

"Bria. Are you okay?"

I snap back to the present, try to push aside my depressed thoughts, and focus on Storm. "Of course. Why?"

"You weren't listening to me." Her forehead crinkles.

"Of course I was listening." I feel a twinge of guilt for lying, but I don't want her to think I don't care about her.

She sighs deeply and shakes her head back and forth. "No, you weren't. I just told you I got eaten by a snake, and you said, 'that's nice.'" Her voice goes into a high falsetto as she mimics me. Then she gives me a pointed look.

I bite my lip and then grin at her. "Fine. You're right. I was a little distracted."

Her childish face turns serious. "Why? What's wrong?"

"Nothing. I just didn't hear your silly story." I try to laugh it off, but she doesn't even crack a smile. I take a bite of my meal. "How's your lunch?"

She kneels on her chair, then puts her hands on my face and turns my head so I'm looking her in the eye. "I know it's hard and scary here." She inhales deeply, and her shoulders rise and then fall. "But we can't let them win."

My eyebrows scrunch together. "What do you mean?"

Her gaze searches mine. "Even though they took so much from us, they won't win unless we let them."

I tuck a strand of hair behind her ear, still not understanding. She's so serious right now, so confident in what she's saying. "I think they already won, Storm. We're here, and," a sigh rises from deep within me and forces its way out, "I don't know if I can do what it takes to get out."

She whips her head back and forth. "That's not what I mean. It doesn't matter if we get out or not." Her lips press together, determination lining her face. "They only really win when we give up. When we stop believing in the things that are really true. When we lose hope and faith."

A lump forms in my throat. If I had just an ounce of the faith this girl has, maybe I'd be the one encouraging *her* not to give up, instead of her telling me.

"Okay." I don't actually know how to respond, so I just agree with her.

"How's your lunch?"

The conversation turns lighter, and I'm thankful for it. I doubt I could continue under her scrutiny much longer. Storm's right. I can't give up everything. I can't stay trapped here like this. Maybe I can borrow some of her determination, even though I don't have her faith. Her head is bowed as she slurps up some soup.

She looks up. "Why are you staring at me?"

I smile at her. "Just thinking that you're a pretty great kid."

I glance down at my wristband to check the time and sigh. "I need to go, little squirrel."

Storm gives me a long hug before I leave, and I promise her I'll be back to see her again soon. Damara tells Storm she can go play and then walks me out the back door.

"She's different. I can tell things have been hard on her." I gaze outside. "But she seems happy with you." I look back at Damara. "Thanks for caring."

Damara inclines her head slightly. "I'm not sure it's possible not to care for her." The hint of a smile plays on her lips and then vanishes. "You're welcome back anytime, Bria. As long as you're sure that my promise to Storm will be kept."

"I would never do anything to harm her."

Damara scrutinizes me, and I shift under her gaze. "I believe you." She turns to reenter the house.

As I jog back to the Recruits Living Quarters, I can't help but see the sadness in Storm's eyes that never seemed to fully leave, even when she was laughing. They're destroying her, and they don't care. All that matters to them is that they get out of her all they want. I need to get her out of here before they've demolished her. I picture my brothers' impish faces, their smiles and antics. No matter what it takes, I can't let them be the next ones destroyed by Talionis.

THIRTY-SEVEN

The two weeks until the Evaluation pass in a blur.

I visit with Storm whenever I can, and Cade has come a few times as well. He and Nika both waved off the way I acted when I found them praying, which was a relief since I'm not sure how to explain my reaction to the scene to *myself,* let alone someone else.

Matthias has continued to help me in hand-to-hand combat, and I've grown more comfortable around him. He seems to spend more time with me and my friends than he does with other cadets, which is something I don't know what to do with, but I don't hate his company.

I sneak out a few times each week to train and plan with Cai. The training has been strange, but he insists I do exactly what he says, so I've cleared cobwebs, beaten rugs with two sticks very specifically, and thrown knives. I like the knife throwing the most, since I seem to get better at it each time. The rest is grueling, and feels pointless, but the extra exercise has helped me improve in PT, which I'm not yet willing to admit to Cai.

While I'm training, he goes out and works. I've heard of more soldiers going missing, and there was an incident at one of the guard towers on the wall with some wild dogs. I'd much rather help him in his fight with the soldiers than do his chores, but he keeps telling me I'm not ready.

But our planning is coming along.

We've identified a few different route options and the areas we may need to sabotage, but we'll know more once I advance—which will hopefully begin after tomorrow's evaluation.

Recruits brush past me as they head to the bathroom to wash up for bed, and I walk to my room, consumed by my thoughts. Leaving has seemed like the most important thing for so long, and it was always on my mind. But now, something else fights for my attention even more. Or rather, Someone.

Even before I came to Talionis, I knew there was something missing in my life. After what I did, I assumed I deserved to feel this way, locked away from experiencing anything good, fighting the demons of my past. Before I was brought here, I wasn't happy. My life didn't offer me peace. Or hope of better things. Or joy.

Cai's face fills my mind. The confidence in his words when he spoke of honoring God. His kindness and compassion toward me and the things I'm going through. And the peace he seems to carry around with him everywhere. I kick Nika's comforter out of my way from where it's strewn across the floor. No. My life has never had what Cai has.

I sit on my bed, alone in the room, and brush out my hair.

A part of me doesn't want to go back to the Ruins, but I'm drawn there by more than just the promise of escape. There's something in Cai that pulls at me. A peace, calm. A hope. Every time I'm there, I find myself wishing he would tell me more about his God, explain how he can be so sure God could love me. But he hasn't, and I know it's because he's waiting for me to bring it back up. I almost did last night, but I'm too afraid he'll confirm what I already know—that what I've done is unforgiveable. Maybe I should have asked anyway, because right now, preparing for the challenge of tomorrow, I wish I had something I could be sure of.

Tomorrow.

My stomach knots, and I set my brush on the small table beside my bed. I've been improving in most of my trainings—

excelling in every warfare scenario—but tomorrow's results are what matter. I need to do well enough to land in one of the top three squads in my unit, or I won't be given higher clearance in any area.

Ari steps into the room, bringing me back to the present. Her face is paler than usual, and anxiety seems to cloak her. She sits on her bed and draws in a shaky breath.

"I'm so scared about tomorrow," she says, her voice small.

"Why are you scared? You can just change your stats like you always do." I grin, and Ari gives me a small smile.

"True," she says.

Nika enters, scoops up her comforter, and tosses it onto her bed.

"Plus," I continue, "no matter what the evaluation looks like, you'll do great in the tech part. Just try to get some sleep. Whatever happens tomorrow, you can't do it as well as you need to if you don't get rest."

"That's what Shane said too." Ari pulls her legs up onto her bed and hugs her knees to her chest. "But what if the three of us don't end up in the same squad? I don't want different roommates."

The thought is disturbing. I hadn't thought of what it might be like to *not* have Nika and Ari as my roommates. "Try thinking of something else."

Nika plops onto her bed. "Yeah, like maybe how *Shane* is the person you go to for comfort." She bats her long lashes and purses her lips. I can't help but grin.

"Stop, Nika," Ari says with no conviction. A small smile tilts the corners of her lips, and her face has gone from white to pink.

"Oh, come on! Tell us. What's going on with you and Shane?" Nika asks. "I've seen the two of you together a lot lately."

"Nothing. We're just friends," Ari protests, but her face reddens even more.

"Paahhleease! I have plenty of friends here who are guys—Cade, Belen, your brother. I don't talk to any of them the way you talk to Shane."

Ari grabs her pillow and flings it across the room at Nika, just missing her as she ducks.

I lean back against the wall. "I heard him tell Matthias you helped him with a tech issue he was having."

Nika draws in a breath dramatically. "You helped him with tech? My, it *is* serious!"

Ari tries to look exasperated, but a laugh bursts from her lips. "You two are the worst. Maybe I do want new roommates."

Nika tosses the pillow, and Ari catches it. "You'd miss us, and you know it."

We all laugh, and then Nika asks Ari about something Mandeville mentioned in class, which I'm almost positive is her way of continuing to keep Ari distracted, more than wanting the answer to the question. Ari grabs her screen, pulls up what Nika was asking about, and launches into a lengthy explanation.

Nika's words to Ari echo in my mind. I'd miss them too.

Resolve fills me. Tomorrow, after the evaluation, I'll tell them about Cai and what we're planning. It's risky, dangerous, but we need more people, and I don't want to leave these two behind.

***

I stand with my unit in formation as we wait for our instructions. They have lined all six units up in a two-row grid: Units One, Two, and Three in the front and Units Four, Five, and Six in the back. Each unit is spaced apart so that several people could walk between them. No one talks. No one moves.

We just wait.

The only thing we've been told so far is that the evaluation will take place in the Center. This will be the first time I've entered the Center. My palms sweat.

Sergeant Andor Valarius comes and stands before us. "Transports will take you to the Center for your first evaluation. Regular evaluations are a key component in the training of recruits in Talionis. Today will be difficult, but it is vital that you do your best."

My stomach flips.

He walks through the rows of recruits. "Your instructors will watch you along with various leaders of Talionis. They will assess you individually. You will be tested, evaluated, and then placed into squads to begin your next level of training." He walks back to the front, and his eyes roam through the rows. "Good luck, recruits. You'll need it."

A transport descends, and we're loaded in for the short flight to the Center. Some recruits around me shift back and forth like their bodies won't allow them to be still. One girl is gnawing on her lower lip. A guy is picking at his fingernails. Shadowy circles mar the skin under many eyes, and there's a fearful tension in the air. My gaze collides with Cade's. His jaw is set, and his dark eyes hold none of the fear I see in the others and feel in myself. He offers a small smile and nods his head at me. I nod back.

We approach the Center. It's even bigger than I remembered. The transport arches over the domed roof, passing the silver spikes that glint in the sunlight like teeth eager to devour. I look down through the glass at my feet as the Center's roof yawns open and consumes the transport. With a soft thump, we land in the beast's heart. My nerves are taut as I exit with the other recruits. I sure hope Cai's prayers do something, because I need all the help I can get.

I feel eyes watching me before I notice the stands surrounding us, mounting almost to the ceiling. The stands aren't filled, but hundreds, if not thousands, of people are here. Many more than I expected. There's an excited anticipation pulsating through the air, as though they're eager to watch whatever we're about to go through. They instructed us to stand before a large platform extending from the stands.

I look around as I wait. The Center has been sectioned off into various areas. There's an area with an obstacle course, another for weaponry evaluation. Mandeville is scurrying around a rectangular area with screens and equipment, testing out holograms. And dominating the largest portion are three huge, windowless cubes. Massive screens stretch across the back of the Center, behind the cubes, and most of the crowd is seated near them.

The screen lights up with a live video of Colonel Keenan Valarius as he walks out onto the platform in the middle of the stands. The crowd cheers as he waves at them. I turn my attention to the real

Colonel Valarius instead of the extra-large version on the screen. He motions with his hands for the crowd to quiet down, and soon there's silence.

"Welcome, recruits, to your first evaluation! Before I brief you on what to expect, I want to wish you the best of luck, though I'm confident your instructors have prepared you well, and you are ready to face this day." He beams, and something about his smile pulls at me. He reminds me of someone else.

Before I can place who, he continues. "Your evaluations will include a physical conditioning evaluation, where you will be required to complete an obstacle course quickly and efficiently; a technical evaluation, where you will identify and properly use different pieces of equipment; marksmanship evaluation; and finally, an assessment of your ability in Warfare Strategies. These screens"— he gestures to the massive screens flanking the back of the Center— "will show live feeds of the scenarios. It's time to begin. Your evaluators will lead you to the proper place for your unit to start." He steps away from the microphone, off the stage, and takes a seat.

They bring my unit to the obstacle course, and, at the word from our evaluator, we begin. The course is like many we've done, and I find myself able to keep pace with the rest of my unit. Several distance themselves from the rest of us, and a sudden rush of competitiveness pushes me forward. I leap over the mud pit and then drop to my stomach to crawl under a laser field. My body aches, but I push forward.

I have to do well today.

I move through the different obstacles, forcing myself to push beyond my natural limits. I jump off the wall I climbed for the last obstacle and race across the finish line, coming in somewhere in the middle of my unit. Much better than I've done. But I'm still disappointed I didn't do better.

Next, they evaluate us on our marksmanship. We're assessed in groups of five for this one as we go through a course with digitized targets hidden throughout. When the target appears, there's a limited time where it can be hit before it disappears again. It's like what we've done in weaponry training over the past couple of weeks, but when it's my turn, my nerves get the best of me, and I end up with five direct hits, seven partial hits, and four misses. I've done worse, but I've also done better.

I walk over to where the rest of my unit waits near the stands.

"Nice shooting," a familiar voice above me says.

A strange sense of relief relaxes my shoulders from their scrunched position when I look up into the stands and find Matthias smiling down at me.

"Could be better."

"Just take the compliment." His grin widens.

A smile lifts the corners of my mouth, and I shake my head at him. "Thank you." I try to say the words sarcastically, but the fact that I'm smiling renders any sarcasm ineffective.

"You've got this." He winks.

Something in my stomach lifts and then flutters, and a warm sensation starts at the base of my neck and cascades down my spine. It's the same wink I've seen a dozen times. The wink he gives to cheer me up, to encourage someone, to lighten the mood. But it's never affected me, other than making me smile or pretend annoyance with him. So why does it feel like, in this moment, that one gesture changed everything?

Matthias's eyebrows bunch together in an unasked question, his face turning serious, the expression the same one he wears whenever he's trying to make something better, to help me. My stomach flips again, the rush of a feeling I've never experienced before sweeping over me. It's wonderful and terrifying.

An evaluator comes over to tell us it's time to move to the next section. I pull my gaze away from Matthias, ready for the distraction of the next evaluation. Matthias is just my friend. I could never feel anything more for him...Right?

I move with my unit toward the technical evaluation, and Nika pops up next to me. "You are *so* going to explain what's going on with you and Matthias later," she murmurs.

My face burns. "Nothing's going on," I hiss.

Nika looks at me sideways. "Right."

I open my mouth to argue, but find I don't have any answer.

The unit stops, and I close my eyes for a split second, attempting to move my mind away from whatever just happened back there and onto the tech evaluation. This evaluation is the one I've been most concerned about, and being distracted won't help me.

The space is a vortex of tech. Holograms shoot out from screens, different pieces of equipment are set up on pedestals, and as I stare at it, my brain short-circuits. No matter how hard I've tried, technical training has been a struggle. Ari has offered me pointers, which mostly don't make sense because she can't understand how I don't get the *basics,* let alone the ultra-specific details she tries to relay. Matthias has helped a little in teaching me some functions of more simple equipment, but I'm not sure any of that will be helpful now.

The evaluators divide us into smaller groups, and we're led through the maze of tech, where we must identify what each thing is and demonstrate its use. We're to start with the items on the pedestals and move to the holograms of tech that are more advanced and too expensive to have out for the evaluation.

I'm going to fail this one. I know it already.

As I step up to the first pedestal, I glimpse Ari. She's already at one hologram and using a screen to turn the item and describe how it's used. After a moment, she moves on to another one. She appears so sure of herself. Which is the opposite of how *I'm* feeling at the moment.

"Recruit Averton!" the evaluator's sharp voice causes me to focus on him. "I said, identify and use this piece of equipment."

I look down at the boxy item in front of me. There's something familiar about it, but my mind seems unable to let go of its struggle over what to do with Matthias, and I can't remember what the box does. I pick it up and turn it over, hoping something comes back to me. It's heavier than I expected. After a few moments, I set it back down. No use denying the obvious.

"I don't know," I say.

The evaluator frowns, then asks about two other items. Both of which I don't know.

"What is this?" He holds up the screen in his hands.

I squint, confused. "It's an AVID-screen."

"At least you know something," he mutters, tapping on his screen. "I've seen enough of you. You're finished with this evaluation. Wait over there." He gestures with his head to where a few other recruits, including Ari, wait.

My stomach drops. I can't believe I did so badly. What is *wrong* with me? I shouldn't have let my mind focus on Matthias. There's nothing there other than friendship. He's trying to be a good friend, and my exhausted brain is making more of it than it is. I push all thoughts of him aside.

Ari smiles as I approach. "This one was easier than I expected!" she says.

I just look at her.

"What's wrong? Weren't you able to do it?"

"I'm not as..." I clear my throat and glance away, "... skilled in this area."

"No talking, recruits!" one of the evaluator's yells at us.

Ari gives me a sympathetic look that stings my already bruised pride, and we stay quiet as we wait for the rest of our unit to complete the evaluation.

CHAPTER

THIRTY-EIGHT

It's time for our final evaluation.

Warfare Strategies.

Once again, we're divided into smaller groups to be evaluated in one of the three cubes. All of our evaluators get into a booth where they will monitor our progress. They designate my group to go first.

I bounce twice on the balls of my feet, hands fisted tightly at my sides. My nerves are on edge, just like they are every time before I enter one of these. There's something about watching people you know get shot, getting shot yourself, that's unnerving, even though it's fake. I step forward. Doesn't matter how nervous I feel. It's time to go in.

Usually there are six to a group, but today there are only four of us: Shane, Cade, Shay, and me. This will be my first scenario without Nika and Ari. It feels weird entering without them, and I'm not thrilled about working with Shay.

The door slides shut behind us with the same clang as in Warfare Strategies. For a moment, there's nothing except the thick darkness. I wait. Sometimes we have to guess what we're supposed to do in the scenario they put us in, other times we find our orders, and then there are the times where a voice comes over speakers we can't see and tells us what to do. I wonder which it will be this time.

Click. It'll be the speaker.

"You will infiltrate the IPC Office and extract a man, Yosef Vinterbin, from block D, office number one-eighty-five. Your prep bag will have guard uniforms and IDs to facilitate your entrance. It is important that Yosef be taken alive, no matter the cost."

The voice clicks off. The room rumbles. No one says anything as we wait for the scene to unfold around us. Soon the room brightens. The windows in the building we're in look out at a towering structure with the words *IPC Office* emblazoned on the doors. The sun is setting, and the city seems to glow.

"Well," Shane says, "let's find the prep bag and do this."

The four of us search the room we're in for a few moments.

"Here it is." Cade pulls a duffle bag out from a hidden compartment in the floor.

Shay, Shane, and I crowd closer to him as he unzips the bag and reveals royal blue uniforms and four IDs. And weapons. I swallow hard as my eyes focus on the four compact guns and holsters. There was a recent scenario where we were issued guns, and I couldn't bring myself to use mine. I failed in that scenario. There's no way I can afford to fail this time, but will I be able to do whatever it takes to succeed? Even if it means shooting someone?

Cade hands out the uniforms to Shane and Shay and then to me. His eyes hold mine before he relinquishes the uniform, and I know he can see my anxiety.

"We'd better change." I turn away from Cade, unable to continue looking him in the eye.

I pull the uniform on over my clothes, making sure everything is tucked in and buttoned. I knot my hair into a low bun and then stuff the guard hat on my head. Last, I cinch the belt around my waist, the attached holster and gun immediately weighing me down.

Shay steps forward. "We need to succeed in this mission."

I roll my eyes. *No kidding.* I really miss having Nika and Ari with me.

"We'll report for duty in pairs," Shane says, taking charge. "Bria and Cade will go in first, and Shay and I will enter three minutes later."

"Once we find him, how will we get him out?" Shay asks.

There's silence as the four of us stare at each other. It's a valid question.

"We'll need a distraction," I say. "Something big enough that no one will pay attention to us while we get Yosef out."

Shane nods thoughtfully, and then his eyes brighten. "I had a prison scenario before…I think I might know a way to give you that distraction."

I tilt my head. "How?"

"Don't worry about that part." Shane waves his hand, brushing away my question. "Shay and I will handle the distraction. You and Cade find Yosef and get him out."

I cross my arms over my chest. "But how will we know when your little distraction is happening?"

Shane frowns. "It won't be little. You'll know."

"Let's set our bands for thirty minutes," Cade suggests. "We can try to coordinate the extraction and the distraction so that everything is taking place at the same time."

We all agree and set our bands for the time limit.

Shane spins on his heel and faces the office. "Let's go."

We leave the building, and Cade and I break off from Shane and Shay. As we approach the doors of the office, several guards exit.

"Looks like we made it in time for the next shift," Cade whispers.

We enter the building, and two guards are inside in front of another set of doors. A man whose height might rival Major Vasco's stands on one side, and a woman with an upturned nose and narrow eyes stands on the other. I keep my face neutral, even though my heart is racing. What if they realize we're not the normal guards?

"IDs," the man barks.

Cade and I both hold out our identification. The guard scans our IDs against a bar on the door.

"*Night guard for block D.*" A voice chirps.

The man then nods at the woman. She types in a code, presses another button, and the door opens.

"Wait," the woman says as we're about to pass.

We both stop, and sweat forms on my forehead. This is it. She knows we aren't two of the guards.

"Don't forget your block D badges." She hands us each a badge.

A small dose of relief cools my anxiety, and I give her a curt nod. "Thanks."

Cade and I enter the building and head down a long corridor. The door clanks shut behind us, and the feeling of being trapped presses in on me. Cade doesn't seem at all worried. I force my breathing to remain even.

The walls are white, and our feet rap against the gleaming floor as we near a desk that's flanked on either side by doors. A large woman sits behind the desk, hair pulled back from her face so tightly that it seems to stretch her skin. Glasses perch on the end of her nose, and she peers over them at us.

"Block assignment?" she asks in a bored tone.

We hold up our badges, and she presses a button. A door toward our left opens.

Cade nods at her. "Have a good one."

The woman snorts but says nothing. Cade and I walk through the door. It closes behind us, and then we're required to scan our IDs at the next sets of doors in order to get through.

I glance up at a camera in the corner of the ceiling. "Security is tight."

"No kidding," Cade says.

"I hope Shane's distraction works."

"It'd better, or we're sunk."

I flinch at Cade's words, even though he's voicing my thoughts. The fact that he feels that way too makes this whole thing even more nerve-wracking.

We swipe our IDs on yet another set of doors and then enter block D. There's a reception area with couches and two desks with two men behind them. They barely glance up from their screens when we enter, and I find myself immensely grateful for the uniforms. At least we can appear to fit in, even though I don't feel like I do at all.

Cade and I pass through the reception area and back into offices of block D. They fill this first level, and hover ramps provide access to upper levels. Very few people are around since it's the end of the day.

Cade glances at his watch. "Only fifteen minutes left. We'd better find him fast." He adjusts his hat. "Maybe we should split up."

The idea of being in this building on my own isn't one I find appealing at all. I look at the nearest office. The number on the door is *15-76*. "Wait. How high do you think this building is?"

Cade shrugs. "I'd guess around fourteen or fifteen stories."

I point at the closed office door. "I think it's fifteen. So if the number of Yoseph's office is one-eighty-five—"

"He's probably on the fifteenth floor," Cade says, instantly understanding. "Let's go."

We rush to the nearest hover ramp and swipe our IDs and badges before stepping on. I press the button for level fifteen. The hover ramp rises, each level passing in a blur. It stops, and we step off.

Without a word to each other, we move down the hallway, our pace just short of a run. The room numbers are lowest near the hover ramp, and we have to go down several hallways before we hit numbers in the seventies. I glance at my wristband. Two minutes left.

Cade increases his speed as though I spoke the time out loud. Maybe I did. My heart's pounding so loudly, I doubt I'd be able to hear anything else. We pass office 1-83, then 1-84, and then we skid to a halt in front of the closed door of office 1-85. Thirty seconds until Shane's distraction.

My fingertips seem to throb with the intensity of the adrenaline racing through me. Cade scans his ID, then places his badge over the reader. I stop breathing. What if the door doesn't open? His fingers curl around the handle, and he presses it down. There's a soft click before the door swings forward.

Cade enters first, with me close behind him. "Yosef Vinterbin?"

"Yes. What is it, guard?" a man's thickly accented voice asks.

"We need you to come with us," Cade responds.

"What?" Yosef asks incredulously.

I move so that I'm standing next to Cade. An older man sits

behind a desk surrounded by windows that offer a view of the city. His mouth is pinched into a scowl.

"Is there a threat I'm unaware of? Because unless there is, I'm not going anywhere with you." He stands, hands planted on his desk as he glowers at us.

In that instant, the entire building seems to shudder, and alarms start blaring. That must be Shane's distraction.

Yosef stands up straight. "What is going on?"

"We'd better move quickly," I say.

Cade nods, and we both head toward Yosef. His eyes narrow. "You aren't the normal guards."

Something in the pit of my stomach tightens, and I hesitate. Cade continues moving and is almost at Yosef, when Yosef draws a small gun from under his suit jacket. He points it at me, and for the second time in under a minute, I stop breathing, waiting to see what will happen.

Cade's leg shoots out and collides with Yosef's hand, sending the gun spiraling to the floor. In the next instant, Cade puts him in a sleeper hold. Yosef struggles at first, but then his movements slow and finally stop. Cade loops an arm around Yosef's now limp frame, and I hurry over to help him.

"Thanks," I say.

We half carry, half drag Yosef from the room. There's no one in the hallway when we emerge from the office, but the alarms sound even louder, and the lights flash. Shouting from the lower levels as guards work to evacuate the building, echo through the clamor. Cade moves back toward the hover ramp.

I stop. "We can't go that way. They'll catch us for sure."

His eyebrows lift. "There's no other option."

My mind whirls, and I look wildly around me. There *has* to be another option. Then I see it: *Maintenance Hover Ramp.*

"This way!" We stumble in the direction of the maintenance hover ramp.

Yosef's weight presses against my shoulders, and my breathing comes in shorter gasps. I glance over at Cade and see that, even though he's not breathing hard, there's a thin sheen of sweat on his forehead. We reach the maintenance hover ramp, and he fumbles for his ID and then scans it. The hover ramp door opens, and we drag Yosef in, collapsing against the wall.

I press the button for level one, and the hover ramp whooshes down. "I hope Shane's distraction works well enough to keep anyone from noticing us."

The hover ramp comes to a stop, and Cade readjusts his hold on Yosef but says nothing.

I loop my arm back around Yosef's waist, and we move as fast as we can through the first level's back hallways and then through the reception area. The men are no longer working at their desks, and the guards we see are all searching the different offices. No one seems to think anything of us.

We get through the hallway that leads back to the building entry. The woman who checked us into block D has abandoned her desk, and the door to freedom is in sight. A guard rounds the corner. Her eyes catch first on Yosef and then on Cade and me. Yosef becomes a heavier weight than I can handle as I realize she knows. Her fingers twitch, and then her gun is drawn and pointed at me.

I brace myself for the pain I know I'll feel. The bullet explodes from the chamber. Then Cade is diving in front of me. The bullet hits his shoulder. His hat flies off his head, and his body falls to the ground. The sounds of the alarms fade from my consciousness, and I drop Yosef as I look down at Cade.

The light is quickly fading from his eyes. "Run, Bria," he croaks out. His head falls back.

A cry lodges beneath my breastbone, and I hear another bullet being fired. But it doesn't hit me.

"Bria!" Shay is shouting at me. "We have to go!"

"But Cade..." My mouth is dry, and the words stick inside it like cotton.

Shane races up next to me, grabs Yosef by the arms, and begins dragging him to the door. Shay grabs my arm and forces me to leave.

We exit the building, and I wrench my arm from Shay's grip. I can't leave Cade in there. I turn to go back.

Everything goes black.

The door to the cube opens. Our warfare scenario is complete. Cade stands, and I can't stop a sigh of relief. Even though I know you can't die in a scenario, there's always a part of me that won't relax until I'm sure the person I thought died is okay. I flash a grateful smile at Cade.

We exit the cube to the sound of cheering.

"What's going on?" I ask.

The evaluator approaches, and we snap to attention. Her face is flushed with excitement. "The Commander observed your scenario." The words gush from her mouth.

Shay gasps. "He did? Do we get to meet him?"

The evaluator shakes her head. "He just left." She clears her throat and fans her face before glancing down at her screen.

It's like they all lost their mind for a moment just because the man showed up. The fact makes me more uneasy than anything.

The evaluator focuses on us, more composed. "You successfully completed your Warfare Strategies Scenario. You are the only group so far to do so. Congratulations." She studies her screen again. "This was a basic extraction scenario, and it provided a solid test of your handle on Warfare Strategies. Averton and Renatus, good job finding and extracting the target. Malton and Bellingdon, your distraction proved useful. Well done. Though one of your team was lost, overall, you showed the skills we wanted to see."

I clench my fist tighter over my heart, wishing I could have prevented Cade from dying in the scenario.

She dismisses us to go to the stands where the other recruits who have finished their evaluation wait.

We sit for another hour as the rest of the units complete their stations and join us. Finally, everyone is done. Exhaustion plasters everyone's faces. Probably mine too. This day was as difficult as I expected. Harder, actually. My stomach rumbles, reminding me I skipped breakfast and lunch.

Colonel Keenan Valarius takes his place on the platform he occupied earlier. "Congratulations, recruits. You have completed your first evaluation. Some of you impressed me today, and I look forward to working more directly with you in the future. Your rankings for each area and squad placement will be listed on a screen in the dining hall shortly. If you have questions about your ranking, you may ask Staff Sergeant Valarius and Sergeant Meritas. They will be in the dining hall during your dinner hour for this purpose. You are dismissed to go to your rooms and clean yourselves up. Dinner will be served at 1800 hours."

He steps off the platform and exits the Center, two soldiers falling into step behind him.

THIRTY-NINE

A large screen dominates one wall in the Dining Hall, and, despite the tantalizing aroma and look of the food lining the center tables, every recruit heads directly to it to find out what their ranking is. I shoulder my way through the crowd, earning a few dirty looks in the process until I can get a clear view.

My eyes scan the screen. Recruits are listed by last name in alphabetical order, along with their ranking in each category. It doesn't take long before I find my name near the top.

Averton, Bria:

Physical Conditioning: 62nd percentile

Technical Evaluation: 7th percentile

Marksmanship Evaluation: 74th percentile

Warfare Strategies: 99th percentile

Okay. What in the world does that mean?

"Before you all ask me to help you understand your rankings," Sergeant Valarius bellows from behind us, causing me to jump, "I'm going to explain the basics to you. You were all ranked individually, and then placed in the percentile that rightly reflects your rating in conjunction with the other recruits in every unit. The higher your percentile, the better you did. In the areas where you received a lower percentile, you will need to focus on pushing yourself to do better before the next evaluation."

He strides to the screen. "These rankings will determine your Squad within your unit. Your HaloAct Bands have been updated with your new squad number. The members of Squad 1 in each unit are those who are the very best in at least one category, and who rank over fifty percent in at least two of the other categories."

He pauses, and I pull up my ranking on my band. It takes a moment, and then the squad information loads. My breath hitches. I did it. I'm in Squad 1 of Unit 6.

"From now on," Sergeant Valarius continues, "everything you do will be with your squad. You will eat, train, and work with your squad. Even your room assignments will change—females will be with the other females in their squad and males with the other males. You'll have to rely on one another to make good competency marks for the squad, and the person who is excelling or rewarded for an achievement will take on the role of squad leader. This position is one of respect and honor, and it can be earned by any member of the squad."

I roll my shoulders. Okay. More change. But it can't be any worse than what I've done so far. I subtly glance around the room, searching for Nika and Ari. Hopefully at least one of them made it into Squad 1 with me.

"Over the next four months, you will have three more evaluations. The next will be six weeks from today. We expect to see an improvement in every category. In the third evaluation, we will determine which recruits show the most promise and place them in the Elite Recruit unit, a specialized unit with intensive trainings. The fourth evaluation will determine which roles you assume in the city, and then the Commencement will take place."

Laban jumps in. "The Commencement is the day you will achieve your true potential and become assets for the Commander. The city will gather to celebrate with you. How well you do in your final evaluations will determine the places you'll be able to ascend to as citizens and potential leaders for the Commander. Or they will seal your fate as mere workers in Talionis, rather than those who will truly make a difference."

Sergeant Valarius's eyes scan the group. "If you have any questions, you may approach us individually."

Like anyone would want to do that.

They move off to the side, and I study my rankings again. I made it into Squad 1, but now I have another goal to push for: Elite Recruit. For Cai's plan to work, that's where I'll need to be. And that means I have some work to do. Fatigue washes over me, and I stifle a yawn.

For now, I need food and rest.

Ari and Nika find me a moment later.

"Which squad are you in?" Ari asks, eyes glowing.

"One."

Nika pumps her arm. "Yes! Me too. Now, Ari," Nika rolls her head to focus on her, "will you finally tell me which squad you're in? She made me wait until you were here."

Ari looks like she's about to burst. "I'm in Squad 1 too!"

"Girl, I wanna ask how, but now is probably not the time for you to tell me." Nika shakes her head, but there's a smile in her eyes.

Other than in tech, there's no way Ari should have hit the marks needed to make it into Squad 1, but apparently she had enough time to adjust her ranking before the squad assignments registered. I smirk as the three of us get in line for our dinner. I can't wait for Ari to meet Cai. She'll probably redo every bit of tech he has set up in the Ruins. The thought makes me want to laugh.

Tonight. I'll tell them tonight when we're back in our room.

It's not until after I have a tray of food that I realize the tables have been assigned. Nika, Ari, and I make our way through the room until we find the table for Unit 6 Squad 1. But when I see who's there, my muscles tense.

Perched on the edge of her seat, nose upturned as she watches me approach, is Shay.

Somehow I get through dinner, only able to endure her gushing excitement about being in Squad 1 and regular mini-lectures about how we all need to work hard to make good competency marks because of the occasional look of annoyance Nika gives me. As I'm finishing the last of my chicken and potatoes, Laban enters. I frown. Perfect. The one other person I didn't want to see again today is here.

"Listen up," he shouts. "Your uniforms need to be updated with your squad information. Before you go to your barracks for tonight, you need to visit the tailors. Squad one from each unit, you're dismissed first. Leave your trays. Squad six from your unit will clear your dishes."

Our table gets up, and I strap my rifle to my back and then reach for my tray.

Shay shoves my hand away. "You heard Sergeant Meritas. We don't have to clear our table."

"I can clean up my own mess," I say through clenched teeth.

She cocks her head. "Then maybe you aren't worthy of this squad." With that, she spins and saunters to the door.

I ball my hands into fists. I've seen Shay in hand-to-hand combat, and I could take her.

"She's not worth it," Nika says.

I blow air out between my teeth but follow Nika from the room. She's right. But I'm not sure how long I'll be able to deal with Shay before I vent my frustration with my fists.

"Next!" Presidia yells.

I step up to the counter and hand her my shirts, and she groans.

"Positively atrocious," she mutters before placing one shirt beneath a machine. Seconds later, *Squad 1* is printed below my name and unit number.

"What is that?" Laban asks Sampta, the vein in his temple throbbing.

"Purple thread," Sampta states, refusing to look Laban in the eye.

"Ooh let me see!" Presidia abandons my second shirt and rushes over to Sampta.

"You cannot use purple thread on a recruit's uniform," Laban says.

Again, I'm amazed by how even he's keeping his tone, especially considering how his golden eyes are flashing.

"But it looks so lovely," Presidia whines. "Ah! What if we dyed the uniform—"

Laban slashes his hand through the air. "Silence. Both of you. The uniforms must be *uniform*. You cannot change any of them. Use black thread."

"But—"

"No. Buts." Each word is sharp, and Laban seems ready to lose his cool. "These are the Commander's specifications. Follow them."

With a huff, Sampta and Presidia resume their work, but as soon as Presidia gives me back my uniform, she uses disinfectant gel and grumbles to herself about how she and her sister are wasting their talents doing such menial work.

I leave the tailors, amused and thankful for the distraction.

"Recruit."

I turn at the word to find a soldier with a screen watching me. "Yes, sir?"

"Your room is now on the second floor of the Recruits Living Quarters." He goes back to his screen.

"Thank you, sir," I say, but he's distracted by his screen, so I leave.

As I'm about to go up the stairs, Ari catches up to me and starts chatting about how excited she is that we're in the same squad. I shake my head, wondering if she'll be as excited once our more intense PT starts. Maybe Cai will help get her into shape the way he's helped me. If he can get her away from his tech long enough.

We exit the stairwell, and Ari finds our names on the door to a room halfway down the hall. It's a little more spacious than the room we had downstairs, but there are four beds instead of three. Nika's waiting inside already.

"I'm so tired," Ari says, refolding her uniform and placing it in the drawer by her new bed.

"I have something to tell you guys before we go to sleep," I say. I'm nervous about telling them about Cai and our plan, and I need to get it done before I lose my nerve.

"I'm shocked that you made it into this squad," Shay's voice precedes her into the room, and everything in me recoils.

She enters and stares down her nose at me. "Don't get in my way. I want the Commander to see how loyal I am to him and his cause. If you mess that up, you'll regret it."

"She earned her place here," Nika says, tone colder than I've ever heard it. "We all did."

Shay's glare moves from me to Ari, and she looks her up and down, disgust painting her face. She focuses on Nika. "We'll see about that."

Ari slumps on her bed and retrieves her screen, burying her face in it. All traces of her excitement are gone, and we have Shay to thank for that.

"What were you gonna say, Bria?" Nika asks me with her back turned to Shay and voice quiet.

I shake my head. "Never mind."

There's no way I can tell Nika and Ari about Cai, not with Shay here. She'd report us immediately and with joy.

I get ready for bed and climb beneath my covers, unease wrapping itself around me. I'm where I need to be, and I'll receive higher security clearance like I need to, but the stakes have gotten higher. Shay's going to be watching my every move, waiting for me to mess up, ready to turn me in and get me kicked out of the squad... or worse.

I turn onto my side and stare at the wall, wishing I could go see Cai and ask him what to do, how he thinks I should navigate this. But sneaking out tonight is too risky.

As I fall asleep, the memory of Cade jumping in front of me, taking my bullet, pierces me. My body shakes, and cold sweat breaks out. It wasn't real. I know that. But the horror of the moment won't leave me alone.

Each time I close my eyes and start to fall asleep, the memory assaults me. When the digital clock on the wall reads 23:19, I make my decision. I need to go see Cai. Now. I need someone to tell me this is all wrong, that I shouldn't have to experience watching my friend get shot, even if it's not real.

I sit up and swing my legs out of bed.

"Where are you going?" Shay asks.

Defeat smacks me in the face. "To the bathroom. If that's alright with you, *ma'am.*"

I get up and go to the bathroom, loneliness consuming me.

I t's been a week and a half since I've been to the Ruins. Ten days of Shay watching me like she's a coyote, and I'm her prey, waiting for me to slip up. Which has made me push harder in every training, much to her annoyance. Shane's our squad leader right now, but I'm second in command because of my skills in Kill Zones and in the Warfare Scenarios we go through. And Shay hates it, so it's worth the sickening praise I'm receiving from our instructors.

Tonight's the night. Once I'm confident Shay is sleeping, I slip out of our room. I *need* to see Cai.

The wind screams through the air, whipping past leafless branches, scattering fallen leaves. I make my way through the Ruins, wondering if he will even be at the training site. There's a loud crack above me, and I look up in time to see a branch splintering off a tree and careening to the ground. I bolt out of the way. It lands with a thud where I stood moments before. Maybe coming here tonight was a bad idea. The wind storm seems to worsen. I pick up my pace and cover the distance to the training site faster than usual.

I pull back the vines obscuring the door and step into darkness. No Cai, but entering the site should have set off an alert that I'm here. The walls block me from the wind howling outside, but I can't stop the chill wrapping itself around me. Someone or something is watching me.

Could Shay have followed me here? In the wind, I may not have noticed.

I step back until I'm pressed against the wall. I move my hands along the rough boards, searching for something to protect myself. My knuckles bump into the smooth wood of a staff. I grasp it, the soft wood against my palm both comforting and familiar. Since training with Cai, I've held a staff every time I've been in the Ruins. I only wish I felt confident using it.

I clutch it with both hands, my eyes searching the blackness for signs of whoever's lurking in the shadows. A gust of wind rattles the walls, and the sound of trees cracking adds to the cacophony of the night. I shiver. I haven't felt this terrified in the Ruins since my first night here.

The vines shift to my right, and someone enters, blinding me with light. I squint and cringe away. There's a scurrying sound in the back corner, but my eyes are still adjusting from the infringing light, and I'm unable to tell what it is. I blink and look back at the intruder at the door, my staff raised, poised for a fight.

"Bria, it's been a while." Cai lets the vines swing into place behind him. "Are you okay?"

Relief and annoyance replace the tense fear from a moment earlier. I drop the staff. "No."

Cai walks to the fire pit and lets the flames of his torch lick against the dry kindling and logs. Soon the entire site is glowing with warmth.

"What's wrong?" He places his torch in its designated space on the wall.

I glance back at the corner where I heard the rustling. "Something or someone else was in here when I got here."

Cai quirks an eyebrow at me. "Only one alarm went off for this site, and it was when you entered. Are you sure you didn't just hear the wind?"

"Yes, I'm sure!" I snap, even as a whisper of doubt makes me question what I thought I sensed. No. I know something was here, and I can only hope it wasn't Shay.

"And I found a staff," I jab my finger toward where it now lies at my feet, "but guess what? I had no idea what to do with it! Despite what you said it would do, your training with this stuff hasn't been preparing me to face any kind of enemy."

I've been on a knife's edge because of Shay, losing the little freedom I had to talk openly in my room with Ari and Nika, and the scenarios they've been putting our squad through, and I know I'm taking it out on Cai. But I can't stop myself.

Cai does a quick and thorough search of the training site. "I don't see anything, but—" he puts his hand out when I huff out my frustration, "I'll make sure the site is secure before I leave tonight. If I find any reason to doubt its security, we'll clear it and change locations. Okay?"

I cross my arms over my chest. "Fine."

He retrieves his staff and faces me. "Now, let's deal with the issue of your training."

I roll my eyes. "What training?" I'm being unfair, but somehow Cai has become safe enough for me to take out my frustration on him.

"As I said before, your body needed to become conditioned to certain movements." He continues, unflustered by my attitude. "I believe it has been, and furthermore, I think you'll be able to do some things I showed you the first day you came to train."

"Yeah right." There's no way I'm conditioned to do the things he did that day.

"You've become faster at clearing the webs." He scoops up the staff on the floor.

I eye the staff, then him. "Cai, come on—"

"Am I right?"

"Sure, I've gotten faster."

He tosses the staff to me and I catch it.

"Let me show you how that will help you." He twirls his staff in his hand. "I'm going to attack you."

I almost drop the staff. "What?"

"When I'm within striking distance, use your staff the same way you do for clearing the webs."

Without giving me a second to register what he's saying, Cai flies toward me and swings his staff at my head. I thrust my staff forward, whirl it in a wide circle, and Cai's staff is thudding to the floor. I gape at him. How did I do that?

"Not bad. Let's try that again, but with a lower attack."

My mind has a difficult time registering that I'm able to ward off Cai's attacks, but my body easily performs the movements each time.

"Okay." Cai sets his staff aside. "Now get the sticks you use to beat out the rugs."

I twirl the staff in my hand and feel a sense of satisfaction when it completes a full circle without tumbling to the ground. "Wait. Can we you show me what attacks I can do with this first?"

"No," Cai answers. "We're going to work with the sticks. Get them."

I twirl the staff one more time and then set it aside. I retrieve the two sticks, and Cai pulls a similar pair from a leather pouch on the table.

He faces me. "Hold them in the first position for beating out the rugs."

I tuck the stick in my left hand under my right arm and rest the stick in my right hand on my right shoulder.

Cai mirrors my movements. "Go through the movements of beating out the rugs, in the order I've shown you. Don't think."

My eyebrows bunch together. "What?"

"Just do the movements. Ready? Begin."

Still confused, I go through the movements. As soon as I start, Cai moves as well, his sticks clacking against mine.

I hesitate, surprised. As soon as my movements slow, Cai hits me in the arm. "Ow!" I cradle my arm, glaring at him. "That hurt."

"You're fine. Don't stop. Don't think about what's happening. Let your body do what we've trained it to do." Cai positions his sticks back into the first position. "Let's try again."

I eye him, unsure.

"You saw how you could handle the staff," Cai says. "You can handle this as well. Come on, let's go." He shifts on his feet, crouching lower.

I bite my lip. My arm throbs, but I'm intrigued, so I resume my position.

"Begin," Cai chirps.

Our sticks fly, and this time I'm ready for the clack of Cai's sticks against mine. I feel the reverberations through my forearms, and there's something exhilarating about the rhythm of the motions coordinating with the clash of the sticks. My feet and hands move in a practiced cadence, Cai's every movement mirroring mine.

"Faster!"

I pick up the pace the same way I would when moving through the rugs. The sticks clash faster, harder. We hit high, then bend low, again and again moving through fight patterns I would never have believed I could do. Sweat beads my brow, and my breathing becomes heavier, but, even so, I'm not ready to stop when Cai tells me to.

For the next hour, he shows me how his methods have been working to train me to fight and defend myself, even though I didn't realize it. He outmaneuvers me, shows me my weaknesses, and points out that there's much more I need to learn, but when we finish, I can't help but be pleased with what I'm able to do.

Cai hands me a rough rag to wipe away the sweat while he uses another for the same purpose. I rub the fabric over my face, then dab it against my neck.

"There was more going on than you realized each time you came here." He leans against a wall. "Am I right?"

"I suppose," I mumble.

A small smile tilts the corner of his lips. "Remember that."

"Sure." I toss the rag onto the table.

"Sometimes the things you're learning and doing have a greater purpose than what you realize at first. If you give up because you don't understand, or because something doesn't make sense to your logic, you risk missing out."

His words bring with them a rush of realizations. "Talionis is doing the same thing with the recruits. Making us do the same things repeatedly, conditioning us."

Cai straightens. "Like what?"

"From the beginning, they've had us jumping over walls and getting shot at with training bullets. There are Kill Zones all the time—before a meal, in an obstacle course during PT. Even the scenarios they put us through have people shooting at us, usually when we're in a city or town or something." My heart races. "What do you think it's for?"

"Not a mission of peace." His face darkens in anger. "It's not right. No one should have to experience the suffering of war, especially ones so young."

Somehow, his anger toward what I'm being put through loosens my tongue. "I've had to watch my friends die. It's not real, but the scenarios..." I share what I've seen, the pain I've felt in the scenarios I've gone through.

When I finish, Cai places his hands on my shoulders, and his dark eyes bore into mine with a tenderness and compassion that makes me feel safe for the first time in months.

"I'm sorry, Bria. God didn't create us for suffering and death, but brokenness and sin have brought it into this world and all of our lives." He squeezes my shoulders and lets go.

I turn away, eyes burning. Cai fights evil, takes down those who would harm others. What would he say if he knew I was responsible for my brother's death, that some of the most intense suffering in my life, my family's lives, was my fault? Would he still let me be a part of what he's doing to stop Talionis?

I bury my thoughts and questions and join Cai at the table.

I share with him my scores from the evaluation and explain why I haven't been able to make it out here for the past week. Then for the next hour, we review the list of targets we plan to attack, going back and forth about additional options. When I share about the Commencement coming up in a few months, he agrees it will afford the best opportunity to escape, since, from what I understand, most of Talionis will be present for the event except for a skeleton crew of soldiers stationed throughout points of interest in the city.

I tell him about my new squad and the higher security clearance I've received. When I show him the new places I have access to, he pulls out a list of buildings with secret passageways and compartments. There are a few I can look into now that I have access to those areas.

By the time we finish, the wind has died down, and Cai walks me back to the fence. He spontaneously prays for me like he did the first time I was here. It's short but powerful. It seems as natural to him as breathing, and a longing rises in me. A part of me wants what he has —what Nika and Cade and Storm have—but if I can't imagine Cai accepting me after what happened with Ezri, how could God?

Maybe the evil of Talionis is the Hell I deserve.

FORTY-ONE

"Listen up, Squad One!" Sergeant Valarius addresses us in the Arena after the rest of the units and squads have been sent to their stations. "Your training today will incorporate both PT and weaponry skills while you are in a warfare strategies scenario. You must work together as a unit to achieve the highest competency marks possible. Understood?"

"Sir, yes, sir!"

Laban paces in front of us. "This squad needs to be the best squad of your entire unit, and so far, you've done well. Today, you need to show us what you're made of, and, more importantly, show the Commander what you can do. Because he will be watching."

Shay's breath hitches, and several in our squad seem to stand taller, but the thought makes me sick. I'd love to sabotage this whole scenario, embarrass Laban and Sergeant Valarius and Shay in front of their precious commander, but the results of that kind of action could be catastrophic.

"Recruit Averton. Step forward," Sergeant Valarius says.

I tense for an instant before obeying, trying to figure out what I did wrong. I come up blank.

"Because of the skills you've shown in the Warfare Scenarios and in the obstacle course yesterday through both the Kill Zone and in the swimming portion, you will lead your squad through this training today."

"Yes, sir." For once, I'm thankful the words come automatically.

"You may step back into formation."

I salute, turn on my heel, and return to my place next to Nika. Shay's face is red, her eyes narrow. She's livid.

Sergeant Valarius marches us to Warfare Strategies, where Major Vasco takes over and brings us to Zone One's staging area. It could be my nerves, but every soldier we pass seems more on edge than usual. Probably because the Commander is making an appearance to watch our scenario.

Before we go in, Major Vasco gives us our instructions. "The ten of you are tasked with taking out a bridge to prevent soldiers from crossing. Your scenario will begin three miles from your target, and you will need to enter a city, retrieve your supplies, traverse dangerous terrain, and set your explosives all within one hour. If you're late, your mission fails. If you're caught while retrieving your supplies, your mission fails. The only way it will be a success is if the bridge is destroyed, no matter what the casualties. Do you understand?"

"Sir, yes, sir!"

"You will have fifteen minutes to review a map and plan how you will proceed." He gives me a screen and then leaves us in the staging area.

For an instant, the weight of responsibility before me is crushing, but I catch Cade's eye. He gives the slightest nod and smile, and it's enough to give me the courage to step forward.

"Okay, let's prepare." I give Ari the screen, and she pulls up the map. I study it for a moment, determining our route, seeing what needs to be done.

"Are you going to give us instructions, *Squad Leader,* or just stare at the map?" Shay's caustic remark brings my head up. "I don't know why you're the one in charge of such an important scenario."

"Are you questioning Sergeant Valarius's decision?" I ask, keeping my voice even.

Shay's face pales. "Of course not, no. Never."

I stare at her until she looks away and then give my instructions, finding more confidence as I do. I know my squad, the skills of each member, and because of that, I can lead them through this scenario.

Ari is the tech genius.

Cade can read people better than anyone else, and he sees the signs when something's about to happen.

Nika is a beast with hand-to-hand combat, and she's also become incredibly skilled in weaponry.

Shane is strong and fast, and he will follow orders, even if he doesn't understand them. A skill I rarely appreciate, but it will come in handy today.

Belen has achieved sniper status in weaponry.

Maze enjoys explosives far more than he should, but he understands them, which we need for this scenario.

And Shay. Shay is ruthless. No matter what the cost, she'll make sure we complete this mission successfully. And, because we need to, I'll give her the detonator.

I'll lead my squad to the best of my ability, and I'll use my skills of getting through dangerous situations to bring them all out safely. Because none of this squad is going to die on my watch.

The fifteen minutes ends, and I exit the staging area first and enter Zone 1.

Here we go.

THE SCENARIO ENDS, AND MAJOR VASCO RETRIEVES US FROM ZONE 1.

"That was a risky plan, Recruit Averton, but it paid off. Well done." Major Vasco taps on his screen. "The Commander was pleased with your performance—all of you."

Our bands buzz.

"He's granted you a pass for the rest of the day as a reward for a job well done. Your dinners tonight will be from his kitchen and served at your table, so you do not have to wait in line with the other recruits. You're dismissed."

Before he can walk away, Shay catches him. "Major Vasco, I have a report on two recruits from Unit 6, Squad 3. They skipped Educational Training."

"Come with me," he says.

Shay trails after him, and my stomach twists. She's gained the reputation of turning recruits in for punishment, and most fear her and stay away, except for her friend in Squad 2 and the small gang they've surrounded themselves with. The girl from Squad 2 follows Shay around at every opportunity, mimics what she says, and feeds Shay information Shay then uses against others. The rest of the gang gives Shay some space but report to her like she's their leader. It's sickening to watch.

Most of the time, she goes to Laban, but I guess, since she has free time now, she figured Major Vasco was a good option.

The rest of us head for the exit.

"Nice job in there," Shane says to me. "You're a good squad leader. I wouldn't have thought to wire the bridge that way."

"That was Maze's idea," I say. "I just let him do what he thought was best."

The scenario went well. Almost too well. Our squad performed perfectly, and Shay even listened to the orders I gave her. The most troublesome part was the time pressure of the scenario, which forced us to move quickly and felt like we were going through an obstacle course in Physical Conditioning.

At the end, when we were attacked by soldiers, it was intense, but we got through it because of how I split our group in half. The best marksmen were ready for any attack, while the rest of us wired the bridge. In the end, we all got through and completed the assigned mission successfully, even though I ordered Shay to delay detonating the bridge until the last possible moment, so Maze could get to safety.

She didn't like the order, but she obeyed.

"What do you want to do with this free time?" Nika asks when we step outside.

The guys walk toward the Weaponry Training Complex, talking about getting in some extra practice.

For the first time in the three weeks I've been in Squad 1, I'm alone with my two friends.

"Let's go for a walk," I suggest. I'll finally be able to tell them about Cai.

An alarm blares, and my band vibrates.

Seriously? Now?

The map feature opens, and a voice comes over the speakers. *"Recruits proceed to bunkers. This is not a drill. Black out procedure in effect. Recruits proceed to bunkers."*

"Guess that's a no to the walk," Nika says.

The three of us join the swarm of recruits being ushered to the bunkers. There's an intensity among the soldiers as they direct us, and they bring out their shock sticks, hitting recruits with more frequency than I've seen since we first arrived.

If what Ari told Nika and me is right, a Sitreean delegation is coming to inspect the city, and there can be no trace of us when they arrive. With the way the soldiers are acting, it seems like this must be a surprise visit.

Once I'm in the bunker, I do a quick search for Storm.

"She's not here," Cade says, joining us.

"Who's not here?" Nika asks.

"Storm."

Our little group makes its way to a corner farther into the bunker.

"How's she doing?" Ari asks. "Have you seen her lately?"

Cade and I both hesitate. Storm isn't herself, but considering everything she's going through, she's doing okay. Probably holding up better than I am in reality.

"I'm just glad it looks like they're not sending her down here for this drill," Cade says.

My thoughts darken, and, as though he could sense it, Matthias shows up, a wide grin on his face. Since I've been in Squad 1, I haven't seen him as often, but he still appears in more places than he probably should.

"How's it going?" He asks, sitting down next to me.

Nika looks between the two of us, and a mischievous grin spreads over her face. "Looks like some of us are better now that you're here."

Matthias raises his eyebrows, and before he or anyone else can ask what Nika means, I grab for a different conversation.

"Why is there a Sitreean military base in North America?" I ask.

Again, Matthias's eyebrows rise. "Trill told you that?"

"Uh, well no…" I'm glad I'm not sitting next to Nika at the moment, since I'd be getting elbowed right about now. "I guessed."

Matthias shrugs, accepting my lame excuse. "It's all about power and information. Things are settled in the nations around the globe, but it's tenuous."

"How much power do you really have if you just kidnap teens and force them to do what you want? They're all just a bunch of cowards and bullies, the Commander more than anyone." I spew the words without thinking, and all four of my friends stare at me.

"May want to keep some of those thoughts to yourself in here," Nika says quietly. "Not bad points, though."

I rub a hand over my face. That was foolish. "Sorry."

Matthias squeezes my shoulder, and a shock zips through me. "It's okay," he says. "You're safe among friends."

Ari spots Shane and waves him over, and the conversation shifts to other things, but my mind is muddled by my sudden over-whelming awareness of Matthias. Each time he laughs, the way his shoulder brushes mine when he's using his hands to say something, all of it is distracting me, pulling at me. What is my problem? Matthias is my friend, nothing more. But even as I think the thought, I know it's a lie.

How am I letting myself fall for a cadet from Talionis?

FORTY-TWO

It's dinner time as I enter the Warfare Strategies building. We spent the rest of the afternoon in the bunker, and they just released us, but I need some time by myself, so I decided to check one of the secret compartments I now have access to. It's quiet in the building now as most are finishing up their tasks after the visit from the Sitreean Delegation.

Using my HaloACT Band, I enter the right wing and pass zones I've trained in and then an observation room until I come to a large mural of Talionis with a raised, small, triangular marking resting on the image of the Warfare Strategies building. The same marking Cai said he used to indicate the entrance for a secret room in this building.

I finger the triangle, glance up and down the hallway to make sure I'm still alone, and then press the center of the marking. The triangle depresses into the wall first and then lifts up. I turn it sideways. The wall creaks, and then the section beneath the triangle raises up, revealing an opening large enough to crawl through. I shimmy through, and then the opening closes.

The darkness ebbs away as the light sensors on the wall pick up on my body heat and fill the room with a dim glow. The room is small since it's pressed between two observation rooms, but I'm able to stand and move around a little. I'm not sure we'll be able to use it for anything in our escape, but at least I can tell Cai it's still accessible.

The murmur of voices catches my attention, and I ease over to the wall on my left. There's a viewing access into the room, and I peer through.

A group of men and women are gathered. The hologram on the table is a map of a territory that's becoming more and more familiar. Sitreea. The country is situated with mountainous territory to their north, a large body of water to the southeast, and a dense forest to the west. Colonel Keenan Valarius and Sergeant Andor Valarius are in the room, as are Major Vasco and Elva Trill. I recognize a few other faces as those who sat on the Council that sentenced me to my punishment in the Ruins, but there are some who are unfamiliar.

The person talking has a slight accent, but I can't see him.

"I want the timetable moved up."

"Commander, we're not ready," Colonel Valarius says.

"Then *get* ready."

So this is what Commander Demetrius Ark sounds like. I shift, trying to see him, but he's sitting out of my view. His voice is powerful, full of authority, and it resonates through the room.

"When do you think you can have them prepared?"

"Within a year, sir. We need more recruits brought in, and they'll need to be trained."

"Very well. Find me the Elite recruits, and get them trained. The Chancellor is becoming far too interested in what we're doing here. The other invasions will happen as scheduled, but I want stage one moved up to this summer."

"Yes, sir," Colonel Valarius says. "There may be more casualties as a result of the accelerated timeline."

"They're expendable. If they die, they die. Enough of them need to survive to take the Chancellor alive, but that's all. The mission must go on, as you know, Colonel."

"Of course, Commander."

The conversation shifts as Ark asks Mandeville a question, but none of it registers. The Commander's words ring in my ears. *They're expendable...If they die, they die...*

He doesn't care if any of us die—he's expecting it. All that matters is whatever his mission is. And he wants the Elite Recruits sent out first. I need to become an Elite Recruit, but now the thought terrifies me even more. I'm not ready to die. Cai's plan has to work.

A door closes and jars me back to the moment. Mandeville is still droning on. There's probably more information for me to gather from their conversation, but I can't process anything else right now. I press away from the viewing access and find the triangular marking on this side of the wall that opens the secret door.

My mind spinning, I emerge back into the hallway. The access closes. I turn to walk down the hall and run straight into Sergeant Andor Valarius.

He puts his massive hands on my shoulders and sets me back from him. I look up into his eyes, and my stomach drops. It's over for me now. I'm not supposed to be here unsupervised — let alone crawling out from a hidden compartment in the wall — and we both know it. He folds his arms across his chest and stares at me, his scar pulled taut by his frown.

"I, uh..." My voice cracks, and I clear my throat. "I forgot—"

"Save it, Averton," he says. "If you're going to sneak around, I suggest you pay better attention so you don't get caught."

I feel the blood leave my face. Does he know what I just saw and heard? If so, they'll never let me live.

"Now get out of here before I change my mind and bring you before others who won't be so understanding."

He steps aside, and I walk past him. His eyes are boring into my back. I pick up my pace and don't stop moving until I'm outside and down the street.

I slip between two buildings and lean against the wall. My hands look like leaves tossed by the wind. My legs weaken, and I dissolve to the ground.

That was too close. My distraction could have cost me my life. It probably would have if I had run into someone else. Maybe Cai's God is looking out for me after all.

FORTY-THREE

Nika and I circle each other on the mat. We've been sparring for the past twenty minutes, and she's landed me on the mat far more times than I've gotten her. I rush her, and an instant later I'm staring up at the ceiling.

"Gotta be faster than that," she says, reaching down a hand to help me up.

"How are you this good?" I roll my shoulders, then bring my hands back into a fighting position.

She's almost as good as Cai.

Nika presses her lips together before answering. "I never want to be in the position where someone can force me to do something again. Now stop jabbering. Give me a bit of a challenge."

"Averton, off the mat," Laban shouts up at me. "Now!"

I give Nika a quizzical look, then obey.

"Come with me." The way he says the words hits me harder than Nika's right hook.

The only reason a recruit walks somewhere with Laban is because they're in trouble. Did Sergeant Valarius report me to his superiors? But that was two days ago now, and I've been continuing as Squad Leader—why would he wait so long?

Laban brings me to a private office in the Arena, and Shay and Matthias are waiting outside. Now I'm even more confused.

"What's going on?" I ask.

"Shut up, recruit," Laban says. "Inside now. The two of you, wait until I'm done."

Matthias offers me a small smile as I pass him, and it warms me as I follow Laban into the room. Knowing he's right outside the door strangely comforts me.

Laban slams the door. "I knew you couldn't be trusted."

"I don't understand, sir." The last word is hard to force out, but I manage it.

"Recruit Shay Bellingdon and Cadet Matthias Valarius have reported that you called the Commander a bully and a coward. What do you have to say for yourself? Not that it matters, since we have the word of an exemplary recruit and of the son of Colonel Keenan Valarius."

My insides shred as Laban's words crash on my ears, and I hardly register the hatred in his eyes. Matthias is Matthias *Valarius*. Colonel Valarius's son. His dad isn't dead like he told me. He lied to me. And he told Shay and Laban what I said in the bunker about the Commander.

That's why he became my friend, why he kept showing up—to spy on me for his father, and with Shay, of all people. He betrayed me, set me up.

Just like my aunt.

"I am loyal to the Commander and Talionis." The lie burns as it comes out, but I know the words I need to say. I keep my gaze fixed on Laban, even as my heart feels ready to rip in half. "I believe I have proven that."

Laban's lip curls in a sneer, and he stalks closer. "Prove it some more, then. And watch your mouth from now on. Do you understand me, recruit?" He shouts the words in my face.

"Sir, yes, sir!" I shout back.

"Your rifle will be taken for the next three days, and you'll be relieved of your duties as Squad Leader. Against my better judgement, Sergeant Valarius thinks you still have something to offer Squad 1, so you'll remain in the squad."

"Thank you, sir!"

"Don't thank me, Averton." His voice becomes a growl. "I'd beat you within an inch of your life for what you said about the Commander. And if I ever hear you say something like that again, I guarantee you'll regret it. Get out of here."

I salute and then march out the door. When I move to pass Matthias without sparing him a glance, he stops me with a hand on my arm.

"Bria—"

"Don't touch me." I yank my arm away. "Cadet Valarius."

His eyes widen.

"Valarius and Bellingdon, get in here," Laban shouts.

Shay immediately obeys, but Matthias stares at me.

"I know who you are now, what all this"—I gesture between the two of us—"was about. Stay away from me and my friends."

Matthias shakes his head no. "Bria, whatever he told you, whatever's going on, it's not what you think."

He reaches toward me, and I shove his hand away.

"Please talk to me. Give me a chance to explain—"

"Save it." With that, I walk away, out of the Arena, and to the side of the building.

He acted like he cared about helping me, like he cared about *me*, but it was all a lie.

How could I have been so clueless? How am I *always* so clueless?

Everything he said, everything he did, was to trick me into befriending him. Just like how everything Aunt Elena did was to betray me. And it worked.

Both times, it worked.

I clench my fists digging my nails into the palms of my hands, but I hardly register the pain. I should have been more adamant about him leaving me alone, shouldn't have let him help with my training. I should have realized he was Colonel Valarius's son.

I pound my hands into the wall and then rest my forehead against it. My eyes burn from unshed tears. I slide down to the floor, turn so my back is resting against the wall, and cover my face with my hands. A sob is lodged beneath my breastbone, but I won't let it out. I won't cry. Not now. Not for him.

***

It's strange walking around the city without my rifle, and the looks of disgust I receive from almost everyone I pass—recruits and soldiers alike—make the experience all the worse. I get into line for dinner with the rest of the rifle-less recruits, bile rising in my throat. I thought I was done eating gruel, but here I am again.

All the work I've done, all the training, and I'm back where I started when I was failing on purpose. Thanks to Matthias and Shay. I grip my tray, ready to hurl it across the room, clinging to the anger rather than allowing the dull ache of hurt to throb through me.

"Hey, girl." Nika pops up next to me. "I heard what happened."

I shrug and move forward as the line moves. "I shoulda seen it coming. Why are you in this line, Nika?"

"Because I'm not sure how else to get two minutes to talk to you without certain people listening." She picks up a bowl and ladles in a spoonful of the mush. Her nose wrinkles when it lands with a *splat.* "I am an excellent friend."

The comment elicits a tiny smile from me. I ladle the nasty stuff into my bowl.

"I believe Shay would turn you in—I think she'd turn in her own mother if she thought it would make the Commander happy. But I can't believe Matthias would do this."

We weave our way between tables, Nika's pace ridiculously slow.

"He's from Talionis. I should have stayed away from him. Not started to fall for him." I'm almost as angry with myself as I am with Matthias.

"I knew you liked him." Nika smirks, but the smile dies quickly. "Sorry. Bad timing. But seriously, girl, there's gotta be another explanation."

We're close to our table now, but there's enough time for me to tell her. "He told Laban what I said in the bunker about the Commander. So much for being safe among friends," I add bitterly.

"No, Cai! I won't do it!" I yell. Maybe volume will get through to him. Nothing else has. I pace the floor, frustrated and angry, while Cai sits on a stool.

"We need him," Cai replies, his voice as steady as it was when he first dropped this bomb on me.

"Gah! What don't you get about 'I. Won't. Do. It.'?" I clench my fists, wishing I could throw something.

I know we need more people, and I've been trying to tell Nika and Ari, maybe Cade. But this? Him? How does he expect me to trust him? How can Cai trust him?

"Matthias can be trusted, Bria. What's more, we need his help. I know you don't like it, but you need to bring him here."

I grab a knife from the table and fling it forcefully across the room at nothing in particular. "How can you be serious? He's one of them! He's from Talionis." I point in the direction of the city. "He has loyalties there!"

My hands fly into the air. "His dad is Keenan Valarius! You honestly think he's going to agree to help us escape?"

The words rush out of my mouth, but by the look on Cai's face, they aren't making any impact.

He remains on the stool, hands resting on his knees, unmoved by my outburst. "I know him."

"You knew him," I correct. "Before you left Talionis and came to the Ruins."

"All the same, I trust him. There's more to Matthias than you realize."

"He was spying on me, Cai! Watching me for his father to make sure I did everything they wanted me to." Saying the words out loud makes the reality of what happened with Matthias hit me again. A fresh wave of hurt and an ache for what I lost jams itself against me.

"What?" Cai shakes his head, incredulous. He shifts backward. "That's impossible."

"This is ridiculous." I grab my jacket off the floor and thrust my arms into the sleeves with more force than necessary. "I don't know why I keep coming back here. It's pointless."

I shrug, and an overwhelming sadness smothers my anger. First, I found out the truth about Matthias, and now I'm about to turn my back on the one place where I was finally starting to find a little hope. Everything that made this captivity somewhat bearable has been torn away from me.

I turn from Cai and walk toward the exit.

"Bria." His quiet voice pulls at me.

As much as I want to keep walking, pretend I didn't hear, I can't. I stop but keep my back toward him.

"Look at me."

Reluctantly, I face him.

He's standing there with an unreadable expression on his face. "Are you sure Matthias was spying on you?"

"Yes." I fold my arms tightly over my chest. "Laban Meritas brought me in for punishment three days ago because Matthias and Shay turned me in."

"Do you believe everything Laban Meritas claims?"

I open my mouth, then close it. I shake my head no.

"You find proof that Matthias was really spying on you, and we'll forget that I ever wanted him to be a part of this."

"Seriously?"

"Yes. I think there's more to this than what Meritas told you. I don't believe Matthias would ever do something like that, but if he did, you're right." He rubs his neck. "We can't trust him. However, I need to know for sure before I make that decision."

I tilt my head slightly. "What kind of proof?"

"Anything that shows he was willingly passing along information about you."

I bark out a humorless laugh. "You need more proof than the obvious? Keenan Valarius is his father. Of course he was spying on me."

Cai walks over and stops directly in front of me, his piercing gaze searching my face. "If you knew Matthias the way I know Matthias, knew all he's endured, then it wouldn't seem obvious to you at all."

I swallow, taken aback by the intensity in Cai's face and words. "Okay, I'll find you your proof."

"Very well. Next time you're here, I'll take you out into the Ruins with me. You're ready."

I leave the Ruins, my mind as tangled as the knotted vines in the trees surrounding me. Cai's fierce objections to Matthias spying on me for his father create a shard of doubt that punctures my certainty. Nika was convinced there was more to the story too.

Memories of the time I spent with Matthias bombard me as I crawl through the fence, make my way through the abandoned building, and step into Talionis. How often he ended up helping me during my trainings, how he'd show up at the oddest of times, the look on his face when he said he wanted to be friends, the moment of vulnerability in the old church under the window when he told me of his loss, his insistence on assisting me in hand-to-hand combat.

My suspicion returns. He was there for every moment I could have failed. Waiting for me to fail, to say something wrong. And he lied about losing his parents. His father is very much alive.

I brush away the bramble and debris on my clothing. No, Cai can't be right. It doesn't matter how certain he thinks he is. I'll find the evidence and prove to Cai that Matthias is as terrible as his father.

I return to my room, climb into my bed, and fight the tears ready to consume me.

FORTY-FOUR

Two Weeks Later

I slide into my seat in tech training next to Ari. There are still a few minutes until class, and Shay hasn't arrived yet. Everything is harder with her around, watching, waiting for me to do something she can catch and report. Getting to the Ruins at night, checking on the hidden rooms and passageways Cai told me about, even having a real conversation with one of my friends—all of it is almost impossible.

But at least now I have a moment with Ari.

"Since you never pay attention in this class," I say, "can you do something for me?"

"I pay attention!" Ari protests.

Nika plops into her chair. "She saying she pays attention in tech training?"

"Yup."

"Not a chance."

Ari makes a face at us. "Whatever. What do you need, Bria?"

I lick my lips. "Can you do some digging and find out more about Matthias? Prove that he's reporting on recruits?"

"I don't think he is," Ari says quickly. "I mean, it's *Matthias*. There must have been a misunderstanding about what happened to you."

"Ari—"

"I think it's a good idea," Nika says. "Clear the air. If you find something proving he is who Bria thinks, we all need to know."

"Fine," Ari huffs. "Not like I had other things I was going to do…"

"You can do them later," Nika says.

"Thanks, Ari," I say.

Shay sits on Nika's other side, but Ari gives me a smile.

The clock chimes out the hour, and Mandeville starts class. Ari types at her screen, and, though I don't understand the code she's searching through, a mix of relief and anxiety dance through me. If there's anything to find on Matthias, she'll dig it up.

I need the proof to bring to Cai so we can keep moving forward, but a small part of me is clinging to the chance Ari won't find any. It's ridiculous—Matthias lied to me about his dad already. But with each person's defense of him, I almost hope I'm wrong, that it *was* a misunderstanding.

Which is exactly why I'm the perfect target to betray.

Disgust for myself pinches my shoulders together, so I turn my mind to other things.

Winter has officially arrived, bringing with it a dusting of snow a few days ago, but I've still gotten out to the Ruins at least three times a week. As long as it doesn't snow enough for my tracks to be visible, I should be able to continue getting in my training with Cai.

He's moved my training to working with him in the Ruins. Two nights ago, we demolished a building when the transport with the next shift of soldiers for the wall towers was overhead. As soon as the building went down, the transport began taking evasive action. Cai said timing was vital in any act of sabotage. Something he wants me to learn well for when we escape.

He took me to different places through the Ruins, occasionally attacking me or telling me to go on ahead and prepare to attack him. I never get the best of him, but I hold my own, and the exercise heightens my awareness of my surroundings to another level.

If it wasn't for this mess with Matthias, I might almost be excited about the things I'm learning with Cai. I could pretend I was training to be a scout, that my brothers and Storm weren't in danger. That Talionis didn't exist. But pretending will only get me killed.

My training matters, not just for my life, but for others. Even if Matthias isn't as terrible as he seems, I can't let myself be distracted.

The clock chimes, and Mandeville ends class. Shay pops to her feet but doesn't walk away immediately, so I take my time packing up my things. After a moment, she leaves to go to our next training.

"Anything?" I ask.

Ari shakes her head. "No. He has more write-ups and disciplinary actions in his file than you did when we first got here."

"What? That doesn't seem right."

Ari shrugs. "I'll keep looking, but I don't think he's turning in recruits. It looks like he's pretty busy trying to keep *himself* out of trouble."

<hr>

Cold air swirls around me, flinging icy flakes into my face, echoing the turmoil inside of me. If Matthias isn't turning in recruits, then why was he there with Shay when Laban confronted me about speaking against the Commander?

I pause at the end of the alley, crouch low, and peer around the side of the building. No one is in sight. I prepare to cross. Something rustles behind me. I freeze, press my body against the building, melting into the shadows. I wait. Not breathing. Not moving. My senses are fully alert now, every distraction gone. Seconds tick by. I hear nothing else and finally let out a breath. Must have been an animal or the wind.

I check again, and the street is clear.

"Recruit, halt!"

Ice freezes in my veins, and I spin around, but no one is coming toward me. Three soldiers are running toward the alley I just vacated. A moment later, they're dragging Shay into the street.

"No, you don't understand," she says. "I was following another recruit—"

Without listening to the rest of her explanation, I take two back alleys and race back to the recruits' living quarters and up to my room. I have to get back before Shay.

I enter the room and trip over one of Nika's rifles and send it clattering across the floor, waking both Nika and Ari up.

"What's going on?" Nika asks, voice slurred with sleep.

Ari turns on the light, and they both stare at me. I'm fully dressed, with ice crystals still clinging to my clothes.

"I'll explain everything later. But Shay's coming back, and if you guys don't help me, I'm in trouble."

Nika springs out of bed, more alert than I've ever seen her after just waking up. "What do you need?"

I quickly change, and they hide my wet clothes. Then Ari and I get in our beds just as footsteps sound in the hallway.

The door crashes open, and a soldier peers in.

"See?" Shay says from the hall. "I told you she wasn't—" She enters the room and stops talking as her eyes collide with mine.

"There you are, girl!" Nika says. "I woke up Bria and Ari because I was worried about you. Heard you leave, and then you weren't in the bathroom. We were just about to call someone and make sure you were okay."

"That's, but, no. That's not what happened," Shay stutters.

"Take her to Sergeant Meritas," a soldier who remained in the hallway says.

The soldier in our room takes Shay by the upper arm. "Let's go, recruit. You know you're not allowed to be out after curfew."

"No, wait. It was her." Shay points at me. "She left. I-I was just following her—"

"I was here," I say.

Ari and Nika nod their agreement.

"That's enough. Sorry to disturb the rest of you." The woman drags Shay from the room, and her protests echo back to us until the door to the stairway clangs shut.

Nika closes our door, and my heartbeat finds a normal rhythm.

"Thank you, guys."

"Okay, what is going on?" Nika asks. "Why were you outside?"

She sits on the edge of my bed, and Ari comes to join us.

"I was going back to the Ruins."

Between the two of them, they ask a dozen questions so rapidly, I can't respond, so I wait. When they pause, I share with them about Cai and what he does in the Ruins, our plan to escape and take down Demetrius Ark, and how I want them to be a part of it. Each thing I share brings with it relief. I've wanted to tell them for so long, and this night that almost brought disaster ended up providing the perfect opportunity.

They both stare at me when I finish, and I suddenly realize how dangerous and overwhelming everything sounds. A new frightening thought occurs to me. What if they don't want to be a part of it?

"You're really doing this?" Nika asks.

"Yes."

"Then I am too," she says.

"Can my brother come too?" Ari asks. "And Shane?"

"We will need more help, but we can't tell them yet."

Ari tilts her head. "Okay, then I'm in too."

Nika nudges me with her shoulder. "I wish you told us sooner."

"Me too." I gesture toward Shay's bed. "I didn't know how to with her around so much."

My friends nod their understanding.

"There's one more thing." I pause.

"Girl, just spit it out. You can't shock us more than you already have."

I tell them about what I overheard Ark say, sharing it for the first time since I listened to the meeting from the secret compartment. The more I share, the more serious they become.

"This escape plan of yours is risky," Nika says. "But we've got to do something. When do we meet Cai?"

FORTY-FIVE

Shay is no longer staying in our room. Part of her disciplinary action was that her room has been moved to the first floor again. They've allowed her to continue to train in Squad 1, but it's probationary. They've put her under higher surveillance and removed some of her Squad 1 privileges. She's furious with me, and I know I'm in a dangerous place with her, but the changes have allowed the opportunity for me to bring Nika to the Ruins tonight.

Ari stayed behind to monitor our progress. Somehow, she set our bands to register that we're still in our room, but she can access a tracking feature she implanted that no one else can find. It seemed a little risky, but her confidence helped ease my fears. She said she'll come with us next time, and that this was important for her to do, but I think she's nervous about the whole thing and wants to wait until she can go in with Shane or Bryson.

Nika follows me as I squirm through the hole in the fence, and I retrieve the torchlight on the other side.

"It's weird being out here," Nika says. "Everyone makes such a big deal about what a dangerous place the Ruins is, and we just came here voluntarily. You promise I'm not about to die, right?"

I chuckle. "You're fine. Cai's got this place set up to scare the people he wants to scare, but I know the way through his traps. At least on this stretch."

We walk for a few minutes in silence.

"My sister and I used to go on hikes," Nika says. "She was always looking out for me, making sure I ate well, stayed hydrated, and got outside. I called them 'mandatory walks.'"

I hear the smile in her voice.

"What's your mom like?" I ask. I've never heard her mention her mom. Always her older sister.

Nika flinches. "My mom, uh. Well, my mom and I have a tough history."

She takes the opposite side of the boulder we go around but not before I see the flash of pain that mars her face. She clears her throat when we're on the other side.

"But my sister is ten years older than me, and she helped me through a lot. I ended up moving in with her a few years ago." A wistful smile crosses her face. "If she so much as *thought* I needed to talk about something or deal with something, she would literally march me out of the house, drag me to somewhere quiet, and stare at me. If I tried to leave, she would just raise her eyebrows. I used to hate that." She swallows. "Now, I'd give anything for it."

"I guess you learned some of your stubbornness from your sister." The side of my mouth tilts up.

Nika laughs, but it doesn't sound like her normal laugh. "Funny the things you take for granted until they're gone."

I exhale deeply. "You're right." I kick at the underbrush in our path. "That's how I feel about my brothers."

Nika cocks her head to the side. "I didn't know you have brothers."

"Yeah." I almost feel guilty for not telling her about them sooner, but I've been afraid to talk about them. Afraid of the pain it would let in. But I want to share now. "They're a little younger than Storm. Twins." I lift my eyebrows in mock horror, and Nika grins.

"What are their names?"

"Eli and Zeke. They're the best little brothers. Super funny and always getting into trouble, but they can be really sweet." I chuckle. "They can also drive me crazy. Talk about no personal space."

We're getting closer to the site now, but I'm not walking as fast as I normally do.

"I hear you there. My little brothers and sisters are the same way. I mean, don't they get that we really don't need their help going to the bathroom?"

"Right?"

We both laugh, but sober quickly.

"Now I miss them and their craziness so much that it hurts," I admit.

"Me too. Can't say I always understand why God allows the things to happen that He does." She sighs. "But my sister always loved to remind me that God's ways aren't my ways, because if I always had my way, we'd never get the rain we need for the crops. She'd say, 'I know you love the sunshine, baby girl, but God brings the rain for a plan much better than one we could come up with on our own. God allows the hard things, the painful things for a reason.'" A tear rolls unchecked down Nika's cheek.

For an instant, I'm struck by our openness and candor. We're friends, but we haven't shared anything this personal before. "Think she'd say that to us now?"

Nika's eyes lock on mine. "I know she would."

"Do you believe it?"

A shadow of something I can't identify flashes through Nika's eyes. "Yes. I have to believe, even if I don't always feel like it's true." We walk the final steps to the site. "It's the only thing that's gotten me through this so far."

We enter the training site to find Cai with his head bent over a small, leather-bound book. His Bible. He carries it with him everywhere, and when I asked him why, he said it's the thing that brings him comfort, no matter what he's facing.

Without looking up at us, he speaks. "You brought a friend, Bria."

"He's good," Nika says.

Cai closes his Bible and gets to his feet. "Heard voices before you entered the site, and my sensor at the fence showed two people."

I make the introductions, and Cai is clearly pleased that I've brought someone else into our plan.

Before we can share more with Nika, an alarm goes off on Cai's screen.

"Ah, I planned a few exercises for Bria tonight," Cai says. "Can you handle yourself in hand-to-hand combat?" He asks Nika.

"Better than Bria," she says.

"I've gotten better!" I protest. "But yeah, she's good," I admit grudgingly.

"Alright, let's go." Cai tosses me a staff and offers Nika one as well, and then we leave the site.

We hike west, toward the old city ruins. "Any updates?" Cai asks.

"They've moved up the selection of the Elite Recruits to the next evaluation," I say. I can picture Colonel Valarius's smile when he announced the change—now that I know he's Matthias's dad, it's hard *not* to see the resemblance.

Cai spins and attacks me with his staff, pulling me from my thoughts. We spar for a minute. He gets in two strikes, which makes this one of my personal best matches, then he goes at Nika.

She doesn't miss a beat, and Cai spars with her longer than he did with me.

"Staffs down," Cai says, and they stop. "She's good."

He leads us to the shell of an old warehouse that no longer has a roof. "Do you think you'll make it into the Elite Recruit unit?"

"Yes, I think we will," Nika answers.

I already explained to her how important it was for us to get the clearance they're promising to the highest ranked recruits. "Bria and I are among the best in our unit."

Her confidence is comforting.

"Good." He hands me a package of explosives. "Let's give the west wall guards a little light show, shall we?"

"Sure," I drawl. There's always a catch when Cai suggests something like this. He's doing more than just striking terror into his enemies. He's training me, teaching me. "And what else?"

Cai almost smiles. "Nika and I will patrol the perimeter. You need to get in, set the explosives, and get out without us stopping you. You have three minutes. Go."

I duck into the old building, torchlight set on low. It's eerie being in a place like this, but I've grown more used to it with Cai's trainings throughout the Ruins. I find a pillar in the middle of the structure that's supporting walls. Perfect. The explosion will take out multiple parts of the building.

I secure it in place like Cai taught me, set the charge and timer, and then jog out of the building. I pause at the fringes, listen for Nika and Cai, but hear nothing, so I slip out. When I'm twenty yards away from the site, something presses into my back.

"Better but not perfect," Cai says. "Let's get to cover."

Cai and I jog, and Nika trails behind a little.

"Cover for what?" she asks.

We duck behind a wall, and seconds later, the explosion rips through the night. I no longer shake with fear at the explosions, even though they still remind me of the scenarios. When these go off, I know Cai is with me and that I'm safe.

"Wait," Nika says, once the roar of the blast has died down. "That was a *real* explosive you gave her?"

"Of course," Cai says.

"Ya'll are crazy enough that this plan just might work," she says.

Cai brings us to another building not too far from the first, and this time he brings Nika in and teaches her how to set the explosive. When we exit the building, Nika runs ahead of us to find cover.

We leave the burning buildings behind us and head to the intel gathering site Cai first brought me to. As we walk, we share with Nika the plan to escape during the Commencement, sabotaging key areas of the city, including Communications and Tracking in the Tech Building, the Weaponry Complex, and the Main Headquarters building, since those areas will require immediate attention from the soldiers because of their security levels, and draw the focus away from the transportation dock where we will meet up, plant explosives, and steal a transport in order to get out of Talionis and make a quick journey to Eryndale. Before sabotaging the key areas, we'll create distractions by setting fire to empty or abandoned buildings and minor explosions scattered throughout the city.

"Sounds good to me," Nika says, when we finish explaining. "What else needs to be done?"

"Gather supplies and steal the map for the journey to Eryndale, figure out how to disengage the tracking on the transport we take, and determine what we need to steal from the tech building." I rattle off the list.

We enter Cai's intel site, and Nika lets out a low whistle.

"How do you have all of this out here?" she asks, taking in his desk with multiple screens.

"Let's call them donations," Cai says, powering on the screens. "From soldiers passing through."

"Ari is going to love this," Nika says.

"Who's Ari?" Cai asks.

"Our friend," I say. "She's the one who's a genius with tech."

"Ah yes."

"She'll be able to tell us what we need from tech and how to disengage the tracking on the transport," Nika says.

"Good." Cai pulls up a screen with a camera feed of the guards on the west wall tower, and a smile spreads across his face.

All of them are freaking out, yelling at one another, and radioing in the explosion to Talionis. It's humorous to watch, though I can't blame them. We successfully destroyed their peaceful evening.

"We're going to need more people for this," Nika says.

"Agreed," Cai says. "I think five or six more would be ideal."

Nika nods. "Okay, so Ari, Cade, Bryson, Shane," she counts them off on her fingers, "and maybe Nalani?" She directs the question to me.

I shrug. "Ari trusts her, but I don't know her very well. And we'll have Damara and Storm."

"Perfect." Cai turns to me, and I tense, knowing what's coming. "And Matthias." His voice is calm, but firm.

I haven't provided him with the proof he needs, but the very thought of having Matthias in this with us, of having to trust him... it's more than I can handle.

"I think he's a good choice." Nika keeps her gaze away from me.

My stomach sinks. "No. How can we trust him? He told Shay and Laban something I shared with all of you in confidence."

Nika faces me now. "That whole thing hasn't made sense to me from the beginning, girl. Why would he be working with Shay? And Ari dug as deep as she could—there's nothing in his records to say he would do something like that. If anything, he does more *against* Talionis than in obedience to their demands."

"But..." Fear of letting Matthias close, of trusting him despite all the reasons logic says I shouldn't, makes my voice shake. I spin toward Cai. "Why him? Why are you so desperate to have Matthias be a part of this?"

Cai adjusts a screen. "He's like a son to me." He stares across the room. "I left a son once because of these people. I won't leave another one." He clears his throat and focuses on us again. "Before you bring anyone else out here, I want you to bring him."

"I can't." Fear, desperation, and anger sear the words in the air, burning as hot as the explosions we set earlier. I can't trust Matthias, can't put the lives of Storm and Eli and Zeke in his hands. "I'm sorry."

And I am, but not sorry enough to bring Matthias into this.

"Then I'm not working with you anymore," he says quietly.

My mouth falls open.

"Bria, if you can't trust me in this, how are we going to move forward?"

I snap my jaw closed, look away, and cross my arms over my chest.

"Well, Nika,"—I feel Cai's eyes burning into me still as he talks to Nika—"I'm sorry to say that it looks like we won't be planning anything at this time."

"What?" Nika sputters.

"We will not move ahead until Bria brings Matthias to me."

Nika points at herself. "I'll bring him. This plan will work. I know it. We have to move forward!"

"No, Bria is the one who needs to bring him. I refuse to continue working toward the escape until she does."

"Cai—" I start, preparing my excuses.

"That's all there is to it." There's a stern look on his face but compassion in his eyes as he studies me. "You can come any time you'd like and talk to me. Come with your questions about God. I know you have them." He tilts his head slightly. "And it's more important that those questions get answered than anything else. Even than escaping."

My heartbeat quickens at his words. I do want answers, *need* answers. But Cai doesn't know. He doesn't know the reason those answers won't change anything for me. Doesn't know that his God would never accept me.

I shove the longing back down and focus on my frustration with Cai and his stubbornness. "But we need to escape, Cai. You've said it yourself. We can't let what they're doing continue."

"I agree, Bria." He shakes his head sadly. "But I will not help you with your training or work on this plan until you come with Matthias."

Our gazes remain locked for several moments. Tension radiates from my body, my jaw locked, arms folded tightly across my chest. He won't change his mind. Cai's as strong-willed as I am. But, despite what I've seen of him, I'm not ready to include Matthias in any part of my life. Let alone this.

"Understood," I finally say.

Then I walk out of the building. Away from Cai. Away from Nika. Away from a plan that just took a turn I can't handle. How could Cai ask this of me? How could he put me in this position? He knows how important it is for us to leave!

"Bria! Wait up!" Nika calls from behind me.

I ignore her and continue forward, increasing my pace.

"Hold on a second!"

I hear her moving faster through the woods behind me, and then she's grabbing my wrist, pulling me to a stop.

"I know you heard me," Nika says, her eyes flashing in the moonlight.

"I really don't want to talk right now." I pull my arm from her grasp and start walking again. She falls into step beside me.

"Well, that's too bad, because we're gonna talk. Are you crazy? If Cai trusts Matthias, you should too! Not to mention, we both know he's a good guy."

I step around a rock, wishing I could as easily step away from this conversation.

"This plan, it's the only thing that's given me hope I might see my sister again," Nika continues. "Bria!" Her arm comes in front of me. "Look at me."

I whip my head around and stare at her, hoping all of my frustration and annoyance are coming through clear enough.

"You know what he did," I snap. "You're my friend. You're supposed to have my back!"

"Ask him if he did it, if he told Sergeant Meritas what you said." She grasps both of my arms. "Think about it, girl. It's *Shay* and *Sergeant Meritas* we're talking about. How do you know they didn't just set him up?"

Her words pierce me, picking at my certainty about Matthias's involvement in my punishment. "He lied to me about his dad. Told me he was dead, Nika. I can't trust him."

Her lips press together. "Sometimes it's easier to lie than to admit who your parents are when you're ashamed of them." She lets go of my arms, and her voice softens. "Just think about what you're doing here, what you're giving up." She pauses. "And what you're forcing the rest of us to give up."

She walks away, but her words ring in my ears.

FORTY-SIX

Storm flies down the slide, a wide smile stretched across her face, and I can't help but smile back at her from the park bench I'm sitting on with Damara. She's having a good day today. Each week is different for her, and when I make my visit, I'm not sure how she'll be. Some days, I can see the nightmares reflected in her eyes, haunting her. Haunting me. Today, the shadows are faded, and I see glimpses of the Storm I first met—her smile, her laugh.

Yet, there's always a hint of the fear and difficulty she's facing in her words, how she flinches at loud noises, in her desperate hugs each time I leave. The smile fades from my face. I wish I could erase these past months and bring back the carefree girl that I only see once in a while now. But I can't. My fear is that that girl is lost forever.

Storm waves at me, and I smile and wave back, trying to clear away the dark thoughts. They haven't fully destroyed her, and I don't know if she'll let them. She still tries to laugh. She still smiles. And she still loves fiercely. They may have stripped her of her little girl innocence and trust, but they haven't taken her spirit.

Can I really deny her the chance to escape?

Storm runs over to get a drink. "It was nice when Matthias dropped off the chicken yesterday."

I've gotten used to how she starts conversations out of nowhere, but her words make me freeze.

"What?" I try to keep my voice calm.

She guzzles another drink of water. "I said it was nice when Matthias dropped off the chicken."

I grip the rail of the bench and feel it leaving a mark on my palm. "Why did he drop off chicken?"

Storm shrugs. "Watch this!" She races back to the slide and runs up it.

"Those of us who live in the modified housing district are given very limited quantities of meat and fresh produce," Damara says. "Usually only a small portion every month or two. Less in winter. Over the past several days, Matthias has been by with meat and produce. He drops it off and stays for a bit to see if there's anything else we need. And he's great with Storm." Her face softens. "He seems to be able to tell when it's been a hard day for her, and he'll stay a little longer."

Why would Matthias try to take care of Storm and Damara?

"Why do you allow Matthias to come if you're so afraid of your promise to Storm being broken? Don't you know who he is?"

Damara sighs. "Yes, I know. He told me who his father is the first day he came."

My mouth parts in surprise. He told her right away, but decided it was a detail I didn't need to know?

"But he's proven repeatedly to me he is not Keenan Valarius and that I can trust him. And I do."

I don't respond. I don't *have* a response. Could Nika and Cai be right? Could Matthias be who I thought he was before everything happened?

My band buzzes, signaling my break is ending, and I need to get back. I stand up from the bench.

Storm runs over, one side of her face pulled up in her expression of disappointment. "You have to go?"

"Yeah." I tuck her hair behind her ear, wishing I had a different answer.

"Okay." She flings her arms around me and squeezes until it almost hurts. "See you soon."

I pull back from her and smile. "Yes, you will."

I make myself leave before I can change my mind and direct my attention to the area I'm passing through.

The park is a little over a thirty-minute walk from the sections of Talionis I spend most of my time in. It's near the residential district, where the soldiers, sentries, and their families live. I take careful note of the area, searching for a weakness, or something of significance that Cai and I can use. That is, if Cai and I continue our planning...if I bring Matthias to him.

Maybe I can. Maybe I have to risk it to save Storm and help my friends escape. I don't have to let him close again. Just bring him to Cai.

"What are you doing out here?"

The familiar raspy voice behind me curdles my stomach. Laban Meritas. I turn and come to attention.

"I was on a break, sir," I say the word, and bile rises in my throat.

I swallow it back. *Keep it together.*

He stalks toward me, his golden eyes flashing like lightning. "I don't trust you, recruit. What're you trying to do?"

My breath catches in my throat. "Serve the Commander however I can, sir." My voice trembles slightly.

He closes the distance between us and grabs my shoulder in a painful grip. "Don't give me that!" he yells. "You've spoken against the Commander. You're not serving him!"

"That allegation against me was unfounded, made by a recruit who is now under disciplinary action for sneaking out at night." Maybe focusing on Shay will distract him.

He shakes me. I clench my jaw to keep from crying out in pain. "Somehow, I trust Recruit Bellingdon more than you."

Breathe. Keep breathing. Ignore the pain. Ignore the fear. Don't react. "Then perhaps you don't wish to see a recruit faithfully serving the Commander, sir."

He smacks me across the face with such force that I would have fallen over if he wasn't still gripping my arm. Tears spring to my eyes from the pain, but I blink them away.

"How dare you," he growls.

He releases his hold, then shoves me. I try to keep my balance, but I fall to the ground. His foot connects with my rib cage. A groan escapes. I know how to protect myself now, how to retaliate, but I can't. Not against him. No one would ever believe my side of the story, not with the record I have.

He crouches to the ground in front of me, his face inches from mine. "I've given everything to the Commander. No one questions my loyalty."

He whips me across the face with the back of his hand, knocking me back to the ground. The skin breaks, and I feel blood bubbling to the surface of my cheek. Pain pulses across my brain, dulling my emotions.

A wicked gleam lights Laban's eyes. "Let's try this again. What are you up to?"

I wipe my cheek, the warm blood sticky against my fingertips. "Nothing."

"Liar!" He hates me as much as I loathe him. "I guess we'll have to do this the hard way."

He stands up and kicks me again. And again. I curl up, trying to protect myself.

God, if You're there, I could really use some help right now.

My reaction time slows as he repeatedly strikes blows to my body. I cry out, unable to stop myself. Pain dulls my mind. I can't think clearly. My vision blurs. The blows keep coming.

As I fade into unconsciousness, I hear another voice yelling, "Stop! What are you doing?"

Laban stops, but before I can see who it is who saved me, I black out.

FORTY-SEVEN

eep. Beep. Beep. Beep. The low, steady sound pulls me from the comfortable blackness. I open my eyes and then squeeze them shut against the blinding light in the room. I shift and regret it as pain ricochets through my body.

Someone says my name, but I fade back into the pain-free oblivion I just emerged from.

Pulsing pain brings me back to consciousness. Slowly, I open my eyes. It isn't as bright as it was before. With as little movement as possible, I scan the room. I'm in the infirmary. The white walls and ceiling, along with the machines hooked up to me, make it pretty obvious. A noise at the door draws my attention.

Two nurses bustle into the room.

"Oh good, you're awake," one says.

They spend a few minutes checking the screens of the machines monitoring me and prodding several painful areas. As much as I try not to, I can't help but moan throughout the process.

"Just let it out, honey," the older of the two nurses says. "You took quite a spill." She props a couple more pillows behind me, then hands me a glass of water. I gulp it down.

The nurse pulls the cup away. "You need to slow down."

When I shift to face her, pain rips through my ribcage and cuts across my lungs. I gasp and fall back, black spots dancing in front of my eyes.

"I'm still thirsty," I finally manage, my voice scratchy.

"Well, don't drink it so fast, and I'll let you have the cup back."

She hands me the cup but doesn't let go until she sees that I'm drinking slower.

It takes a while, but eventually I empty the glass.

She takes the cup and hands it to the other nurse, who then leaves. "How do you feel?"

I arch my eyebrows. Does she think that's a legitimate question?

She doesn't seem to notice my incredulous look. Or she's choosing to ignore it. "Well?"

"I'm not feeling so great," I say, a bit of sarcasm coming through.

"Not surprising." She pulls down a personal screen from the wall beside my bed. "You have some bruised ribs and several bad contusions. But no broken bones."

"Could have fooled me," I mumble.

"You'll be feeling good as new soon enough. We have a special ointment we'll be applying to the bruised areas and medication to help the pain and speed up the healing process. You're a lucky one. The Commander himself approved the use of the ointment. It's quite expensive and difficult to procure."

Even my pain-fogged brain registers the significance of the Commander being involved in a recruit's stay in the infirmary.

"How long have I been here?"

"Twenty-four hours."

That would make it Wednesday evening.

"How long do I have to stay?"

"Oh, about two more days," the nurse replies.

"But what about my training?" I ask.

The next evaluation is coming up, and I need to be an Elite Recruit. We have to escape, even if it means bringing Matthias in—something else I can't do if I'm stuck in the infirmary.

"Don't you worry a bit about your training." She pats my shoulder lightly. "You'll be back at it soon enough."

She reviews my treatment plan, then leaves the room. Before I can process everything that's happened, sleep takes over again.

———

I LIFT MY SHIRT UP ENOUGH TO SEE THE UGLY GREENISH BLACK AND BLUE marks marring my sides. My left thigh is covered in a bruise as well, and an enormous lump on my right shin makes its presence known when I try to cross my left leg over it. The bruise and cut on my cheek isn't as swollen as it was, but it still hurts if I accidentally press it against the pillow. Even my arms have bruises. But it all looks better today than it did last night. Whatever is in the ointment they've been making me apply, it's working. The pain has lessened as well. I can sit up without groaning now.

I drop my shirt at the sound of the door opening and tug the light blanket back in place. A woman enters, wearing the uniform of the kitchen staff and carrying a tray with my breakfast. She says nothing as she sets the tray down on the table next to my bed and leaves.

I eat my food, envisioning how boring this day is going to be. There's nothing to do in the infirmary, but "rest and recover" according to the nurse. It never occurred to me how the activity of my trainings has kept me occupied and made the days pass until I woke up this morning and was left alone for hours. Well, except for the moments when a nurse would come in and check my vitals and injuries and apply more of the ointment. I shove aside my tray. Today is going to leave me with way too much time to sit and think.

The door bursts open.

"Girl. What is going on?" Nika whooshes into the room, followed by Ari.

I spread my hands. "Isn't it kind of obvious? I'm in the infirmary." A smile edges its way out.

Ari hurries to the side of the bed. "Are you okay?" Her hands flutter up as though she's going to hug me, but then she drops them back to her side.

"I'm fine."

Nika flops into the chair and props her feet up on my bed. "So this is what you do to get out of trainings and nightly duties? Fall out the second-story window of an old building?"

My brow furrows. "What?"

"They told us how you fell out of the building and banged yourself up. What were you doing leaning out the window, anyway?"

I shake my head, wondering what she's talking about, and then I realize that, of course, they would make it seem like my injuries were because of an accident of my own making. They would never say that Laban beat me up for no reason. Nika's eyes narrow as she watches me, and I see the moment she registers that what she heard isn't accurate.

"We just found out you were here." Ari perches on the side of the bed. "We would have been by earlier, but no one seemed to know what happened to you."

"Which was concerning," Nika adds pointedly.

My band buzzes, and I glance down to find a message from Ari.

Can't talk freely. They monitor everything in the infirmary.

I give a subtle nod. "How much have I missed in training?" That should be a safe enough subject.

For the next half hour, Nika and Ari catch me up on what's happened the past two days, Ari's explanation about what she's been learning in Advanced Technical Training going over my head. They share stories, and Ari has Nika and me both laughing as she describes how her brother had a run-in with Sampta and Presidia.

The visit isn't very long, but I'm worn out by the time they leave to go to their next training. I lean back into my pillow and start to drift off to sleep, disturbed at the thought that Laban could get away with what he did. If he had killed me, like I'm pretty sure he wanted to, would they have pushed that aside too? Probably.

Sleep drifts in like a slow fog. At least the mystery person came along when he did and stopped Laban. Otherwise, I don't think I'd be here right now.

FORTY-EIGHT

arfare Strategies, two days later

W I wait in the center of the Warfare Strategies compound with my squad and several cadets. We've been informed that today's training will be different, and we're waiting for instructions. Last night was my first night back from the infirmary, and I shared with Nika and Ari about what happened with Laban. Nika asked me what I was going to do about it, and I told her I know what I need to do. But that doesn't mean I'm thrilled.

Matthias is one of the cadets here today, of course. I need to talk to him—soon—but the thought is unsettling.

He visited me in the infirmary, but I pretended I was sleeping. He sat there for two hours, asked the nurses how I was doing, and got answers from them, probably with his outrageous smile. Watched me. Talked to me quietly, telling me he was sorry I was hurt, how he wished he had been honest with me about his father so I would have understood that he's nothing like him. He even said he doesn't know how Shay and Laban found out about what I said in the bunker, but it wasn't him.

And he told me he hoped one day we could be friends so he could go back to annoying me. I could hear the smile in his voice. Then he said he missed me. I was considering opening my eyes when the nurses came in again and shooed him out. When he left, I felt even more lonely than I had before.

Now he's here. He catches me looking at him, and his lips twitch. I look away before he smiles. I can't watch him smile.

Major Vasco enters.

"Both of your squads have shown promise in your scenarios, so today you will begin Advanced Warfare Strategies." His dark eyes assess and measure each of us. "You will most likely come to regret your placement. This training will not be easy. You will be tested to the point of breaking. We will place you in scenarios you never would have dreamed of. You will be forced to persevere through hardships. But that is what the Elite do. Prove to us, prove to me, you are worthy of that title, and you will find yourself training to take a place among the greatest soldiers of Talionis."

A soldier hands out individual screens.

"You will be placed in pairs," Major Vasco says, "and given the rest of the morning to prepare a plan for a scenario in private staging areas. In the scenario, you will go against another set who will prepare a counter-attack to your attack. The first team to successfully complete their mission wins. The screens you now have contain the files you need, and they tell you who we've paired you with."

I turn on my screen and drop my head. They've placed me with Shay.

Shay and I are brought to a staging room and told we have four hours to prepare.

As soon as the soldier closes the door, Shay faces me, hands on her hips.

"I'm no happier about this than you are," she says. "But I don't want to fail, so we have to work together. Agreed?"

"Agreed."

With our temporary truce in place, I turn on my screen.

The words *Warfare Strategies, Advanced Scenario Preparation* appear. I lean forward. We've never *prepared* for a scenario before. A moment later, the words disappear, and a hologram of a large compound with massive walls emerges from the screen. A voice speaks.

"Your mission in this scenario will be to enter a secure military base, disarm its security protocols, and disable its communication ability. You will have ninety minutes to complete your mission, at the end of which, you must arrive at the extraction point."

The hologram slowly rotates, showing the sides of the base, and then a view from overhead.

"The base is well guarded and on an island." The hologram pans out and shows the water surrounding the base. *"Entry points for the military base at this compound are by air"*—a small helicopter appears and descends into the center of the base—*"and by sea."*

The hologram shifts and shows a boat entering through a narrow passage. Then a bridge is lifted so the boat can go under it. Finally it reaches a docking station where lines of soldiers guard the entrance, checking documentation, and identifying those on board.

"Both of these options will be unavailable to you. You must find an alternative way in. The security measures for this base are on the eastern quadrant of the wall, although the exact location is unclear. You must first disarm this before you will be able to disable its communication network."

The hologram zooms in on the eastern quadrant of the wall. Swarms of armed men and women patrol the area.

I pick at my fingernail. This will be difficult.

"Once you have successfully disarmed the security, you must then enter the communications network tower."

The hologram shifts toward the center of the compound to show a tower that rises higher than every other building.

"This compound houses an advanced communications database. In order to disable it, you must enter the tower, acquire an access badge for the top floor"—the hologram shows a video of each stage of the process—*"and plug in a fireworm lightning retractor, which will be provided to you at the onset of this mission. Once the FLR has been inserted, you will have thirty seconds to clear the area before it self-destructs."*

I watch the images playing from the hologram, my mind racing to keep up. This differs from every other scenario we've faced.

"Once you've cleared the area, you must exit the compound through the Western Quadrant and go to the extraction point: a beach a half mile

away, where a transport will be waiting for you. You must arrive at the extraction point no later than ninety minutes after you begin your mission. If you are late, the transport will be gone."

The hologram shows the transport taking off from the beach, and then it disappears.

"During this scenario, you will face many hazards and complications. Do not forget that you will undertake this mission against others whose purpose will be to stop you from completing your assignment. In order to help you prepare for your mission, this screen is equipped with Hologram Planning Technology. You will be able to access the map of the compound, the extraction point, the details made available for you, enact theories through Hologram Speculative Maneuvers (HSM), and make notes for yourselves on the best possible way to accomplish your task for this scenario. Remember that the events you plan for will be in real time, and you must account for the potential for unexpected changes."

The hologram for the scenario disappears, and the screen lights up with a list of categories for us to choose from so we can prepare. Shay and I both stare at the screen.

"When they said advanced, they meant it," I say.

"We better get started."

There's so much information that we end up watching the briefing again. Then, for the next hour, we work through the different categories on the screen, go through the hologram diagrams of the compound, try various entry possibilities, and find a hundred ways to *fail* this mission. Just finding an entrance into the compound is proving to be a challenge.

"Okay, let's work around the base again. Maybe we can find an entry point." Shay taps on the hologram, zooms in on the base, and begins rotating it slowly. The first wall is along the water.

"Wait." I put my hand on Shay's arm, which earns me a glare.

I let go. "Go back a little."

She does but doesn't look happy about it.

"There. Do you see that?" The water laps against the wall, but at one point, the water is darker, like it's deeper than the rest.

"What is that?"

"Zoom in."

Shay's eyes narrow. "Stop telling me what to do."

"Seriously? Shay, come on. Just zoom in."

"You're not in charge of this, Bria." Shay does nothing.

I grind my teeth. "*Please* zoom in."

Why did I have to be in this with Shay, of all people?

She finally acquiesces.

I lean in closer. "Look at that. I think there's something there." I press on the spot on the hologram, and it suddenly opens, revealing an underwater tunnel.

"That's it. That's our way in," Shay says, like she's the one who found it.

I push past my irritation and input a new spec maneuver, making our entrance the underwater tunnel. The hologram shows two figures swimming down the tunnel and coming to a laser barred entrance. "Stink. How do we get past that?"

"We need a lasitrix to disburse the laser field." Shay depresses the button and tells the hologram to use a lasitrix. The lasers shift, and the two figures in the hologram swim through.

"We're in."

Now that we've found an entrance, we work on ways to get through the compound to the eastern wall quadrant. We spend the next three hours watching the hologram flash MISSION FAILED more times than I care to count. The furthest we go is inserting the fireworm lightning retractor into the Communications Network Tower, but before we're able to get back out of the tower, soldiers stop us. I slam my fist against the table.

Shay pushes back from the table and scrubs her hands over her face. "This is impossible."

I inhale deeply, refocusing. "It can't be impossible. We're just not seeing something." I stare at the hologram of the compound, searching for weaknesses we can exploit. My body is stiff from being hunched over for so long, but I can't stop until I solve this.

I stretch my arms over my head and wince at my still-tight bruised ribs.

Shay's watching me. "How do you always find trouble? And get me in trouble? You've been this way since we were kids."

"You're the one who left the room the other night, Shay. Don't blame me because you got caught."

She glares at me. "We both know there's more going on here. Plus, whatever you did to get yourself in *this* condition."

I stare back at her. This is Shay. The one person here from my home, the only person around who's known me since I was a kid.

"Don't you miss it? Home? Our families?"

Shay blinks and leans back in her chair, surprised by the question. But then her face hardens even more. "No. Derbe was a dingy old town, stuck in the past. Talionis is the future. *My* future. Stop living in the past, Bria, and don't get in my way again."

We stare at each other for a few moments.

"I wouldn't dream of it," I finally say. "Let's figure this out."

We come up with a tentative plan using zip-packs to get out of the tower. The small backpack has a crossbow-like attachment that shoots out a heavy-duty cable with a pointed end that embeds itself in whatever you shoot it at. Once the cable has been shot, the backpack activates and splits in half. One half clamps down and secures the cable. The other half is used as a harness and allows you to travel down the cable.

The plan will require us to split up—one going for the zip-packs, the other disabling the main security. It's a big risk, but with the tension between the two of us, it seems to be our best option.

Major Vasco enters our room. "Time for your scenario. You'll be competing against Recruit Shane Malton and Cadet Matthias Valarius."

Stress tightens my muscles. This will not be an easy match.

We follow him from the room.

"Recruit Averton," Major Vasco says as we walk. "You've been excelling in your scenarios, and I like what I see. Keep up the good work, and give us a show today."

"Yes, sir," I say.

The look of hatred on Shay's face sends a chill through me.

We arrive in our zone, and Shane and Matthias are waiting.

"Averton and Bellingdon, you'll enter here," Major Vasco says. "Malton and Valarius, you'll be entering through a different door."

Major Vasco gives Shay and me waterproof packs and then presses the button to open the door. We enter, and a moment later, the door clangs shut. Blackness envelopes us. The room rumbles and shifts, and the sound of rushing water fills my ears.

The solid floor is no longer beneath my feet. Instead, I'm standing in a small raft. It rocks up and down in the water, and I sit before I fall out. The rumbling stops, and a half moon brightens the scene. Shay sits in the front of the boat, and in the distance, the compound we're tasked to enter is lit up. A small motor rests at the rear of the raft near me.

"Well, you better start that thing if we're going to accomplish our mission." Shay's facing me, but I can't read her expression.

I turn the motor on and begin navigating us toward the compound.

We're going up against Shane and Matthias with a plan that's weak, and I have to work with someone who hates me, all the while knowing Major Vasco is expecting me to do well.

It's hard to imagine how this will end successfully.

I cut the engine as we near the wall. We locate the general area where we'll be entering, and Shay pulls a lasitrix from her pack of gear. Without a word to each other, we slip from the raft into the water and swim toward the entry point.

We dive under before we enter the water that's illuminated by the lights on the wall. Shay follows me as I run my hand along the wall, feeling for the tunnel. I find it. There's only room for us to go through one at a time, so I motion for Shay to go ahead of me. She swims in with the lasitrix, and I follow.

She activates the device, and soon the laser barring our entrance moves aside, and we're able to swim through. My lungs are burning now. I kick harder. A moment later, Shay swims upward. We surface in the bowels of the compound, both of us breathing hard. Old stone stairs ascend to our right.

Shay puts the lasitrix back in her pack. "Alright. I'm going to go disable the security system. You get the zip packs." She steps out of the water and begins walking to the stairs.

"No." I follow behind her. "I think I should be the one to disable the—"

"Bria!" She hisses, whirling around to face me. "For *once*, do something someone tells you to do without fighting it."

"Fine," I say through clenched teeth. "Why are you still standing around? Let's go."

Shay stalks up the stairs. When we reach the top, we peek through the door. A movement to the side catches my eye, and I motion for Shay to wait. But she's not looking at me. She opens the door and steps out.

"*Wait!*" The word is barely a whisper, and Shay doesn't show any sign that she heard me. I scramble after her, even as I recognize that something's about to go wrong.

When I'm close, I reach for her arm.

"Halt!" Shane yells from behind us.

Neither of us look back. We just start running. An alarm sounds through the compound. I hear Shane running after us, yelling for help into his com system. All the noises merge, and then they're overshadowed by the blood pounding in my ears. We barely began this mission, and we're about to fail.

Shay screams in pain and then drops to the ground. I skid to a halt as blood pours from her side. A flashing pain rips through my chest. A blinding light. Then nothing.

———

"That was pathetic." Major Vasco paces in front of Shay and me as we stand at attention, staring straight ahead. "I expected much more from both of you. I'm disappointed." He stops his pacing and looms over us. "I do not like to be disappointed."

I couldn't argue with him even if I dared to. He's right.

"As a result, your entire squad will be assigned trash duty today. And I'll be sure to tell them they have you to thank."

Shay releases the hiss of a breath. Trash duty is an assignment usually given to recruits failing in multiple areas of training.

"Dismissed!"

FORTY-NINE

I operate the small trash transport to the dump area, the back filled with the trash we collected at the designated pickup points. The transport is so slow, I think it would actually be faster to walk. And the smell is horrendous. Nika sits next to me, foot up on the dash, her shirt pulled up over her nose. I doubt it helps. When I first stepped onto it, I thought I was going to lose my lunch.

"This is not okay." Nika's voice is muffled beneath the fabric of her shirt.

We're nearing the dump, and my eyes are watering from the smell of rotting food and sewage. It's in the back corner of Talionis. Once every week and a half, they incinerate all the trash. That day is tomorrow, so the dump is as full as it ever gets. If it smells this bad in the cold of winter, I never want to smell it in the heat of summer. I stop the transport, and Nika and I jump out and unload the bags of trash into the dump.

The rest of our squad is paired up, doing the same.

I throw in bag after bag, Nika working alongside me. The last remaining bag is heavier than the others, and halfway between the transport and the dump, it rips open and spills its contents onto the ground.

"Ahh! Come on!"

I march over to the transport, retrieve a new bag, and go back to the debris scattered on the ground. Thankful for the gloves I'm wearing, I shove the trash back into the bag. Nika stoops next to me and helps. Halfway through the pile, a piece of fabric under other pieces of trash captures my attention.

It's red.

Blood red.

The blood drains from my face. I know I don't want to see what that is, don't want to touch it. I don't want to know the story of why it's here. But a part of me has to know.

"Bria?" Nika's voice barely penetrates my concentration.

I don't move—can't move. I just stare at the strip of fabric that's visible.

"Bria. What's wrong?" Her voice is hesitant. "You're kind of freaking me out."

Without a word, I force myself into action. I pull the fabric out from under the pile. It's part of a recruit uniform. Ice cuts through my veins. The uniform is torn, shredded almost, and covered in blood. The name in the corner is still visible: *Mason Percleon*. This is what happened to the dark-haired Hispanic boy who spoke up. They got rid of him.

Nika's mouth falls open, her eyes widening. "What in the world...?"

I drop the uniform. A hundred emotions should be assaulting me right now. Fear. Anger. Resentment. But I'm numb. I don't feel anything.

I watch Nika carefully pick up the garment. Her eyes catch on the name, and she swallows hard before gently placing the uniform in the bag. "What do you think happened?"

"Something they don't want any of us to know about." My voice is detached, like it's coming from somewhere else.

"I don't think...Probably couldn't..." Nika clears her throat and tries again. "Do you think he's," she pauses, "alive?"

I stare at the bag where she just placed the blood-soaked uniform and envision the faces of those in Talionis who I've crossed. Keenan Valarius. Tay Vasco. Laban Meritas. Andor Valarius.

And then I hear the Commander's voice. *"They're expendable. If they die, they die."*

"No." I choke on the word.

Nika doesn't respond. Or maybe she does, but I don't hear it.

I kneel and drag the uniform back out of the bag and force myself to stare at it, see it for what it is. Recognize what it means. A sense of urgency gnaws at my numb brain. If I do nothing, whose uniform will I be holding next? My fingers clutch the fabric tighter. The urgency devours me. Whose blood will they not care about shedding? Nika's? Ari's? Cade's? I swallow. Mine?

I drop the uniform like it burned me as a horrifying picture paints itself across my mind. What if it's Storm? Or my brothers?

No.

I stand up. It won't be them. It can't be them, because they will *never* come here. They'll never face this. I won't let it happen. I'll get Storm out of here. Before it can reach my brothers, I will stop this. And I'll do whatever it takes to make that happen. Or I'll die trying. I won't fail them. I *can't* fail them.

I WAIT IN THE ALLEY, PERIODICALLY LOOKING OUT INTO THE STREET TO SEE IF Matthias is nearby. Nika offered to join me for this, but I told her I'd do it alone. It's time I faced him,

Especially since I'm about to give everything he needs to turn me in if that's what he wants to do. I hope Cai, Nika, and Ari are right about him.

I peer out at the street. Matthias strolls out of the Tech building and begins walking down the road toward me.

He's a few feet away when I poke my head out of the alley. "Matthias."

He looks over at me, surprise written across his face. I gesture for him to follow me. After a moment's hesitation, he enters the alley.

"Bria. What's up?"

I twist my hands together. It's so easy to be angry with him, to push him away when he's not standing in front of me. His gaze is watchful and sincere, almost hopeful. Like he's anticipating me giving him the chance he asked for to explain himself. My stomach twists tighter than my hands. What if I gave him that opportunity? What if I heard what he had to say instead of focusing all of my attention on what Laban said happened? My heart hammers in my chest.

He's proven that he's different from his dad. He does things for others, and he's helped take care of Storm. He even cared enough to come and see me in the infirmary. I snap out of my haze when he cocks his head. I know enough to believe I can include him in the escape plan without him betraying us, but we can't be friends again.

"Are you okay?" His voice is uncertain.

"I'm fine," I say, a little sharper than I intended. I stare down at my feet and take a deep breath.

I have to tell him about Cai. I look up. His expression is filled with concern.

"Why?" I blurt out the question.

Matthias' forehead furrows in confusion.

"Why do you care about what happens to me? Why can't you just be like everyone else here?" I shake my head. "I don't get you."

"I don't want to be like them." He licks his lips. "This place," he sweeps his arm out, "isn't something I want to be a part of. I think you know that." He shrugs. "But I know God put me here, so I'm just trying to figure out why."

We stare at each other—me trying to understand, to grasp what he's saying, his eyes imploring me to believe him.

God, why do You keep coming up? What do You want from me?

I swallow hard. I can't deal with this right now. There're more important things going on.

"Cai wants to see you."

Matthias's jaw goes slack, and all the color drains from his face. He takes a stuttering step backward and half leans, half falls against the wall. His mouth opens and closes like a fish that just got thrown onto land.

"What?" The word is between a breath and a whisper. "How do you...? Cai's dead."

I cringe. Maybe I shouldn't have been so blunt. "No, he's alive. And he wants to see you."

"How is this possible?" He lifts a shaking hand and runs it through his hair. "He was dead. They told me he was dead."

I keep my voice low. "He lives in the Ruins."

His jaw drops again.

Before he can say anything, I rush on. "He wants me to bring you to him. Tonight." Okay, so maybe Cai isn't the one who said it has to be tonight, but I know if I don't do it soon, I might lose my nerve.

"I can't believe Cai's alive." He shakes his head slightly. "Why did he let me believe he was dead? How do you know him? Why does he want to see me?" His voice is getting stronger now, and louder.

I take a step toward him and put my hands up, stalling his questions. "Matthias. He'll answer your questions if you come with me."

He doesn't respond.

"Will you come tonight or not?" My voice is hard, because I'm suddenly afraid he won't come. That's not a scenario I ever played out, but I doubt Cai or Nika will believe me if I tell them I *tried* to bring him.

He still doesn't respond, his face unreadable.

"You know what"—I take a step back—"never mind."

This was pointless. No, it was worse than pointless. It was stupid. I just told Matthias Valarius about Cai and implied that I can get into the Ruins to see him. This will not end well. I turn to leave, frustrated with myself and everyone who put me in this position.

"Wait." Matthias's voice stops me. "I'll come."

I eye him cautiously. "Really?"

He nods. "Just tell me when and where." Some color has come back to his face, but he's still pale.

I almost feel bad for the guy. This has been a pretty big shock, but I shake it off. As long as he's agreeing to come with me, what does it matter how he feels?

"Good. Meet me right here at 2300 hours. Don't be late."

He nods his agreement. "Alright."

We both begin to exit the alley, but I stop him with a hand on his arm. He looks at me, an unspoken question in his eyes. "Promise me you won't tell anyone."

His eyes narrow, piercing into mine, and for a moment I think he can see everything in me, my deepest secrets, my greatest longings. My fears. Cai is the only other one who ever seemed to do that. I want to look away. But I don't. I need him to agree to keep this quiet.

"I won't, Bria," he finally says, his voice serious. Then his hand is on my shoulder. "I trust you. I'm sorry I lied to you about my dad, but I promise I never betrayed you to Sergeant Meritas. You can trust me."

He drops his hand and walks away, leaving me staring after him. His words both comfort and terrify me.

I LAY IN BED, FULLY DRESSED, AND WAIT. TONIGHT IS THE NIGHT WE'RE going to start planning again. Tonight, I'm bringing someone I was sure was my enemy to meet my only hope of escape, of saving the ones I love. This is crazy. *You can trust me.* Once again, Matthias's words replay in my mind. My heartbeat quickens. I don't really have a choice tonight.

I put my head under the covers and check the time on my band. 22:50. This is it.

I slip out of bed, and Nika joins me. Ari's staying back tonight, but she'll be coming with us next time.

We go downstairs to the kitchen, melting into the shadows, alert to any sounds or movement, the stale smell of dinner hanging in the surrounding air. We open the same window I've used every time I've left the recruits' quarters to visit Cai.

The night is frigid, fully in the clutches of winter, but I hardly notice. My nerves are taut. Adrenaline courses through me. What if Matthias told others? What if he's waiting for us in the alley with Laban and a group of soldiers? What if he wanted me to see him doing all of those good things just so I would get lulled into believing he's not like his father? What if—

I stumble on a rock and almost fall, but Nika catches me by the arm.

"Keep it together!" she hisses in my ear. "If you keep making that kind of racket, someone's bound to catch us."

I nod. Taking a deep breath, I continue forward. When we're almost to the alley where Matthias is waiting, I slow down. Nika bumps into me. I don't even have to see her face to know she's annoyed and wondering what my problem is. Every fear and uncertainty about what I'm going to find when I turn into the alley floods through me. This could be the end. If Matthias decided to betray me, then this is likely the last night I'll be alive. I reach for my necklace, the old habit, but my necklace isn't there. Hasn't been there for months. Nika's hand presses into my back, urging me forward.

Inhale. Exhale. I step forward, turn the corner.

And see no one.

CHAPTER

FIFTY

Where is he? My eyes scan the dark alley, searching for movement in the shadows. Nothing. It has to be past 2300 hours now. I told him not to be late. I step further into the alley, Nika close behind.

"Where's Matthias?" she asks, her voice low and close to my ear.

Anger coils in my stomach and then begins rapidly winding its way through my limbs. I press my fist into the wall, wishing I could punch it without making any noise. I should have seen this coming. He's not here and probably is at this moment informing on us. He's who I thought he was all along. Everything else was a lie, a facade. Just like with Aunt Elena. I should never have told him. I should have—

A hand comes out of the shadows and touches my arm. My reflexes kick in, and I grab the arm, twist my body, using the force and momentum to flip the stranger over my shoulder. The person lands on their back, and I kneel into their abdomen, one hand twisted into their shirt, the other raised, poised to strike.

"Remind me never to startle you again," Matthias wheezes.

I relax my grip on his shirt and slowly lower my arm as his voice registers.

"Mind getting off?" he asks in a quiet voice, but I detect a hint of humor.

"Why were you lurking in the shadows?" I demand, my voice a harsh whisper as I stand up.

"I didn't want to be seen by anyone." Matthias gets to his feet.

"Well then, why didn't you step out once you saw us enter the alley?"

"I had to make sure it was you. Come on, Bria. You told me to be careful!"

Nika clears her throat. "I hate to break this up, you two, but I think we should get moving before someone walks by and hears you," she whispers.

"Let's go." I jab my finger into Matthias's chest before we start walking. "Never do that again."

"I don't plan to," he says, sounding like he's about to laugh. "You're fast, by the way. Much faster than the last time we trained together. I'm impressed."

I roll my eyes, even though he can't see the gesture in the dark, and walk away. His praise pleases me a little, but I push it aside. It's safer to be annoyed.

I lead the way to the Ruins, and we arrive at the abandoned building with no further incidents. We wind our way through the debris and to the fence. I pull my hood up, crouch down, and push through the vines and vegetation until I'm on the other side. I wait for Nika and Matthias to come through, and then we continue on.

A dog howls in the distance. The sound still makes me shudder, even though Cai has assured me they're "safe." We traverse the jumble of a path to the training site, Nika and Matthias sticking close to me. The air smells cold, like it's trying to decide if it will burst into snowflakes.

As we near the site, my heart beats harder and harder in my chest with new fears about what's about to happen. Did I wait too long to bring Matthias in? What if they decide I'm too much of a risk? After all, I didn't immediately agree to Cai's request. And I have caused my share of problems. But I need to get out of Talionis. I can't stay trapped here. My hands shake slightly, and I clench them into fists at my sides. No. They need me, need my help. Why am I even thinking like this? Cai's been saying all along that we need a good group of people involved in order for our plan to work. And he wouldn't give up on me that quickly.

Right?

We step around the final bend in the trail and into the small clearing in front of the site. Anxiety continues to gnaw at my chest, making it difficult to breathe normally. I know I'm expendable, too much of a risk. I can only hope the rest of them don't discover that fact. I have to get out of here for Storm and my brothers. I have to protect them.

I walk forward, determination in every step. I'll convince them they need me, need my expertise. After all, I don't think any of them are as good with directions and maps as I am. I push through the door and into the site. Cai turns from the table and whatever he's working on and faces me. A smile softens his features.

"Bria. How can I help you?" There's a tenderness in his voice that brings me to the verge of tears.

I swallow the emotion and step aside, allowing Nika and Matthias to enter. Cai's gaze collides with Matthias's, and emotion clouds both of their faces. Matthias swallows hard, and his eyes redden.

"Matthias," Cai says, voice cracking.

A tear escapes, and Matthias brushes it away. "I can't believe it's you. I can't believe," he takes a shuddering breath, "you're alive." His voice is hoarse and raw with emotion.

The distance between them vanishes, and they embrace. Nika and I watch the scene unfold, neither of us saying a word. I feel like an intruder, but I'm afraid to leave for fear of breaking up their reunion.

Matthias pulls away so that he's looking Cai in the face. "I thought you were dead." His voice is choked.

Sadness sweeps over Cai's face. "I'm sorry for that."

"I'm just glad I was wrong." Matthias gives Cai another firm hug, then steps back.

The next hour is spent with the two men catching up. They try to include Nika and me in the conversation, but the camaraderie between them and the depth of a relationship that time has not tainted, leave the two of us as observers. But neither of us mind. Listening to them talk, laughing at some stories they tell and reminisce about, is a pleasant reprieve from the stark realities of what we're all living. And the danger we're about to walk into.

"Well, we should probably get down to business," Cai says after some time. He explains the details of our plan with Matthias interrupting occasionally to ask a question or clarify a detail.

Once he finishes, Matthias nods. "I'm in."

"Good," Cai says, matter-of-factly, but I can see a small smile playing around the corners of his mouth.

Matthias leans forward. "I don't think Ark's plan is just about Talionis. I think it's about his home, Sitreea."

I clear my throat. "I think it's about more than just Sitreea." I share what I overheard about invasions and kidnapping the Chancellor of Sitreea, information Nika knows but that I haven't shared with Cai yet.

"What I don't understand is why kidnap the Chancellor?" Nika says. "If he's training an army to invade who-knows-where, what does the Chancellor matter?"

"Because Demetrius Ark is his illegitimate son," Matthias says. "And he can prove it." Matthias taps his leg. "And I think one place he's planning to invade is Sitreea."

"Why do you think that?" I eye Matthias curiously.

"The Warfare Scenarios. A lot of them take place in Sitreea. He's finding the weaknesses, forming recruits who can exploit them." Matthias shrugs. "I thought he just wanted to be Chancellor, but from what Bria heard, he has his eyes set on a lot more."

"If he wants to be Chancellor, why *attack* Sitreea?" Nika asks. "I don't think the citizens of the country are going to be excited to have the person who attacked them as their ruler."

"They'd never know it was him." All of us look at Cai. "The recruits aren't from Sitreea, or anywhere in that region. He can use them without anyone knowing he was the one behind it. He saves the day, and the people love him. And then he attacks other nations with the recruits and his soldiers, claiming he's avenging his father's death."

It makes sense. Too much sense.

We lapse into silence. The fire crackles, pops, hisses, each sound sending a spark along my nerves. If this is true, we won't have any hope of stopping him once he leaves Talionis.

"How much time do we have?" Nika asks.

"He wants to send the Elite Recruits in to kidnap the Chancellor within the next six months," I say. "But the rest of his plan can't happen for at least a year. He needs more recruits."

Even though I say the words, they send a chill through me. I get up and go stand in front of the fire, but it doesn't warm me. He's going to bring in more recruits. He's not done taking people from their homes, their families, and making them his slaves.

This isn't just a fight to escape or a fight for our lives. It's a fight for the lives of every recruit now in Talionis and every one they plan to drag in. It's a fight for the children and young people of this region. A fight we can't afford to lose.

THE MORNING IS STILL. THERE'S NO BREEZE BLOWING, BUT IT'S TOO COLD for the birds to be singing. Faint rays of light finger the edges of the horizon, testing the sky before the sun emerges. The houses I pass are shut tight against the wintery morning, but I occasionally catch glimpses of movement within. It's early, but the inhabitants of this housing section are already up and preparing for their duties for the day.

I shove my hands deeper into my pockets and pick up my pace. After the conversation last night, I wasn't able to sleep, so I laid in bed until I couldn't stand to any longer. An early morning walk seemed to be the only option I could settle on, and now my destination looms in front of me, beckoning me forward. I've only been back here one other time since Matthias brought me.

Since I've been mad at him for weeks, I haven't even considered returning to the old place. But right now, I don't care that he was the one who showed it to me. If I can find even a taste of the peace and comfort I felt staring at that window the first time I saw it, I might just be able to get through this day.

The sky has lightened a little more by the time I enter the dark interior. The familiar musty smell of the place greets me almost comfortingly. I blink and wait a moment for my eyes to adjust before cautiously making my way to the back where the stained-glass window is. When I enter the room, the curtain is already pulled away from the window. It's not lit up as majestically as it was the first time I saw it, but it still glows, even in the faint light of dawn. I sigh and step further into the room, my eyes caressing the blues and golds of the window. Some of the weight of what I learned lifts off my shoulders.

Something creaks to my left, shattering my respite. A person stands up from one of the broken benches, cloaked in thick shadows. I take a hesitant step backward. Maybe they haven't seen me yet. The person turns and looks at me. My heart slams into my chest like a trapped rabbit.

"Hi, Bria."

My heart freezes, and I wish even more that I could disappear back through the building. Why didn't it occur to me that Matthias might be here? He walks toward me. My mind screams at me to leave, but my feet seem stuck to the floor. More light seeps in through the windows, and the shadows slip off him as he comes closer. There's probably something I should say or do, but I remain exactly where I am, mouth sealed shut.

He stops near me. "I know you probably came here to think, but since we're both here, can we talk?"

Saying no and leaving would be the safe thing to do.

"Okay." The word slips past the guard of my lips and I can't stop it.

Matthias sighs in relief and motions for me to sit on the bench. I know I should leave even though I just agreed to talk to him, but it's like I'm watching someone else go through the motions of walking to the bench and sitting down, and there's nothing I can do to keep this conversation from happening. Maybe because a part of me wants it to finally happen and be over with. I tell myself I don't want to know his reasons for what he did, that I don't want to trust him, but is that true?

Matthias paces one way and then the other before coming to a stop in front of me. "We're going to work together now, and I have to clear the air before we do."

I watch wordlessly, not sure what to say, not willing to interrupt.

"I lied to you, and I'm sorry I did." He lifts one hand and then lets it fall back to his side. "You don't know how sorry I am. But I need to tell you why, not that it makes it right. I just want you to know my reasons."

He pauses, like he's waiting for me to object. I curl my fingers around the seat of the bench, the old wood smooth in some places and rough in others.

"Fine," I whisper.

He bobs his head and then sits down a few feet away from me. "You remind me of my mom," he blurts out.

I blink, unsure of what that has to do with anything. "Okay..." I draw the word out.

Matthias clears his throat. "My mom died when I was thirteen. I don't believe my father ever loved me much, but whatever love he had for me died when my mother died. So it didn't feel like I was lying to you when I said I lost both of my parents because," his one shoulder lifts wearily, "I believe I did."

My fingers twitch, preparing to reach out and comfort Matthias and the young boy who was so hurt, but I squeeze the bench tighter instead.

"When I heard about how you tried to run when you were taken by the extraction unit, the fight you put up, how you were defying orders, I knew I had to meet you. Because I haven't known anyone to fight against what's going on in Talionis that hard since my mom."

The impact of his words hits me a few seconds after he says them. "Your mom fought against Talionis?"

Matthias nods. "Yeah. She made it clear that she didn't agree with what Ark was doing, or what she believed he was planning. So they silenced her."

They killed her? "I'm sorry, Matthias."

He tilts his head. "I'm proud of who she was, of what she did, but I miss her...every day." He hesitates. "I wanted to be your friend because I saw some of that same strength in you. But I was afraid that if you knew who my father is, you wouldn't speak two words to me."

He's right. There's no way I would have let him hang around me as much as he did.

When I say nothing for a while, Matthias stands up.

"I just needed you to know." He sounds defeated and exhausted.

I stare down at my hands so I don't have to see those emotions reflected in his eyes.

"I hope we get out of here, Bria, and that one day you can forgive me, maybe even let me be your friend again." He clears his throat. "I told you you could trust me, but I don't deserve that, so thank you for bringing me to Cai, for allowing me to be a part of stopping what Ark is trying to do."

He moves to leave.

"Matthias."

He pauses.

"How did Laban find out what I said in the bunker? If it wasn't you, why were you brought in with Shay?"

"I don't know. Shay was hanging around me a lot when you weren't around. Flirting with me. I think she found out who my dad is and thought I'd be a good connection for her."

Sounds like Shay.

"But I swear, Bria, I didn't say a word to her."

Then he leaves. His footsteps echo around the room and fade to the hallway. I stare at my hands and imagine him exiting and walking down the street, back toward the center of the city. I'm too tired to process all he said, too overwhelmed by what he shared to even know what to do with it.

What if Matthias hadn't lied to me? What if he had told me who his father was? I would never have cared enough about him for it to matter what he said or did. He never would have heard what I said in the bunker. It was because of his lie that we became friends, that I could see more of him. That I started to care. My stomach folds in on itself, and I stand abruptly, causing the bench to creak. As much as I wish they didn't, his reasons make sense, but I can't *excuse* what he did. And I can't allow him that close again.

CHAPTER

FIFTY-ONE

I wait in the Ruins for everyone else to arrive, nerves on edge.

Ari and Shane are with me. Nika should arrive with Nalani and Bryson any moment, and Matthias and Cade are supposed to arrive ten minutes after. Breaking the group up into three sets made sense, but waiting is killing me.

"He really has tech out here?" Ari asks for the fourth time in the past two minutes.

I'm not sure if I want to laugh or strangle her. "Yes."

"Do you think he'll let me take a look at it?"

"Sure." I've said "I don't know" the past few times, and that hasn't gotten me anywhere.

Nika comes through the fence, followed by Nalani. Matthias enters with his group on time.

I lead the way to Cai's intel site, breathing a little easier. Somehow, we all made it through. Hopefully, getting back will be just as easy.

When the building Cai uses for his site comes into view, and I head toward it, a few of those with us hesitate.

"Buildings collapse out here," Bryson says, warily.

"Not this one."

I enter the building, and the rest follow. As soon as Ari sees Cai's set up, she heads right for it, before Cai can say hello. Everyone else just stares, reminding me of my shock upon finding this place when I first arrived.

"What system are you using?" Ari asks, making herself comfortable in Cai's chair, and powering on the screens. "Do you have a secure channel? Ever experience any interference with —"

Cai watches, amused.

"Girl," Nika says. "You have to ask before you touch someone else's stuff."

"Sorry," Ari says sheepishly, hand poised over a screen.

Cai laughs. "It's okay. Your friends told me you'd be excited. Check it out."

His kindness and gentle nature are so different from the soldiers in Talionis, I wonder how I could have ever suspected he was one of them.

Ari barely says thanks before she's engrossed in the screens, hands typing on two different keypads at the same time.

We do a quick round of introductions, and then Cai shares that this is more than just escaping. It's about stopping Demetrius Ark from what he's planning to do, which means going to Eryndale and gathering those who can help us.

He passes it over to me to share what we need to do before escaping.

"We'll need items for our journey to Eryndale. Basic things like food, blankets, medical supplies, and weapons." I tick the items off on my fingers. "We'll store the supplies here until the day before the Commencement. Since we'll steal a transport to get us to Eryndale, we should have room for everything."

Ari makes a disgruntled noise, but I can't tell if it's because of something I said or something she's doing on the screens.

"Hopefully, the soldiers and the Commander don't see us as a threat or anything worth pursuing, but we have to assume they'll try to stop us. Which is why it's important we sabotage as much as possible before we leave."

Matthias nods. "Right."

Matthias walks over to a big screen with a map of Talionis and shifts it so everyone can see. He's helped us choose a few other areas to hit in order to cause distraction and mayhem so we can escape, and we've marked those with an X.

"The escape will happen during the Commencement, so there will be minimum security throughout Talionis. We'll separate into three groups and begin by setting fires to these abandoned buildings"—he points to three buildings in different sections on the outskirts of Talionis—"as well as to the Physical Training Arena and the Education Center. Both will be empty, but when the alarms sound, they'll provide a distraction. We'll also be setting off minor explosions in several areas." He taps one of the small red X's that indicate an explosion scattered all over the map. "We'll set the explosives in place the night before, so all we'll need to do is trigger them."

"We also want to set off as many alarms as possible throughout the city," Nika adds. "Specifically, in the areas we don't need to be in. We're still trying to figure out how to remotely activate the alarms so we don't have to actually be there."

"Well, that's easy," Ari says.

I could have guessed that would be her response.

She's squinting at a screen. "As long as I have the right equipment, I shouldn't have any problem activating the alarms."

"Will this setup work?" Cai asks.

Ari glances over. "It's not bad. I'll make some necessary adjustments and updates. But I could use a few more things."

"We'll get you what you need," Matthias says confidently. "In the chaos we're hoping this creates, each group will be given one of these specific major targets to first acquire items and then sabotage: the Main Headquarters, Weaponry, and Tech buildings. Those tasked with the Weaponry building will retrieve weapons and then detonate an explosive to cause a major distraction. Those in the Tech building will gather the gear we'll need, such as night-vision glasses, and then disable the Communications and Tracking, and those tasked with the Main Headquarters building will need to retrieve the maps from Ark's safe."

Matthias's gaze darts to mine. We've already discussed that I'll be the one to retrieve the maps. He looks away.

"Once this has all been done, we'll meet at the Transportation Dock, where we'll rig explosives to destroy most, if not all, the transports. We'll steal one transport, and once we've cleared the building, set off the charge."

I take a deep breath as he finishes. The plan is good. This is going to work.

"The transport part won't work," Ari and Bryson say at the same time.

"What?" Nika's voice borders between uncertain and incredulous.

Ari leans away from the screens. "The transports are all equipped with antitheft panels, pilot sensory systems, and four-lock key generators."

My memory swims in search of the moment where I may have learned the definition of at least one thing she just said, but nothing comes back to me.

"Right," Bryson says. "Even if you could get past the antitheft panels and override the four-lock key generators, there's no way you could fly a transport without a pilot."

"But, why?" I sound desperate, but not nearly as desperate as I feel.

The tech-whiz siblings are poking a hole in the most crucial part of this plan. We *have* to steal a transport.

"Because of the pilot sensory system," Ari says, matter-of-factly.

"Sorry, but even I don't know what that is." Matthias's face looks calm, but he's gripping a paper so tightly it's crumpling.

"Oh." Ari's eyes widen. "In order to activate a transport, you need that specific transport's pilot. The pilot sensory system is what will operate the transport. The pilot speaks a specific voice activation code for the system to turn on. Then it does a body scan and reads the vitals of its pilot to ensure he or she is in proper health. It scans their eyes for retinal confirmation, and both of the pilot's hands must be placed on the activation board before the engine will start." She lifts a hand apologetically. "There's no way you could steal a transport and make it fly on your own."

The site is silent when Ari finishes. My head pulses as I try to find a way around what she's saying. We're running out of time to come up with a different plan. Cai stands, hands resting on the table as he leans over the map, studying it, likely looking for an answer to our massive new problem.

A thought flickers into my mind, and I blurt it out. "Well then, we just need to kidnap the pilot."

Cai's head flies up from his inspection of the map. "Too risky."

I stand up. "We don't have a choice."

"That is not an option," Cai says.

The hope that was almost palpable in the room as Matthias shared the plan has shattered.

I can't believe this is happening. We were so close to getting out of here, to escaping, to stopping Ark for good. But of course, it was all too good to be true. I'm going to remain trapped here, unable to protect my brothers, unable to free Storm. My knees weaken, and I sink back into my chair.

"Could we get out on foot?" Bryson asks.

Cai shakes his head. "The Wall is impenetrable with the electric current racing through it and the guards stationed all around it. The transport would have gotten us over it." He sounds strong, confident, the same as he always does, but his shoulders are stooped in defeat.

Silence clutches us in its depressing embrace again.

"It might not be impenetrable," Ari says slowly. She types on one screen, and then a hologram of the wall emerges. She studies it for a moment. "We could create a power surge. Flood the primary power source with so much energy that the system will crash and need to reboot itself, causing the Wall to shut down."

The possibility of another way out makes my heart lift tentatively.

A few keystrokes later, the Wall has disappeared, and something else appears. "If we can overload this server, then create a large voltage surge, like the equivalent of a lightning strike, we may succeed in not only shutting down the electric current in the Wall in order for us to escape, but also in frying some of the technology that runs off the same server." She smiles and tucks a piece of blond hair behind her ear. "A nice bonus. The Wall is a vital feature in Talionis, so we won't be able to fry that. But we should be able to shut it down long enough to get over it."

"This could work," Cai says, standing straighter.

"It might," Matthias says. "But it's risky. They're going to make it their top priority to get the Wall fully functioning. A lot rides on it. Including the Net."

"What's the Net?" I ask.

"I learned about that in Advanced Tech Training," Ari says. "It's like a shield that keeps Talionis hidden from the rest of the world."

"Right." Matthias nods. "It blocks all technology that could otherwise detect a city or any kind of movement. Only those in the very highest levels of the Sitreean government know where Talionis is. If other nations knew what Sitreea was doing, it could start another war. Trust me, they're not going to let much time go by before they get the Wall back up."

"As long as we have enough time to get over it." I face Ari. "How difficult would it be to create the surge?"

"Well," she pauses and types. "It looks like they keep that server in the classified wing of the tech building."

Even though she's looking at us, I can see her thinking.

"I'll need something to create crydrospheric charge, which should be enough voltage." She focuses on her brother, and he shrugs and nods. "If I can get what I need, it shouldn't take that long."

Cai strokes his beard. "Okay. This is our only option. Ari, if you think you can do this, we will adjust the plan and make it work."

His eyes bore into Ari, but she nods confidently.

"I can do it."

"Very well," Cai says. "We'll keep most of the plan the same, but we'll change the location of some of our distractions and create a path to the Ruins to give us the best chance to get out of Talionis undetected." He folds his arms across his chest. "The Commencement is only two months away. There's a lot to do, and it's going to take all of us working together to accomplish this."

Everyone nods.

The rest of our time together is spent dividing up duties and responsibilities. Since Nika, Shane, and I are the most advanced recruits in our little group, it is decided we will be the ones, along with Matthias, to find out as much as we can about Ark's plan and confirm the secret rooms and accesses that Cai knows about. The others will find ways to gather supplies.

As Cai details lists of the supplies needed, my mind drifts to Storm. I'll need to talk to her and prepare her. Because there is no way I'm leaving without that girl.

I don't know what I expected from Storm when I told her about leaving, but this was certainly not it. I hold her close, her tear-soaked face pressed into my shoulder. Her little body shudders. Damara watches us, her face empty of emotion. What is she thinking?

"Why do we have to go?" Storm asks, her voice muffled and choked with tears.

"Don't you want to leave?" I feel completely helpless. "Why stay here?"

"Am I gonna go back to my mommy and daddy?"

I open my mouth to say yes, then close it. I can't lie to her. "Not right away. We'll need to travel a little first. There're some important things we need to do."

I pull away from her slightly and tilt her chin so she's looking at me. She hiccups.

"Don't you trust me, little squirrel?" I smile, hoping the nickname lightens the mood.

"Yes." She rubs her arm across her face, smearing the tears. "Miss Damara, you're gonna come too, right?"

"Yes." Damara's eyes turn tender as she looks at Storm. "Honey, why don't you go dry your face." Storm leaves the room, and Damara's gaze lands on me. "When do we need to be ready?"

"The Commencement."

Damara nods. "I need your word that you will do everything in your power to keep Storm safe."

"Of course."

"Very well. It's dangerous, but I don't think we have another choice." She pauses. "They killed my husband. I'm sure they'll soon find they don't have a use for me." She links her hands together on her lap.

She told me before that her husband was supposed to be a watcher for Talionis but refused to do what they wanted. It's hard to believe that he's dead, even though she knew he was in danger. "Fill me in on what I need to know, and we'll be ready when the day comes."

"TODAY WE ARE GOING TO RECOGNIZE THE TOP RECRUITS." COLONEL KEENAN Valarius addresses all the recruits where we stand at attention in the middle of the Center. "After yesterday's evaluation, seventeen recruits rose to the top. This day marks the day that they become Elite Recruits. They will receive greater responsibilities and greater rewards. Their training will be difficult and push them to the extreme, but they have proven that they are strong, and I trust they will succeed."

We haven't seen the rankings from our evaluation yet. I need to be one of the Elite recruits. Everything depends on it.

"I am now going to call out the names of those recruits. If your name is called, make your way up to the platform. Seffrin Johand. Adira Kamalani. Shane Malton…"

Colonel Valarius continues listing the names, and those recruits are now lining the platform. He's called fifteen names already. Only two more. Maybe I didn't make it.

"Nika Bromeliad."

Nika moves from her position next to me and goes to the platform. It feels like there's a fist inside of me, slamming into my ribs and bruising them. This is it. If I didn't make it, what will I do? I'll be expendable. They might not actually need me to escape.

"And finally, Bria Averton."

I'm frozen in place for a moment. Then I'm walking forward. Somehow, I did it. I made it into the highest ranking of recruits. I stand at attention next to Nika.

"Congratulations," Colonel Valarius says, facing us. "I'm honored to announce to you that your reward for this magnificent accomplishment will be dinner with the Commander tonight. Proper attire will be provided, and a transport will pick you up at 1800 hours." He turns his attention back to the other recruits. "To the rest of you, I hope these few will become a new standard that you yourselves will attempt to achieve."

He snaps his fingers, and his aide steps forward and hands him a slip of paper.

"For further motivation," he consults his paper, "Dex Tildon, step forward."

A scrawny guy steps away from his unit.

"Recruit Tildon received the lowest marks of all the recruits in every area of training. This is unacceptable. While we do not have the unrealistic expectation that every recruit will attain the status of Elite, we expect each recruit to work at and excel in at least one level of their training."

Dex ducks his head, his shoulders hunched by his ears, hands twisted together. I don't blame him. I've been where he is, and facing an angry Colonel Valarius is a terrifying prospect.

Colonel Valarius makes a slight gesture with his hand, and Laban, Major Vasco, and Sergeant Valarius all come and surround Dex.

"You will all witness what it means to fail so completely," Colonel Valarius spits the word. "Recruit Tildon, you'll now face these three soldiers of Talionis and engage them in hand-to-hand combat. You'll fight until you succeed in getting the better of one of them, or until you are unconscious. I hope this teaches you a lesson.

And to the rest of you, let this be a warning. Do not take your training lightly."

Colonel Valarius settles into a chair, crossing one leg over the other. "Begin."

The three soldiers move as one toward Dex, who doesn't even get into a protective stance. This will not be good. Every part of me wants to cry out, to tell them to stop. But I can't draw that kind of attention to myself.

Instead, I'm forced to watch as blow after blow is landed on Dex, and all of his feeble attempts to fight back are turned against him. His cries of pain echo around us. It's not long before he's on the ground, blood oozing from his nose and a gash above his eye, bruises already forming on his face. He's curled into a ball, not moving.

Major Vasco and Sergeant Valarius step back, but Laban moves forward and kicks him in the gut. Once. Twice. He picks him up off the ground, spins him one and a half times, then flings his limp body through the air. Laban closes the distance to Dex. His booted foot rises into the air above Dex's head. He's going to kill him. I take a half-step forward. I can't let this happen.

"That's enough," Colonel Valarius says. "I believe he's already unconscious." There's a hint of amusement in his voice.

My stomach churns. Evil men are commending me.

Laban steps back, and his golden eyes lock on mine. A look of pure hatred cloaks his face. It doesn't matter that I stand among the Elite Recruits. He hates me, and that isn't ever going to change.

<hr>

THEY HAVE ISSUED ME A NEW UNIFORM, AND I DIDN'T HAVE TO GO TO THE tailors to get it. It was waiting for me in my room.

Instead of the green camo I've worn since I came to Talionis, I now have a white uniform with a red stripe on it that goes from my right shoulder down to my hip on the front and the back. My left sleeve has a black band with the words Elite Recruit printed on it in red. My name is stitched in red over my heart. I pull it on, and it fits me perfectly. Like it was designed specifically for me. My boots slide easily over the pant legs, and I lace them up, the black a stark contrast to the white. A reminder of the contrast of who I was and who I am now.

I am an elite recruit.

I'm one of only seventeen who have achieved the status. And the fact makes me physically sick. The uniform clings to me like a new skin. I've been stripped of who I was, and they've crafted me into who they wanted me to be. It doesn't matter at this moment that I let them, that it's part of the plan, that it's how we're going to destroy them.

All that matters is that they think they've won.

Maybe, in some ways, they have.

Nika enters the room. "Woah." Her eyes quickly assess me before taking in the similar uniform laying on her bed. "Guess we got new uniforms."

"Yeah," I say.

Nika picks up her uniform and holds it out in front of her. "What do you think about the dinner tonight with the Commander?"

I give her a wry smile. "Well, I suppose it's about time we meet our host."

She gives me one of her looks, but a smile starts in her eyes, then steals across her face. "You're crazy."

A light knock sounds on the door, and it's pushed open before either of us can respond.

Sampta and Presidia enter, arms overladen with boxes. Nika and I exchange a look. I thought we got out of having to see them.

"Good evening," Sampta says. She almost sounds giddy with excitement. "We are here to prepare you for your dinner with the Commander."

"Finally, a design worthy of our talents," Presidia says.

Sampta's gray eyes run up and down me. "Your new uniform is considerably better than the rotten thing you've been wearing. But you will not be wearing it to such an important engagement." She turns to Presidia. "I'm appalled to think she would even consider such a thing, honestly."

Presidia clicks her tongue. "Indeed."

Ari opens the door and comes into the room, stopping short when she sees the two women.

"You are not welcome right now," Presidia says. "Please leave." She gives an impatient flick of her wrist toward the door.

Ari's eyes widen. She mumbles an apology, grabs the screen on her bedstead, and flees the room.

A protectiveness fills me. "You didn't need to do that." I gesture toward Ari's bed. "This is her room too."

Presidia's eyes narrow. "It is unnecessary and highly irregular for her to be here for this process." Her words are clipped.

"Well, you didn't need to be rude about it."

"Bria." Nika puts on an unnatural smile, but there's a clear warning in her voice.

I clamp my mouth shut against the sharp words bursting to come out. Presidia lets out a huff.

Sampta waves her hand, as though dismissing the exchange. "Enough of that. We have much to do in order to prepare you for tonight. Let's get started."

For the next few hours, Nika and I are prepared for our meeting with the Commander. First we are bathed. Then every "excess hair" is removed, a process that is both painful and completely unnecessary in my mind. Next, they apply cosmetics and style our hair.

Finally, the women step back and open the two remaining boxes. They remove gowns that are unlike anything I've ever seen before, let alone worn. The one Presidia brings to Nika is gold and shimmers in the light. Sampta brings me one that is emerald in color. I step into it, and she laces it up my back. The material glides over my skin and brushes the ground at my feet. She hands me a pair of shoes that look completely impractical, but I slip them on, anyway.

"Amazing. Miraculous almost." Sampta steps back. "You are ready."

Presidia says something similar to Nika, and I turn toward her. My jaw drops. She looks like a different person. The gold of the dress is perfect against her dark skin. Her hair has been intricately braided, and the cosmetics they applied to her face accent her natural beauty. She glows like she's from another world.

"Wow, girl," Nika says. "You clean up nice."

I smooth my hands down the sides of my dress and slowly turn to look in the mirror.

I don't recognize the girl staring back at me. Every flaw I'm used to seeing on my face and neck, every scar, every mark, is covered. My eyes match the emerald color of the dress, and somehow Sampta wrestled my curls into order. My hair is swept up, twisted, and tucked and pinned in such a way that I'm wondering how I'll ever get it back to normal. A golden thread is woven through the strands.

I tentatively touch it, amazed.

"The transport will arrive shortly," Presidia says. "I suggest you make your way out front."

"And please do your best not to spoil all our hard work," Sampta says.

Nika and I both nod, and I realize she was staring at herself as well.

We exit the room with our rifles, but soldiers in their dress uniforms inform us we are to leave the guns behind. They flank us in the hallway and lead us down to the first floor. It takes several steps for me to adjust to the high-heeled shoes I'm wearing, but as we exit the building, I begin to feel more comfortable.

I almost stop walking.

All of the recruits are lined up in formation, as Nika, me, and the other Elites are led down a red carpet to the waiting transport. The other Elite girls are in gowns like Nika and me, and the Elite guys are dressed in different colored suits, each accenting the looks of the guy wearing it.

I notice a few girls from my unit staring at me. They glance away when I catch them looking but can't help but look back again. It's strange being watched like this, but I don't blame them. I'd be staring at us too.

"This is one of the craziest things I've ever experienced," Nika says out of the side of her mouth. "And that's saying something."

When we are halfway to the transport, one of the female soldiers with us shouts, "These are the ones the Commander delights to honor!"

My face burns, though I'm not sure anyone can tell through all the cosmetics. The walk to the transport feels like it takes an eternity, but we finally arrive. It's more luxurious than any I've ridden in before. We are told that this is one of the Commander's personal transports.

A thick, plush carpet covers the floor. The seats are large and roomy. The windows darken as we ascend, cutting down the glare from the setting sun. By looking out at the passing city, I know we're moving fast, but the transport hardly makes a sound as it glides through the air. I sit next to Nika, and a table rises from the floor between our chairs. A woman appears.

"Would you like a beverage for your journey? Or a light snack?" she asks.

"I'm fine," I say.

"No, thank you," Nika says.

"Very well." The woman disappears.

Nika leans toward me. "Fancy."

"No kidding."

We pass over the main part of Talionis and eventually come to a large building on the river. The transport descends onto the flat roof. The door opens, and we stand.

FIFTY-THREE

A large, familiar silhouette fills the doorway. "Welcome to the Commander's home," Colonel Valarius says.

He's still wearing a uniform, but this one is much dressier—all white with gold buttons and threading and various medals dripping from his chest. His dark hair has even been freshly trimmed for the occasion.

"Follow me."

We file out after him onto the roof of the largest home I've ever encountered. He leads us inside, and we go down a flight of stairs. Double doors open before us into a high-ceilinged dining room with windows on the western wall offering a perfect view of the setting sun. A table stretches across the center of the room, the silver of the platters and utensils glittering in the light of the massive chandelier overhead.

"All stand at attention for the Commander of Talionis, our leader, Demetrius Ark," Colonel Valarius bellows.

We all snap to attention, though the movement feels strange in the extravagant dress. A set of double doors across the room from us are opened by two high-ranking soldiers who immediately stand at attention as the Commander enters the room.

A chill of nervous anticipation washes over me. I'm about to finally meet the man responsible for everything that has happened. The light of the setting sun shadows him from my view, allowing me only a glimpse of his silhouette, and there's something powerful even in that. He appears to be shorter than Major Vasco and the Valarius brothers, but his stride is purposeful, his shoulders squared. I can see why they call him the Commander. His presence is...commanding.

He comes toward us, and as the light shines on his features, I'm struck by how handsome he is. He's not very young, perhaps mid-forties, but there's a youthfulness to him. Dark brown hair lies in thick waves on his head, each hair perfectly in place. Thick eyebrows perch over eyes so dark, they almost look black. He stops in front of us and smiles, revealing straight white teeth. A dimple appears on his left cheek.

"Welcome to my home," he says, his voice smooth and resonating. His accent is unique, different from the others, and there's something in the way he talks that almost makes me want to hear what he's going to say. "I've been looking forward to this night for some time now. Colonel," Ark looks to Colonel Valarius, who steps forward, "please do me the honor of introducing me to these fine young people."

"Of course, sir," Colonel Valarius inclines his head.

I stand at the far left in the line of Elite Recruits, and he begins making introductions with those on the right. I observe the Commander as he meets each recruit. He makes eye contact, remarks on something personal to that recruit, smiles, shakes their hand, then moves on to the next one. With the female recruits, he bends over their hands and kisses them. He stops before Nika.

"Beauty and strength. Miss Bromeliad, you do not disappoint." He smiles.

"Thank you, sir." Nika's face is unreadable as the Commander bends over her hand and kisses it, but a muscle twitches in her cheek when he makes contact, like she's flinching.

He straightens and turns his attention to me. Our eyes connect. From the point of my heeled shoes to the gold thread in my hair, goosebumps coat my body. This is a man to be feared.

"May I present," Colonel Valarius begins, "Recruit Bria—"

"Averton, yes," the Commander interrupts, his eyes remaining locked on mine. "I must say, Bria—I do hope you don't mind the familiarity—that I'm quite glad to see you here. You look exquisite this evening."

He picks up my hand, and my skin crawls at his touch, but I keep from yanking it back.

"I have been intimately following your progress." His words and demeanor seem sincere, but there's something else behind them, something I can't identify, something that terrifies me.

"I understand that there was some struggle and adjustment in the beginning, but I'm pleased to see and hear how far you've come. You will be a credit to Talionis. Of this I have no doubt." He squeezes my hand slightly. "Indeed, I've believed so from the beginning."

He brings my hand up to his lips and presses a kiss to the back of it, lingering. Everything in me screams to yank it away, but I know I can't. This must be what it feels like to be kissed by a serpent.

He straightens, and I think he's going to release my hand and move on with the rest of the evening. But he doesn't.

Rather, he addresses me again. "I truly am pleased you have come to recognize how much Talionis offers and that you've let go of those foolish notions of returning to the primitive life you once had."

I swallow and hope my face remains neutral as I nod in acknowledgement of his words. Have I really fooled them all so much that they believe I care about this place? Or is he taunting me? Does he know I'm not who I'm pretending to me?

He smiles, and his eyes glimmer in the setting sun. "I look forward to getting to know you better." He's beautiful, cunning. Deadly.

"And I you, Commander." I hope my voice sounds strong and confident. Because at this moment, I feel completely the opposite. How can we ever outwit this man?

We're seated at the elegant dining table, and soon servants appear, bringing tray after tray of food. The meal begins with a large assortment of appetizers, each looking and smelling more delicious than the one that came before it. My stomach is twisted in knots, and I struggle to force down the food, though it's tastier than any I've had in a long time. I sense the Commander's attention on me and know I can't appear nervous. I force myself to take a bite of the blue cheese and steak crostini that was just set before me. I chew slowly but barely taste it. Why was I seated so close to him?

There isn't much conversation.

The Commander carefully cuts a small bite of the crostini. "Well, it's a little quiet in here." He winks at Adira, and she blushes. "Tell me, what's your favorite spot to visit in the city?"

He eats the bite on his fork, his eyes surveying those at the table.

At first, no one speaks, but then someone mentions a small park, and others jump in. When that discussion dies down, the Commander brings up another. He freely sprinkles the conversation with his own thoughts and his smiles. Every word, every topic, is intended to put us at ease. Yet with each passing moment, I'm more tense.

This man is not who he seems to be, but he's a master at making people believe he is. I keep up my guard, afraid of being sucked into his spell. He's behind everything that's happened so far. I know just a bit of what he has planned, and it's terrifying.

The main course is served. My stomach protests at the thought of more food, but I pick at it anyway. Maybe if I appear like I'm eating and enjoying this, no one will notice me.

"Bria," the Commander says, as the surrounding conversation continues to flow. "Is everything okay? You've hardly touched your meal."

Of course he would notice. "Oh, yes. I'm just so overwhelmed by all that's happened today. I don't seem to have much of an appetite," I say, satisfied with my response and hoping he will be as well.

"It's been quite a day of accomplishment for you." He gives me another of his congenial smirks. "I understand. When I was first rising in the ranks, there were days where my head practically spun with the enormity of all that was happening."

He reaches over and pats my hand, and I manage a smile.

"Have you seen young Storm lately?"

My smile dies. "Not the past few days, sir." The words are airy, but at least I got them out.

"She's doing well, the little one, don't you think?" The question sounds innocent, but I'm afraid it's anything but.

I nod, and he smirks again. He focuses on another recruit. I release my breath. This man is a cunning snake. And I've just walked straight into his den.

FIFTY-FOUR

Dinner has been cleared from the table. Everyone seems relaxed and comfortable, as though they are fully enjoying their time here. I try to mimic their attitudes and hope my true feelings don't show through. Maybe all the cosmetics Sampta applied will help. Nika catches my eye, and her eyebrows lift ever so slightly. She's much better at masking her feelings than I am, but that small look tells me everything I need to know. She's uncomfortable too.

The Commander stands, and everyone immediately pushes back from the table to stand as well.

"This has been an enjoyable evening. It is exciting to see all of you in your quest to be all you can be for yourselves and for Talionis. As I am sure you are aware, your training as Elite Recruits will differ from the training the other recruits will continue in."

He folds his hands together in front of himself. "That being the case, you will all be moved to different quarters so you can maintain the proper focus needed during this time. From here, you will be taken to your new rooms. We have moved all of your items for you. I hope you find the arrangements comfortable." He smiles, his dimple flashing. "I will take my leave of you now and allow you to settle in.

You have a big day of training tomorrow. I look forward to watching your continued progress."

His gaze rests on me with those last words. My stomach revolts, making me regret the small amount of food I ate, but I maintain eye contact. Then he turns and leaves.

Our new living quarters are very different from what we had before. We are in a building in the center of Talionis, and our rooms are on the top floor. Nika and I share a room. Tall windows line the wall, giving us a perfect view of the city. Our beds are large and comfortable, yet they take up only a small portion of the space. I feel sorry for Ari since she's still in our old, cramped room, alone, and I already miss her chatter. I wonder how she'll handle the change.

Two overstuffed chairs are nestled in one corner with end tables next to them. The lighting in the room isn't the harsh lighting I've become accustomed to in Talionis but soft, and with the windows, the natural light during the day will be nice. A door off to the side leads to our own bathroom, and there's a walk-in closet for each of us stocked with more clothes than I've ever seen in one place.

"Well," Nika says, "I'd say this is an upgrade."

"That's an understatement." I sigh. "The security is probably tighter in this section of the city."

Tomorrow night we're scheduled to go see Cai, and I'm wondering how that will play out with our change in accommodations.

"We'll get Ari to figure it out." She kicks off her shoes. "For now, I'm beat. And so full! The guy might be crazy, but he sure knows how to throw a feast. That food was something else!"

"If you say so." I plop myself down on the bed.

"What do you mean, 'if you say so'? Please tell me you weren't so paranoid that you didn't eat anything!"

I gaze out the window. "I didn't have much of an appetite."

Wind howls around Nika and me as we walk through the dark on our new route to the Ruins. It took us most of our second night in our new accommodations to find a way to get into the Ruins undetected. The security in our building and in that section of the city is different from the security we were used to. More soldiers patrol the streets, not on guard, but busy going about their duties. There are surveillance cameras positioned around the main buildings, and most of the alleys are well lit.

Thanks to Ari, we finally found a route where we only had to cross three major streets and that avoided the main surveillance areas. It's a longer route, but so far, it's been working.

An icy raindrop splashes on my cheek. Then another. A moment later, it's steadily raining. The frigid water finds its way onto every exposed area of skin. I wear my old uniform, which provides some level of protection, but by the time we've entered the Ruins, I can feel the rain soaking through. The one good thing is that there are minimal guards out on nights like this, and we could cross the streets without needing to wait as long for breaks between soldiers.

When we enter the site, the only part of me still dry is my feet. At least my boots are waterproof. I gravitate toward the fire, letting the warmth soak into me. The others trickle in, dropping the supplies they've gathered into the pile. It's grown steadily over the past couple of weeks, but it still doesn't look like enough.

Soon everyone has arrived, and we congregate around the fire.

"I wasn't sure you'd all make it tonight in this storm." The wind howls outside, the rain pelting the earth, accentuating Cai's words. He gestures to the fire where we're all huddled. "Finish warming up. We have things we need to discuss."

I walk away from the fire and take my seat near the table.

Cai leans against the wall, arms crossed, observing everyone settle into place. As usual, I can't read his expression.

"Supplies." He states the one word, starting the process we've all become familiar with—going over the plan.

Cade stands up. He's the one responsible for keeping track of supplies, and he sums up what we have and what we still need.

"Very well," Cai says.

"Wait," Shane cuts in. "We still need a lot, and we're running low on time."

"He's right," Ari says, looking defeated.

A few others nod their agreement.

"We'll have what we need." Cai is confident, and his tone leaves no room for anyone to disagree. "Any new intel?"

Nalani suggests we add destroying the lab in the tech building to our sabotage. She's advanced in the medical and tech areas, and she discovered the drugs being created in the lab are how they can extract recruits from their homes without them or their families knowing what's happening.

We add it to the list. Anything that can be done to stop Ark's plan.

Finally, we review who will do what on the day of our escape. It's clear that Ari and Bryson are the most qualified to handle the Tech building, gathering the gear, creating the surge to temporarily take down the Wall, and disabling the Communications and Tracking systems.

Shane and Cade are assigned to the Weaponry building. Since it's the closest building to Damara and Storm, they'll be meeting them once they've finished the sabotage on the building and bringing them back over the Wall.

"There's a false wall in the Transportation Dock," Cai mentions. "The Commander's transports are kept on the other side of that wall. Nika, if you'll assist me, I believe the two of us will be able to disable the transports."

Nika nods her agreement.

"That leaves the Main Headquarters building, and the retrieval of the maps." Cai looks pointedly at me. "Bria, you *and* Matthias will be the ones to handle that."

Everyone stares at me, waiting for my reaction. Or maybe it just *feels* like that. *I'm* waiting for my reaction. Well, at least the reaction I know I need to have. Instead of feeling upset about the idea of Matthias going in with me, I feel relieved. And that scares me.

I clear my throat. "I, uh, think Matthias should probably assist you and Nika at the Transportation Dock."

Cai watches me, unblinking, his lips set into a line.

"I can handle the map retrieval on my own." I say the words thoughtfully, but the relief at the possibility of Matthias helping me melts away as I decline the offer, and it's replaced with the same uncertainty I've felt every time I've considered sneaking into the Commander's office to get the maps.

"Very well." Cai nods curtly, sealing my decision to work alone.

Everyone goes back to discussing what else needs to be done, but I'm hardly aware of what they're saying. My throat thickens. I don't want to handle the Commander's office alone, but now I don't have a choice.

———

THE LIGHTS FLASH ON IN MY ROOM. I GROAN AND PULL THE COVERS OVER MY head. Didn't I just fall asleep? It took me forever to get warm and dry after coming back from the Ruins in the pouring rain. Exhaustion weights my entire body.

A loud beep sounds through the room. Then a speaker clicks on.

"Attention Elite Recruits. Report to the Physical Training Arena in twenty minutes for endurance training."

"You have got to be kidding me!" I mumble.

"What time is it?" Nika asks, her speech slurred from sleep.

I throw my covers back and roll onto my side to look at a clock.

"0340." I yawn and force myself to sit up, knowing if I don't, I'll fall back to sleep. Another yawn escapes, and I look at Nika. She's lying on her stomach, arms and legs completely spread out, face buried in her pillow.

"Nika!"

Her head pops up. "What? Yeah? What do you need?"

"Wake up. We need to get ready." I drop my legs to the floor. "Get out of bed."

"Right. Yeah, girl, I'm up. Don't worry." Her head drops back onto her pillow, and her sentence ends with a snore.

Perfect. I walk over to her bed and yank the blankets off her. She doesn't move. "Nika, get up!" I shake her. And I'm not gentle.

"Alright, alright. I'm awake. Just give me a second."

"Fine."

I change into my uniform and use the bathroom. After splashing some water on my face, I go back into the bedroom. Nika is still in bed, and the clock now says it's 0350. We only have ten more minutes until we need to be at the Arena.

I get a cup and fill it with water. She is going to be livid, but it's better than her facing the consequences of not showing up on time.

I dump the contents of the glass on Nika's head and jump back as she flails her arms. She springs out of bed.

"What was that for?" She glares at me as she wipes her hand over her face.

"You have five minutes to get ready, or I'm going to the Arena without you."

Nika gives me a scathing look, then walks away muttering something about rude people who don't know how to give proper wake-up calls. I smile, glad her back is to me. Because if she saw it, I would be dead.

Nika gets herself ready in under the five-minute time allotment, and we jog to the Arena, barely making it on time. The rest of the elite recruits have already arrived. Laban and Sergeant Andor Valarius enter, and we come to attention.

Sergeant Valarius speaks. "All right recruits! This is the beginning of Deprivation Week. As Elite Recruits, we expect you to persevere through physical and mental exhaustion and to withstand intense stress." He paces in front of us. "At the point others would break, we expect you to endure."

He shouts the word inches from Nika's face. She doesn't flinch, but I'm pretty sure she's wide awake now.

"If you can't, then you have no place in elite training. Quitting is not an option. Failure is not an option." Each sentence is accentuated by Laban yelling it into the face of one of the elites. "You've made it this far, true."

Out of the corner of my eye, I watch Laban walk down the row toward me. He stops in front of me and bends down so that we're at eye level. His voice drops in volume, but increases in intensity. "Prove to me you deserve a place in this group."

I will myself not to blink or flinch when he doesn't immediately move away. He's so close that I can see every pore on his face, each eyelash that surrounds his strange, golden eyes, the scar on his nose. One thing is clear: he doesn't think I should be standing here.

Finally, he backs away, and I exhale a slow, somewhat shaky, breath. As Sergeant Valarius explains what we will be required to do, I wonder if maybe Laban's right. Maybe I don't have what it takes to be in this group.

When he finishes, I grab my fifty-pound pack and put it on, securing my rifle across the front of my body.

Nika adjusts her shoulder straps directly in front of me and speaks without moving her lips. "Don't let him psych you out. You've got this."

I nod.

At Sergeant Valarius's command, we start the ten-mile hike that will begin our day.

We move at a quick pace, remaining together as a unit. Shane and Seffrin lead us. A light drizzle starts as we go into the outdoor portion of the Arena. The first few miles, I barely notice the weight of my pack. By the fifth mile, it's cutting into my shoulders. At the eighth mile, each time I take a step, it feels like the pack is crashing into me with bruising force.

The hike ends, and we all catch our breath. I rotate my shoulders, and they scream at me under the weight. Sweat trickles down my face, mixing with the rain. I lift my head toward the icy droplets.

"Mud pits with your guns! Let's go!" Sergeant Valarius shouts at us. "No one said to take a break! Move! Move! Move!"

We race to the mud pits, shedding our packs along the way. My turn comes, giving me no time to savor the relief from carrying the pack. The rain continues to fall as I drop to my stomach and push my way under the first laser field. Mud oozes through my uniform, coating my hands and my rifle as I shove it forward.

"Faster!" Laban bellows.

I reach forward, dragging myself through. They've increased the length of the mud pit we use for training to triple the size of the one the other recruits use. My thighs burn. Rain water trickles down my neck. The end nears. I give a last burst and clamber out of the pit. I look down at my mud caked uniform. Why do they make us wear white?

"You need your packs, recruits!" Sergeant Valarius yells. "Go back through and get them!" He jabs his finger back toward the pits.

I grit my teeth and obey the command.

After we all go back through the pits and retrieve our packs, Sergeant Valarius makes us double time it to the river. Ice crystals catch at the edges of the water.

"Walk a mile upstream, keeping your gun above your head the entire time. It had better not hit the water! Go!"

I enter and suck in a sharp breath as the water swirls around my legs, piercing through my clothes and numbing my skin. Any bit of warmth I had from the exertion is a distant memory in the icy water. Despite my obsession with swimming, I've never attempted it in water this cold.

We trudge through the river in a single file line. With each step, the water deepens. It's now at my stomach. The rain falls harder. I hold my gun high above me and keep my eyes fixed on Adira's head directly ahead of me. With her next step forward, she drops deeper into the water. I take a step, and now the water swirls around my neck, the current pushing against me, fighting me, reminding me of its power.

My foot slips on a rock, and my head goes under, water seeping into my nose and mouth. A flash of panic rips through me as the memory surfaces. I try to force it down, to stand up. My pack pulls against me, and I lose my footing. Maybe this is how I deserve to die.

A strong hand grips my arm and pulls me up. I gasp, spewing the water from my mouth, choking.

"You're good," Shane says from behind me. "Keep moving. Don't stop, or they'll notice."

I nod, still choking, and press forward, soon closing the distance between myself and Adira. With each step, I become more determined, the memory retreating to its proper place. I can't let the water control me. Not today. Not ever again.

CHAPTER

FIFTY-FIVE

I finish pulling on my uniform. It bags around my waist. At least Deprivation Week is over. Every day this week, we were awakened early and not allowed to sleep until late, and they gave us very little food. The trainings tested me not only physically, but mentally, bringing with them nightmares each moment I arrived at the short time where sleep was an option. It's like they want to break us.

Nika knocks on the bathroom door.

"You almost done in there?" Her voice is hoarse, but she claims she's fine.

I open the door and step out. Dark circles shadow her eyes, and her cheek-bones are more pronounced. Weary lines crisscross her forehead.

"It's all yours."

"Thanks." She yawns as she plods into the bathroom.

Once we're both finished getting ready for the day, we go to the main dining hall for breakfast. My stomach rumbles at the thought. This will be my first hot meal in a week. At this point, I might even eat gruel if it was warm enough.

As Elite Recruits, we are given preferential treatment, and they force the other recruits to allow us ahead of them in the line. Normally, it bothers me. Today I couldn't be happier about it.

I greedily fill my plate high, taking a bite of a warm biscuit as I make my way to the Elite Recruit's table. They've set us apart from the rest of the recruits and like to point to us as an example of what they should aspire to. But observing us now, each of us with shoulders stooped, bagging uniforms, and fatigue written all over our features, I can't imagine that we're inspiring any of them to want to become like us.

"Anyone hear about how Blake and Adira are doing?" Seffrin sets his tray down and drops into his seat.

Both of them ended up in the infirmary this week.

"Last word on Adira was she still has a high fever," Nika says. "And I heard Blake's arm is broken."

"I wonder if they'll let them continue training with us," Seffrin muses.

"Unlikely," Shane says. "You all heard Sergeant Meritas's speech, same as I did. Failure is not an option." He takes a swig of water. "My guess is they consider Blake and Adira failures."

A soldier enters.

"May I have your attention please," he says. "All recruits, including the Elites, are required to present themselves in twenty minutes at the Physical Training Arena. Failure to do so will result in punishment."

He lists ten recruits who he needs to go with him immediately, and they follow him from the room.

"I wonder what this is about," Nika murmurs.

I shovel the rest of my food into my mouth, not responding. We'll find out soon enough.

Once everyone has been accounted for at the Arena, we're led to the roughest portion of the river. A long rope has been strung across it. The ten recruits who were led out earlier stand along the bank of the river behind Colonel Keenan Valarius, their eyes filled with fear.

Laban instructs the Elite Recruits to stand off to the side with him. Everyone else waits in a cluster to find out why we've been brought here. Of the ten recruits, I only recognize Ava, the girl Laban almost drowned in the river early on in our time here.

"You all know we reward those who do well," Colonel Valarius says, shouting over the noise of the rushing water. "You have watched your peers who are now Elite Recruits rise in the ranks and receive recompense for their efforts."

He waves a hand toward us. "They still continue to persevere through training more difficult than anything the rest of you can imagine in order to be the best they can be. I have observed them endure great difficulty over this past week in order to become those who will better serve Talionis and our Commander. They could have given up. They could have quit. But they didn't!" He pounds his fist into his hand. "And they will be rewarded. But for some of you, merely seeing us reward those who excel isn't enough. You still rest in a complacency that is abhorrent. We expect better of recruits of Talionis."

He steps to the side. "So today, I bring before you ten of your fellow recruits who have been slacking in their training." He spreads his arm wide, gesturing to the recruits next to him. "Ten who do not seem to understand the honor that it is to be a recruit of Talionis. For those of you who have not learned from the success of the Elites, perhaps today you will learn from the punishment of these!"

He turns to the ten. "You choose not to push yourselves to be better through your trainings. Perhaps you will push yourselves to be better when your life is on the line." He pauses, the raging river stressing his words. "Your punishment will be a dead hang over the river from the rope. You will hang from your arms until I decide you should be done. If you fall before that time comes, the rapids should take care of you. If they don't, we will."

He faces the recruits in formation. "Do you all agree that this punishment is warranted?"

"Sir, yes, sir!" all the recruits chant.

"Let 'em drown!" A recruit shouts.

Others cheer in agreement.

Colonel Valarius smiles. "That's what I like to hear."

The cheers grow louder.

He turns back to the ten waiting. "Now go!"

Dread coats me, turning the food in my stomach to acid. The ten recruits climb up the tree and out onto the rope. A few are crying. All of them look petrified. The acid burns up my esophagus. It swirls in my mouth. Ava glances back at us when she is halfway up the tree, her face pulled tight. Her skin is pale and drawn. She looks sick, but there's still a bit of fire in her eyes.

She reminds me of Lencie, sick and fragile, but not yet defeated by it. The fire in Ava's eyes wavers as she turns to make her way up to the rope. A coughing spasm doubles her over halfway up the tree, and my dread turns to fear. Then I'm angry. Protectiveness marches through me, as though Lencie were the one now grasping the rope above the river. How could they make a sick girl do this?

"This is ridiculous," I mutter.

Laban whips around to face me. "Do you have something to say, Averton?"

I clutch my fists and look straight ahead.

"If you care so much about them, then why don't you get up there with them?"

I glance over at him. Is he serious?

He stretches his arm out and points at them. "Go. Then maybe next time you'll think twice before you criticize the way we handle things in Talionis."

I clench my jaw and move to join them.

Colonel Valarius looks at me in surprise as I climb the tree. "Recruit Averton. What are you doing?"

"I instructed her to join them, sir," Laban responds. "She was having a moment of unnecessary pity, and I thought this might drive it out of her."

Colonel Valarius gives a curt nod. "Very well."

I reach the top and grab the rope, allowing my body to drop so that I'm now hanging over the river. I shimmy myself out until I'm next to the girl who was the last one of the ten to go out. Ava.

She coughs, wracking her entire body. The rope shudders beneath my grip.

"Keep holding on, Ava." I search for something to say. I don't like the look on her face. "You'll get through this."

"I don't think so." The fire I saw flashing through her eyes moments ago seems to have been extinguished by the fits of coughing.

I squeeze the rope tighter, its fibers poking between my fingers. She might be weak, and even certain of her failure, but I refuse to believe it will happen. I won't let it happen.

"Where are you from?" Maybe distraction will work.

"Leddington." Her breathing is more labored.

For the next several minutes, I ask any question I can think of. My arms are burning. Normally, this type of exertion wouldn't bother me much, but because of the week I just endured, I'm finding it to be a challenge. If my arms are burning, I can't imagine how Ava's feeling. I talk to her, trying to keep her attention off the water raging below us.

"Have any siblings?"

She doesn't respond for a moment. I glance over. Sweat is dotting her upper lip, and her fingers are white against the rope. She coughs again, the sound rattling through the air. "I have a sister," she says finally.

"What's her name?" The question comes out rushed. Desperate.

She's getting weaker. I can feel it, just like I could tell when Lencie had pushed herself too hard and needed extra rest.

"Ridenna." She looks at me, and there's a sadness in her eyes. "I wish I could have seen her one more time. I'm not going to get to say goodbye to her or tell her I loved her."

"*Don't* give up, Ava." Desperation tingles my lips as the words cascade from my mouth. I can't let this happen. "You'll see Ridenna again. We're almost done. Just hold on a little longer."

"I'm not sure I can." Her words are almost drowned out as the turbulent water below seems to increase in volume.

Like it doesn't want to give her a chance to say anything else. Like it's ready to swallow her whole.

Pressure builds within me. "Ava, please. Hold on just a little longer."

"I'm slipping!" A trace of panic emphasizes her words.

I look up at her hands and confirm what I hoped wasn't true. "No! Ava—"

"Time!" Colonel Valarius yells from below. "Everyone off."

"We're done. Come on." I nod my head back toward the riverbank.

She's hanging on by her fingertips now. The rational part of my brain is trying to tell me she won't make it, but I refuse to listen. She can't go like this! If she falls, there's no way she'll survive the rapids. I release one hand from the rope, reach for her, grabbing her arm just as her hands slip. The rope cuts into my hand as I support both of our weight.

Another cough rips through her, and the hand that is weakly grasping mine loosens as energy drains out of her. "I've known from the beginning I wouldn't survive here."

"We can get to the side!" Panic claws at my throat, its sharp edge cutting through each word. "I'm going to try swinging you over!"

She isn't able to respond as the hoarse, grating sound of her cough consumes her. I hold tighter, but feel her slipping from my grasp. Her fingers squeeze mine lightly as she tries to hold on, but the pressure fades as quickly as it came. She looks up. Fear and resignation fill her hazel eyes.

I try to lift her higher, but her fingers slip from mine.

"*No!*" I scream, as she falls into the clutches of the raging river below.

As soon as her body is within its reach, the angry torrent grabs ahold of her and sucks her under. No. No. I can't lose someone else to a watery grave. Someone else I should have saved.

I swing back to the tree and down to the ground as quickly as possible, my eyes searching for her and finding nothing. My body shakes as my mind screams out, rebelling at what just happened. I failed. I didn't save her. And now she's gone. It's the same...I choke back a sob and start running toward the river. Maybe there's still a chance—

Colonel Valarius grabs my arm and spins me around.

"I do not want to see you try to pull a stunt like that again," he hisses at me. "Don't interfere with a punishment. Understood?"

I want to scream. I want to cry. I want to beat my fists against him.

"Yes, sir." My words are stripped of all emotion.

"Good. Now get back to the others."

I return to my place with the other Elites. Nika touches my hand, but I pull away. I don't deserve comfort.

FIFTY-SIX

The night is dark and moonless and silent, shunning me, judging me. But no more harshly than I'm judging myself. My feet carry me to the Ruins, my mind not even registering the journey through Talionis. I find myself at the training site, but it's dark. Empty. I'm walking again. Wandering. I don't pay attention to where I'm going as my mind ferociously replays Ava's fall. I crunch through leaves but hear her crashing into the water. Hear my scream again and again.

Remember how I failed.

Anger and guilt are my companions. Anger toward Colonel Valarius. Anger toward Laban. Anger toward the Commander who's behind all of their actions. Anger with myself for being someone they praise. But mostly anger toward myself for failing to help Ava. Guilt for not thinking of another way to keep her from falling to her death. She was found lifeless on the bank of the river a few hours after her fall. I couldn't save her. Just like I couldn't save Ezri.

"Bria!"

I stop walking and blink. I don't recognize where I am, don't remember walking here.

Cai stands next to me. His hood cloaks his face. "The alarm triggered in the training site, and then I heard you scream. Are you okay?"

I shrug. A lump lodges in my throat, burning with unshed tears. My screams must have been more than just memory. When I don't say anything, Cai takes me by the arm and leads me to one of his sites that I haven't been in before. A warm fire dances inside. Cai closes the door and removes his cloak. He turns me to face him, but I keep my eyes downcast. I can't look at him, because as soon as he knows what I did, I'll see the same judgment in his eyes that I see when I look at myself. Somehow, I don't think I could bear it coming from Cai.

"What happened?" His voice is more gentle than I've ever heard it.

Something cracks in me, and a tear slips down my cheek.

"Why are you here?"

"I didn't know where else to go." My voice breaks, and the tears flow. And I can't stop them.

Cai doesn't say a word, and I drop my head against his chest, soaking his shirt with my tears. His arm comes around me, and he holds me and lets me cry. This is the first time I've felt the comfort of an embrace since arriving in Talionis, and I know I don't deserve it, but I sink into it more, the tears falling harder. After some time, my tears dry, and he leads me to a handmade bench near the fire. I sit. He sits across from me. I feel him studying me, but he remains silent.

I still can't look at him, but suddenly words pour out of my mouth. "Do you want to know why your God could never love me, Cai? Because I'm responsible for the death of two innocent people." I raise my head now.

His eyes are watchful, but I don't see the condemnation I expected, so I press on. I tell him about what happened to Ava, how I couldn't save her, how she slipped from my grasp. How the river swept away her life.

"That wasn't your fault, Bria." Cai's voice is quiet, almost a whisper.

I wish he was right, but he's not.

"I should have thought faster, done something. She shouldn't have died!" I shift so I'm looking him directly in the eye. "And my brother should never have died. But because of me, they're both gone."

A sob rips through me, and the memory is dragged to the surface. The wall I built to keep it hidden crumbles to the ground, and every second of that horrifying day plays out before me.

"Tell me, Bria." Cai's voice is still soft, but I hear the command.

Maybe it's because I've grown used to doing exactly as Cai commands, or maybe it's because I need someone else to help me shoulder the burden of the memory—this monster—pressing down on me, suffocating me, trapping me, but I find myself ready to do just as he says.

"His name was Ezri. He was only a year and a half younger than me, and we were best friends." My throat closes, as though the monster is clutching it. But I have to tell Cai, I have to share this with someone. "We did everything together, and Ezri usually did what I wanted. I wish I could change that fact, make it so he would have said no to me that day. Because maybe things would be different. Maybe he would still be alive."

I stare into the fire, watch it lap over the logs. Like waves. "I was eleven, and he was nine. Almost ten. It's my fault he never turned ten, my fault he died."

The log cracks, shooting sparks up the chimney. Cai remains quiet, motionless. I keep staring at the fire.

"Winter was coming, and the ocean was getting colder, but I just had to swim that day. Even though my parents said I wasn't allowed to." I glance briefly at Cai. "That's the last day I remember actually *wanting* to swim." My nails press crescent moons into my palms.

"The water was rough, even in the bay, but I plunged in anyway. Ezri followed me. Everything was fine at first. Normal. But then...Ezri wasn't coming to the surface. I still don't know what happened."

My face is wet from crying. My brain is numb, but my heart is still breaking and telling my eyes to shed the tears Ezri deserves.

I force myself to continue. "I panicked. I kept diving under, trying to find him. The water got rougher, and I was getting tossed around. Then it started raining. I choked on mouthfuls of water while I screamed his name, like the ocean itself was determined to silence me."

The first day I met the monster who is the water.

There's a loud crack, and the log in the fire splits in half, the flames eagerly capturing the space between the pieces, forever separating them.

"Finally, he bobbed to the surface. Everything was okay, I thought. He didn't respond when I pulled him onto the beach. I screamed and screamed for him to wake up. I shook him. I cried. But he wouldn't answer me." My voice catches, and the tears run in a torrent down my cheeks. I sniff. "Then my dad was racing toward us. I was half lying on top of Ezri, crying, begging God to do *something*, to make my brother wake up."

I rub my sleeve over my face to make room for the new tears. "My dad pushed me off Ezri, pressed on his chest and breathed into his mouth for an eternity. Then he stopped and pulled Ezri into his arms, and he did something I had never seen him do before. He cried. Sobbed."

The log crumbles, dissolving into pieces.

"He carried my brother home, and I followed, asking if Ezri would be okay. And he said 'No baby, Ezri's not going to be okay.'"

I draw in a shuddering breath, the weight of guilt on my chest making it almost impossible, as I relive every emotion I felt. "Ezri died that day, and it was my fault."

I force myself to look at Cai, to see the judgment in his face, to feel his censure. Now he knows my darkest secret. But I see compassion in his eyes.

"I'm sorry for your loss, Bria."

His gentle words pierce me, and I ask the questions I've been afraid to ask since Ezri died. "How could God let him die? Why didn't He save him? It's because of me, isn't it? Because it was my fault."

Cai reaches into his pocket and pulls out a cloth. He strokes it with his thumb, then lifts it up. It's worn and tattered and looks like a ripped piece of a garment. "This is the only thing I have left of my son. It's a piece of his shirt that ripped off in my hands. We were arguing."

His hand drops back into his lap, and he stares at the cloth.

I listen even as I wonder why he's telling me this.

"The last moments I had with my son, we were arguing." He pauses, lost in the memory. "I don't remember why. I was so frustrated that I insisted my wife and I go visit her younger sister without our son, even though she was desperate to have him meet his aunt."

He swallows hard. "It was on our journey there that I was taken captive while they held my wife at gunpoint."

His face is lined with grief. "I lost them both that day because of actions I have regretted ever since." He scrubs a hand over his beard, and his eyes find mine. "But the thing I found in these years since is that, no matter what I've done, God has forgiven me. And even though it's hard, and some days the grief still overwhelms me, in Him, I have peace."

Peace.

The idea of real peace is something I long for but know I don't deserve. Yet I can't deny that Cai has it, despite all he's been through.

"Why did it have to happen, Cai? Why did you have to get torn away from your family? Why did my brother have to die?" I ask the questions, searching for an answer.

"I don't always understand why God allows certain things to occur. We live in a messed-up world, and it's marred because of us and our mistakes and the ugliness of our actions at times." His hands grip the cloth. "Our actions have consequences. But I know this—despite who we are, despite what we've done, God is gracious and, even though we don't deserve it, He offers us forgiveness and life and hope and peace through His Son, Jesus. He offers freedom from the guilt of all that we've done. We just need to reach out and accept that gift."

"But those in Talionis should pay for what they've done, for what happened to Ava." I look again at the fire.

It's dying, turning to ashes. Useless.

My voice drops. "I should pay for what happened to Ezri."

"You're right."

My gaze flies to Cai as he confirms what I knew but wish wasn't true.

"We all owe a debt because of what we've done wrong, and someone needs to pay for it. God is perfect, and He won't let evil go without consequences. And the debt we all owe because of what we've done is death." He pauses, his eyes gentle as he watches me. "But Jesus paid the price for all you've ever done wrong, for what happened with Ezri. He died for you, and He rose back to life, defeating death. If you reach out to Him, He'll forgive you and free you from the weight of your past and give you hope for your future."

"I don't deserve that."

"None of us do."

A yearning unlike anything I've ever felt rises from deep within me. I long to have what Cai's talking about. Then I remember Ezri's lifeless body, Ava slipping from my fingers. The yearning is swallowed up by guilt. There's no way I can ever have his peace. There's no way I deserve to be forgiven.

"Where were you last night?" Nika asks as we make our way to the Weaponry Training Compound.

"Just needed a walk," I say.

"Let me rephrase. Why did you go see Cai?"

I spin toward her a few yards from the compound.

"You were so out of it, Ari had to adjust your band for you," Nika murmurs. "You've gotta be more careful, girl. I know yesterday was rough, but…"

She trails off, and I swallow hard and nod. "Sorry."

The word is lame, broken. But all I have to offer. I wasn't thinking last night, and my actions could have destroyed everything we're working for if Ari and Nika didn't have my back.

"Bromeliad, Averton, get in here!" Corporal Sidon shouts at us.

We jog toward the door, our conversation abandoned. It's time to train, and neither of us can afford any slip-ups. The plan requires Nika and me to remain at the pinnacle of elite recruits, which means we have to continue to excel in every area of training until the Commencement. No mistakes. No distractions.

Maybe if I can immerse myself in the trainings, I can forget what happened with Ava, forget the pain of telling Cai about Ezri. And maybe keep myself from drowning in guilt.

When we arrive inside, Corporal Sidon guides us through the compound and back to the course area. There's a quickness to his movements but also...excitement. Like he can barely contain a smile. Something I've only witnessed when he's talking about weapons.

He brings us to course three, where the rest of the Elite recruits, as well as recruits from Squad One of each unit, are already waiting.

"What's going on?" Nika mutters.

"Wait over there." Corporal Sidon points to where Shane and Belen are standing.

Nika and I obey.

"Rifles out!" Corporal Sidon shouts, the "attention" equivalent for Weaponry Training.

As one, we all take our rifles, left hand on the barrel, right hand near the trigger, thrust the weapons in front of us, and then snap them back into place at an angle across our bodies.

"Beautifully done." The voice comes from behind me, but I know who it is before he steps into view.

The Commander.

"Thank you, sir!" Corporal Sidon says, almost bursting with pride.

My neck prickles. What is the Commander doing *here*, in our scheduled weaponry lesson?

"For those of you who don't know, I am Commander Ark."

A few recruits inhale sharply. From my position, I have a clear line of sight to Shay, whose face has turned almost completely red, though she still holds the perfect position for rifles out.

Commander Ark strides into the center of the room, giving smiles and making eye contact with recruits in the squad one of each unit. Every recruit smiles back at him.

My shoulders burn with apprehension.

"You've all been doing splendidly in your weaponry training, according to Corporal Sidon. I trust his opinion, for he is a master weaponsmith." He nods to Corporal Sidon, who appears to require every muscle in his face to keep from grinning like a fool.

Pathetic. It's like the praise and presence of the *glorious* Commander are rewards to be coveted.

"… and Bria Averton."

The sound of the Commander saying my name snaps me back into focus.

"These four," the Commander continues, "have shown incredible skills in weaponry, and it is my delight to be here today to watch them perform."

Watch us…The Commander rarely observes recruits, and when he does, it's never in person like this.

Shay's acidic gaze catches me. Her lip is curled up, jaw clenched. She hates me for beating her out as an Elite Recruit and now as someone the Commander is honoring with his attention, and she'd hate me all the more if she knew *why* I'm doing it. I drag my eyes away, but most of the other recruits I look at appear upset or jealous. They'd do anything to trade places with me.

Corporal Sidon offers his observation desk to Commander Ark with great flourish and then he leads Nika, Shane, Belen, and me downstairs to course three. He places a small camera on each of us so the Commander will have a view of our different perspectives as we go through the course. There are cameras throughout the course as well, and all of them project onto screens in the observation area, but from the observation desk, the Commander can also look down and see us.

I force myself to focus on Corporal Sidon's instructions, though I've been through course three multiple times. The course has a specific path with targets to both sides, in front of and behind you and, sometimes, overhead. We'll be using standard issue guns, electrofitted bows and arrows, and knives for this. Guns will be used for the first leg of the course, then the bow, then the knives. We can choose to work as a unit to hit all the targets, or attempt the course on our own.

"And remember," he says, right before sending us in, "the Commander is watching."

In our elite weaponry training, they put us through different courses, some using a variety of weapons, others focusing on one specific weapon. All designed to determine our skill, accuracy, speed, and ability to respond quickly to imminent threats. So far I've improved my score each time, but I haven't yet achieved sniper status.

Which makes my placement as one of the four Commander Ark wants to observe seem...odd. There are at least three other Elites who are more skilled in weaponry than I am.

The four of us decide to go in as a unit, and Shane keys it into the screen at the start of the course. This will change the amount of targets and our path through the course, but it will also give us the advantage of knowing others have our back. None of us wants to fail today.

A buzzer sounds, and we enter the course.

We move in a tight formation, with almost no space between us. I press the butt of the gun into my shoulder, alert for the slightest movement, and I know the others are doing the same. Between the scenarios and these courses, we've learned to be alert and ready for an attack...or *to* attack.

Targets materialize, and an instant later, the sound of guns firing echoes around me. I shoot along with my team, hitting targets, vigilant to the slightest movement. The targets look like people and can appear anywhere. As much as I hate myself for it, there's no hesitation in my shooting now. When I see a target, I shoot, and I shoot to kill. Every time.

The four of us rapidly make our way through the first stretch of the course, hitting every target and sustaining no return fire.

There's a brief break in the course where we exchange our guns for electrofitted bows and arrows. This section has been my weak point each time I've gone through, but I've taken extra time working with the weapon and becoming more familiar with it. I release the arrows into the targets with a new speed, though I don't have to worry about hitting as many because Nika and Belen are both experts with the bows.

When we come to the end of the section, we break formation in order to keep from cutting each other with the knives. I drop my bow and draw two knives from the belt at my waist, mentally thanking Cai for his expert training in this area. Each knife I'm given flies from my hands, and I turn from the targets before even confirming a hit, confident in my accuracy. I tuck and roll to avoid an incoming "attack" and, while still in a crouched position, fling my final knife at the target above me, allowing myself the satisfaction of watching it stick in the dead center.

Nika is throwing a knife at a target above her, but another attack target is coming from behind her.

"Knife!" I yell.

Shane is closest, and he presses one into my hand. I fling it at the target about to attack Nika, and it dies.

Another buzzer sounds, indicating the completion of the course.

Our bands reflect the fact that none of us were hit, and we all cheer and laugh and pat each other on the backs.

We head to the scoreboard as we exit.

"New high score, baby!" Belen says, pumping his arm in the air. "That's what I'm talking about!"

He and Shane high-five, and the slap is so hard it sounds painful.

Nika and I grin at each other. Then her face grows more serious. "Thanks for having my back in there."

"Anytime. Thanks for having mine." I know she knows I mean for more than just the course.

"Impressive."

The sound of the Commander's voice through the speaker causes the celebrations to cease. We come to attention.

He chuckles. "At ease. You may come up to the observation area."

We obey, marching up the stairs. The other elites and recruits are still there, though no longer standing in rifles out position. As soon as we enter the room, Commander Ark claps, a warm smile on his face. Like a proud dad.

Everyone else in the room claps as well, and my cheeks warm.

I hate myself right now, because I *like* the attention, like knowing I impressed Ark with my performance. Am I as much of a fool as Shay and just about every other recruit in this blasted place? Maybe.

I need to get out of here before I become just like those I despise.

After a moment, Ark holds up his hand, and the clapping ends. "Nicely done, Shane, Bria, Nika, and Belen." As he says our names, he looks each of us in the eye. "As a reward for a job well done, I would like to invite the four of you to an intimate dinner party I'm having tonight." He smiles, his dimple flashing. "You've earned a pleasant diversion from your training."

Alarms go off in my head. The last thing I want is to spend an evening with Commander Ark.

"I'll send a transport to pick you up at 1900 hours. Until then." He tips his head to us and then leaves, not acknowledging the other recruits in his exit.

THE FOUR OF US ARE DISMISSED FROM THE REST OF OUR TRAINING FOR THE day and sent back to our rooms. Sampta and Presidia meet Nika and me to prepare us for our dinner with the Commander, and we go through a similar process as before, although they style our hair differently, and our gowns are new. When I suggested we wear the gowns we already have, the idea was met with scorn. I think if Sampta hadn't already spent an hour on my cosmetics, she might have spit on me for even *thinking* such a thing. Whatever. Focusing on what I'm wearing is the last thing I need to be doing.

This dinner tonight is dangerous. I'm not ready to speak with Ark as though I admire him, want to be around him, crave his approval. But he's devious and disarming. A deadly combination.

And I'm afraid I'll either be sucked in by his lies or do something I'll regret.

Several hours later, Nika and I are once again transformed by Sampta and Presidia. My gown for tonight is a deep red, and they've swept my hair to the side, my curls cascading down my shoulder. Dark eyeliner and eye shadow make my eyes the central focus. I imagine some would say I look beautiful, but I've never seen myself look more hideous. I wear the mask of a favored one, and, even though there are good reasons, I hate myself for it.

Nika's gown is ivory and shimmers in the light from the windows. Gold and purple eyeshadows combine to give her an ethereal look, her thick, dark lashes curling perfectly.

Sampta and Presidia exit, and Nika and I are left alone to wait.

We have close to an hour before the transport is scheduled to arrive. I force myself to turn away from the mirror.

"I'm nervous about this." Nika scratches behind her ear, taking care to leave her hair undisturbed.

"Me too," I admit.

"He's hard to resist, you know? Like when he talks, I *want* to listen to what he says. And I was a little happy we impressed him today. I'm afraid this place is getting to me." Her words echo my thoughts so closely, I almost want to laugh.

I sit on a chair, hoping my dress wrinkles. "Maybe we'll learn something while we're there. Something useful."

Nika sits on the other chair. "I don't know. Somehow I get the impression Commander Demetrius Ark knows how to relay only the information he wants you to know and nothing more."

NIKA AND I ARE ABOUT TO ENTER THE COMMANDER'S DINING HALL, WHERE the rest of the dinner party awaits, when Sergeant Andor Valarius emerges from the shadows.

"A word, Averton," he says, his face unreadable.

I glance at Nika. She raises her eyebrows but says nothing.

Sergeant Valarius leads me down the corridor until we're out of Nika's earshot. He glances to the side. "Be careful."

His words are quiet, and I'm not sure if I heard him correctly.

"What?" There's no way he really just told me to be careful.

"You heard me." His eyes lock on mine. "The Commander does the unexpected to determine where loyalties are. That he has asked you here tonight means he likes what he sees in you. But I can guarantee he is going to test you."

This seems more like a test to me. "How?"

His face twitches, bunching his scar. "I don't know."

Sergeant Valarius must be baiting me. "But if he likes what he's seeing, why test me?" I push back. "Can't he already tell I've given everything to Talionis?"

His eyes narrow. Something tells me he isn't convinced I'm as committed as I say I am. I shift uneasily.

"If you're not careful, he'll see what I see. And that will get you killed."

Ice races through my veins, bringing goosebumps to my skin. "Why are you telling me this?"

He steps back, and I watch the same shift happen I witnessed when he was escorting me back from my punishment in the Ruins. The man is an enigma.

"Because I believe you have great potential, and I do not want to see that wasted." He spreads his arm wide, back toward Nika. "The Commander will be waiting. Enjoy your evening."

He bows slightly and disappears back into the shadows. I rejoin Nika.

"What was that all about?"

"He was warning me. Said the Commander is going to test me. But it felt like the entire conversation was a test."

"Either way, we'd better be careful."

As we approach the doors to the dining room, a sense of foreboding wraps itself around me. If Sergeant Valarius really can see my contempt for this place, how long will it be before he tells the Commander? Or before the Commander notices?

CHAPTER

FIFTY-EIGHT

"Welcome!" The Commander says, halting all other conversation. He stands from his seat at the table. "We had begun to wonder what happened to you. I received word that the transport arrived, and I expected you several minutes ago."

I hear the unspoken question and challenge in his words. The air seems to tighten, and I struggle to breathe.

"I beg your pardon, sir. I had need of the facilities upon arrival, and I asked Bria to wait for me," Nika says easily.

He smiles, and oxygen finds its way into my lungs. "Well, I'm glad to know all is well." He snaps his fingers. "I'm famished. Let's enjoy our dinner, shall we?"

Nika and I take the seats Ark indicates for us, and his servants come bustling into the room, filling the table with tray after tray of food. Besides us, the only other recruits present are Shane and Belen. The Commander sits at the head of the table. On his right is Colonel Keenan Valarius, and on his left is Elva Trill. Major Tay Vasco sits on the other side of Colonel Valarius, and next to him is Shane and then a cadet who I don't know. On the other side of Trill, is Belen and then Matthias.

Matthias is staring at me. I can feel it. Trying to avoid making eye contact with him seems impossible. My eyes connect with his. He swallows and then smiles, appearing almost dazed. Heat flares in my cheeks, and I can't stop a small smile. His grin widens more.

He's wearing a blue shirt that matches his eyes, and his dark hair is set perfectly in place, not the slightly messy look I'm used to. I feel safer with him here, even after Sergeant Valarius's strange warning, and I realize with a start the real reason I've pushed Matthias away. I pull my eyes away from his, the smile slipping from my lips and my worry over Sergeant Valarius overshadowed in light of the realization.

I trust Matthias.

I believe what he's told me about himself. About him not knowing about Laban disciplining me. I haven't been keeping him at a distance, trying to stay mad at him because of who his father is. It's because I'm terrified that he'll reject me once he discovers more about who *I* am. Maybe Cai didn't judge me for what happened with Ezri, but there's no way I could expect the same thing from Matthias.

I glance at him and find he's now focused on something Belen is saying. He nods and then grins, and my heart clenches painfully. If Matthias rejected me, if he wanted nothing to do with me, I'm not sure how I would handle it.

A server comes behind me and leans over to set a napkin on my lap. I smooth it into place, grappling with this new insight. Breathing out slowly, I force Matthias from my thoughts. Now isn't the time to wrestle through this. I'll deal with it later.

I scan the table. No other places have been set. Interesting group of people. I wonder what the Commander has planned for this evening.

The conversation is kept light as course after course is brought out. Soup. Salad. Appetizers. I eat and listen, doing my best to keep from dwelling on my thoughts about Matthias and from recalling my conversation with Sergeant Valarius, though his words keep gnawing at me. They bring the main course out—glazed duck, andouille sausage, sautéed asparagus, buttered turnips, roasted fingerling potatoes, and fresh bread.

If my stomach wasn't filled with apprehension, I'm sure the food would look delicious. As it is, what I've already eaten bubbles in my stomach like the gruel heating on the back of the kitchen stove. I force down half of the plate of food.

"Let's retire to the parlor." Ark pushes back from the table.

I stand with Nika, and we follow the rest into the parlor. The room is large, lavishly decorated, and everything is pristine. I doubt a speck of dust would even dare to make an appearance. Everyone seats themselves on the chairs and couches set in a semi-circle around the room. I stiffly lower myself to an ornate, and somewhat scratchy, couch. The Commander stands in the center, waiting until we're settled.

"This is a special evening," he begins, "and I've invited you all here for a special reason. Three of my most trusted advisors"—he nods toward Major Vasco, Colonel Valarius, and Ms. Trill—"and six young people whom I believe show great potential." He smiles at Belen, Nika, the cadet, Shane, Matthias, and then me.

My heart pounds so loudly, I worry the others can hear it. Could the Commander possibly know that four of us are planning a way to escape, to stop him?

"You all push yourselves to be the best you can be. To be stronger, more powerful, wiser than the rest. You serve Talionis, and therefore me, with everything. Tonight, I wanted to reward you for your efforts." He chuckles softly. "Now, I know a mere dinner cannot do that. But I have found that a gift along with a satisfying meal can go a long way in showing one's gratitude."

He snaps his fingers, and nine of his servants enter the room, each bearing something in their arms. "So I would like to give each of you a small gift. You've earned it."

The servants each head to a particular person and present the Commander's gift. A young woman approaches me, hands me a small rectangular box, then walks away. I hold the box with the tips of my fingers and stare at it. I sense someone approach me, but I don't look up. I know it's the Commander.

"You won't know what it is unless you open it." His voice is amused, and when I look up, I find his expression matches the tone. "Go on now. You'll like it."

Even his command for me to open the gift grates against me.

"Just savoring the moment." I duck my head down before he can read behind my words and tentatively remove the lid.

I gasp, unable to stop myself, like I've been drowning underwater and finally surfaced to find air. I stare, but my vision blurs, wavers. It can't be...can it?

I reach out one finger. Ezri's necklace. The one they took from me when I first arrived. I thought they'd destroyed it, at least thrown it away. Never did I expect to have it again. Not like this. Not from the man responsible for everything I've gone through.

Tenderly, I run my fingers over the sea-glass pendant and then notice the chain has been changed. Instead of the leather strap, it's on a delicate gold chain.

"I thought you'd want it back," the Commander says, reminding me he's still here, but I can't pull my eyes away from the necklace.

This is *my* necklace, my one remnant from home. The last tie I have to my brother. Yes, I wanted it back, but I never dreamed it would be possible. My eyes burn, and I squeeze them closed for an instant. With a shaking breath, I open them and look up at the Commander.

"Thank you," I say, the words thick with emotions I don't want to feel in this place, let alone express. But I can't stop myself.

He gestures to the box. "May I?"

I nod as confused emotions torment me. I feel indebted to this man whom I want to hate, this man who's responsible for the necklace being ripped from me in the first place. But gratitude fills me.

He comes behind me, places it on my neck, and fastens it. It rests against me, both familiar and foreign. I grasp the pendant, and waves of memories wash over me, from the first moment Ezri gave it to me, to the moment he died, to the moment a recruit yanked it from me so he could have a drink of water.

"The chain was irreparable," Commander Ark says as though he can read my thoughts. "But perhaps this now represents you more fully. Your past," he gestures to the pendant, "and your present," he points to the chain, "combined to make you stronger than ever."

I tilt my head. "Thank you, sir."

He joins me on the couch, his dark gaze searching mine. "Our pasts shape us, define us. And what happens in our youth, our childhood, can change the course of our destinies... and others' destinies as well."

The chain on my neck seems to grow heavier. What is he saying?

"A mere child can cause heartache and destruction. Or, like Storm," he says her name with a smile that stiffens my shoulders, "bring joy and show incredible potential. And you, Bria, know both of these truths better than most. The tragedy of your past," he lightly taps the pendant, "has shaped you to become who you need to be now."

My jaw quivers, and I clench my teeth together. He knows about Ezri, about my part in his death. How does he *know?*

He continues. "You have become more valuable to Talionis, to me, than you realize. As you move up in the ranks, I look forward to having you take those younger than you under your wing, teach them, help them. Like you have with dear little Storm."

"Of course, sir," I choke out the words. My voice sounds far away, unnatural, but Ark doesn't seem to care.

"Wonderful," he says, standing. "Perhaps I'll have you work more with Storm to be better prepared for when others arrive."

His words pummel me, making it difficult to breathe or process all he's saying. I feel the blood draining from my face even as I attempt to mask all emotions. He excuses himself and walks away.

The itchy fibers of the couch prick through the fabric of my dress and scratch my skin, pulling me back to this moment, this awful reality.

I'm not indebted to Demetrius Ark. This whole thing was a test, like Sergeant Valarius warned me about. He saved the necklace for this moment, to disarm me, watch me, test my loyalty. Taunt me with the possibility of me being a part of the *training* of young children, of perpetuating his city of horrors.

I hold the sea glass, remembering Ezri's excitement when he gave it to me. Everything I ever cared about has been torn from me. Or destroyed by me.

The glass falls from my fingers. I'm as dangerous to those I care about as Demetrius Ark is.

The couch shifts, and I glance over to find Matthias has joined me.

"How are you this evening?" His voice is smooth, calm, and there's a smile on his face, but his eyes hold concern. "Your necklace is lovely."

He leans forward as though he's examining it. "Whatever just happened," his voice is so quiet, I almost can't hear him even though he's inches away, "you need to stop reacting. He's watching you." He pulls back. "Did you enjoy the meal?"

I swallow. Matthias is right. I need to pretend this test hasn't phased me, that I'm excited to be where I am. But I don't know how to do that.

"It was delicious." My voice sounds almost normal, which should make me feel grateful. Instead, I feel like it's betraying me. Everything is not normal. Everything is not fine. My voice shouldn't be acting like it is.

Then there's a muffled gasp from Nika, who's sitting a few feet away from where I am. Her eyes are wide, mouth gaping. She looks stricken, and it unnerves me.

Nika doesn't get like that. Ever. No matter what's happening.

Ark pats her hand and then moves on to someone else.

I go to Nika. She has a bracelet clutched in her hand, but I'm not sure she realizes it. I decide to follow Matthias's lead with me.

"Your bracelet's beautiful," I say, leaning closer than necessary to look at it. "He's watching us. Try not to react," I whisper.

The words seem to be enough to snap Nika out of her stupor. She smiles, transforming back into her normal self, though if I look close enough, I can still see the haunted look in her eyes.

Over the next hour, Nika and I interact with the others, though we're not the only ones who seem shaken. Sergeant Valarius was right. Ark's testing us.

This is a game for him. He's enjoying toying with us, taunting us, waiting for us to react, to fail. A steely resolve stiffens my spine. I won't let him have the pleasure of seeing me dissolve, of seeing me crushed by what he shared. I force myself to engage further in the surrounding conversation.

My band buzzes, and I casually glance down to find a message from Ari to both Nika and me.

Meet me in your room as soon as you can.

There's nothing else, but the message disappears almost instantly this time.

Somehow, I stay engaged in the conversation for the rest of the evening, even laughing at a stupid joke Colonel Valarius made, but the pulsing dread in the pit of my stomach promises that the worst part of this evening is yet to come.

What does Ari have to share with us? And why would she risk messaging us while we're here?

CHAPTER

FIFTY-NINE

The Commander finally dismisses us, and Shane, Belen, Nika, and I are brought back to our quarters. As soon as Nika and I are away from Shane and Belen, I turn to her.

"What happened in there?" I ask. "Whatever he said got to you."

"Mmm." Nika's jaw bunches, and she keeps her gaze ahead as we walk down the hallway to our room. "Looked like he got to you too." There's an edge to her tone that warns me to back off.

"Sorry," I say.

She slows her pace and rubs the back of her neck. "Sorry, girl. He just...he knew things. Things from my past that he shouldn't have known."

From the haunted look on my friend's face, I know whatever Ark probed tonight touched on a deep pain. Which is something I understand. "Same with me."

She looks at me then, and, without another word, we both know we understand each other.

"The Commencement can't come soon enough," Nika says.

We enter our room, and Ari is perched on the edge of my bed, hunched over a screen. She doesn't glance up when we enter.

"Girl," Nika says as soon as the door is closed. "You just sitting right out in the open for the fun of it? What if someone else came in? We'd all be in trouble!"

This brings Ari's head up. "I'd know way before they got here."

She's so confident in her abilities and shocked by Nika's questions that a laugh bursts out of me.

Nika rolls her eyes.

"What's funny?" Ari asks.

I laugh again, and Nika chuckles as well. Ari's brilliant but clueless sometimes.

"Give me one second, and then you can show us what you found." Nika goes into the bathroom and shuts the door.

I kick off my shoes as Ari becomes engrossed once more in her screen. I change out of my gaudy dress in my closet and put my uniform back on. It's comfortable, normal. And I might even prefer it over the clothes from home now. How have they changed me so much?

"Bria, we're ready," Nika calls in to me.

I take a deep breath, grip my necklace for a moment, then tuck it under my shirt, and join my friends.

Nika changed as well. But it's the serious expression on Ari's face that captures my attention.

"What did you find?" I ask.

"You won't like it."

I perch on the edge of a chair. "It can't be much worse than what I've already gone through tonight."

"Amen to that," Nika agrees.

Ari doesn't say a word, which unsettles me more. She approaches me, holding out her screen. Ari *never* parts from her tech. She points to things, holds it for other people to see, but she never offers it to anyone else.

So why is she handing it to me?

I bounce my leg up and down and take the device, but I don't look at it. "What is it?"

She nods at the screen. "Look." One word from the girl who likes to over-describe everything.

The last thing I want to do is look at whatever this is. I can't handle another blow tonight. But I grip the screen and focus on the words.

Phase One Youth Extraction

Recruit List: Derbe

Before I can stop myself, I keep reading.

Averton, Elijah (Eli)

Averton, Ezekiel (Zeke)

`The screen falls from my hands, clatters to the floor, and a scream builds in my throat, choking me, refusing to fall from my lips.

This can't be happening. Not my brothers, not my baby brothers.

I'm vaguely aware of Nika retrieving the screen, reading the words, gasping in horror. I grip my face, rock back and forth. No, no, no, no. Not them.

How could Aunt Elena betray not only me but the boys? She had her issues with me, but everyone loves Eli and Zeke, even her. At least, I thought she did.

I lurch to my feet. I can't stay here. Something has to be done, anything. I head to the door.

"Bria, wait." Nika steps into my path. "We'll get them in time. Their extraction is set for two months from now—that's after the Commencement. We'll be able to get to them."

Some of my panic is eased, but the need to act, to do something right now, pulses through me.

"I'll be back soon." I push past Nika and stride to the door.

She calls my name, but I ignore her, and, thankfully, she doesn't follow me.

I want to kill Demetrius Ark, end things once and for all. But I'm not convinced killing Ark would be enough. Another person would just take his place, continue his mission.

Cold, early spring air stings my exposed skin, but I barely notice. It's more important than ever that we escape, that we destroy Ark and his plans and all those who would fight for him. But tonight, I'm going to do what it takes to save the one child I can from experiencing one more second of horror in this place.

I jog toward the Modified Housing District.

Whether or not it's part of our plan, I don't care. Tonight, I'll bring Storm and Damara to Cai. They can stay with him in the Ruins for the next few weeks until we escape.

It's not the safest place for a child, but the Ruins with Cai are far safer than a house in the city of Talionis, under the watchful eyes of Demetrius Ark.

It took more convincing than I expected to get Damara to pack herself and Storm up and go with me to the Ruins, but my desperation won out, and she finally agreed to go. Cai was surprised to see them, but he won Storm over with the promise of taking her to meet some puppies in the morning, and by the time I left the three of them, Cai was settling Storm and Damara in a site near the river, completely hidden.

By the time I return to Talionis, it's almost curfew, but I catch Cade before he goes to his room and let him know Storm is safe but no longer where she was. He looks concerned at the thought, and I can see him calculating the potential outcomes from the situation, but he thanks me for the information and goes to bed.

Now I just have to tell Nika and Ari.

I feel calmer now than I have all night. I acted, did *something*, and protected the one child I could. Ark will be upset when he can't find her, but he'll think Damara took her and is hiding somewhere in the city. They'll probably search for her, but then it'll pass. And she'll be safe.

My hand is on the doorknob to my room when the door is yanked open.

"Girl, what were you thinking?" Nika hisses, then pulls me into the room.

Ari is still here.

"I was just—"

"We know what you were doing," Nika snaps. "Ari tracked you as soon as you left—and made sure to make it look like you were in the room the whole time since you didn't bother setting your band. Do you know how dangerous it is to take Storm to the Ruins? They'll look for her!"

"I know, but—"

"We have a plan. We need to stick to it. Running around and acting without thinking is going to get us in trouble."

"Nika. I had to do something." My voice cracks, and a tidal wave of emotion washes over me. "I had to protect her."

Nika releases a long sigh. "I know. Sorry. I just got freaked out, and this whole night—it's got me on edge."

I nod in understanding.

Ari comes over. "We'll get out of here and stop them from getting those kids."

"And that is why," Mandeville says, "you must—"

"*All recruits and personnel, report to the Center.*"

The speaker cuts Mandeville off, and his face reddens. "Class is not supposed to end for another eight minutes and twenty-four seconds."

"*All recruits and personnel report to the Center for a special appearance by the Commander.*"

Mandeville inhales quickly. "Alright, well get going, all of you! I won't have any from my class late for the Commander."

I turn off my screen and shoulder my rifle, giving Nika a sideways glance. "What do you think this is about?"

She presses her lips into a thin line. "I don't know, but I can't say I'm happy to see the man again so soon."

I'm still not sure what the Commander said to Nika last night, but it's had her shaken all day and not quite herself. Then again, I'm not quite myself either. The man knows exactly how to disarm you enough to make his attack even more brutal. And he's lauded for it.

Everyone loves the man. At least that's how it seems.

The soldiers, recruits, and personnel flocking to the Center are pulsating with excitement. Some chatter among themselves, thrilled to see the Commander. A group of female recruits are straightening their uniforms and redoing their hair. Many walk taller, with a purpose. The few who seem hesitant, maybe even a little afraid, are the ones who aren't carrying rifles. The lowest of the recruits.

I'm an Elite, but I resonate with their trepidation.

This is the first time the Commander has made a public appearance to all the recruits. Typically, he shows up unannounced to small groups, those doing particularly well in different areas. But this is different.

The sudden announcement.

The call to *everyone* to come to the Center.

It's meant to feel random, spontaneous. But I can't help but feel that it's all calculated.

Nika and I say nothing as we walk along with everyone else, but recruits step out of our way, letting us pass. Some salute. All of it sickens me. This stupid white uniform, the weight of the rifle on my back, even my necklace pressed against my chest—it marks me, makes me appear as brainwashed by all of this as everyone else.

We enter the Center in the swarm of people. A soldier calls Nika and me over and leads us to an elevated platform with the other Elite Recruits. Everyone else crowds the ground. No one is given access to the stands. They bring the recruits into formation, the soldiers forming behind them, and the rest of the crowd—personnel and workers—is scattered behind them.

Thousands of people.

Then Commander Demetrius Ark steps onto a platform halfway up the stands, higher than the platform I'm on with the other Elites, and his image is projected onto the massive screens throughout the Center.

The crowd erupts in a deafening cheer, and he smiles and waves, and I'm forced to join them or risk exposing myself. Every clap of my hands, each shout from my mouth, burns with bitterness, but I don't stop. To save my brothers, to get Storm out of here, to stop that man, I'll do this.

"Com-mander Ark! Com-mander Ark!" Someone chants, and then the entire Center has joined in until my ears throb with the volume and intensity. It lasts for a solid minute but feels like an hour.

Finally, Ark raises his hands, silencing the crowd.

"Hello, my friends," he says.

Another cheer.

Another smile from Commander Ark.

Then silence.

He looks out over the throng, a smile softening his features. Then he points to different people in the crowd—recruits, soldiers, even some workers—calling them by name. Most of them are names I don't know. They're not recruits who are excelling. Not ones who the soldiers typically recognize. But Ark knows them. When he says their names, a camera focuses on that person, projecting their faces onto the screen beside the image of Ark.

For the next twenty minutes, he calls out different people, thanking them for their hard work, how they labor faithfully. Every person smiles, thrilled by the praise of the Commander.

And as I watch, I realize one important thing. He's won their hearts. They may not know him well, may only know what Trill has been indoctrinating us with, but they love this evil man. And they'll follow him anywhere, do whatever he says.

We have to escape and then return and expose him, defeat him, before it's too late.

"My Elites," Ark says.

We all snap to attention as one.

He smiles. "At ease. Please. Relax."

I drop to the at ease position, but the last thing I can do is relax.

"Thank you for your hard work, how you labor to be the best. Your loyalty to Talionis." He places his hand on his chest, bowing his head slightly. "Your loyalty to me." He pauses, appearing to collect himself, and then spreads his arms wide and addresses the crowd. "Are they not remarkable?"

The crowd bursts into cheers and applause. For us.

It's unbearable.

Ark silences them again, places his hands on the railing. "Talionis is more than just a city, your training grounds. It's more than the place where you're pushed to be the best you can be. From the lowest recruit to the greatest Elite, from the highest ranking soldiers to the lowest worker, we are a *family*. And Talionis is our home."

More cheering. More soaking in the lies of this twisted man. I want to blame them all for their stupidity, shout at them that they're walking into a trap. But, like the dozens of Kill Zones I've navigated, what's clearly propaganda to me looks like a safe place to them. And how could it not? Ark is the best speaker I've ever heard. If I hadn't seen the things I've seen, hadn't fought the way I've fought, if I didn't have Nika, Ari, Cade, Cai, and Matthias in this with me, maybe I would cheer right alongside them.

Ark speaks again, repeating rhetoric Elva Trill has spouted from day one of our time here. Then there's a commotion on the stage, cutting Ark off mid-sentence. He spins, and the camera zooms in on Laban as he drags a bloodied and beaten Cade onto the stage.

Nika and I gasp.

"I've uncovered the traitor, sir," Laban says, his voice amplified in the silent stadium.

Commander Ark waves his hand, inviting Laban forward.

A twitching begins in my neck, fluttering, desperate. I want to clamp my hand over it to make it stop, but I can't.

Laban shoves Cade, who stumbles, then falls to his knees. His eyes find mine, one swollen almost shut, blood trickling from a gash in his head. And he smiles. A soft, pain-filled smile, full of peace.

My breath locks itself in my lungs.

"What have you discovered, Sergeant?" Commander Ark asks.

"Recruit Cade Renatus," Laban's rasping voice grates over my ears, "has committed treason against Talionis, and you, my Commander. And I will not stand for it."

There are some boos and jeering remarks from the crowd directed at Cade, and then the Commander holds up his hand, and they stop.

"What has he done?" His voice is still calm, confident.

"He's the one responsible for the youngest recruit going missing."

It's like the monster of the ocean is drowning me while I'm on land, distorting everything. This isn't right. This can't be happening.

"We've been searching for the girl all night and day, and one of the tech personnel came to me with proof he's the one responsible for her disappearance. His band shows him traveling throughout Talionis all last night. We have retraced his steps, but his movements were erratic, and we haven't found the girl anywhere."

My heart pounds behind my ribs with bruising intensity. This isn't right. Why would Cade do this?

Commander Ark approaches Cade. "Where is Storm?"

Cade doesn't look up at Ark. "No child should have to endure the things you put that girl through. I won't let you touch her again."

Ark's perfect composure cracks for an instant, and he bares his teeth like an angry wolf. Then he's calm again. He faces the crowd.

"How should Recruit Renatus be punished for his insubordination?" Ark asks the crowd at large.

"He's committed treason!" The voice rises, a shout. A voice I know. Shay. "He should die!"

A chant rises from the crowd: "Execute him, execute him!"

"This can't be happening," I say.

Nika grips my hand. We're both shaking.

"He knows what he's doing," she says, close to my ear so I can hear her over the crowd.

Ark throws his hands into the air. The crowd goes quiet. He focuses on Cade again. "One last chance, Cade. Your actions will lead to your punishment, yes, but you can prove your loyalty. Where is Storm?"

Cade gets to his feet, flinching, and then his eyes find mine again. He's chosen to take my place, given them all the evidence they need to charge him with this crime. *My* crime.

"I'm ready—I'm not afraid to die. And I *will* die to protect the innocent and those who aren't ready for death and what comes after."

Again, I'm amazed at the peace on his face. He smiles.

Ark takes a step back, shaking his head.

The chanting for Cade's execution begins again. Ark gives the subtlest of nods to Laban, who smirks. My brain is reaching to process what I'm seeing—

Bang!

The blast of a gun cuts above the noise of the crowd. Cade falls to the ground, blood pooling around him. The camera focuses on him, his dark eyes staring lifelessly into the sky. Eyes that just looked at me.

Laban steps forward, arms held out like a champion. The crowd cheers, louder than any other moment.

"No!" The word tears through me, ripping me in half, but I can barely hear it myself over the deafening crowd.

Nika's arm comes around my shoulders. "Keep it together, Bria." She has to shout the words into my ear so I can hear them. "He chose this. Don't let him die in vain."

A sob punches me, but I choke it back, leaning into my friend. Her body shudders as she draws in a shaking breath.

Cade died for me, made himself the one they looked to for Storm's disappearance, to protect me.

Why?

The crowd continues to cheer.

CHAPTER
SIXTY

I don't know how I made it back to my room. The only thing I see over and over is Cade being shot and falling to the ground. Dead. It's all my fault. He's dead because of me, because I couldn't stand the thought of Storm having one more day here.

His words to me right before he died echo in my mind. *I'm ready—I'm not afraid to die. And I will die to protect those who aren't ready for death and what comes after.* What did he mean? And why would he choose to take my place? Tears flow down my face, starting as a trickle, but quickly becoming a torrent.

My entire body convulses as the sobs rip through me, each one dissolving more of me. They should have shot me. I should be dead. But I'm not. Because of Cade.

"Oh God, *why?*" I cry out, crumbling to the floor. "Why is Cade dead, and why am I still alive?"

Fresh tears pour out, and I do nothing to stop them. Sorrow and devastation pierce through me, tearing me apart. My throat and chest ache from the fierceness of my crying.

"Bria?" Nika's voice is raw, like she's been crying too, but there's a strength to it as well.

I place my hand over my mouth, trying to quiet the sobs, but my body won't let me contain my grief, my guilt.

Nika kneels next to me. "Oh, girl," she says softly, a compassion in her voice I've never heard before. "Cade knew what he was doing."

I open my mouth to respond, but I can't. I just cry. Nika sits on the floor next to me, wraps her arms around me, and we both cry together.

"I deserve to die," I say, once I'm able to control myself. "I should be dead. If I was dead, then people wouldn't be dying because of me."

Even as I speak the words, I know they're true. Ezri is dead because of my actions. Ava's dead because I couldn't save her. And now Cade's dead because he took my place. My eyes burn and feel swollen, and more tears leak out.

Nika rubs my back.

"Why did he do it? Why would he take my place? I told him where Storm was so he wouldn't worry, not so he would cover for me." I shudder. "Nika I just, I don't understand."

She stops rubbing my back and shifts so she's directly in front of me. "Cade loved Storm as much as you do, and he wanted to protect her too. But he was ready for something that you're not ready for."

"I don't understand." I don't attempt to wipe the tears pouring down my face. "What does that even mean?"

"He was ready to die. You're not."

Her words land on top of me with crushing force, an echo of Cade's last words. I know I deserve to die, should be dead, but she's right. The idea of death terrifies me. "But who *is* ready? You can't seriously be okay with dying."

Nika cocks her head to the side. Her eyes are red from crying, but her face is dry now. "No, not *okay* with dying. Death is always hard to handle. It's scary. But you *can* be prepared for it, and Cade was."

I knot my hands together in my lap, focusing on them. "How?"

"If there's one thing I knew about Cade, it's that he trusted God. He had heaven waiting for him." Nika tilts my chin up and forces me to look at her. "He died, yes, and it hurts, and it won't be easy to get over, and we will miss him." Her voice cracks. "But he was ready to die, and his death is giving you the chance for something you desperately need. Something Cade already had." Her eyes bore into mine. "Freedom."

I shake my head. "But he was trapped here, the same as I am."

"Yeah, he was trapped in Talionis. But he wasn't trapped by his past or by guilt like you are. He was free from all of that in Jesus." She rests her hand on my shoulder. "The question is, will you remain locked away in your guilt, or will you accept the freedom, the forgiveness that God is offering to you?"

I gnaw on my lip. Could it be that simple?

Doubt creeps in. "It's too late for me. There's no way God would want me."

"You're wrong," Nika says, urgently. "God loves you, Bria. Jesus paid the price to forgive you, even though He knows everything you've ever done. He died in your place, just like Cade did. He was innocent, perfect, but He took your place because He loves you. He died so you could live. He paid the price so you could be free, and He's offering you the key to release you from your prison. Will you take it?"

I want to believe. I want what Nika has. What Cade had. I want the freedom Nika's talking about. But I'm afraid. A fresh tear tracks its way down my cheek.

Nika unknots my hands from my lap and holds them tight. "Just reach out to Him, girl. Ask Him to forgive you. Ask Him to free you. Ask Him to come and be with you. You'll find everything you're looking for." A sad smile lifts the corner of her mouth. "What do you have to lose?"

A spark ignites in my soul, a glimmer of hope. I can't go forward on my own anymore. I can't keep trying to live my life without God. Even if I got out of Talionis, I wouldn't *really* be free. I need God's forgiveness. I need His love. I need Him to free me.

I need *Him.*

I lean back against the wall, and it supports me. Firm. Solid. Strong. The opposite of me and my crippled life because I haven't been able to move past the things I've done and the things I've allowed to happen...and the things that have been done to me. I can't do it anymore. I can't live with the burden that has weighed me down. And I don't have to.

Jesus, I'm done trying to run. I need You. I don't understand why You died for me, just like I don't understand why Cade died for me. Please forgive me, because I haven't been able to forgive myself. Help me trust You. Trusting myself isn't working. If You want me, You can have me.

I still feel the pain of Cade's death, the loss of Ezri, fear over what's coming, but the crushing weight of guilt seems to lift, like someone unlocked chains that have bound me. I stand and then reach down to help Nika to her feet. I don't release her hand.

"Okay." My gaze connects with hers, and I hope she can see that I believe her, believe what she just shared. "I'm done trying to do this on my own."

I release her hand and then step forward and wrap my arms around her. She tenses in surprise for a moment, and then she hugs me back.

Something rests on me, something different from any other feeling I've experienced in my life.

Peace.

SIXTY-ONE

The Commencement is only a week away, and this is likely our final meeting. I look around the room at the group of nine gathered. There should be ten of us escaping. I feel a pang at the absence of Cade. His death not only saved my life, it *changed* my life. Tears threaten. It's only been a few days, and I'm still raw.

"Where's Cade?" Cai asks. "We really need to begin."

"He's not coming," Shane says, his tone icy, but with a tinge of sadness. "He's dead."

There's a tense silence after Shane's words, an ache of loss. Storm sits next to me and faces me, eyes wide. Only a handful of people here know I'm the one who brought her to the Ruins, not Cade.

"What?" Cai's question cuts through the air.

I swallow the lump in my throat. *Okay, God, I could really use some help right now.* The prayer rises from my heart, and I hope He hears it.

"It's my fault. Cade's dead because of me." My voice cracks, and I press my eyes closed to keep from crying. I inhale and continue.

They all deserve to know.

"He took responsibility for my actions the other night, set himself up as the one who helped Storm and Damara escape."

I don't look at Storm—can't look at her. She's already lost so much, and I don't want her to think this is her fault in any way. I attempt to keep myself from crying, but feel my mouth is pulling down into a frown with the suppressed emotions. A tear rolls down my cheek, and I wish I could permanently block the haunting memories of that night.

Storm leans into me, her warm tears seeping through my sleeve. I hold her tight. Cade wanted to protect her too—Nika was right about that.

"It all happened so fast," I continue. "I couldn't stop it, didn't understand what was going on until it was too late to stop it." The ache in my throat intensifies as I try to hold back the tears. "He took the bullet that should have been mine. He died in my place."

Silence fills the site, broken by Storm's muffled sobs. I hold her against me, and Damara sits on her other side, stroking her hair. Her eyes meet mine, but there's no censure. Only compassion and understanding.

"Why would he do that?" Ari asks after several moments.

"Cade loved Jesus," Nika responds, and I'm glad I don't have to. "He was ready to die, but he knew Bria wasn't."

Ari presses her lips together. "I don't get what his God had to do with him being willing to die for Bria."

I don't respond to Ari, and I don't know if Nika does. I face Cai, who's watching me. His face is void of emotions. "I'm ready now."

Cai is one of the strongest men I've ever known. If I had to wager whether or not I'd ever see him cry, I'd put my money on never. Yet, as what I say registers, his face cracks with emotion, and a single tear trails down his cheek.

"I'm glad." He abruptly turns away and adds a log to the fire. But it doesn't bother me. I know the two words he spoke were genuine.

We spend some time remembering Cade, those who knew him sharing about him, those who didn't listening. Storm talks about how Cade was like a brother to her, how he always made her feel safe. She cries again when she says she'll miss him and buries her head in my side, which almost starts my tears flowing, partly for the pain she feels but also because she still trusts me.

Cai says he's thankful that out of death, God can bring life.

Several of the others look confused by his statement, but I know what he means now.

After we finish, we turn our attention to planning. Ari powers on the screens, pulling up the map of Talionis on the largest screen. She's reconfigured Cai's entire tech set-up, not only here, but throughout the Ruins. I'm not sure Cai understands half of what he's working with anymore.

"There are only a few days left," Cai says. "We're ready, except for our need for additional weapons. Shane, you'll need to gather those from the Weaponry Building before starting the fire." He hesitates. "You'll need someone to help you."

There's an awkward silence.

"I could help him," Bryson chimes in. "Ari and Nalani should be able to handle what needs to be done in the tech building."

"I was actually going to suggest Nalani come out here and handle some of the alarms from the Ruins." Ari chews on her lip. "But I could show Damara what to do."

"Remember to use simple terms," Nika says. "Not all of us understand advanced tech."

Ari rolls her eyes, and a chuckle ripples through the room.

Cai looks at Damara. "What do you think?"

"I can do it," she says.

"Okay," Cai says. "Shane and Bryson, once you've set fire to this building," he taps one of the abandoned buildings we're targeting, "and you've activated the five explosives on your route," he traces the blue route to the weaponry building that they'll be taking, "you'll have fifteen minutes to gather the weapons and set the fire."

"Right." Shane agrees, and Bryson nods his head. "Then, we meet Damara and Storm here and take this path," he points his finger to a path on the map, "through the Ruins, over the disabled Wall, and to the rendezvous point a mile into the forest behind the Wall."

"Correct," Cai says.

"We could get over the Wall ourselves," Damara says.

Cai shakes his head no. "You'll need an escort past the wild dogs."

Damara quirks an eyebrow at a dog resting in the corner. "They don't look very wild to me."

"Not my dogs," Cai says. "The wild dogs. My dogs keep them away from here, but they prowl near the Wall."

Damara inclines her head in acquiescence and Cai continues. "Speaking of the Wall—Ari, are you prepared to disable it?"

"Yes," she says. "I've discovered a weakness, and I'm going to use the transfinton to create the crydrospheric charge. It should be strong enough to crash the electromagnetic field on the Wall, as well as destroying communications between the Wall towers and Talionis."

"Those are big words, girl," Nika mutters.

"However," Ari ignores Nika and continues, "once I trigger the surge, we will only have thirty minutes to get over the Wall before it reboots itself."

Cai rubs his beard. "Right. Wait to trigger it until the last possible moment. From your position here," he points to where Ari will be, near the Tech building, "you should be able to see the smoke from the fire Shane and Bryson start in the Weaponry building, and you'll undoubtedly hear the explosion from transports being disabled. Be sure to wait until after those things before you trigger the power surge."

"Okay," Ari says.

"And before you disable the Wall, I'll set off alarms in secure buildings throughout Talionis?" Damara asks.

"Yes," Ari says. "I think the best places to activate the alarms are here, here, and here, since none of us will be in any of those buildings. And I'll show you how to disable the alarms in the buildings we'll be in. Nalani will gather the gear we need and disable the communications and tracking while I work on the prep in order to disable the Wall."

"Excellent," Cai says. "Before anything begins, I'll create some disturbances throughout the Ruins to...discourage," he smirks, "soldiers from any patrols. Then Nika, Matthias, and I will disable the transports and do our best to destroy as many as possible."

Cai expels a deep breath. "Crippling their transportation is going to be vital in order for us to get to Eryndale without them finding and stopping us." He seems to say the words more to himself than to any of us, but several people nod in agreement.

"Alright." Cai moves on and focuses on me. "And Bria, you'll be infiltrating Ark's office and stealing the maps of the area so we can find Eryndale."

I nod as my heart thunders. How am I going to pull this off?

"Ari, do you have what Bria needs to access the safe?"

"Yes." She pulls a slip of paper from her pocket and picks up a small satchel at her feet. "I wrote the instructions." She hands them to me, and I hold them without looking while she types something on a screen.

"It's true. I can gain access to the building and possibly the higher level offices—"

"You will," Ari interrupts me. "I just gave you the highest security clearance possible."

Everyone stares at her.

She shrugs. "I lifted a clearance card from Mandeville. Didn't want to do it before now in case he got suspicious, but I was able to use the data on his card to find the code needed to update Bria's band. When she goes through, it'll look like Mandeville is accessing the rooms."

"Okay...but I'm still unsure the best way to get into Demetrius Ark's office." I hesitate. "I think Matthias should come with me."

A stunned silence fills the site. Part of me wants to rescind the suggestion, but I don't. I know I need his help with this. I know I need to trust him.

Cai recovers first. "Fine. Matthias, do you think you'll be able to help Bria gain access to Ark's office?"

"Um..." Matthias clears his throat. "Yeah, I've been in it a few times over the years."

"Very good. Nika and I should be okay dealing with the Transportation Dock. The only problem is that Matthias will get there after you, Bria, since he needs to set off the explosives in the Physical Training Arena."

I finger my necklace and glance at Matthias. "That's okay. I'll open the door into Colonel Valarius's office and wait for him there."

"Very well," Cai says.

We finalize our plans and, before we dissipate, Cai addresses us once more. "I'm proud of you all. You are taking a stand against a powerful regime. This will not be easy, and I can almost guarantee that all will not go according to our plans."

My stomach knots, and fear overshadows me. What if we fail?

"But we will do our best and trust that, no matter what, God is in control. Be strong, my friends. We face a great evil, but God is greater. I, for one, will pray that He guides us through this."

Even after Cai's reminder, a tendril of fear remains woven through me. Tomorrow will not be easy. Damara and Storm join Ari at the screens, and Ari explains what they will need to do—Storm understands more tech than Damara does, and she does a surprisingly good job of explaining what Ari wants them to do. The two of them should be fine out here until Shane and Bryson can get to them.

The others leave in small groups.

Picking up a handful of knives, I walk over to some old practice boards set up in the corner and begin throwing them. It's one way to pass the time while I wait for everyone to go. I need to speak with Cai alone. Storm comes and gives me a hug goodbye, squeezing me tight. I hug her back, kiss the top of her head, and wave to Damara as the two exit to return to their site. Then I retrieve the knives and throw them again.

After a while, I turn so my back is to the board and fling the knife over my shoulder.

"Nice throw." Cai leans against the wall.

I tuck the other knife still in my hand into my belt. "I wanted to talk to you, tell you what happened."

"I know." He nods his head toward the pile of supplies. "Help me pack some of these up while we talk."

We fill packs with clothes, small weapons, and packets of food, and I talk. I unload everything to Cai, recounting the details of that night and all that occurred. I tell him about Ark giving me back my necklace, how he seems to know things about my past and Ezri's death, his words about Storm. Ari showing me the list with my brothers' names on it, how my aunt is a Watcher for Talionis. I share how I reacted, explain that's the reason I brought Storm here. And then I tell him about Ark's speech, Laban dragging Cade in. How Cade made it seem like he was the one who hid Storm. The chanting crowd crying for his execution. Laban killing Cade. The cheers.

Then, I softly speak about how Nika talked with me and, in my darkest moment, led me to Jesus and how His peace filled me and comforted me.

Cai's rolling up a blanket when I finish. "This is an answer to prayer for me, Bria." He puts the blanket into a pack. He reaches across two packs between us and places a hand on my shoulder. "Whether or not we're successful in our escape, I know my time in Talionis hasn't been in vain."

I pick up a small crossbow and work to attach it to one of the larger packs, suddenly hesitant to share the other thing on my mind.

"What is it?"

A grin briefly flits across my face. Of course he would notice that there was something else. The grin dies.

"I'm still struggling with my aunt's betrayal. How do I move past it?" I grit my teeth. "I could push it down, ignore it mostly when it was just me. But now she's selling out my baby brothers. How could Aunt Elena do that? She gave me over to be kidnapped, torn from Derbe, from my family, and now *this*."

Cai's face pales as I talk.

"Are you okay, Cai?"

He opens his mouth, but no words come out. He shuts it, and his Adam's apple bobs as he swallows. "What's your aunt's last name?"

I raise my eyebrows. What does that have to do with anything? "Blyweiss."

He pales even more. "Your aunt is my wife."

"What?"

"Elena Blyweiss is my wife. Bria, you're my niece."

I'M STILL REELING FROM CAI'S REVELATION ABOUT BEING MY UNCLE AS I LAY in bed. I'm happy about it in one sense, but trying to imagine the woman Cai talked about as his wife and the woman I know as Aunt Elena as the same person...well, it's not working for me.

I suppose when Cai was taken, she changed. Anyone would, I guess. But change enough to go from being a supporting wife to a betraying aunt? I roll onto my side. A tendril of bitterness slithers into my heart. How could she do what she did to me? Cai was certain she would never do something so treacherous, but I can't deny the facts I saw with my own eyes. She's a Watcher for Talionis. She gave them my name, told them to abduct me, and now she's doing it to my brothers.

Forgive her.

The words whisper into my heart. I punch my pillow and drop my head back onto it. How can I forgive her for what she's done?

Cai's parting words replay in my mind. "*I understand you're hurt, Bria. But don't hold on to bitterness. Jesus forgave the ones who hurt Him the most. He forgave you. You need to forgive her. Forgiveness sets us free.*"

I blow out a sigh and turn onto my back, staring up at the ceiling. *Okay, God. I don't know how You forgave those who hurt You so badly, but I know You've forgiven me, and that fact has changed my life. Help me to forgive my aunt, because there's no way I can do it on my own.*

The agitation I felt moments ago releases. I curl into a ball and fall asleep.

SIXTY-TWO

Nika pulls the sheet up on her bed. It's the first time I've ever seen her actually *make* her bed. Usually she just leaves the blankets in a ball on top. "You nervous?"

Today is the day of the Commencement.

Today, we will either escape from Talionis or die trying. Of course I'm nervous.

I duck my head under the end table, looking for anything I don't want to leave behind. "Yeah." I stand. "Are you?"

"Please. I'd be crazy *not* to be nervous. Everything rests on this."

I touch my necklace where it lies on my bed. I haven't put it on yet, can't decide *what* to do with it. It's my last remnant of Ezri, but it's been tainted by Demetrius Ark.

"From the Commander?" Nika asks.

"Sort of." I pick it up. "It's partly my necklace from my brother, the one that got taken from me when we first arrived." I hold out the sea glass. "But the chain is from Ark."

"He gave me a bracelet." She flops onto the bed. "I flushed it down the toilet."

Laughter bubbles up inside me and forces its way out. Her act of defiance cracks me up. I can't stop laughing. Nika grins, and then her laughter starts too. Maybe it's the stress we've been under for months. Maybe it's the tension and importance of today. Or maybe it's the only way my body can handle dealing with every emotion I've experienced lately. Whatever it is, the laughter feels amazing. We both end up sinking to the floor, clutching our sides. I laugh until tears run down my face, and it's hard to breathe.

Eventually, we get ourselves back under control. "Thanks for that." I sigh.

"Laughter is good medicine." Nika stands up and brushes her hands over her new uniform. They issued everyone new uniforms for the Commencement. She reaches a hand down and helps me to my feet.

"Whatever happens, I'm glad we're in this together." I smile and release her hand.

"Same."

The buzzer sounds, alerting us it's time to go to the Center.

The Commencement is about to begin.

All traces of laughter and lightheartedness evaporate faster than the early morning dew on a summer day. I take a deep breath. A few hours from now, we'll either be out of Talionis, or we'll be facing the muzzle of a gun.

Nika and I grab our packs and rifles, and then I follow her as she leaves the room. I shut the door for the last time. We walk down the hall, and I mentally trace the route I'll take when I sneak away from the Commencement.

Once outside our building, we join the rest of the recruits making their way to the Center. It rises before us, and Nika and I slip away, hiding our packs in nearby alleys. My fingers tingle in anticipation as I step into one line wrapping around the Center. Minutes from now, the processional will begin. That's when we'll slip from our places in line. We're counting on all the leaders, soldiers, and citizens of Talionis who were instructed to attend the Commencement being in the Center at that point.

Anticipation swirls through me. I'm nervous, but I'm also excited. I'm finally about to do something that could actually make a difference. Several soldiers with screens move through the lines, checking in each recruit. I give my name, and they make me press my hand against the screen.

Elite Recruit Bria Averton, Accounted for.

The soldiers move on.

Soon music plays from the Center, and then the recruits in front of me move forward. Soldiers are stationed at the entrance to the Center and at the corner. There are five lines of recruits, and I'm near the back. I walk until I'm several yards away from the corner and then drop, pretending to tie my boot. The recruit directly behind me pauses, then she walks around me and closes the gap. The recruits behind her follow her lead. I ease up, turn in the opposite direction, and sprint away.

God, please don't let anyone notice me.

Adrenaline courses through me, my heart thumping in rhythm with my feet pounding on the ground. I don't stop running until I get to my first mark at an alley a quarter of a mile away from the Center. Once I'm in the alley, I press against the wall and peer back. There's no one in sight. I breathe a sigh of relief, retrieve my pack, slinging it over my body, and remove my rifle and lean it against the building. Our rifles are too big to carry with us out of Talionis. Shane and Bryson will get us smaller weapons and firearms, but as I continue forward, I can't help but feel like I'm missing something. I shake off the feeling and follow the route laid out for me.

Pass two cross streets, turn right at the third, left at the next street, straight for several blocks, right again, and then I'm at the back of the Main Headquarters Building. I cautiously move around to the right side of the building, alert for any sign of a soldier or citizen of Talionis being nearby.

The side door comes into view. I scan my band over the lock on the door. There's a click as the lock releases, and I ease the door open a crack so I can see into the hallway. No one. I open the door wide enough to enter the building and close it behind me.

I go left down the hallway. Then up two flights of stairs. I pass security zones and keep my head low, even though I know that action won't do me any good if Damara hasn't been able to disable the security. Since no alarms sound, and I don't hear footsteps rushing toward me, I'm inclined to think she's been successful.

I move down a long hallway at the end of which I'll go right and up three more flights of stairs. I jog up one flight of stairs, briefly wondering if the others were able to slip away from the Commencement undetected. Whether or not they were, it won't be long before they realize we're missing. Especially since several of us are Elites. I take the steps two at a time.

Once I climb the third flight of stairs, I find myself in the wing of the Main Headquarters building that houses the offices of the senior officials and leaders of Talionis. I count off four doorways before standing in front of the office of Colonel Keenan Valarius.

My heart hammers into my rib cage as I try the door. Locked. I force myself to stay calm. This is what we expected. I still have my security clearance. And Ari equipped me with Mandeville's security level. I stretch my band forward, preparing to swipe it over the lock.

I hesitate.

This isn't going to work. Sweat beads on my forehead. I start to pull my hand back, then force myself to scan the badge. A low beep sounds. I need higher clearance. My hand shakes, and I glance down the hallway. I feel every pulse in my body working overtime to pump blood to my erratically beating heart.

I try again. The beep sounds again.

Mandeville doesn't have clearance high enough to get into Colonel Valarius's office. None of us expected this.

I walk away from the door, force myself to take a deep breath. There's still another option. Colonel Valarius's office was the easiest way to access Ark's, but since it won't work, it's time for option two.

My badge grants me access to the utility closet at the end of the corridor. The potent smell of cleaners permeates the small room. I push aside cleaning supplies and the janitors' tools until I find what I'm looking for.

The air shaft.

Stacking a couple of buckets on top of each other, I climb onto them, precariously balancing myself. The bucket under my feet shifts with a crunching sound. I freeze, but it shifts again. My fingers can just reach the vent, and I'm able to flick it open. *Crack!* One bucket breaks. I spring off the bucket and grab hold of the air shaft, dangling from it as the buckets crash to the ground.

The noise sounds like an explosion in the silence. I hoist myself into the shaft and close the vent. Everything finds a new place to settle in, and the noise subsides. I wait with bated breath.

When no one comes rushing in, I breathe a sigh of relief, adjust my pack, and crawl through the shaft. It branches off in three different directions, and I take the one on the left, following it until it dead ends. Access point number two into Colonel Valarius's office.

I peer through the slits in the grate. The office is empty. I open the vent and drop to the ground, tucking into a roll and then coming to my feet.

I give a wide berth to Colonel Valarius's desk as I go to the office door. Matthias should be there waiting for me. I ease open the door and peer out into the empty hallway.

Where is he? What if something happened? What if they captured him? Or worse: what if he's been setting us up for a trap this entire time?

I shake my head. No. I can't think like that. He'll be here.

I step away from the door, back into Colonel Valarius's office. I need to work on figuring out how to get into Ark's office. If I don't do what I'm supposed to do, then it doesn't matter if Matthias is betraying us or not. We won't be able to get to Eryndale.

I start to close the door but hesitate. Matthias is probably on his way. I leave the door cracked open, staring at it for a minute, willing Matthias to come through. He doesn't. I can't stand here waiting forever. Guess I'm on my own.

My eyes comb over the room. If Colonel Valarius catches me in here, I can guarantee we will replay my last visit to this office, though with a much different ending. I walk over to the bookshelves, shoving the thought away.

Matthias was supposed to help me open the entrance to Ark's office, but it looks like I'll need to figure it out for myself. I close my eyes and envision the wall sliding open and Colonel Valarius walking through. I open my eyes and run my fingers over the book bindings.

It was this wall, but there's no sign of a secret doorway. So how do they make the door open?

I push on different books, pull some. Nothing happens.

"Oh, come on!"

Boom!

A nearby explosion shakes the items on the shelves. Alarms sound in several of the buildings nearby. An alarm inside of me goes off. Time is running out. I need to find the entrance. Now.

I frantically try everything I can think of, pulling at a light fixture, yanking a picture of a woman from the wall. Nothing is working.

What if Ari already created the power surge? I'll only have thirty minutes to get out of here, through the Ruins, and over the wall. I might not make it. Even if I leave now, if we don't have the maps...

Why can't I find the way in? I slam my hand into a panel, frustration forcing out the fear.

There's a scraping noise, and something shifts. I jump back. The wall transforms into the entrance to a passageway.

Thank You!

I rush into the passage, and moments later, everything moves back into place, sealing me in. Well, hopefully getting out of here is easier than getting in was.

I blink. The passageway is dimly lit, and it's difficult to see far ahead. It doesn't matter if I can't tell where I'm going. This is the only way to Ark's office that I could access. I step forward. The lights brighten, illuminating my way.

The path is curved, and roughhewn stones line the walls. There's a cave-like quality to it. Even the air is cool and damp, erasing any warmth that early spring has brought with it to the outside world. Though I know there are alarms sounding throughout Talionis, no sounds penetrate the thick walls. All I hear are my own footsteps. I round a bend, and a stairway rises before me. I take the steps two at a time, an urgency pushing me on.

When I reach the top landing, an arched doorway greets me. I twist the knob and enter an office that takes up the entire top floor of the building. Thick drapes are drawn over the windows on one side of the room, but they're pulled aside on the windows facing east, looking over the city. I allow myself a moment to glance out of them. Smoke billows from several areas. It appears things are moving forward.

Ark's desk is in the far corner, placed in front of floor-to-ceiling bookcases. The wall across from the desk holds a fireplace big enough for me to walk into. A sitting area with chairs and couches is set away from his desk and to the right. On the left is a hologram table surrounded by chairs. Screens with images of Talionis cover the wall nearest the windows. I watch the live feed of soldiers streaming from the Center and racing toward the various buildings in Talionis where trouble is indicated. The red words *Alarm Triggered* flash over different buildings. All buildings where we wanted alarms triggered.

Nice job, Damara and Storm.

A new building shows an alarm. I suck in a sharp breath. The Weaponry Building. How did that happen? There must be security measures we didn't know about. Bryson and Shane are in there. What if they're caught? Who will get Storm?

Fear clouds my mind.

I turn toward the door, ready to race to the Ruins and get Storm, but something stops me. Like a gentle hand on my shoulder. I can't fall back into that way of thinking. I need to trust the others on my team, trust God. No matter what, He's in control. I try to take a deep breath, but it catches in my throat.

What if that's not the only security measure we were unaware of?

My stomach swirls. I need to work quickly. Turning away from the screens, I recall the instructions Cai and Ari gave me concerning Ark's safe.

It's behind a large painting of a woman. I scan the room until my eyes come to rest on the painting near Ark's desk, amidst the book-shelves. I approach it, remove my pack, and place it on the floor.

Cai said he triggered it to open when a book near the painting was pressed, but he didn't know which book Ark used as the trigger. I search the nearby books. One on the history of Sitreea catches my eye. I press two fingers into the spine of the book, and an instant later, the painting swings away from the wall.

The safe gleams at me.

I retrieve the electronic-ion rare-earth magnetic device from my satchel. Ari collected the materials needed to make it and designed it from plans she had seen. She said it should open the safe, deactivating the alarm.

The word that's bothered me most about her speech on how to use this thing is that it *should* work. I'd much rather have a guarantee at the moment.

But I won't get one.

Only one way to see if she's right. I hold the round magnetic device in my hand, wrapping the cloth around it like she instructed before placing it over the door of the safe.

Click. The safe opens. I stare inside at two small pouches and a stack of papers, some bound, others stacked loosely. Which ones are the maps?

Voices from a corridor to the left, different from the one I came through, snag my attention. It sounds like two people arguing. And they're coming closer. I reach into the safe and pull out all the contents, loading them into my bag. I yank the magnet off the door of the safe, close it quickly, secure the painting back in place and duck under Ark's desk just as the door opens with a groan.

I clutch my bag to my chest, my knuckles turning white.

"I can't believe nobody saw this coming!" The voice belongs to Colonel Valarius. "You were supposed to oversee the recruits during the Commencement, Andor. How did you not notice the ones who were *missing*?" Colonel Valarius is almost screaming.

Their footsteps reverberate through the floor as they walk through the room. I curl up tighter in the black space under the desk.

"Calm down," Sergeant Valarius says, his voice low and steady.

"Calm down? How can you tell me to calm down! The Commander does not stand for mistakes, let alone of this magnitude. I guarantee someone is going to pay for this. But that person will not be me." There's a deadly quality to his voice.

"That person is never you," Sergeant Valarius says, a hard edge to his tone. They're right near the desk now. I'm barely breathing.

"What's that supposed to mean?" Colonel Valarius barks.

"The Commander's office is clear. Let's go back down and search the rest of the building."

"Don't tell me what to do," Colonel Valarius says. "You may be older, but I still outrank you."

The sound of their footsteps retreating the way they came allows air to return to my lungs. Colonel Valarius is still ranting about the "chaos that should have been stopped before it could start," but Sergeant Valarius is quiet. Their voices fade until I can't hear them at all.

I scramble out from under the desk. By now, Ari probably activated the power surge. I need to get out of here. I hurry back to the door I came through and race down the stairs and through the corridor, my pack beating a steady rhythm against my back. For a fleeting moment, I wonder what happened to Matthias. He should have been here long ago.

I skid to a halt in front of the door leading back into Colonel Valarius's office. No time to worry about Matthias. I need to focus on getting back through Talionis without being caught.

Two lights flank the door, and under the one on the right, there's a button. I assume that will open the door. But I'm suddenly apprehensive about who might be on the other side. Once that door opens, there'll be no hiding.

I feel the seconds ticking away, time running out. The musty smell of the corridor chokes me. I have no other choice.

Taking a deep breath, I press the button. The passageway opens, and I peer into the part of the office revealed to me, searching for any sign of another person in there. No one is visible. I clutch the strap of my pack and step into the office as everything slides into place behind me, hiding all signs of the passageway.

"Well, what do we have here?"

SIXTY-THREE

I skid backward, and my heart stutters to a stop before racing.

Demetrius Ark emerges from the shadows, alone.

My hands tighten on the strap of the bag, and I edge away from him.

He clicks his tongue at me, slowly shaking his head back and forth. "Bria, Bria, Bria. Why did you think for even a moment that you could outsmart me?" With each word, he steps closer, stalking me like a predator with his prey. "You foolish girl. I have given you so much, and this is how you repay me?"

I back up until I'm pressed against Colonel Valarius's desk. Ark stands between me and the door.

"Tell me, what was your plan? Did you turn some of my soldiers against me?" His lip curls into a snarl. "If you cooperate with me now, I *might* consider sparing your life."

My voice is locked inside.

"Who else is involved? Tell me!" He growls the words.

I expect fear to rip its angry claws through me, but instead, I find my voice. "I'm not telling you anything." I spit the words at him.

His eyes narrow into deadly slits, and I feel the rage radiating from him. He reaches inside his jacket and pulls out a gun.

I take a deep breath. At least now, I'm ready to meet God. I don't want to die, but I realize I'm not afraid to anymore.

"You had so much potential. It's a shame to see it wasted." He cocks his head to the side. "You can't stop me, Bria. You lose." He loads a bullet into place. "My plans will be carried out, and no one is going to get in my way."

"No, you're *wrong*." I take a step toward him, away from the desk. "Maybe we've failed today, but one day, you *will* be stopped." I quietly enunciate each word with a conviction I shouldn't be feeling as I prepare to die.

Ark's eyes widen, and the tendons in his jaw tighten. "You insolent, wretched..." His nostrils flare, and his chin juts forward. "You see, Bria—"

The door to Colonel Valarius's office opens, distracting Ark.

A spark of hope ignites in me...and then instantly dies.

Laban Meritas enters the room. As he takes in the scene, a smug expression tightens his features. "I *knew* she couldn't possibly be who she was pretending to be. Commander, let me take care of this tra—"

"Ah, are you here because you're a part of this, Sergeant?" Ark's voice is calm.

Laban's eyes widen, and he gapes at Ark for a moment. "Of course not. Sir, you know I'm completely loyal to you. I'll put her in custody, shoot her—anything you want!"

"Get out. I'll deal with you later."

Sweat breaks out on Laban's upper lip. He takes a hesitant step back. "I'd never work with her, sir. I'm loyal to you! Always!"

Ark's lips tilt up. He's toying with Laban, taunting him. "We'll speak later, sergeant."

Laban bolts away, leaving the door wide open and Ark momentarily distracted. This might be my only chance. I prepare to rush Ark when he swings the gun back at me. My small window of opportunity slams in my face.

"You see, Bria," he says, as though we were never interrupted. "I'm not a forgiving man. Once I've been betrayed, I can't move past it until that person pays for their betrayal. My father," his face twitches with the word, "ignored me, acted like I didn't exist. He didn't *want* me to exist." He spits the words out, but there's a hint of hurt in them.

For an instant, I feel almost sad for Ark. Then he shifts the gun in front of my face, and the feeling vanishes. Whatever his childhood was, what he's doing now isn't right.

"I'm going to make him regret that. He wasn't the father he should have been. He betrayed me. But I'll show him I can rule a country, and I'll rule the greatest empire in the world by the time I'm done."

My heart beats a steady rhythm in my chest, and peace fills me. *No matter what happens to me, would You please stop Demetrius Ark?*

"I am not an unreasonable man," Ark continues. "Those who are loyal to me, I reward. But traitors like you must pay the price."

A slight movement over Ark's shoulder catches my eye. Matthias is in the doorway. I bite my cheek to keep from reacting. He holds a finger to his lips and lifts a blunt metal stick, pointing with it toward Ark. He steps forward. The floor creaks.

Everything seems to slow down. Ark begins turning toward Matthias, and I know he'll kill him. I scream and rush Ark. His attention latches back onto me.

He releases the safety on the gun. His fingertip whitens as he puts pressure on the trigger. I flinch, anticipating the bullet. But before Ark can completely depress the trigger, Matthias slams the metal pipe down on his head.

The gun goes off. Ark crumbles to the floor, unconscious. The bullet hits the ceiling. My ears ring from the shot, but I step over Ark toward Matthias. "Thank yo—"

Matthias grabs my hand. "Save it for later. We gotta go!" He pulls me from the room.

"Do you know how much time we have?" I ask as we rush down flights of stairs.

"No, but it can't be much. My guess is Ari already set the power surge, so we have less than thirty minutes."

We crash through the side doorway and into the alley. The sirens blare all around us, and the acrid smell of smoke tickles my nostrils.

We run through the alleyways of Talionis, Matthias pulling me to a stop more than once to wait as soldiers rush by.

The minutes tick by, and I'm acutely aware of the limited time we have until the Wall is rebooted. If we don't get over it in time, we'll be stuck.

The abandoned building is finally in sight.

"Over there!" A soldier shouts behind us. We've been seen.

Matthias clutches my hand tighter, and we run faster. We burst into the abandoned building, racing through it to the hole to the Ruins. Matthias pushes me through first, just as I hear the clatter of boots searching the building. We emerge in the Ruins. I doubt the soldiers will think to look for us here, but we don't wait around to find out.

The paths have become familiar. I jump over rocks and skirt trees in our way with ease. Soon, we're past the training site. There's no time to stop and make sure the others gathered all the supplies. We need to get to the Wall.

"We have to go faster, Bria!" Matthias says, increasing his speed before the words are out of his mouth.

I pick up my pace as we follow the part of the path that is less familiar now. Cai has marked our way by putting three slashes on the trunks of the trees. We pick our way through a graveyard of old buildings and are forced to slow down in order to climb over partial walls in our way. A building creaks and sways, ready to topple. I drop on the other side of the last wall and crest a hill. The Wall looms ahead of us. There's no hum of electricity coursing through it.

"We're in time!" The words are just out of my mouth when I hear the low growl to my left. I freeze in horror. How could we get so close and have it end like this?

Matthias faces the dogs, pulls a gun from his belt. "Bria! Run!" There are two quick blasts from his gun, and then a moment later he's caught up with me. He grabs my hand and pulls me faster. There's a whimpering, and then one of the dogs howls. The earth shakes as they chase us.

Where is Cai and his whistle now?

We reach the Wall and get several feet off the ground before the dogs catch up to us. They bark at our feet, snarling. One leaps into the air and snaps its jaw inches from my ankle.

"Don't look down. Just keep climbing," Matthias says.

Even with my fear gnawing at me, I find hand and footholds in the metal spikes jutting from the Wall. We reach the top, and I stop. The dogs pace at the base of the Wall, barking up at us. In the distance, smoke rises from the buildings of Talionis. Is this really happening right now? Am I really about to leave this nightmare?

"Bria!" Matthias is ready to begin the descent. "We need to go down. *Now*. The Wall could come back online at any moment and fry us."

"I'm coming!" I reply, jarred back to the danger at hand.

I'm almost to the bottom when there's a slight rumble in the Wall.

"It's coming back on! Jump!" Matthias yells.

I jump off the Wall. Before I hit the ground, the hum of the electrical current fills the air. I land in a heap and let myself lay there a second. I sit up and pull a leaf from my hair. Matthias and I grin at each other.

I say the words that mere moments ago I thought I would never be able to say. "We did it. We escaped from Talionis."

CHAPTER

SIXTY-FOUR

Towering trees sway before us. Pine. Evergreen. Small leaves have begun to paint the trees with color again. Dogwoods burst with flowers. Squirrels scamper limb to limb as birds sing their songs from the tops of the trees. Spring has consumed the forest. The air is fresh, intoxicating. Free.

I'm free.

I close my eyes and breathe deeply, filling my lungs, letting the slight breeze wash over me. Leaves rustle in the wind. My curls dance around my shoulders.

"We're not there yet." Matthias nudges my arm. "Come on, slowpoke."

"Whatever. Don't even pretend like you didn't pick that flower back there." I point at where the yellow bud pokes its head out of his pocket.

His eyes sparkle. "At least I kept walking."

I roll my eyes, even as a traitorous grin splits my lips. "Fine. Lead the way."

I sweep my hand forward. We should have less than half a mile left to go before we reach the others.

We walk in companionable silence, the forest floor crunching beneath our feet, and I feel a deep sense of contentment walking next to Matthias.

I tuck a flyaway curl behind my ear. "I haven't thanked you."

"Sure you did."

I place my hand on his arm and stop him.

He smirks. "Bria, you really need to stop delaying our progress."

I remain serious. "Matthias, really. Thank you. If it wasn't for you...I'd be dead."

The humor disappears from his eyes, and he flinches. "It was too close. I should have been there sooner." His jaw tightens, but he maintains eye contact. "I don't know what happened. Everything was going like it should. I set off the explosives in the Physical Training Arena and was nearing the Weaponry Building when the alarm went off." He rubs the back of his neck. "Soldiers started arriving way faster than they should have, and it forced me to take a different route." His voice rises. "What if I had been later?"

"But you weren't. You saved my life. Don't downplay that." I would never have thought a few months ago that I'd be the one trying to comfort Matthias Valarius. Yet, I can't stop myself.

We walk again. "I just don't get it."

"What?" I ask.

"How was that alarm triggered? I've played it over and over again. It shouldn't have happened." He kicks at a stone, and it skips ahead of us.

I shrug. "Maybe Shane and Bryson will tell us."

"If they made it."

The forest seems less cheerful after those words. We continue in silence. After several minutes, we see Cai and a few others. I jog forward, eager to be with them, to make sure everyone is there.

Cai's the first to see us approach. "Bria. Matthias. We weren't sure if you made it."

"I almost didn't. Matthias saved me." Something in Cai's face causes me to pause. "Did everyone else make it?"

Cai doesn't say anything. No one says anything. I search the faces of the others, trying to determine what's going on. Nika, Ari, Nalani,

Shane, Bryson. They're all here, but they all look away as my eyes meet theirs. I turn to Cai again.

Something burns in my gut. "Where's Storm? She's here. Right?" Even as I ask, I know the answer isn't the one I want.

Cai takes my hand. "Storm and Damara didn't make it out."

"What?" I pull my hand away, whipping my head back and forth. "No. No, that *can't* be right. He's here," I point at Shane, "so she should be too."

Cai's lips form a thin line, and he doesn't have to say a word. I know it's true. But I still don't want to believe it.

"She was the reason…" My words fall away. I step toward Shane. "You said you'd get them out! How could you escape and *leave* them there?" My voice rises in frustration. Desperation. This can't be happening.

Shane's cheek flinches. "Bryson had to go help Ari and Nalani, and by the time I finished, I didn't have time to get them. The alarms—"

I march toward him, grabbing the front of his shirt in my fists. "Are you kidding me? You didn't have *time?* She's just a little girl!" I shake him. "What kind of man leaves a little girl to fend for herself in the Ruins!"

A hand on my shoulder pulls me away from Shane. "Bria, we don't know what happened. Maybe he didn't have a choice," Matthias says, his gaze probing Shane.

"There wasn't enough time, and it was too much of a risk. I'm sorry, Bria."

"Sorry?" I shake my head, incredulous. "Sometimes, Shane, sorry just isn't good enough." I press my lips together, then whirl away from him. "I'm going back for her."

Cai blocks my way. "You can't. The Wall is back up."

I grip my head, desperation devouring my logic. "I have to try!"

"No." Cai folds his arms across his chest. "We have to continue forward to Eryndale. That's the only way you can save Storm now." His voice drops so that only I can hear him. "Trust God with this, Bria. Don't do something rash."

My jaw hurts, and I realize I'm clenching it. I gaze back toward Talionis. I know he's right. There's no way for me to go back and save her right now. My insides twist themselves into knots as I imagine what Ark might do to her if he finds her in the Ruins. *Oh God. Why did this have to happen?* I swallow hard. *Protect Storm. Keep her and Damara hidden from the soldiers.*

I drag in a ragged breath. "Okay."

"Where are the maps?" Cai moves on in his no-nonsense way. "We need to get moving."

I don't move. I *can't* move. I just stare back toward Talionis. What will happen to her?

"Bria." Nika's hand is on my arm. "Give me your bag."

She doesn't give me a chance to agree. She just pulls the satchel over my head and sets it on the ground. Someone else takes my hand and squeezes it before letting go, but the attempt to comfort barely registers.

"Why is there so much in here?" Nika is rummaging through the pile. "I thought you were just getting the maps."

I draw in a fortifying breath and try to reengage myself in the task at hand. The only thing I can do for Storm now is get to Eryn- dale, send word to my family to get out of Derbe before the next extraction—something Cai assured me we could do in refuge city— and stop Ark. "I was almost caught, so I took everything."

Nika empties the contents onto the ground. Everyone else gathers closer.

"Here they are." Nika pulls a thick, multi-dimensional map out and opens it up one layer. She hands it up to Cai. "I'm not exactly sure how this thing works. What's the rest of this stuff?" She pokes at a stack of what looks like old letters bundled together with a journal of some sort. There's another bundle of papers that seem to be newer correspondences.

I shrug. "Don't know."

Ari picks up one of the two pouches and opens it. A compass slides out.

"That's useful," Bryson says.

My curiosity eases some of my desperation to get to Storm. I bend down and scoop up the other package. I open it and dump it out into my hand. A weird key. "Interesting."

"What's that?" Matthias presses himself closer, his voice strange.

"Just a key."

"Can I see it?"

When I hand it to him, his face blanches. "Oh, no."

"What?" He looks like he just got handed a death sentence.

Matthias doesn't answer. He leans over and picks up first the newer stack of papers, then the older one. "This is not good."

"Matthias, what's going on?" I ask, apprehension swirling in my stomach.

Finally, he looks at me. "You stole Ark's proof, his plans."

"You're not making any sense."

He clutches the key and the letters. "This is what Ark needs to prove that he has the right to become Chancellor of Sitreea." He holds up the key. "This is a key to the Sitreean armory's most powerful weapons. Only one who can become Chancellor possesses a key like this." He flips through the letters.

"I think these are love letters between the Chancellor and Ark's mother from before Ark was born. And these," he picks up the newer stack of papers, "look like they're written plans and notes for his invasions into surrounding countries. These are the things he doesn't tell anyone else, but everything he has hinges on them." His hands fall to his sides with the letters and key. "My father always suspected Ark had more intel than he shared with his advisors."

A small tingle of excitement zips through me. "So we stopped him."

Matthias shakes his head no, lips pressed into a line. My excitement turns to dread before he speaks his next words.

"Demetrius Ark can't carry out his plan without these things. He'll stop at *nothing* to get them back."

———————

WHICH RECRUIT OF TALIONIS CHARACTER ARE YOU MOST LIKE?

TAKE THE QUIZ TO FIND OUT!

About the Author

CJ Milacci seeks to take her readers on a grand adventure that begins with a single word. As a referee, she is always relearning the hard lesson that it's impossible to make everyone happy, and she's discovered that stories can be found anywhere, even on a lacrosse field. She is passionate about crafting stories of good overcoming evil, finding hope in the midst of seemingly hopeless circumstances, and true acceptance. Always willing to get real about hard issues, C.J. also enjoys the cheesiest of puns. She chats about writing, her faith and the hope found in Jesus, bubble tea, and other fun adventures online (@cjmilacci) and at cjmilacci.com.

Find out more and sign up for her newsletter to be the first to know about Book 2 in The Talionis Series:

SPREAD THE WORD

Can you think of two people who could use this book in their lives? Maybe they are your friends, teens in your church, someone you know who loves young adult fiction. Maybe they are avid readers and always looking for a new book. Or maybe it's someone you know who needs an escape from the crazy life she is immersed in, someone desperate for hope.

If so, I would love it if you could connect them to this book so they can experience the hope found in this book.

Thanks again for reading!

ACKNOWLEDGMENTS

First and foremost, thank you to my Lord and Savior, Jesus Christ. Without Him, this book would never have existed. Thank You! Creating with You is the best possible journey.

I have been so blessed to have many amazing people who have poured into this story and those who have been willing to take a chance and read my story and give me their honest feedback.

My incredible parents. Thank you, Dad, for loving it and becoming one of my most hype supporters, even though you didn't think you'd like the book ;) and Mom, thank you for being my sounding board, for listening to this story and every iteration over and over again — it wouldn't be what it is today without you listening... and begging me not to mess it up.

Rachael Jacques, my cousin who was my brainstorming buddy, character creation cohort, and all around a lover of this story from the very beginning. Recruit of Talionis has your fingerprints all over it! Thank you!

To the little sister of my heart. Ani, I'm so thankful God blessed me with you. Thank you for being excited about this story and supporting me each step of the way.

My early beta readers. Katie Robles, Sara and Alan Collins, Gabby Peters, Maria Jacques, Auntie Id, and Megan Kontz. Your feedback, encouragement, and insights helped make this book better.

To my incredible family. I have the most supportive crew around me, and I'm so thankful for all of you.

My YOP writers group. I am amazed at how God pulled our little writing crew together, and I'm blown away by how much of a blessing this group has been to me. I look forward to our

Friday meetings each week and I'm a better writer as a result of being in this group with all of you. Jon, Chris, Kristin, Kelly, and Peter — thank you for your encouragement, support, and friendship.

Chris Pearce, my proofreader, who can catch the littlest of mistakes. Thank you for cleaning this up so I can be all the more confident in sharing it with the world.

Jonathan Shuerger, my military expert and developmental editor. If there is any accuracy in the military aspects of this book, the credit is owed to Jon. He was the Drill Sergeant I needed to help whip *Recruit of Talionis* into shape and bring it to a whole other level. (Now, if you're in the military and you read my story and find things that *don't* ring true, I'm the one to blame.) Thank you, Jon, for all of your hard work.

Emilie Haney, my cover designer, who was amazing to work with. I didn't have a picture in my head of what this cover should be, but she patiently worked with me through the entire process and produced a cover that I absolutely LOVE. Thank you, Emilie! It's better than I could have imagined.

My Word Weavers Group: Page 31, I'm honored to be in a group with such talented writers. I learn more from each meeting, and I've come away a better writer. Eva, Clare, Jake, Jennifer, Bethany, and Margaret, thank you for being such an encouraging and fun critique group.

My BLB Marketing Mastermind Group, Candace, Katie, and Karyne, you guys are the best!

Erynn Newman, my line-editor, was patient, kind, and helped clean up my story and make it better than ever. Thank you, Erynn!

The Brain Trust. Megan and Jewell, you are both wonderful friends and supports in this entrepreneurial life and I'm so thankful for our monthly meetings!

Erica Martin, my life-long friend and the backer of The Commander Pledge, thank you for believing in this story!

And to my Kickstarter backers who made all this possible and helped bring this book to life in ways I never imagined, thank you. You all made this project an amazing experience, and I'm honored that you chose to be a part of this. Without further ado, here's the list of Kickstarter backers (in order of when they backed):

Maria Jacques, Bill & Brenda Milacci (Mom and Dad), Uncle Fred and Aunt Tommie, Kristin Cooney, Karah, Karyne Norton, Rachael Jacques, Kelly, Alicia Jacques, Aunt Michelle, Liz Skidmore Edwards, Cayla, Naomi Thompson, Elizabeth Fraley-Hogg, Deb McGuire, Willy Milacci, Charlene Ducane, Peter DeHaan, The Broomes, Ariana Marie, Kathy Brasby, Thomas Umstattd Jr., Rob and Jewell Rowlands, Josh Sorensen, Kristin Flanagan, Tori Reed, Ani, Kristopher Ecklof, Jonathan Shuerger, Candace, Michele Meszaros, The Emma Family, Pat Zab, Chris Pearce, Sara Collins, Curt and Cadence W., Uncle Gene and Aunt Judy, Jonathan, Jerry Paradise, Jerry Buck, Libby, Andrew and Joice Milacci, Megan, Keith & Becky Woods, McMoogle, Mr. & Mrs. Jose P. Ortiz, Rebecca Webb, Jake Stoddard, Donna FitzPatrick, Amanda Trumpower, Todd, Ella Evans, Jonas, Dan and Ashley Jacques, Janet DiAntonio, Joelle DiAntonio, Bridgette Findley, Jason, Gabriella Peters, Ambre Sautter, Katie Robles, Diane Plappert, Hannah, Bobby, Megan, John D. Smith, Bernadette Botz, Karen Grunst, Shari Weise, Kristin Hendrick, Aunt Kelly, Leonora Teale, Doug Erling, Remington Cloutier, Leah E. Good, Uncle Paul and Aunt Linda, Joshua C. Chadd, Angel Gonzalez, Margaret Hamlin, Jeff Chandler, Taylor Belser Yinger, Bentley Searing, Abbie, Vitina Marino, Becca Wierwille, Jamie Foley, Eddie Joo, Jeanna Simmons, Emily L., Zachary Dale, Pierluca Morando, Marcus ‚Nanoska' Bruckner, Geoff Emberlyn, Jennifer Dyer, Joey Ehrgott, Marie-Hélène Ayotte, Katherine Briggs, Patricia Cameron, Caroline Doughty, Dawn and Bill, Jennifer Arndt, Galina, Maria Jung, Brian Cooper, David Swisher, Kathryn Maris, Steve Guglich, Mary T, Sarah, Jill Cooper, Jane Ashcroft, Jacob H Joseph, Emilie Haney, Conor Neilson, Gage "SpaceGhoat" Troy, Gabriel Rivers, Harold van Bolhuis, Connie Hendryx, Erin Griffin, Jane Maree, Elisha Snowdon, Dianne Gardner, Nancy, and Meghan Krouse.